# PRAISE FOR *DOWN THE STEEP*

"*Down the Steep* elegantly scrutinizes the horrors of the Jim Crow south, heroism gone awry, and the family and home you can never fully flee. A. D. Nauman writes with compassion and understanding about characters who don't always understand themselves—and she keeps the pages turning. An engaging novel and a beautiful coming-of-age story."

—Rebecca Makkai, author of *I Have Some Questions for You*

"*Down the Steep* travels into dark places where lesser authors might fear to tread. A. D. Nauman has created an unforgettable narrator, a pulse-pounding plot, and an ending that will leave readers haunted and changed. This book is unflinching in its honesty and breathtaking in its beauty."

—Abby Geni, author of *The Wildlands*

"It's increasingly rare to encounter a work of fiction that truly allows us—no, compels us—to witness a character's profound moral growth, their making and re-making, but with Willa Mc-Coy, the teenaged protagonist of *Down the Steep*, A. D. Nauman accomplishes just that. This fast-moving novel of the heart and mind builds, one impeccable small-town detail after another, to a devastating conclusion. You'll never forget this emotionally wrenching and beautiful book."

—Kimberly Elkins, author of *What Is Visible*

"As a child growing up in 1960s Virginia, in a chillingly genteel atmosphere of racism and patriarchy, Willa McCoy has an awakening that changes the course of her life and her family's. This is a beautifully written novel of great depth and pathos."

—Elizabeth McKenzie, author of *The Dog of the North*

"The clear-eyed honesty of a young girl's voice describes the brutality of racism and the prison of misogyny in A. D. Nauman's *Down the Steep*. I read this novel with rapt attention, as unable to stop thinking about it as I was reluctant to put it down. Fresh and tough and beautifully crafted, this is a novel that begs to be read."

—Chris Cander, author of *A Gracious Neighbor*

"Sharply observed and alight with fury, A. D. Nauman's novel scrutinizes the devastation of hate and the scarcity of courage. Her characters will break your heart more times than you can count."

—Adam Shafer, author of *Never Walk Back*

"I couldn't stop turning the pages of this propulsive novel. *Down the Steep* is historical fiction at its best. Nauman effortlessly conjures the textures of small-town Virginia and the way the setting affects the characters' behavior and psychology. The white, teenaged narrator's sense of herself as both victim and savior, as powerless and all-powerful, is achingly palpable, and I held my breath as the stakes ratcheted up and her muddled good intentions threatened horrific damage. Nauman is not afraid to look at the way racism is born and bred into white people. That there is no easy path forward doesn't make the search for redemption any less urgent, and this novel about the past underscores how true this remains today."

—Zoe Zolbrod, author of *The Telling*

"As seen through the eyes of a wise and rebellious teenager, *Down the Steep* is a vivid, poignant, and boldly wrought account of the Jim Crow South on the cusp of the civil rights movement. One can't help but cheer for Willa as she seeks social justice as well as justice for herself with passion and charm. In a world of wrong, she is a spark of right. A. D. Nauman has given us a compelling, thought-provoking book."

—Louise Marburg, author of *You Have Reached Your Destination*

# DOWN THE STEEP

A. D. Nauman

Regal House Publishing

Published by
Regal House Publishing, LLC
Raleigh, NC 27605
All rights reserved

ISBN -13 (paperback): 9781646033706
ISBN -13 (epub): 9781646033713
Library of Congress Control Number: 2022949371

Cover design by © C. B. Royal

Regal House Publishing, LLC
https://regalhousepublishing.com

The following is a work of fiction created by the author. All names, individuals, characters, places, items, brands, events, etc. were either the product of the author or were used fictitiously. Any name, place, event, person, brand, or item, current or past, is entirely coincidental.

Printed in the United States of America

For Maggie,
Connie,
and especially June

# PROLOGUE

By now I can recite from memory the history of the Ku Klux Klan. I tell it mid-semester, when I'm sure my students feel safe within the snug walls of our classroom. I stand at the podium and let the settling subside—backpacks dropped next to feet, laptops pried open on narrow desks, bodies shifted adequately on hard chairs. Our cinderblock room is scuffed and not big enough for thirty of us, but we don't mind. The lone window usually bares a square of grimy dusk—I teach evening classes—but tonight the Chicago winter has turned the view silver. I wait for the faces to turn my way. Most are smiling. Then I begin:

Picture this. The Civil War has just ended, and across the devastated landscape come the soldiers of the Confederacy, defeated. They've fought with all their might; they've watched their best friends blown to bits. They lost anyway. They reach home to find their fields gashed and ragged, pooling with humiliation, and into this open wound ride Northerners, carpetbaggers, the federal government, interlopers here not only to take land but to encourage freed Black men to *vote*. Now Black men will *vote*. The Confederacy shakes with rage.

*Kuklos* is the Greek word for "circle." The agitated soldiers who founded the Ku Klux Klan thought of themselves as a social circle. They were a men's club, with a mission: to prevent Blacks from voting. They were drinking buddies who donned robes and hoods and rode through the night terrorizing families, beating resisters, burning down their homes.

In the 1870s, Congress passed the Enforcement Acts to curtail violence against Black people, and Klan activity waned, but in the late 1910s, the mood of the country shifted. The US had gone to war—the one to end all wars. Fears of "anti-American elements" roiled; hatred of "the other" seethed.

Black soldiers came home from World War I acting "uppity," presuming respect. Theaters across the country aired *Birth of a Nation*, flashing giant moving pictures of bestial, pitch-black men lusting after white women—images that burrowed deep into the minds of white audiences. Klan resurgence blazed through the 1920s and '30s. New immigration laws were passed to shut out darker-hued immigrants, those deemed genetically inferior to whites. The eugenics movement flourished. Hitler admired us. Between the two world wars, more than a thousand Black people were lynched in the US, many at so-called picnics, where crowds of whites cheered and laughed and had their photos taken with a body dangling in the background.

Here I have to pause and take a long breath. I survey my students' faces, which are no longer smiling. They are ashen, stricken, petrified, appalled. I continue:

The exposure of Nazi atrocities after World War II shifted public sentiment again. Horrified Americans needed to distance themselves from that loud and brutal form of hatred. Klan activity subsided, somewhat, until 1954, when the US Supreme Court decided *Brown v. Board of Education* in favor of desegregating schools. Suddenly all those violent, brainless, genetically inferior, oversexed beasts were to be in classrooms alongside everyone's lovely and chaste white daughters. The Klan rose again.

I emphasize to my students: white supremacy comes in waves. It may recede over a decade or two, but that kind of hatred—hatred of the other—never truly goes away. That kind of hatred is tidal. It hovers beneath glassy surfaces, then rises, rushing toward us in a low bump of water, in a towering surge, or in a tsunami. Hatred of the other drowns everyone, even those born with privileged skin.

Through all its iterations, I tell my students, white supremacy has one enduring righteous conviction: that people of Northern European descent are better than those who came from other places. After all, it was the Northern Europeans, with their clever ships and weapons, who sailed around the world colonizing it. Personally, I don't think superior intellect is signified by a quickness to judge and a willingness to harm others for personal profit. My own ancestors were Scots Irish. Forfeiting our claim to superiority need not imply that other races are superior to us. But the white supremacist brain is apparently hardwired to compare and rank, unable to envision humankind on a level field, atavistically obsessed with pecking orders.

Then I tell my students about Virginia, where I "mostly grew up." After *Brown v. Board of Education*, Virginia launched a campaign of *massive resistance* to desegregation. In 1959, officials in Prince Edward County avoided integration by closing all public schools—for five years. When the Supreme Court ruled that tax dollars couldn't be used for whites-only private schools, state legislators crafted a strategy of *passive resistance*, a web of laws making it hard for Blacks to enroll in white schools. By 1962, only one percent of Virginia schools were integrated. By 1964, five percent were.

Ironically, in the midst of growing Klan reactions to desegregation, state legislators also passed laws prohibiting cross burnings and masked rallies. But, I tell my students, this was not because Virginia's political elites questioned the truth of white supremacy; rather, they viewed the Klan as ill-mannered, ill-bred, an embarrassment to their genteel sensibilities.

I do not tell my students that my father was a Klansman. I don't tell anyone this, not even my closest friends.

When class ends, my students file out of the room, bunch up momentarily in the corridor, and trickle away. I sit down at the desk to reflect. Silence grows heavy in my ears. I'm exhausted and unsettled, as usual, after telling this history. Of course I'm still ashamed of my personal history, of who my father was, of who I was. Although I've spent decades doggedly transforming myself—I'm an advocate for social justice now, a history teacher, a city-dweller, even a Northerner—that doesn't erase the past. Like any white American, I would rather keep the bad stuff submerged. I'd rather believe in moving on, talk excitedly about the future, imagine myself as someone different—someone better. But hatred of the other has risen again, and I fear we're all hurling ourselves toward collective destruction. So, alone in the silence, I make the decision: I will face my history.

It's time to tell.

# 1

When I was thirteen years old, in 1963, I realized some people in this world are extras—born to be peripheral—and I was one of them.

My parents had four children: boy, girl, girl, boy. As girl number two, I served as a backup if anything happened to girl number one. Worse, it was clear my parents had wanted another boy. They'd planned to name the new baby William, without bothering to choose a girl's name, and when I turned out to be me, they lazily named me Willa. After my little brother Billy was born, they quit having kids.

We lived in southeast Virginia, in the low-lying coastal region known as the Tidewater. Our town was small but bigger than its neighbors, its industry hardy, thanks to lumber, hogs, and peanuts. In summer the air hung thick as a swamp, rattling with insects. The smell of sawdust and tree lilies mingled with the rotting-cabbage stench of the paper mill. I used to fly my bike up Main Street through our downtown—five blocks of white-painted brick facades. Across the Blackwater River was the lumberyard, where towers of skinny pine logs rose up beside stacks of slender sheets of wood. *That's what will become of you*, I'd say out loud to the logs, then zoom past them toward the peanut silo, embossed with its monocled cartoon peanut kicking up a merry leg. Beyond the silo, hunched along the railroad tracks, were shacks cobbled together with scraps of wood, corrugated Plexiglas, and pieces of billboard sign. This was where the most impoverished Black people lived.

Of course, in that place and time, all the African Americans were extras, part of the blurred backdrop erected for those standing center stage. Blacks who behaved well were allowed to serve whites. Tidewater was where the first shackled Africans

were brought in 1619 to be sold as slaves, though that fact did
not tend to come up in polite conversation, and our conversation
was always polite. We were a gracious folk, eager to distinguish
ourselves from those coarse inhabitants of the Deep South:
Tidewater was not a place where churches blew up or police
battered marchers with water hoses on national television.
Southeast Virginians were descendants of the first-ever Brits
to land in the New World, settlers who'd lived in Jamestown,
who'd met Pocahontas. In my hometown, Kingsfield, people
felt their worth. They also understood the value of avoiding
trouble, and so they offered a restrained sort of benevolence
to their coloreds. "Coloreds" was what we called Black people
back then, in polite society. Other times, I am ashamed to say,
we called them the "n" word—a word I refuse to use now.

On my bike I would soar up High Street, past the sprawling white clapboard houses with wide lawns of purple phlox
and azaleas, through puddles of shade cast by grand weeping
willows. In June, the crepe myrtles would bloom in their aston-
ishing red- and purple-pinks. The trunks of crepe myrtles split
at the base into a chaos of pale gray stems and, when I lived in
Kingsfield, gardeners debated the proper treatment of them.
Some insisted on pruning the trees down to three or four even
trunks, while others believed the bloom was fuller when the
trees grew free from the human impulse toward uniformity. It
seems likely this debate continues, but I don't know. When I
was fourteen, I destroyed our family and my parents sent me
away, and I have never been back.

I was, after all, only an extra.

The important people in my family were as follows: first, my
father—head of household, knower of all things, celestial object around which we were all naturally to revolve. Second was
eldest son Ricky, expected to someday morph into my father.
Third was Billy, a backup for Ricky, should anything untoward
happen to him. Tied for fourth place was my mother, with
her many uses, and my eye-catching sister, Barb. Then me. In
the era of my childhood, women and girls were viewed as not

quite people, existing in a state of foggy ineptitude, requiring guidance and long explanations of how things were and why. A woman's purpose in life was to make sure her husband felt important and comfortable, attended to and in charge. A good woman was someone who accomplished this pleasantly, without noisily voicing needs of her own.

My mother was a good woman. My father often told her this. In response she would smile and try to look proud but not prideful. She was, in fact, an ideal female for the times: dutiful, acquiescent, reliable, attentive, homebound—entirely dependent on her husband. Although she was a Kingsfield outsider, having grown up in southern Ohio, people had an admiration for her. She was considered smart for a woman. She'd finished two years of college before quitting to get married, and while my father was off fighting Japs in the Pacific, she'd worked as a secretary in a doctor's office. She knew how to pronounce and spell medical terms. Impressive, everyone agreed.

My mother was also a renowned hard worker, doing all the cooking and housework herself at a time when middle-class ladies in Kingsfield had colored maids—the labor was that cheap. My mother told people she just loved doing housework; it was so gratifying, she said. In truth, she was trying to save every penny. A family of six was costly, especially on an assistant principal's salary, and Daddy was a spender, his eye caught by shiny shoes and elegant suits. He wanted to *appear* rich, and in quiet obedience, my mother ensured he did. The other ladies never suspected financial stress; if anything, they thought my mother did all that work herself because Daddy wouldn't allow coloreds in our house. That was also true. *If we let coloreds in the house*, he said, *they'd steal things.* Coloreds in the yard pulling weeds were okay, but not in the house.

Women's Lib was slow in coming to Tidewater, but even at the age of thirteen, I could see that my mother's existence was small, focused on bits of food stuck to the insides of pots, threads hanging from the hems of skirts. I wanted to be like my father, a significant person in the world, someone who stood center stage. I wanted to be like my father, striding out of the house every morning with flapping lapels, briefcase in hand, leaping into our Oldsmobile and speeding backward out of the driveway, not nervously hesitating at the narrow path across our steep ditch. I wanted to *be* my father, coming home in the late afternoon with important news, telling my mother about his day while she stood over a frying pan humming and clucking and sympathizing. I wanted to sit in a cushiony chair after dinner and read the newspaper, not scamper around with dirty plates and a towel over my shoulder. Men had interesting things to talk about—politics, foreign countries, wars. Women talked about how to hard-boil eggs so the shell wouldn't stick to the skin and leave pocks, rendering your deviled-egg tray ugly and shameful. Women shared urgent tips on how to get all the silks off the cobs after shucking the sweet corn so your husband wouldn't get strings caught in his teeth. Women's lives contracted as they aged; men's expanded. Men went to meetings and made decisions that changed things. Recently our town council had decided to build a new municipal pool—*Olympic*-sized, with three levels of diving boards. They'd voted to give the old crumbling public pool to the coloreds, which everyone agreed was so generous.

One night at dinner, I attempted to step into the affairs of men. At the time I didn't know it, but this was to be the opening act of the drama that ended in my family's ruin. I was about to start eighth grade, and I was ready to be grown up. It was mid-August 1963. The March on Washington for Jobs and Freedom was about to happen; 200,000 people would soon pour into the nation's capital to hear a speech by Martin Luther King, Jr. But such a showy, distasteful event would not have been a topic for our supper conversation.

My father and Ricky were already seated at the table, at the head and foot, respectively. I was already in my chair, too, because if you wanted to be an important person in the world, you had to be near men. Our dining room, papered in faded pine wreaths, was kept dim to help us imagine we weren't so hot.

But the room was laden with dark furniture: a mahogany-colored china cabinet slumping in the corner, almost matching our hand-me-down table and the hardwood chairs crowded tight around it. As uncomfortable as those chairs were, I loved their square backs, open and framing the curlicue shapes of harps.

Through the archway between our living and dining rooms came seven-year-old Billy, romping toward us in an embroidered-trim cowboy shirt that was surely too hot for the season. Our living room was always drenched in shadow, the hefty gold-hued drapes blocking the sun. In the window behind me wheezed the air conditioner, whipping up the edges of the napkins around our forks. My mother and Barb came through the swinging kitchen door, shuttling in bowls of butter beans, corn on the cob, biscuits, a platter of pork chops.

"Willa," my mother sighed.

"I got it," Barb said, rushing back for the serving spoons.

Billy clambered into the chair next to mine, scalp sweat visible through his fresh crew cut. My father said, "Ready to start school, buckaroo?"

"Yes, sir!" Billy's feet jittered under the table.

"Question number one!" my father boomed. He loved giving pop quizzes at supper. He'd been a science teacher at the high school before his recent promotion to assistant principal. "What is the difference between a tidal marsh and a pocosin?" Billy's eyes sprang open, his shoulders leaping up in a shrug, and my father laughed with affection. My hand shot up, but my father called, "Ricky?"

My older brother's eyeballs rolled skyward and eventually found the answer in his skull: "Pocosin's not tidal."

"Good job!"

Barb took her seat across from me, but my mother remained standing, an ecstatic grin pushing apart her narrow cheeks. "Dick," she said, "I have something to show you." My father frowned. Something before we ate? From behind her back she whipped out a copy of the *Tidewater Times*, opened to an inside page, and gave it to him.

"Well," he exclaimed. "Look at this!" None of us could see it. Together our parents gawked at it, their faces aglow.

The rest of us waited. Despite his short stature and slight build, my father had complete authority over us all—even Ricky, who was several inches taller and broader. As my father read, I studied his forehead, shiny and lumpy with veins. His patchy eyebrows ascended in delight. His ears, near-perfect circles, stuck out from either side of his head like little stop signs. On the back side of the paper was an ad for the grand opening of the new Be-Lo Supermarket: everyone was invited, and you could win a fourteen-foot frost-free refrigerator-freezer combination.

"I didn't know you took this picture over, Trudy," my father said. "Good job!"

At last, he showed us the paper. There, on the *Women in the News* page, was a giant photo of Barb and her friend Patsy, accompanied by a ridiculously long article about how they'd brought lemonade to the football players during practice at the high school on account of the heat wave. The photo of Barb was stunning, her short tennis dress clinging to her perfect proportions. Barb was fifteen but looked twenty-one, willowy tall and overdeveloped. The black-and-white picture did not do justice to the soft coppery tint of her blond hair, bouncing in its signature ponytail. My father gave the paper back to my mother, who tidied it before circulating it among us. The pork chop platter followed.

"Barbie," our father glowed, dumping food onto his plate. "That Beale girl's got nothin' on you."

This was true. The newspaper had come to rest at my elbow. Poor Patsy Beale, her face immense and square, peering weirdly over Barb's splendid shoulder. Barb looked like Kim Novak. Much later I'd turn out pretty, too, but at the time no one would've predicted it. Two Christmases earlier my father had bought me a doll named Barbie—invented, he said, by a *lady* entrepreneur. Wasn't that something? I couldn't believe it. Someone had made a doll of my sister, and the dolls were sell-

ing out as fast as they could be manufactured. Barb was everywhere; I was nowhere. So I did the meanest thing I could think
to do to that doll—colored in her face with a brown magic
marker. Then I threw her under my bed with the stupid Chatty
Cathy doll.

I ate my beans and skimmed the other articles on the *Women
in the News* page. Miss Cynthia Forbes had celebrated her tenth
birthday. In attendance were Mrs. John Morehead and daughter
Margaret, Mrs. Russell Barnes and daughters Clara and Rose,
Mrs. Joseph Darden, Mrs. Lloyd Pretlow and daughter Dorothy,
on and on—all the families with streets and parks named after
them. If my father had seen this, he would have been stung.
Like my mother, he too was a Kingsfield outsider, born and
raised in western Virginia. Since neither of my parents' families
originated in Warwick County, they were excluded from Kingsfield's true circle of elites. It didn't matter how smart my father
was; he'd never be a Barnes or a Forbes or a Darden. Mrs. Rich-
ard McCoy and daughters would never be invited to Cynthia
Forbes's birthday celebration. I was worrying about this, sawing
away at my leathery pork chop, when my elbow knocked into
my glass and the milk sloshed around the rim in a stormy sea.

"Willa, pass that back, please." My mother stretched her
hand across the table for the paper. I refolded it first, like an
adult, and caught sight of the headline for the week's editorial:
*Should the Poll Tax Be Repealed?*

I had no idea what a poll tax was, but as I handed back the
paper, I remarked, "I certainly hope they repeal that poll tax."

A confused silence ensued. Looking back, I suppose those
words in the squeaky voice of a pubescent girl caused a kind
of cognitive dissonance in everyone's head. Finally my father
said, "We need that tax to fund the schools, Willa. Two million
comes in every year from that tax to fund Virginia schools."

"Oh." My face burned. "I thought taxes were bad."

"Depends what they're for." My father's voice was terse
and tense. Across the table Barb giggled at me—some trilling
movie-star laugh she'd been cultivating—and said, "Willa's

tryin' to be smart again," which made Ricky bust out, "Keep tryin', Willa."

Ricky snatched the last pork chop from the platter, which no one objected to. Ricky rarely got corrected. Handsome, popular, good enough in school, star tennis player, eldest son, all Ricky ever had to do was bask in my parents' adoration. By some inexplicable and inevitable mechanism, this had turned him into a jerk.

My mother exclaimed, "Billy hit a double today! Jimmy Poole on second scored a run, thanks to Billy!"

"Good job, son!"

"Daddy?" I asked in a sudden panic. "If they get rid of that poll tax, how'll the schools pay everyone's salary?" For example, his.

"That's not the only money the schools get." He replied as if I should have known this. "There're other types of taxes."

"Like what?"

My father took a bite of pork chop and chewed and gazed at a patch of air as though he hadn't heard me. Billy munched on his corn cob.

Barb offered, "There's…sales tax, right? There's…income tax, right?"

"Why is it called a *poll* tax?" I blurted.

"Duh, Willa," Ricky said. "It's the tax you pay at the *polls*, when you vote."

"Oh," I said. I looked at my father, who was still chewing, his cheeks puffing out, drawing in. I said, "So it's like, people have to pay to vote?"

Again his response was slow to surface. He nodded once and shoveled some beans into his mouth. I persisted: "So, are people gonna vote on whether people pay to vote?"

This time his reply was immediate. "Should be. Should be the people of the state decidin' it, not just one guy, not just one senator from Norfolk tellin' the whole state what to do. *Our* senator's on the right side, wants the people to vote on it. Good man, Bill Rawlings."

Forks clinked and everyone continued to eat except for me, my brain stuck thinking how it was the people who could afford to pay to vote who were voting on whether people should pay to vote. "Thing is," I couldn't help saying, "what if someone's really poor and can't afford it?" My father, we all knew, had grown up poor.

My mother erupted, "Death and taxes! My goodness! Surely there's a nicer topic of conversation!" My mother was responsible for everyone's happiness, particularly my father's. "Dick, tell the kids that funny story about the muskrat in the school parking lot."

A muskrat story followed, and the conversation lurched from there. Ricky updated us on his tennis wins. Barb wished aloud for the Featherlite crescent toe pumps she'd seen in the Sears, Roebuck & Company catalog. I studied the kernels of corn running crooked along my cob. Then I watched the butter melt on my biscuit. I had so many questions to ask, so many thoughts to voice, and it always felt like a door had slammed shut before I could get into the room. What room? It seemed like there was a room somewhere—high-ceilinged, plush-chaired, full of carved wood and important people with secrets—which I'd been shut out of. What did I have to do to get in?

My skull began to feel numb, and I had a sensation of floating upward, of rising like a helium balloon and wafting away from the table. I looked at my father, his face contented now, nodding at something Ricky was saying. I looked at my mother, carefully nodding in sync with my father. I looked at Barb, then Ricky, then Billy, and suddenly I understood I didn't belong with these people: I wasn't really a part of this family. I was untethered, alone, about to be lost.

I set down my fork and stared at my plate, at the dripping half biscuit I could no longer lift to my mouth. My mother's gaze kept fluttering over to me, her eyebrows sinking together, and after a while she asked if I was all right. I told her yeah, and my father told her to order those shoes for Barb.

&

Later that evening, with the dishes washed and dried and tucked back into their cabinets, I felt normal again. Billy and I sprawled together on our scratchy plaid couch in the family room to watch TV. The fall season hadn't started yet—we were still in reruns, but we didn't mind. Thursdays were Dobie Gillis. It was the episode where Dobie's cousin, Dunky, accidentally has a canister of nitroglycerin. The picture was flipping, the image scrolling upward slowly until the top half of the screen was Dunky's legs and feet and the bottom half was Dunky's head and torso. Messing with the rabbit ears only made it speed up, so we resigned ourselves to it. When the commercials came on, we sang along: "…*Viceroy's got the taste that's right!*" Then, "…*The name that's known is…Firestone!*" Next came the commercial for Gaines-Burgers, which didn't have a song, and I realized that, even though the TV volume was turned up high, my parents' voices in the living room were suspiciously low. I leaned toward the wall between us. Had someone said my name?

I sprang into spy mode. A few years earlier, before I decided to become a newspaper reporter when I grew up, I'd wanted to be a spy. I even bought a Secret Sam Spy Kit with my own allowance money—an attaché case with a periscope and hidden camera. Needless to say, I'd developed superb spying skills. Hiding in the coat closet, the sliding door crunched open half an inch, I could hear the adult talk in the living room. My mother was saying, "I thought you didn't care much for them."

"Naw, they're harmless," my father replied. "The missus wouldn't make trouble, and all the reverend does is talk about brotherhood. Willa's not gonna pick anything up from that." A silence intervened, and he added, "She's not that bright."

"What do you mean?"

"I mean, she's not that bright," he repeated.

My memory of this moment is distinct: the feel of plaster, hard against my spine, the oily exterior of someone's galoshes soft beneath my curled hand. I inhaled stuffy closet air and wondered what "she" he was talking about. Someone's "missus" was not that bright. Who could it be? I thought of Mrs.

Vaughan—she seemed pretty dense. Or maybe Mrs. Bunch, a complete moron. Mrs. Darden struck me as not that bright, but she seemed too important for my father to criticize.

My mother replied, "She does pretty well in school."

"She gets Bs. Anybody can get Bs."

"She needs to try harder, that's all."

"You're a nice mama, but you heard her tonight. She's just not that bright."

As his meaning grew clearer, my brain grew darker, as though dimming its own light so the meaning would remain indistinct. But it was there—the meaning. I could feel it—a hard, sharp thing poking at me, piercing me, making me shrink away from it, forcing me backward, downward, down and down until I was sliding into a morass. I sank and kept sinking. My thoughts, underwater, floundered upward, flailed into a grotto, thrashing until the realization crystallized into an ugly stalagmite: my father had meant *me*. My father was talking about *me*. I tried to swallow. My father thought *I* was not that bright. The shame of it scorched me. At the far end of the closet, the dark forms of our winter coats hung like legless, headless people. From the family room, a laugh track rose to a static-filled roar. The whole world was laughing at me.

I tried to breathe. I was *stupid*. In my family, *stupid* was the worst thing someone could be. My father had no tolerance for people who didn't know things. He'd ridicule them at the supper table or in the car: Mr. Bowman didn't know how big the Great Dismal Swamp was; Mrs. Councill had never heard of the Battle of Makin. My father was contemptuous of people who forgot items at the grocery store, who couldn't judge distances, who had to ask if their phone still worked when the power went out. My father had finished college in three years—that's how brilliant he was—and then he kept going for a master's degree in science. And he'd done it all immediately after the war, on the GI Bill. My father had been on the *Liscome Bay* when the Japs torpedoed it; he'd seen 600 men die, including his closest friend, but that didn't stop him. As soon as he got home, he enrolled in college—that's how tough he was—and he got straight As his first semester. That's how smart. Being smart made him better than other people. We were all expected to be better than other people, in some way. Ricky was the best tennis player in the county; Barb was the prettiest girl. What was I? I panicked. I'd thought I could be smart, like my father, but I couldn't be, I just wasn't. I was nothing.

My throat filled up with rocks. He was right—last year I'd gotten all Bs. *Not that bright.* The phrase circled in my head like a vulture looking for a carcass. The carcass was me. I wanted to cry, but I didn't want to be discovered there in the closet; I didn't want to be looked at. *Stupid. Stupid girl.* I heard my mother's shoes clack into the dining room, my father's chair squish. For endless minutes I slumped in the dark of the closet, hiding, trying to disappear.

Then, after a while, after the noise and sting of these thoughts subsided, a different, calmer voice nudged into my consciousness. It was as though another part of my brain was speaking up to express a dissenting view. The thing was, said this other part of my brain, my father's assertion—that I was not bright—seemed unlikely. There was evidence to the contrary. For example, I'd read more books than most of my classmates. I read faster than nearly all of them. When other kids were confused by a math problem, I wondered why. School was never hard; it was just dull. It was more fun to drift off in a big, long daydream. A puff of excitement caught in my chest: I realized I could change this. What if I did what my mama said and *tried harder?* What if I did *not* leave homework till the very last minute, and I checked my work like teachers always nagged us to do? What if I actually listened when teachers were talking?

I reasoned it out: if I got straight As on my next report card, my father would see I wasn't stupid. He would realize, in a flash, that I *was smart.* And then everything would change. He'd respect me. He'd look at me with pride—I wouldn't be invisible anymore. He'd brag about me like he did the others. He'd smile when I walked into the room, he'd ask my opinion, he'd nod along as I spoke. He'd laugh at my jokes. He'd listen. He'd finally love me. The thought of it was like water pouring over my parched heart.

By the time I slipped from the closet and ran upstairs to my room, it was late. Jittery with excitement, I pulled on my night-gown. I didn't see how I would ever sleep. I sat cross-legged on my bed, and my chest pounded with anticipation. I could do this; I knew I could. And for the first time in my life, I was eager for the school year to begin.

The next morning, I woke to the sound of my mother call-ing: "Willa! Come here please!" I trotted down the hall to my parents' bedroom, where a pile of clean white clothes formed a pyramid in the center of their bed. I squeezed alongside it and sprawled on the pillows. As usual, my mother had set up the ironing board in front of the window, so she could catch glimpses of the outside world. Our magnolia tree was there, its branches quiet in the breezeless heat. I raised myself onto my elbows. The nubby bedspread imprinted itself on my forearms.

My mother unfurled one of my father's shirts, then eyed me lounging on the bed. "You watch me while we talk," she said. "Watch how I'm doing this. See how I'm ironing it flat?" The point of the iron nipped onto and off the collar, darting up and back like a nervous squirrel. "See?"

"Yes." I felt exhausted. "I see."

"You're thirteen," she huffed. "By now you should be able to iron more than your father's handkerchiefs."

"*Okay.*"

She glared. My mother was a tall woman, her arms and legs lanky and strong. She had a body designed for farming, though her father owned a butcher shop in their small Ohio town. During the Depression, this had kept him employed, but still, at night, he'd hidden his knives under his mattress for fear the bankers would break in to repossess them. My mother's childhood had instilled a profound fear of spending money. She struggled to stay silent when my father overspent. Last

year he'd wanted to buy the twenty-one-inch RCA Victor Color
TV in the window of Moreheads' Electronics, so we could see
*Disney's Wonderful World of Color* and the tail feathers on the NBC
peacock in color. My mother had to use her feminine wiles to
avert the purchase, pointing out that the wood stain would
clash with the rest of the furniture. My father always deferred
to ladies in matters of home decorating.

I watched her bone-shaped fingers clutch the handle of the
iron. Finally, she said, "What are you gonna do when you get
married? Tell your husband to iron his own shirts?"

"Yep," I replied, seeing this as the only possible response.
"I'll say, 'Ichabod'—that'll be his name, Ichabod. 'Ichabod,' I'll
say, though I'll probably call him Icky—'Icky,' I'll say, 'You'll
just have to iron your own shirts because I refused to learn
how!'"

She tried not to smile, but her eyes glittered. I was the only
one of us kids who could make her laugh.

"Ichabod will leave you," she said.

"Good riddance!" I bellowed. "He was a snorer." And I im-
itated how Ichabod would snore: loud slurpy snorting sounds.

"Be serious."

I was serious, but like everyone else, she didn't believe me
when I said I never wanted to get married. I wanted to be a career gal, like the women in movies who worked in newsrooms,
clacking away at their typewriters with the men. I knew without
being told a girl had to choose between career or marriage—
you couldn't do both, because what if you neglected your
husband? Imagine the poor husband with wrinkled shirts, his
favorite socks still in the hamper, his dinners frozen and served
late by an inattentive wife. I imagined such a man, rumpled
and hungry, sitting forlorn in his chair as the house grew dim,
waiting for his wife to come home and bring him a sweet tea.

She continued. "You won't learn to iron, you refuse to learn
to cook—"

"Is this what you wanted to talk to me about?"

"No." She lifted the shirt, gave it a shake, poked its shoulders one at a time into the arms of a hanger. Another shirt came off the pile and flapped onto the ironing board. "You know Reverend Swanson's wife?"

"Yeah." Not really. Reverend Swanson was our new minister, and I didn't pay much attention in church.

"Did you know Mrs. Swanson has multiple sclerosis?"

I didn't reply. I didn't even know what that was, though I could tell by my mother's tone it was not good. She said, "*MS*. It's a deadly disease."

"Oh."

"They think the move down here caused some kind of flare-up. She's not doing well. You know she has those two little girls."

"Yeah."

"So, your father and I are sending you over to help them out a few days a week. As our gift to the church."

I deflated into the pillows. "What? Why? To do what?"

"To help out. Watch the kids, do some housework."

Now I was incensed. "Why can't they get a colored girl in?"

"Well, I don't know. Maybe they don't like that idea. They're from Minnesota They're Northerners."

"Obviously they're Northerners if they're from Minnesota," I replied in Ricky's sarcastic tone, showing off my knowledge of geography.

"Willa." She sounded tired to death of me. I sat up, tucked my legs together Indian-style and stared furious-faced at her.

"I don't like kids," I proclaimed, a shockingly unfeminine statement. It was like throwing a poisoned dart at her.

"Well, you're gonna like these ones. You start tomorrow. Ride your bike over. When school starts, you go there straight from school three days a week."

"*What?* What about my homework?"

She hung another shirt and gathered my father's regalia from the pile on the bed. The garment overflowed her arms, swallowed the ironing board and its metal legs. "You'll have time for homework."

"Not as much!" I doubted she heard the genuine panic in my voice.

"You'll be fine." She ironed the robe one swath at a time, dragging it toward her.

"Mama. This year I have a *goal*. To get straight As."

"Good," she replied without hesitation. "You can do it. You're a smart girl."

Her response was so sincere, I could tell she was thinking of what my father had said and feeling bad for me. She wanted my father to love me too. I thought I might cry.

I said, "I'll go over to the Swansons' and I won't complain at all if you ask Daddy can I go with him and Ricky to the meeting tonight."

This made her hand stop ironing and her eyes attach to mine, unblinking beneath pale raised eyebrows. "We are not *negotiating* here, young lady." She puckered her lips and resumed ironing. "Anyway, you know he'd say no. You know that. He doesn't want ladies involved because we might blab it all over town."

"*Mama.*"

She shook her head slowly. Her shaggy pale-brown ponytail swayed with each shake. "We do what your daddy says, Willa. Your daddy's a brilliant man and he knows what's best. Lot of people in this town don't understand things the way your daddy does—he sees what's comin'. He's braver than most of those other men too."

"I'm brave. I can see what's comin'." How could I grow up to be like my father if I was excluded from everything he did? "Mama, *please*? Just ask him?"

She kept shaking her head. Then, to console me, "You can help me make the deviled eggs for the meeting. I'll show you the right way to boil eggs so the shells don't stick."

She lifted the regalia from the ironing board and found its special hanger—the extra wide one made of wood that would hold the weight of the garment. She hung it high on the edge of the closet door, and the material shimmered, catching bits of sun that blasted through the window. I saw how artfully she'd sewn the insignia over the breast, the arms of the cross straight in its red circle, the teardrop centered. My mother came toward me to rummage through the clothes on the bed. "Okay?"

"Okay," I croaked.

From the pile she pulled the hood, fitted it over the narrow end of the ironing board, aligned the eye holes, and began ironing from the bottom to the top, where the material formed a point.

❧

When I was growing up, my mother often repeated the sad story of my father's childhood, either to elevate him in our minds or justify his behavior in her own. I don't recall ever not knowing it. He was born in the mountains of western Virginia, at the extreme edge of the state. The scenery was majestic, but there was no bulb of joy there—no raucous uncles getting together to play breathy banjos or bow-slapping fiddle music. My father's family had always been destitute. Then the Great Depression hit. One day his unemployed father, tired of his wife and five children, wandered away. My father's mother was a weak woman, prone to whining and blaming, unable to solve problems without a man's guidance. The children took care of themselves.

Here my mother would pause to emphasize: that's why our father was such a devoted family man who would never abandon us. He had a profound understanding of the importance of the father to the family.

He was one of the younger boys, and he was scrawny, with a weirdly tall head and protruding ears so round and red it was hard not to laugh at them. All his brothers were broad and muscly; my father was called "the runt" and mercilessly bullied. His talent for school—for remembering facts better than other boys—only made the after-school assaults worse. The mountain forests were dense, designed for concealment: it was easy for packs of boys to hide there, primed for a strike.

On the landscape of my father's childhood, life felt threatening and circumscribed, bounded by walls of treetops, gouged with twisted lanes and vanishing dirt paths. When it rained, the mist sank over the mountaintops, making you feel sealed in. My father's brand of poverty was not one you could simply walk away from, across a grassy field: you had to climb out of it in an upward struggle, weighed down by fears and the likelihood of backsliding. You had to pretend to believe in yourself, because you didn't.

By contrast, I grew up on the flat terrain of the Tidewater. On my childhood landscape, things were naturally out in the open. I expected everything to be visible, easily spotted from a distance. Although some roads curved around bends and patches of trees—loblolly pine and hickory nut, poplar, live oak, willow, birch—soon enough you were back out in the open, in a field of hunkering cotton plants or peanuts that stretched tidily toward a faraway horizon. A luminous sky cupped over you, broad and high. You could look up; you could look around. You could predict and anticipate. I did not and never have coped well with surprise, concealment, or sudden revelations of character.

The road ahead of me was going to be rough.

# 2

The reverend's family lived in the church parsonage on Butterwood Road, a flat, red-brick ranch house with no porch, only a concrete step up to the back door. The backyard was packed with southern pines, skinny and sky-high, all the branches concentrated at the top—the lower limbs being too deprived of sun to survive. I tilted my blue Schwinn against one of the trunks, poised for a quick escape. I was irrationally hoping no one would be home.

Then I saw her standing at the back door: Ruth Swanson.

She had the palest skin I'd ever seen. Her face was so white it was almost pewter, sunlight pooling on its smooth planes. She was short—my height—and slight, her shape swallowed up in a turquoise robe, a pinwale cotton corduroy thing with a tie at the neck that was much too heavy for summer in southeast Virginia. She had a nub of a nose and watery eyes tinted like an early morning sky. Her hair, wound wet around curlers, was the color of dry sand. She grinned—closed-lipped, lopsided—and spoke in a voice that floated, as ethereal as the rest of her. "Willa?"

"Yes, ma'am," I said and stepped inside.

"Oh, please, call me Ruth."

She led me on a tour through the family room, kitchen, and living room, as though I hadn't been in the parsonage a thousand times before. In fact, my mother had been great friends with the previous minister's wife, and I'd passed many hours here fidgeting on chairs while church ladies drank coffee. The interior was intentionally plain, being for a minister's family: walls white, kitchen cabinets the standard knotty pine. Church members periodically donated old furniture to the parsonage, so none of the pieces matched, although some were interesting because of their age, like the "bonnet box," a light maple cabinet with drawers on one side and, on the other, under a hinged top, a large compartment for ladies' bonnets. Mrs. Swanson had moved it next to the front door and hung an oval mirror over it. Also in the living room was a sleek green couch too modern to be a parishioner's leftover; the Swansons must have brought it from Minnesota. The enormous oak bookcase against the opposite wall must have been theirs too. Already it was packed with books, weighty hardcovers and paperbacks fat and thin. I gazed at them, and Mrs. Swanson sang out, "*Willa!* Like Willa Cather!" When I didn't respond, she added, "The famous author. Willa Cather."

I'd never heard of her, which embarrassed me, so I blurted out, "I've read *lots* of books. My daddy's the new assistant principal at Kingsfield High."

"That's good," she replied, then, "Impressive!" Her accent was funny, all the vowels squished to barely nothing between hard consonant sounds. She continued: "Your mother is such a sweetheart to send you. I have a ladies' luncheon at church today and look, I can't even get my hair dry! The girls have been underfoot all morning, but now you're here, thank goodness! Your mama is such a sweetie, she even gave me the number of a boy to mow the lawn. I don't think it's been done for weeks, it looks shabby—did you notice?—*shabby*, and we can't have that, now, can we?" A bitterness crept into her tone, with an undercurrent of panic. "The minister's family has to set a good example. The minister's wife has to have everything *just right, all the time.*" Abruptly she concluded, "It's hard being a minister's wife."

I'm sure I looked surprised. It would have been the first time an adult had confided anything personal in me or had spoken to me for a reason other than to instruct or direct or admonish. She turned and waved me down the hall behind her, and I saw how she walked, the right foot dragging, the left foot lurching to maintain balance. *Multiple sclerosis*, I heard in my head, slowly, to ensure all the syllables were there.

In the doorway of a bedroom decorated in cool blues and

greens, we stopped. Two little girls sat together in a sea of toys and books. "Julie, Annette," Mrs. Swanson said. "Say hi to Willa."

"Hi," their squeaky voices said in unison.

"Julie's five, Annette's three. Maybe you could read to them?"

"Okay," I said. She loped across the hall into her bedroom, and I sat on the floor.

I'd never babysat before. People called on Barb, not me. I really had no idea what to do. The girls gazed at me, round-faced and doe-eyed, and I had to admit, they were kind of cute. The older one had long, shiny cinnamon hair, the younger was a frowzy blond, and they were dressed in matching red-and-white-checked playsuits. I was sure my brother Billy was never this adorable. Billy was all knobby knees and elbows and boogers.

I said, "Wanna read?"

A giant copy of Disney's *Cinderella* lay in front of us. Meticulously Julie opened the cover, then looked at me, her eyes intelligent and a bit skeptical, maybe unconvinced I could handle such a complicated book, full of fat paragraphs of small print. I began to read, but mostly we lingered over the pictures, the girls wanting to touch the cartoon birds and mice and the fairy godmother.

I glanced behind me. In the bedroom across the hall, Mrs. Swanson sat stoically with a plastic dryer cap pulled down over her curlers, the roar of hot air through the kinked hose rendering her deaf. She stared at the floor. Her fingers fidgeted with themselves.

"Ooooh!" Annette said, turning the page that revealed Cinderella in her scallop-skirted ball gown. Julie explained each part of the costume—gloves, tiara, shoes made of *glass*. Annette pointed and repeated everything her big sister said. Eventually Mrs. Swanson appeared at the bedroom door, looking more substantial in a fitted daisy-yellow dress, her hair a halo of curls. To the girls she said, "Daddy's here to pick me up." She stepped into the room, picked up a different book and handed it to me. "Here. Let's give Cinderella a rest." She blew kisses to her daughters, then attempted a stern tone: "Be good for Willa. Do everything she says. See you in two hours." We listened to her uneven walk down the hallway, the door opening and closing. I looked at the children. *Two hours?*

"Okay!" I said and held up the book Mrs. Swanson had given me. *The Little Engine That Could.* I proceeded to read with such expression—"I *think* I can, I *think* I can"—that when I finished, Julie asked me to read it again. I did. Then she asked me to read it a third time, then a fourth, then a fifth. Dragging through the sixth read, I swore to myself I'd never touch this annoying book ever again. "Okay!" I slapped it shut and sent it skidding across the floor. "What else do you have?"

They had an infinite supply of *Little Golden Books* about ducklings and puppies, kittens and bunnies and hens, mice and squirrels and a baby elephant. I longed for *Nancy Drew*, or even a *Boxcar Children* book. We read and read, yet only fifteen minutes had passed. How was that possible? At the end of a book about a brave little sparrow, I said, "Let's go look at the books in the living room."

This surprised and thrilled them. They raced ahead of me and stood at the immense bookcase, which rose nearly to the ceiling. On top of it, instead of photos and knickknacks, were more books, squeezed between two white marble bookends chiseled to look like books. These people were nuts about books. Head cocked, I read along the spines: Camus, Sartre, Adler, Kierkegaard—how could there be so many authors I didn't know? Of course I'd only been on the planet for thirteen years, but at the time that didn't occur to me. Instead, I felt dumb, and that made me angry from shame, remembering what my father had said. I pulled a book off the shelf at random and flipped through. It was full of pictures of liberated Nazi Concentration Camps, skeletons dancing next to piles of skeletons. I slammed it shut and put it back. My eyes continued their sideways slide until I spotted a Bible. Surely this would be appropriate for the preacher's kids. Though I was not a particular fan of Bible reading, it would be far more interesting than another story about a baby mouse.

I popped it loose from the shelf and sat on the couch; Julie and Annette snuggled against me. I opened to the Gospel of Matthew—why not?—and began at a random verse, "And when he was come to the other side into the country of the Gadarenes, there met him two possessed with devils, coming forth out of the tombs, exceeding fierce, so that no man could pass by that way." This was some weird old-fashioned version of the Bible, not like the ones in the wood racks on the pew backs at church. "And behold, they cried out, saying, What have we to do with thee, thou Son of God? Art thou come hither to torment us before the time?" The girls could not have understood a word of it—I barely did—but they were captivated by the musical strangeness of the language, sounds from a faraway place and time. "Now there was afar off from them a herd of many swine feeding. And the devils besought him, saying, If thou cast us out, send us away into the herd of swine. And he said unto them, Go. And they came out, and went into the swine: and behold, the whole herd rushed down the steep into the sea, and perished in the waters."

"What's a swine?" Julie asked.

"A pig," I replied, and oinked at her.

"The pigs ran into the sea?" she asked, and Annette followed up, "*Why* did the pigs run into the sea?"

"Because the devils got into them." Instantly I regretted saying this. Maybe the Bible wasn't appropriate for young children after all.

In a somber, instructional tone, Julie said, "The devil is *bad.*"

"Yes," I said. "Yes, he is."

She said, "I didn't know there was more than one."

"Well."

Her eyes grew enormous with fear. "How many devils are there?" I glanced at Annette, who also looked terrified.

"Um. I don't really know."

Solemnly, Julie summed it up, saying, "The devils made the

pigs run down into the sea," and Annette squeaked breathily, "Did the pigs *die?*"

"Uh—"

"Where are all those devils now?" Julie asked in alarm. "Are they still in the pigs?"

Fortunately, I had the sense to pause and think. One of Kingsfield's major industries was ham. We were surrounded by hogs and smiling pink images of hogs gazing down from billboards. I said, "No. No. The devils left. They flew really far away." Then, for no reason: "They're in Romania."

Annette tapped my arm and whispered, "We're getting a kitten. We're going to a farm to pick one out."

Julie tapped my other arm. "Do devils get into cats?"

"Oh no," I replied, dead serious. "Cats would never allow it."

They looked relieved.

"Okay!" I jumped up and pushed the Bible back onto the shelf. "Let's go play!"

We were in Julie's room with a community of Fisher-Price people when we heard the car crunch up the driveway.

"Mommy!"

The girls rushed her at the door. She squealed and hugged them fast and dropped onto the sofa cushions. In a rush the girls told her about everything we read—about the little engine that could and the bunnies and the ducklings and the puppies and the swine that went running down the steep and drowned. She nodded along smilingly. I stood in the doorway and asked her, "Would you like me to get you some lemonade?" She looked so exhausted, her face puffy and red with heat, her halo of curls drooped on her sweat-drenched forehead. She seemed so frail.

"Oh, thank you, no, let me get it. I hate being so useless!" She clucked at herself, stood and teetered and waved me along with her into the kitchen. At the counter she poured three large tumblers of lemonade and handed me two. "One is for the young man mowing the lawn. Could you take it out to him?"

"What?"

"The young man, who came to mow the lawn, he's almost done. Outside. Take it out to him please." I glanced outside: it was a colored boy. I froze. Surely she was not suggesting I serve a colored boy. My eyes fastened to hers. She said, "In the yard. He's almost done."

I remained in place, a tumbler in each hand, the plastic growing ice-cold against my palms. We were like two statues pointed at each other. She repeated, "In the yard," her expression blank, the translucent eyes showing no emotion, no anger or confusion, only determination. I didn't speak, and I didn't move: I protested with inaction. I was never going to fetch and carry for some colored.

Finally she took one of the cups from me and dragged herself to the front door. I heard the squeal of hinges and her singsong voice: "Hello, hello! Come get some lemonade!"

I crept up behind her. I'd seen this boy before—he'd been in our yard a few times, pulling weeds and rotten tree stumps. He was tall, sweating through a limp white T-shirt, shoving his hand mower hard through the dense grasses, up and back, up and back. He didn't seem to know she was speaking to him.

"Hello!" she called again, and he peered up, looking surprised that she was speaking to him. She raised the lemonade. "Come take a break!"

He hesitated, then dropped the mower handle and inched toward us, one little step at a time—giving her the opportunity to change her mind—until he stood, bent at the waist, at the bottom of the front steps. Mrs. Swanson opened the screen door and stretched her arm along it to welcome him inside.

"Please, come in!" she said. "I'm Ruth Swanson." He stepped up and reached for the lemonade but stopped at the threshold.

"Thank you, ma'am," he said.

"Oh, please, call me Ruth. And, I'm sorry, what's your name again?"

"Langston," he said, glancing fast at her, then me, then averting his eyes.

She yelped, "Langston! Willa! I'm surrounded by literary giants!" A silence descended, heavy as the heat. She clarified, "Langston Hughes."

The boy replied, "It Langston *Jones.*"

"Yes," she said. "I was trying to make a joke. Langston Hughes, the great poet. I was an English literature major in college. Now I spend all day reading Dr. Seuss." She laughed at herself. "Please come in and sit, it's *so hot* out there. How does everyone stand it? Thank goodness August is almost over. Come in."

"No, thank you, ma'am," he said, eyes downcast. But he drank the lemonade, all of it in a few gulps. I watched his lip on the rim of the cup. He said, "I have another job to get to."

"Oh, a hard worker! I bet your father's a hard worker too."

What a weird thing to say. I stood behind her, smirking.

"Yes ma'am, he is. He work at the paper mill." He passed the empty tumbler back to her.

"I hope he enjoys it."

It was rude of Mrs. Swanson to be making conversation with him—coloreds got nervous talking to white people. But Northerners didn't understand these things; she wasn't being rude on purpose. As he shuffled toward his mower she called, "Come back when you're done so I can pay you!" She smiled, looking after him, then she turned to me.

"I feel terrible!" she blurted.

"You didn't know," I said too quickly. Puzzlement swept across her face.

"I feel terrible because I wanted to pay you, too, for babysitting, but your mother says not to. Your time is a gift?"

"Oh. Yeah. That's right." It was like a punishment when I hadn't done anything wrong.

"Well, I'm hoping I can do something for you in return." She thought for a moment. "I could teach you to sew."

"No, thank you. My mama tried that once."

"Hm. Well, let me know if you think of anything."

I hesitated. "You said you went to college?"

"I did. University of Minnesota, Class of '56."

"You *graduated?*"

"I did."

"Then maybe you could help me with my homework if I need it. I'm determined to get straight As this year—that's my goal."

I could tell this impressed her; her entire face smiled. "Okay, straight As! That'll be *our* goal!" She continued to smile at me. She seemed to be *thinking* about me. It was an odd sensation, being so acknowledged. It made me feel like a whole person, with a mind as well as a body—sort of like an individual. I was used to being regarded as a label, a group member: an eighth grader, a girl, a McCoy kid. Ruth Swanson made me feel like I existed all on my own.

I rode my bike home light-headed, my brain buzzing. I was sure to get straight As with this smart lady helping me. Had she read all those books on those shelves? I was ticking up to my house, imagining my father's face when I presented him with my first perfect report card, when I spotted an unfamiliar car parked in front: a bright white, silver-trimmed, brand-new Chrysler convertible.

I rode past its sharp rear fin and peered into its soft beige interior. It had no window cranks! My father had told us about power windows, but even he thought they were an unnecessary extravagance. I steered my bike in a U and approached the car from the front, its grill growling, its slanted eyes observing my approach. Why was this seriously gorgeous car at my house?

I leaned my bike against the fence, entered our front door, and stepped into a crowd of teenagers. It wasn't unusual for Ricky and Barb to have friends over. The surprise was that there, lounging on our worn blue couch, was Jim Darden. *Darden.* The Dardens were the epitome of Kingsfield elite. The original Darden founded Kingsfield Ham in 1897, and the family had been amassing wealth ever since. They'd built and still occupied the mansion on High Street, a lofty-roofed, many-gabled place with a wide porch wrapped around all four sides. And here was Jim Darden, youngest son of the president of Kingsfield Ham, sitting in our dingy living room, smoking a cigarette.

I wasn't sure which surprised me more: him or his cigarette. My father was adamantly against smoking—it was unhealthy, he said, and Indian savages were the ones who gave tobacco to the hardworking settlers. Yet Jim Darden's pack of Benson & Hedges lay nonchalant on our coffee table, the top pried open, a row of circular ends peeping out. Beside the pack was an actual ashtray—a white ceramic thing with Monticello embossed in its bowl. My mother must have scrounged it from the back of some closet.

"Hello," I said to the room. Patsy Beale was at the record player, stacking forty-fives onto the spindle. Barb and Cindy Poole were smoothing out two Twister mats on the floor. Warren Bunch sat in one of our wing chairs—Warren and Jim Darden were on the football team, a year ahead of Barb and Patsy—undoubtedly the lucky recipients of Barb and Patsy's generous lemonade, as featured in the *Tidewater Times*. My brother Ricky didn't play football, being a tennis star, but he was there too, draped sardonically across the other wing chair. Barb and Cindy Poole jumped up, both in pink slacks and loose white tops—an embarrassing wardrobe accident, no doubt. Cindy was not especially friends with Barb and Patsy; she must have been invited to be another pretty girl, which she was, in a pug-nosed, flat-faced sort of way.

"Hi, Willa!" Barb bubbled, drunk on popularity. "Y'all know my sister, Willa."

"Willa can be our caller!" Patsy chimed and threw open her arms as though to hug me. I'd noticed, over the past few years, that Patsy's personality had been expanding—her voice louder, her gestures grander—as she established herself as "the fun one," unable to be "the pretty one."

I glanced at Jim Darden, who smiled at me. Despite his ultra-white squares of straight teeth, he was not good-looking. His face was horsey-long with too much forehead—a harbinger of early baldness—and his eyes were dark and round like a vole's. Warren Bunch was far more handsome, hazel-eyed and strong-jawed, the crown of his head smooth enough to look good with a crew cut. Yet Barb had seated herself at Jim's side, giggling, stroking her ponytail. Barb, I understood then, would be trading on her good looks for a wealthy husband. Mrs. James Darden would be on the guest list of anyone's social event. Barbara Darden, I thought—*ar ar ar.*

From the kitchen came my mother's voice, delirious with glee, sounding like someone else entirely: "Willa?" I went in. My father was sitting at the kitchen table reading his newspaper, which was unusual in late afternoon.

My mother stood at the stove plopping Oscar Meyer hot dogs into a boiling pot. On the counter was our good Georgian Eggshell china tray, the one we used at Thanksgiving. On it she'd lined up hot dog buns, each one spread wide, awaiting its wiener. "How was it at the Swansons'?" she asked.

"Fine," I replied.

"Good!" my father boomed.

"Wonderful!" my mother burbled.

Everyone in my house was high that night.

"I really liked babysitting," I said and my parents looked so pleased, as though every last worry was now gone forever, all problems permanently solved.

"Here, honey!" My mother began yanking bottles of Coke and Dr. Pepper from the refrigerator. "Take these in?" I managed to get three bottle necks per hand through my fingers "Oh, wait!" she said and whipped out the bottle opener. *Hiss thunk, hiss thunk.* Somehow I inched into the living room without spilling them and got them safely onto the coffee table, beside the cigarettes.

Across the room a commotion had begun. "Give 'em back!" Patsy shrieked, but laughing, Barb by her side. Warren Bunch had taken all of Patsy's records off the spindle and was holding them over his head. Warren was exceedingly tall, so Patsy and Barb had to leap at his raised hand.

"I just want to see," he said. Cindy Poole sat demurely awkward on the arm of Ricky's chair. Ricky persisted in his slouch; Jim Darden lit another cigarette. Warren looked at the first 45 and in a high-pitched girlie voice said, "Bobby Vee, oh Bobby Vee, you're so dreamy." Ricky belted out a laugh. Warren looked at the next record and began singing in a shrill voice, "*Take good care of my ba...by...*"

"Gaw!" Ricky said.

Then Warren looked at a third record, groaned, and screeched out: "*It's my party—*"

"Hey," Patsy finally said, no longer smiling or lunging. "I like that one."

"Jim," Warren called. "What about this one?" He lobbed a record like a Frisbee to Jim, who raised a lethargic hand to catch it. This caused Barb to prance toward him. He glanced at the record and smiled and held it over his head against the wall. Barb could've easily walked around the end of the couch to get it; instead, she stood at Jim Darden's knees and reached over him, tittering and tilting until she had to steady herself with one knee on the couch beside his thigh. She pitched toward the record, pink-faced with joy, her breasts joggling in his face. His beady eyes widened until she grabbed his wrists and pulled them toward her, all the time laughing and radiating heat, her sexual desire now entangled with the ridiculing of her musical tastes. Finally she got the record from him and fell onto the couch beside him. He said to Warren, "It's okay. It's Elvis."

Barb announced, "I say *Jim* gets to pick out all the records for tonight." Patsy looked stricken, and Ricky looked mad. Just like that—just by sitting on the couch and smoking and being rich—Jim was awarded authority over what everyone would hear and feel all evening. He picked out a Marty Robbins, Freddy Cannon, The Ventures, a few Beach Boys. Silent and dutiful, Patsy stacked them onto the spindle. Then came my mother's voice from the dining room: "Ki-i-ids! Food's on!"

Set majestically on our table was the platter of hot dogs wedged into buns, accompanied by a serving bowl heaped with

Ore-Ida Tater Tots. Ordinarily we did not have such food. My mother must've dashed out to the Be-Lo when Barb told her Jim Darden was coming over. My parents retreated into the kitchen, covering their giddy smiles, and we ate standing up, Barb and Cindy nibbling daintily on the ends of wieners, the boys wolfing down dogs and tots as fast as they could. Patsy and I ate a normal amount, though I snuck a few extra potatoes. Then it was time for Twister.

Everyone gathered at the edges of the mats. I spun and called out commands: "Left foot, red!" Feet slid onto red circles. "Left foot, green!" Feet shifted; girls giggled. "Right hand, yellow!" Down went the hands, all six bodies now curved into arches. *Right foot yellow, right foot green, left hand blue.* Legs stretched, hands clamped, arms entangled, ankles hooked around other ankles. Warren's tall, toned body arced over Cindy Poole's and his shirt pulled up, revealing a stretch of suntanned torso. Ricky's hand slid onto a green circle just below Cindy's breasts, and Patsy had a leg around Warren's thigh. Jim Darden was clearly playing for the sole purpose of touching Barb—shoulders against sides, knees against knees. Barb swung her ponytail against his face. Forty-fives dropped onto the record player one at a time and rhythms pumped, desperate voices sang about wanting, needing, loving, aching, and I could not take my eyes off Warren Bunch, his muscle-rounded shoulders stretching the thin material of his shirt, his back and butt rising and dropping as he reached and balanced and straddled the girls.

I had never been a girlie girl. For as long as I could remember, I'd disliked playing with baby dolls, preferring instead to run and climb and stab trees with cardboard swords. With a sheet tied around my neck, I was Batman. I despised stiff, scratchy Sunday dresses and rock-hard patent-leather shoes. I hated the feel of jewelry, clammy little orbs of stone and strings of metal crawling along my skin. Often I dreamed I was a boy having adventures. I didn't think of myself as "a girl." I thought of myself as "a kid." My androgynous sense of self would be a constant all my life. But the night of that Twister game, I knew

without a doubt I was a hopeless, flaming, raging heterosexual.
I wanted to be on that mat with Warren Bunch's body arcing
over mine, to feel his breath flowing down the side of my neck.

Later, after everyone had gone and Barb was sound asleep
in her bed across the room from me, I lay awake thinking of
Warren Bunch. I imagined his smile, broad and sudden, his
front teeth turned slightly inward. I saw his hands large and
solid on the shiny mat, fingers spread wide—his hands rugged,
strong, scraped, browned by the sun. And in the dream I had
that night, I was definitely a girl.

Our family tradition, on the last Saturday before the start of
the school year, was to rise early, dress in a rush, eat little boxes
of Cocoa Krispies and Frosted Flakes, and go downtown to
Holland's Discount to buy binders and loose-leaf paper and
pencil cases. The morning after Barb's party, we piled into our
new used car—our Oldsmobile Super 88, which made us all
feel fancy. The exterior was a shimmery silver, the interior a
dignified executive gray. My father straightened himself behind
the wheel, my mother and Ricky beside him on the bench seat.
Billy, Barb, and I were in the back, me in the middle, my feet on
the hump. Already the day was drenched with heat. Everyone
madly cranked down their windows, which my father insisted
we keep closed overnight so wandering cats and other critters
wouldn't get in. Our mother turned to smile at us, her eyes
nearly lavender in the rippling shadows of the maple leaves
overhead. Her chestnut waves of hair were soft against her long
neck. You could see how pretty she used to be.

"A new school year!" she chirped. "Exciting!"

Her happiness was genuine. This was Ricky's last year of
high school, my father's first full year as assistant principal; and
now Barb would see Jim Darden every day, catching his eye as
she swished down the corridor. She would be a junior; in two
weeks she'd turn sixteen. When my father turned the key in
the ignition, Ricky clicked on the radio and twisted the dial to
the rock-n-roll station. Amazingly, my father did not lunge to

change it; usually he couldn't stand our jungle music. Today he was glowing with optimism, stretching his arm along the back of the seat, accelerating backward down our gravel drive, flying across the narrow path over the ditch.

As we trundled over the ditch, I peered into its depths, its far-down bottom full of mud, wet leaves, twisted sticks, rocks. When Ricky and Barb and I were younger, we dared each other to leap over the ditch. Now I realized that, for a nine-year-old and a seven-year-old, this might not have been scary; for four-year-old me, it was terrifying.

Buddy Holly came on the radio and still my father didn't lunge at the dial. Instead, remarkably, my mother began to sing along: *"That'll be the day…"* Somehow my mother knew all the words. My father said, "Trudy!" sounding surprised but affectionate. Barb joined in, and Ricky's shoulders twitched in a kind of dance. We rolled down the street, singing and grinning, and suddenly I felt maybe I did belong in this family, surrounded by them, tucked in. I let out a laugh.

Downtown Kingsfield was a seven-minute drive from our house. The shops along the five-block strip were boxy, short, turn-of-the-century buildings of white-washed brick. At one end was the Esso station; at the other end was Rich's Hamburger Stand. We passed our sole movie theater with its sagging marquis; *Gidget Goes to Rome* was still playing. We passed the bank, which was the tallest building on Main Street, though still only three stories—the ceilings were just very high. We passed Priddy's drugstore and rolled into Holland's parking lot. My father stopped the car and everyone jumped out, but then Ricky got back in, and he and Daddy drove away. My mother acted as though this was normal. Barb, Billy, and I followed her into the store.

Inside we wandered up and down the aisles, wanting things we didn't need. Barb saw a Japanese-painted headband; Billy saw matchbox cars. I was intrigued by tiny spiral notebooks in a variety of colors that would fit into a pocket. We were scheming how to get Mama to buy us these items when, through the front window, we saw people lining up along the sidewalk. Was it a parade? Mama stood with an armload of shifting notebooks and boxes of pencils. "Go on," she said, and the three of us ran outside.

It seemed like the whole town was out, crowded onto the sidewalk. The mid-morning sun was ruthless, screeching off car hoods. Overhead a row of stoplights hung on their cables, swaying in an inconsistent breeze. Downtown Kingsfield was a treeless place, barren and bald and dusty, even when it was full of people. Everything was flat and open and wide—the street, the stores. The sky was planed with uniform stripes of cloud—its own distant landscape, mirroring ours.

Looking westward, I saw what the commotion was about. Of course. Ricky and my father had better things to do today than shop for silly school supplies. I burned with envy. Past the Esso Station, three blocks away and coming toward us, were the marchers, robed and hooded, blindingly white in the glare of the sun. The chatter of the crowd on the street faded. Soon all I could hear was the moan of streetlights swinging overhead. The marchers approached in slow motion, their footsteps clattering in sync like hail on the pavement. They came without faces, each one hidden behind empty eyeholes, the group moving in otherworldly anonymity.

I ached, longing to be one of them. This was not just a group of men parading, I knew: this was a force, a belief system, a higher cause, a reason for being, a homeland—a power that was timeless and uncontainable. It was a rolling wave of Southern pride, and I surged with it. This is who we were. This is who I was. I yearned to feel the authority they felt, to belong to them.

The marchers grew nearer, and I tried to pick out my father and Ricky by the way they walked. They both had a distinctive, confident, gliding sort of saunter. But the regalia hid even that. I knew who some of the concealed men were because they met at our house sometimes, but I didn't know them all. I realized that by scanning the crowd and applying the process of elimination, I could figure out who some of others were.

The manager of Holland's was nowhere in sight; all morning I hadn't seen him in the store. On the sidewalk among the watchers were some of the guys who worked at the paper mill, our plumber, the boys who flipped burgers at Rich's Hamburger Stand. But the man who pumped gas at the Esso wasn't there, nor was Dan Cobb the car salesman. The mayor of Kingsfield stood ashen-faced in the doorway of the appliance repair shop across the street, but there was no sign of drugstore mogul Donald Priddy. Down the block, tilted against his car, was Jim Darden, with Warren Bunch by his side. Both wore crisp new polo shirts and sneering expressions, nearly snickering at the approaching men, and suddenly I was furious at both of them. Snobs, I thought, rich snobs who had everything and assumed they always would. Smug, protected, conceited, relaxing against a flashy car without a care in the world, leaving all the hard work to people like my father. I was not going to dream of Warren Bunch again.

Row by row the marchers passed, the onlookers dead-faced, hiding their feelings as the Klansmen hid their faces. Then, through the flicker of hoods, directly across the street from me, I spotted Ruth Swanson. She was motionless, clutching her daughters' wrists in each of her hands. Her ghost-white face had grown pink and hard. Her eyes widened and reddened; she was clearly upset, and I felt bad for her. She didn't understand. The Klan was not a threat to *her*—a nice white lady, a minister's wife, a mom. The Klan was here to *protect* her and everyone like us. My father said it so many times and here was more proof: Northerners just did not get it. Mrs. Swanson ought to be feeling grateful and safe.

The marchers receded up the road and spectators began to shift and shuffle away. Ruth Swanson remained planted, gazing up and down the street with a lost expression. Then two running boys knocked into her, and to steady herself she let go of Annette and grabbed on to a lamp post. I watched as Annette was swept away in a tide of walkers. Mrs. Swanson screamed.

I didn't hesitate. I ran into the crowd and plucked Annette

from the forest of legs. She was fine, just startled. I propped her onto my hip, as I'd seen moms do, and brought her back to Mrs. Swanson. "It's okay!" I tried to sound upbeat. "I got her! She's fine! See? Everything's fine!"

Ruth Swanson burst into tears. It was embarrassing. Silently I walked with her down a side street to her car and she kept crying, gulping, trying to catch her breath, but she couldn't calm down. I wondered if this was a symptom of MS. Again I said, "It's okay, it's okay."

"Thank you," she coughed and with her free hand grabbed on to my shoulder, as much to steady her walking, I think, as to express gratitude. At the car she opened the rear door, and the girls scrambled into the back seat. Then she plopped herself into the driver's seat and wailed, "I want to go home."

"That's a good idea," I replied, thinking she meant the parsonage on Butterwood Road. I leaned into the passenger window. She spent a moment folded up over the steering wheel, then finally caught her breath and turned to smile at me. "You're a good person, Willa."

I didn't know how to respond. I'd never heard anyone called "a good person" before, only a "good woman" or a "good man." She meant something different from either of those, I thought. I said nothing. She started the car and said, "I'll see you next week."

The car drove away and I stood watching, waving and waving to the little perplexed faces pressed against the rear window. The girls waved back and kept waving, like me, then smiled, their trust in caregivers so easily restored.

# 3

The new Kingsfield Elementary School was completed just in time for my last year of elementary school. At least I'd get to spend eighth grade in this incredible, space agey place—the building so modern it didn't look like a school at all. The exterior was like a wide orange shoebox crouched low on the landscape, not the traditional stone-gray haunted asylum style. The interior was bright, with wall-sized windows. The library had pale wood tables that rolled around and molded plastic chairs. The cafeteria walls were painted yellow, and the main office had a green-and-purple checkerboard carpet. I'd never seen so much color in a school. The auditorium had seats that snapped up, just like in a real movie theater, and it was *air conditioned*. The classrooms were luminescent with clean right angles, free of weird nooks and jumbled closets and old woodwork loose on the door frames. Here there were no cobwebbed ceilings, no cracked plaster walls, scuffed floors, or distracting whorls of dust mites hovering in shafts of sun. The main corridor was wide and lined with metal lockers rather than coat hooks. This was for our safety, my father said; a few years earlier there'd been a grisly school fire in Chicago, which had raged down the corridor coat by coat, incinerating dozens of children. We were all issued shiny combination locks with bright green faces, and we had to practice turning the dial one way, then the other way, then back again, then yanking on the horseshoe to open it. It was harder than it looked.

The old Kingsfield Elementary School was renamed Washington Carver, after the peanut guy, and given to the colored children. For a while it was feared we'd have to build a new school for the coloreds. I'd read articles about it in the *Tidewater Times*. One article included an architect's drawing: six small separate buildings in a circle, serving as five classrooms and an office. The architect argued that if you didn't have interior corridors, you wouldn't have to heat them in winter. But someone pointed out there'd be the extra cost of all those exterior walls, and other people were confused over where the bathroom would be, and it all seemed like a series of problems with no solutions until someone thought of building a new school for the white kids and giving the old one to the coloreds. A new elementary school for whites could be located near the new white high school, built two years ago at the epicenter of the white region of town. The old elementary school was at the edge of town, closer to the encroaching colored neighborhood. It would never make sense for the coloreds to come all the way across town into the white neighborhood for school. So everyone was elated with the solution, except for a handful of clergy, who wrote a letter to the editor urging town leaders to start planning for integration—white kids and coloreds in the same building, together. The letter generated a notable silence. But as a kind of concession, apparently, the editors included the *Coloreds in the News* section, which was an occasional insert, in the very next issue. Pictures of happy colored children outside the old school filled its page.

The first day of school arrived with fluster and noise and nervous energy. I was eager to embark on my quest for straight As, though now every day I'd have to see my former best friend, Becky Campbell, who'd heartlessly dumped me at the end of seventh grade. We'd been best friends since the middle of second grade, when her family moved up from Charlotte, and I thought we'd be best friends forever. Becky was different from the other girls—she was smart and funny and tall. She had thick unruly waves of hair and a way of floating across a room, pitched forward on the balls of her feet. Her father had opened the first photography studio in town. He took fancy portraits of brides and families at Christmas and important men. Becky wanted to be a photographer for *National Geographic* when she grew up. I was going to write the articles. That was our plan. We ruminated on all the exotic places we'd see, all the animals she'd take pictures of: giraffes and gazelles and cheetahs.

I made her promise we'd do this—promise she'd never change her mind. I was sure I'd never change mine. I wasn't going to just get married and be a wife. I was going to *be somebody*. I intended to do something important with my life. I told her this time and again.

Then one day, in the middle of seventh grade, Donna Bowman started giving Becky advice about her hair. She could use this or that shampoo and she could put it up in a ponytail and get bangs—wouldn't that be cute? Suddenly Becky and Donna were going to the beauty parlor together, and then they were shopping for outfits at Peeble's, painting each other's fingernails, and walking home from school without me. By March they were including the ridiculous Toy Bracey in their shopping trips. So I told Becky her new friends were *vapid*—a word I'd recently learned—and she told me I was annoying and critical, and that I felt sorry for myself, and also I was getting too big for my britches—talking about doing important things with my life and being some big important person someday. I was conceited, she said; I thought I was better than everyone else. And that was the end of our friendship.

I cried so hard that night I woke Barb on the other side of our room. She came to sit on the side of my bed and pet my shoulder. The moonlight was bright on the surfaces of our maple dresser and the nightstand between our beds. "It'll be okay, Will," she said again and again. "You'll make new friends."

But most of the kids at school—kids I'd known since kindergarten—were already cemented into their cliques. Nancy Vaughan and Tammie Hines were the popular girls, always pretty in their store-bought clothes, with loyal followers Claudia Holland, Judy Pretlow, the Debbies, and half a dozen other girls. Cathy Parker and Eleanor Barnes were the athletic girls everyone wanted on their team in gym class. Of course all the boys were friends with each other. There were a couple of loose kids on the fringes. One was Florence Whipple, with a person-

ality as unpromising as her name, who'd appeared at our school
in the sixth grade, having moved down from Newport News so
her father could work at Kingsfield Ham. In two years she had
managed to make zero friends.

Inevitably, I ended up beside her at lunch. She was nice
enough, and thrilled to be with me, but she was slow witted,
devoid of charisma, describing in great detail how her mother
mixed up the tuna salad for her sandwich and whacked off
the bread crusts with a meat cleaver. After a few days, the
knobby-elbowed, acne-scarred Sue Bates joined us at lunch,
as did Joe Pedicini, the fat kid from Greensboro. I'd become
the rounder-up of misfits. Because my social status was slightly
higher than theirs, they viewed me as their leader, imitating my
mannerisms and way of speaking, which was flattering. Between
this tolerable human contact and my focus on work, school life
without Becky was endurable. Still, I thought about her, and I
missed her, not just at lunch, not just that year at school, but for
decades to come.

A new math teacher had arrived in Kingsfield: young,
broad-smiling, curly-haired Mr. Marcus, from Baltimore, who
wore his shirt sleeves rolled up on his ruddy, muscly forearms.
After two days of math review, he gave us a surprise test,
which enraged everyone but me; I didn't think it was that hard.
Thursday morning, he announced that only one person in the
entire eighth grade had achieved a one hundred percent—Willa McCoy. He turned his fabulous smile toward me, and my
heart jumped into my skull. Three purple-inked mimeographed
pages of solved math problems were presented to me by Mr.
Marcus's manly hand, attached to the virile forearm, and at the
top of the first page was a bold, red, shiny "100%." I was awash
in happiness. But I would have to wait through the rest of the
long day, and then until I got home from the Swansons', to
show my father. Willa McCoy: "100%." Better than *anyone else
in the eighth grade.*

At lunch I propped the test up between my two little cartons
of milk, and my fan club heaped praise on me. "I'm going to be

famous someday!" I burbled at them, and they heartily agreed.
When Becky walked by with Donna and Toy, I couldn't help
but catch her eye—and in a wordless plea begged her to see my
worth and like me again. Instead, she shot me a look of disgust:
there I was once more, *showing off.* I slid the test back into my
binder and trudged through the afternoon. By my last class, history, I was just tired, slouched at my desk with a drooping head.

My history teacher that year was the infamous Miss Cooke.
Renowned for being old and loony, she was a lumbering woman who wore sack dresses patterned with giant blossoms or
geometric shapes or paisleys—designs you'd upholster furniture with. Her cheeks wobbled when she talked, her chin like a
cork afloat on a sea of neck. Rumor was she'd lost her fiancé in
the war—not the Second World War, but the First—and that
he'd died, not in some great battle, but of the flu on the ship
going to France. For decades, young adolescents speculated
about what they would have done with the body. Put it in a
giant icebox? Dump it into the ocean? After this tragedy, Miss
Cooke lived with her parents, and when they died she inherit-
ed their house on Witchduck Lane, which had needed a coat
of paint since 1947. Even the adults wished she'd retire, but
no one wanted to suggest it for fear of being rude. Today she
sat behind her desk telling stories about the War Between the
States, her favorite war. She was prattling on about the Battle of
Smithfield, in which gallant Virginians refused to surrender to
the Northern invaders and sank the *USS Smith-Briggs.* I already
knew about this. I'd been to Smithfield and seen the plaque. So
my mind wandered.

Through the iridescent glass was sunshine, grassy slopes, the
low branches of elms. Two summers ago Becky and I had spent
hours sitting on tree branches, discussing our action-packed
futures and eating peanuts. We squeezed open the soft brittle
shells, shaking out the nuts, raining peanut dust onto the ground.
Triple peanuts were lucky and we could make a wish on them.
I wished for fame and adventure. She wished for more practical things—for her dad's business to pick up, for her mom's

laryngitis to get better soon. Had I thought her wishes were too small? Once I'd said, "Oh, c'mon! You gotta think *big!*" Now I regretted it. I'd been pushy and bossy, and I'd lost her. I was wholly absorbed in my sorrow when the pitch of Miss Cooke's voice startled me back to history class: "Now we got *mobs of coloreds* marchin' on Washington!" she was screeching, rising from her desk, massive and pyramid shaped. "Hordes of 'em! *Singin'!*" She added in disgust, "Why do they have to *sing?*"

I knew vaguely what she was referring to. I'd seen some footage on Walter Cronkite—crowds of coloreds, some white people too, oozing through the streets of Washington, DC— before my father jumped up to turn off the Jew media. Miss Cooke railed on: "*Mobs* of coloreds in our streets and everyone just sittin' around doin' nothin', doin' nothin' because *why? Why?* Because *everyone* is too *stupid* to know their *history*, that's why!" Her voice dropped to a deep, menacing tone: "Who here knows the story of Nat Turner's insurrection?"

The class went dead quiet. I did not know the story, and if anyone else did, they were hardly going to raise their hand and risk being wrong. Miss Cooke lurched toward the front row. Fortunately, I was three rows back, behind the coiffed strawberry-blond head of Claudia Holland.

"Not *one* of you!" Miss Cooke raged. "You kids get stupider every year!"

I'd heard this complaint from teachers before, and I'd always wondered about it. Here was the human race, inventing television, developing vaccines for polio, building spaceships, yet, according to teachers, each generation was dumber than the one before. Much later I would figure out it wasn't the kids getting dumber, it was the teachers getting smarter—every year they acquired another year's worth of knowledge, while their students stayed the same age.

Miss Cooke grumbled on, "People just sittin' around know-in' nothin' while the federal government passes all kinds of laws tellin' us what we can and can't do." Then she hollered, "*Negro* rights! *Negro rights!*" She paused, apparently to get a hold on her emotions, and in a frightening near-whisper said: "Let me tell you a little story about a slave, named…" Pause for effect. "*Nat Turner.*"

She began: "Not *ten* miles from here lived a slave named Nat Turner, treated *kindly* by his masters. Treated like a prince! Not once whipped. Taught to *read.* Allowed to go rabbit huntin' and keep some of the rabbits. Given decent food, decent clothes. Given good solid Bible instruction—so much he fancied himself a *preacher.* But was he grateful? *Was he?*"

We shook our heads no, which was the obvious answer. She tilted toward us; the hem of her dress swung forward over her flabby knees. "Do you think he ever said *thank you?*" Again heads shook. "Did he live out his life like a loyal servant obeying his master, like the *Bible says?*" A few soft *no*'s were vocalized by a couple of boys unable to control themselves.

"No, he did not! Do you know what he did instead?" Her face turned red as a beet. By now we were all riveted to our seats, hands gripping the edges of our desks. "He organized a bunch of wild coons to rise up against their masters! Nat Turner and a horde of wild *coons* went rampaging through the countryside, slaughtering good Christian men and women—and children!—not *ten miles* from where you are sittin' at this very moment in time." I shifted. Ten miles was, in fact, not all that far. "*Butchering* children just like yourselves, children and *babies* slaughtered like hogs, innocent children with their throats split open and their heads chopped off. Right here in Southampton County! Hundreds chopped to pieces! Have any of you seen a body with its *head chopped off?*"

Surely no one had.

"Imagine," she went on. "You wake up in the night to the sound of your mama screamin'. You run out of your room, and there's a horde of big Black bucks whacking her to death with hatchets, chopping her up into bloody bits, pullin' out her intestines all over the floor. Then they go after your *sisters, hacking* them to pieces, *whacking* off their heads. And then, then, they come after *you. Imagine* that."

We all were imagining it, and undoubtedly would be all night long, too terrified to close our eyes.

"Nat Turner's last victim," she gasped, "was a beautiful young lady named Margaret Whitehead. Kind and loving, charitable to all, caring for the sick and the old folks. *Murdered* in cold blood! Lovely young girl, Margaret Whitehead, who loved poetry and animals. Ironically, she was *concerned* with the condition of slaves in Virginia. Ha! What did that get her? *Butchered.* Sliced through by Nat Turner himself, the beast! First he ran her through with a saber, then he *bashed* in her skull with a fence rail."

Soundless and still, many of us forgetting to breathe, we heard the ticking of the clock—a shiny sunny circle rimmed in silver, mounted over the door. Miss Cooke glared at us, and then, perhaps satisfied we were all suitably terrified, continued in a more instructive tone: "Coloreds need to be kept in their place. Strict rules and discipline. Coloreds aren't capable of moral judgment, no more than gorillas in the jungle. Now, we have some gorillas here in the civilized world, don't we? And where are they? *Locked up in cages in the zoo.* That's where they belong. But there are people in this country wanna give the gorillas *rights. Rights.* They think gorillas ought to vote and eat in restaurants with us, *swim in our pools,* go to the same schools as you. You just think about that. You think about Nat Turner, treated so well by his masters. Didn't matter how he was treated because he wasn't a man, he was a *gorilla.* Soon as he could, he got out with the other gorillas and murdered hundreds of good Christian people! You *think* about that."

I did. It was just more proof of what my father always said: it was a scientific fact that colored people were inferior to whites. The colored brain was different, smaller and less developed, incapable of advanced thought or moral reasoning. That's why coloreds did all the terrible and stupid things they did. Science had established the inferiority of the Negro. Obviously my father would know this, having a master's degree in science.

Still, something pricked at my brain. Even then—young as I was, immersed as I was in the quagmire of my culture—something seemed wrong to me. I felt my hand float up into the air. Miss Cooke looked surprised. "Yes?"

"Were there other slave rebellions in Virginia? Besides Nat Turner's?"

"No," she replied with a moral finality. "No, there were not."

"Why not?" I said. "I mean, you'd think the ones treated *badly* would rebel, wouldn't you? Why weren't there more rebellions?"

"I'll tell you why." She squinted her eyes at me, the flesh enveloping all but her pupils. She raised an index finger to emphasize her point. "Because coons are *cowardly* by nature. They don't have the courage or the fortitude of good white Christian men."

Again something rankled in my head, a kind of subtle alarm set off by that part of my brain that noticed adults' inconsistencies, their lapses in logic. The voice that had spoken up before, which had pointed out I could not be as stupid as my father believed, suggesting the adults around me might sometimes be wrong, wanted to speak again.

I said, "So, if they fight back, they're monsters, and if they don't, they're cowards?"

I recall the room filling up with silence. Like a glass filling with water, it seemed to start at the floor and rise over our heads. Slowly it occurred to me I'd challenged the teacher. I don't think I'd meant to. Nervous now, I looked at Miss Cooke. But her face did not look angry; instead, she began to smile and nod. "Exactly," she said, victorious. "Exactly."

*What?* She returned to the Battle of Smithfield, and I sat worrying *I* was the one who didn't understand, that there was some principle of logic I hadn't grasped. I kept working the idea around in my head—whatever the slaves did, rebel or not rebel, was a sign of moral inferiority. I worked it around some more, but back then I wasn't able to see the connection; I couldn't carry the principle forward. Everything colored people did was taken as a sign of inferiority. Yet when white people did something wrong—stole something, struck someone—it was not taken as evidence of the entire race's lack of morals.

It was never a thing done or not done that we hated about Black people; it was simply the fact that they were Black. We just pretended otherwise.

When the final bell rang, I leaped up with my classmates, and in the frenzy of grabbing stuff and racing toward the exit, I forgot about Miss Cooke and Nat Turner. Instead I remembered my stellar math test, and my thoughts turned to glory ahead.


Through the Swansons' screen door, I spotted Julie and Annette sprawled on their tummies on the tile floor, with coloring books and a box of twenty-four Crayola crayons between them, their legs bent at the knees, all four little feet waving like flags on a lazy breeze. "Knock knock," I called out, as my mother always did.

"Willa!" said Julie.

"Wumma!" said Annette.

I walked in. None of the lights were on. I could hear the chug of the whole-house fan in the hall ceiling, and propped on a metal TV tray next to the girls was a roaring box fan.

Ruth appeared in the kitchen doorway and wafted toward me through stripes of shadow. "It is *so* hot," she said, with her slanting grin. "Thank goodness it's finally September—cool weather on the way!" I didn't have the heart to tell her September in southeast Virginia was pretty much like August. Cool weather arrived around Halloween.

The girls were on their feet now, bouncing. Ruth said, "Yes, Willa is here to play with you, but first she has to do her homework. Keep coloring please, and don't bother Daddy while he's working."

I glanced into the living room. Reverend Swanson, gawky-limbed and unkempt, was reclining on the couch, reading one of the books from the giant bookcase. Emanating from a record player beside him was the soothing drone of cellos and violins. Ruth stood watching me. "Ready?" she said, meaning we should go to the kitchen table now to start my homework. But I couldn't wait.

"Look!" I unfurled the math test, its glorious ruby "100%" as thrilling to me now as when I first saw it.

"Oh! Congratulations!" She took the paper. "Wow! Look at all this fancy math!" And she did; she stood and read every question and every right answer, basking in my accomplishment. I'd never felt so acknowledged, so attended to. My parents were always too busy for me, and here was this stranger, giving me all these moments, *looking*. She got to the last question about diameters and tangents and let out a sigh. "I'm not sure I *ever* knew this kind of math! Good for you! Straight As here we come! What do you have today?"

"An essay."

"Oh, thank goodness. Something I know how to do!"

"I have Mrs. Beale for English," I said, tucking away my math test. Ruth turned and headed toward the kitchen. I followed. "Everyone says she's a real *stickler*," I continued, but at least she wasn't crazy like Miss Cooke. Mrs. Beale was a real war widow, whose husband had died on Omaha Beach, and also she was stylish, coming to school in suit dresses and paneled skirts in colors like peacock blue and berry red. We all wondered why she'd never remarried. "She gets very excited about grammar." Once Stevie Hedgepeth claimed he saw the edge of a black bra strap peeping out from her sleeveless blouse. "Today she was talking about 'the joys of gerunds.' At first I thought she—" Abruptly I stopped. There, at the kitchen table, with books and loose-leaf paper spread before him, sat Langston Jones, the colored lawn mower boy.

Ruth chirped, "You remember Langston!" I heard parts of the explanation that followed: joining us for homework... senior at Trackton High... As she talked, her energy returned. "And he's planning to go to college!" *College?* I must have known there were colleges for colored people—there was a colored dentist in town. Ruth sat and motioned for me to sit too, next to her, across from the boy. She was saying, "Langston's mother is the teacher at the Negro school outside of Courtland. Did you know that?"

Of course I didn't know that. How would I know that? Sitting, I noticed my hands trembling. I tried not to look at Langston's face, but he was right across from me. I had to turn my head unnaturally to keep my eyes on Ruth, who burbled on, "It's an old-fashioned one-room schoolhouse, with all ages, up to junior high. Right?"

"Yes'm," Langston said, and my eyes couldn't help but twitch toward him. He had a steep chin and thick straight eyebrows. He looked as uncomfortable as I was. What did Mrs. Swanson think she was doing?

She said, "Hey! You're both teachers' kids! No wonder you're both so smart! Willa just got a one-hundred percent on a math test!" she told Langston, then turned to me. "Langston got straight As in chemistry last year!"

I wondered what kind of chemistry they taught at the colored high school. Maybe something to do with farming. I couldn't help but look at him again, his forehead sloped and shiny, a scrubbed russet potato.

Ruth's voice jumped an octave. "Isn't it a shame you two don't go to school *together*!"

At this, our heads rotated toward her, mirror images of each other. I did not say out loud that if the schools were integrated, Langston's mother would be out of a job. Colored teachers wouldn't be hired to teach white kids. Then I thought of my father, enraged when anyone brought up desegregating the Kingsfield schools. He hadn't worked hard in college and gotten a master's degree in science to teach a bunch of porch monkeys how to sit still.

Silence coagulated, making us all motionless. Then Ruth burst out, "All righty! Let's write essays! Willa, what's your topic?"

Dry-throated, I croaked, "What I did over my summer vacation."

"Oh my goodness, are they still assigning that awful topic? Langston, what's yours?"

He nodded once and mumbled, "Same."

"Is there no creativity left in the world? Well, okay. Let's bounce ideas off each other." She turned her ebullient eyes on me. "What did you do, Willa?"

I'd gone to Virginia Beach with my family for a week. We swam in the ocean and got sunburned. Billy thought he got stung by a jellyfish but he didn't. Ricky wanted to surf, but the waves weren't big enough. The pimply counter boy at the Dairy Queen got a crush on Barb. This was going to make a very dull essay.

"Hmm," Ruth said, then asked Langston the same question.

Langston had gone to North Carolina with his family to see his grandmother. They swam in a lake. His little brother stepped on a nail but it didn't go into his foot and he made too big a deal about it.

"That's just like Billy!" I blurted and was horrified at myself. Ruth bowed her face to conceal a smile. I did not appreciate being tricked.

Langston said, "My summer vacation was as dull as hers," meaning me.

"Maybe you don't have to write about these trips," Ruth proclaimed. "Years from now, looking back on this summer, what will you most remember?"

Immediately I thought, Being alone. This was my first summer without Becky. I'd ridden my bike by myself, down every road and path in a five-mile radius, my tires thudding over gnarly roots, my legs pumping hard along the dirt. Thank goodness for my bike—as hurt as I felt, at least I could still be out in the world; I could feel myself strong and alive, despite being alone. My bike became my best friend. But what I'd remember most about this summer was the absence of Becky. I said, "Most of the summer I was just by myself."

"Oh. Why was that?"

I shrugged. "I need new friends."

"Ah." Her gaze rested on my fidgeting hands. "Then you should write about what it felt like to be alone. Take one ordinary day and relive it on paper—everything you saw and heard and smelled and felt and thought. What do you think?"

I nodded. What a weird idea. We were supposed to write about something unusual, then attach a moral to it, like, "I should not have eaten my ice cream in the car," or, "I should be more patient with my little brother." I was hardly going write something different and risk my A.

She turned to Langston. "What about a typical day in your summer?"

His walnut-colored face lowered and began to smile. He tried to suppress this smile, but it broke loose, broad and full of big beige teeth, peach-pink gums showing above them. Ruth tilted toward him, her forearms folding together on the table, and half-laughing said, "I think you *found* a new friend."

"Yes, ma'am," he said, trying to get the smile under control.

"Does she have a name?"

"Daisy."

"Daisy! What a cheerful name. I love that name. Tell me about *Daisy*."

My skin grew hot. I had no interest in hearing this colored boy talk about his girlfriend. But once he got going, it was hard not to get drawn in. Daisy was a year below him at Trackton. She'd recently moved down from DC to live with her grandma outside of town; her mother had died of lung cancer. Daisy kept a photo of her mother in a fold of cardboard in her purse and showed it at every opportunity—a smartly dressed woman who'd worked as a clerk typist for the government. As he spoke, I kept my eyes on the slope of his broad shoulder, not wanting to accidentally make eye contact. Daisy, he said, was just a little thing, short and thin, but she went down the halls like she owned the place, all determined and focused. She wore big dangly earrings. All the girls liked her too, because of her confidence and her way of encouraging them to speak their minds.

The more Langston talked, I realized, the more he relaxed, and the more intelligent he sounded. He started pronouncing the ends of words, conjugating verbs correctly, using past tense, including the "s" on plurals. He kept talking because

Ruth Swanson kept listening, nodding at him, inviting more. He continued. All winter he'd wanted to ask Daisy on a date but he was too nervous. He snuck around and stared at her and his friends teased him. Finally a friend of his told a friend of hers and one day Daisy found Langston on the front steps at school and struck up a conversation.

"What did she say?" Ruth asked.

"She said, 'Hi, I'm Daisy Wheeler. You're Langston Jones.'" He paused to chuckle joyously. "I said, 'That's right,' and she said, 'I believe there's something you want to ask me.'" Again, the chuckle. "So I said, 'May I walk you home today?' and she said sure, and so I walked her—two miles out of my way!" Then he laughed mightily at himself. I imagined the story told and retold to future generations, an aged Langston and Daisy tittering together in wooden rockers on a sloping porch, surrounded by grandchildren and great-grandchildren.

Then I remembered Nat Turner. I remembered Miss Cooke's arms flailing and her pasty face growing scarlet. Nat Turner, that vicious beast, educated and fooling everyone, playing the well-behaved darky, then leading a pack of wild coons in the slaughter of hundreds of white people—she said *hundreds*—including people who showed him kindness, like Margaret Whitehead. My insides contracted. Just like Ruth Swanson, sweet and well-intentioned, stabbed and battered to death.

Mrs. Swanson should not have this boy in her house. She didn't know what these coloreds were capable of. I appreciated she was trying to be a good Christian—she just didn't know. I turned intentionally and stared at Langston Jones's face, examining him for traces of barbarism. His eyes were acorn-brown, flickering with light as he talked about Daisy, his smile waxing and waning but never disappearing, powered by the ecstasy of his new love. He *seemed* genuine, but you couldn't trust him, you wouldn't want to trust him. Coloreds were like a different species; there was no way to really understand them. I stood up. "I'm gonna take the girls outside."

Ruth looked surprised. "Oh, I'm sorry! We got completely

sidetracked! My fault! Sit down, sweetie, we'll all get a start on the essays."

I was already walking away. "It's okay, I know what to write. I don't want to keep the girls waiting."

Ruth seemed to believe this. She turned an appreciative grin toward me and nodded, and she and Langston resumed their excited discussion of Daisy.

At home I found my mother and Barb in the kitchen, my mother stacking pieces of fried chicken onto a plate, Barb dumping succotash into a bowl. I stood in the doorway, relieved to be home and safe. "Just in time!" my mother sang out. "Table!" Setting the table was my great responsibility.

I asked, "Where's Daddy?"

"Backyard with Billy."

"I have something to show him."

"Table first!"

I ran around the table shoveling plates and silverware and napkins into their approximate spots, then grabbed the math test, crinkled now by all the admiring, and ran to the back door. Appearing from nowhere, as she tended to do, my mother asked, "What is it?"

Barb hovered behind her. I showed her my test score.

"Oh, well, look at that!" my mother said, without really looking at all, calling out to my father and Billy, "Supper!" Barb peered at the test and rolled her eyes.

"What?" I asked.

"No one likes a know-it-all, Willa. And don't tie up the phone tonight—Jim Darden's gonna call."

This seemed intentionally cruel. She knew I didn't have any friends I wanted to talk to on the phone. I shrugged and watched my father amble toward the door, Billy moseying at his side, swinging his bat. Softball with Billy, tennis with Ricky— my father made time for the boys, made sure to be a role model for them. He'd expect wives to attend to girls, of course. Still, I couldn't wait to show him my test, and when my mother attempted to herd me to the table before I had the chance, I wouldn't go.

"Come on," she whispered and pulled the paper from my hand. "We'll show them all at supper."

I thought, Yes! We'll *show them all.* That was exactly what I wanted.

We sat and said our prayer. Then came my father's pop quiz: "Name one species of bird found in the Great Dismal Swamp."

Billy called out, "Wood duck!"

Ricky drawled, "Warbler."

I said, "Pileated woodpecker!"

Then my mother asked Billy to tell us about his day at school, and he embarked on an endless chronicle, from the morning bell to dismissal—a shapeless, meandering narrative, devoid of rising action or a climax or a point, his feet apoplectic under the table, his spoon gently pounding his succotash into mush. When finally his story wandered to something like an end, Barb asked Ricky if he was going to call Cindy Poole. He didn't know. He didn't want Cindy to get the wrong idea, and anyway, he was busy with tennis. The conversation then leaped to the topic of tennis. My father and Ricky spent several minutes recollecting Budge Patty's forty-six career titles. Ricky didn't think Rod Laver was anything special—he was no Pancho Gonzales. My father let out a kind of moo, a vocalization he made at any foreign-sounding name, and in the dip of silence, my mother burst out, "Willa has good news!"

She produced my glorious test and passed it to Barb, who passed it to Ricky, who looked annoyed and passed it across me to Billy, who gulped and gasped dramatically, then gave it to my father. My father had been smiling and kept smiling as he took the paper. Then the smile grew neutral, perfunctory—his anticipatory smile in the process of becoming a different kind of smile. His eyes focused and proceeded down the page line by line, steadily shrinking to a squint. The smile, at last, became a smirk.

"Well, I *hope* you got a hundred percent on this," he said.

"This is all *seventh-grade* math. You're in eighth grade." He passed the test to my mother and resumed eating.

I shrank in my chair. My mother gave the paper back to me and began buttering her biscuit. Barb and Ricky looked at me with actual sympathy.

Of course, my father was right. It was all review: ratios, percents, decimal notations, parallel lines. I was the only one in the eighth grade to get a perfect score, but suddenly that didn't seem to matter. It only underscored how dumb my classmates were. Abruptly, my mother chimed, "She's off to a great start!"

"Yep," my father agreed, concentrating on a drumstick, turning it one way and the other in search of the meatiest side. Then our phone rang, and Barb bolted from the table.

My mother whispered to my father, "Jim Darden," and they exchanged triumphal grins.

Still, I told myself, I was off to a great start. *Yep!*

Quietly my father asked Ricky, "Ready for tonight?"

"What's tonight?" I said too fast.

My mother replied, "Just a few of your father's friends comin' over for pie."

I knew what that meant. The Klan leaders were meeting. My father was treasurer of his klavern, though of course his ambition was to be Klaliff someday, so he had the meetings here as often as he could. I forgot about the stupid math test, snarfed down the rest of my supper, and then jumped up to clear the table. I had to be ready too.

There was an hour to kill before the meeting, so I sat with Billy for part of the Thursday Night Movie. Cowboys were herding cattle and squinting around the horizon for Indians, whose savage whoop finally rose from behind a lump of hills. When the doorbell started to dong, I crept into the closet to take up my spying post. Pleasant greetings were exchanged: "Hello, hello, come in, come in, what can I get you?" I heard Dr. Vaughan, the optometrist: "Hello, Trudy." I recognized the voice of Jerry Owens, one of the peanut farmers; and Mr. Doyle, the football coach and gym teacher at the high school. Other voices I didn't recognize. I listened as the men settled into chairs and my mother clacked from living room to kitchen and back again, bringing them coffee or tea and pie. When she excused herself for good, the voices deepened to their getting-down-to-business tone, their conversation punctuated by the dinging of dessert forks against dainty plates.

Mr. Owens said, "I'm thinkin' it's too soon."

My father's reply was sharp. "This'll be their *third* meetin'."

"Y'all don't think the march'll stop all that?"

Dr. Vaughan cut in. "They weren't even there, did you see 'em there? I didn't see 'em there."

"They would've heard about it."

"I'm with Jerry. Too soon. The march got the point across. I say we lay low for a while and give folks time to think on it."

"Think on what?" My father's voice rose. "About the fact they're meetin' again despite the march? We need to keep up the pressure, show 'em *we're* still in charge and we've got guts. Ricky here's eager to be nighthawk."

*Nighthawk?* Ricky's voice mumbled something. I didn't know what "nighthawk" was, but it sounded daring and heroic, something requiring speed and strength and cunning. I wanted to be it. I wanted to be *nighthawk*. If Ricky could do it, I could.

Mr. Owens's reply was tepid. "I don't know, Dick."

"Dick's right," snapped Dr. Vaughan. "Whites and coloreds meetin' together. You want jigaboos goin' to school with your daughters? You want tar-babies in your family?"

Someone else said, "Virginia's got a *strategy* for dealin' with that. Maybe other states don't, but we do."

Mr. Doyle's voice grew irate. "You think the federal government's *not* gonna come in here and force this down our throats? You know Kennedy listens to coons and you know who's whisperin' to those coons? *Commies*. Coloreds too dumb to do all this organizin' themselves. It's the *Commies*. Kennedy's so stupid he don't see it. Federal government's gonna march right in and force us to desegregate our good schools. Government's already makin' us pay these coons minimum wage. Government's gonna destroy our economy! Commies an' coons! You want them in our schools? Destroyin' our economy? Next thing you know our taxes'll be through the roof!"

Mr. Doyle's thinking seemed a bit all over the map, but I admired his passion. Mr. Owens tried to turn the conversation. "Let's explore all our options. Doesn't have to be a cross burnin'."

Dr. Vaughan retorted, "Symbolism's important here. Christians on fire for the Lord. Takin' back our country."

Ricky's voice squeaked out: "Aren't the Harlans Christian?"

Finally I knew who they were talking about. The Harlans were a Quaker couple who'd been organizing meetings for whites and coloreds to discuss the integration of the schools in Franklin, a town no more than eight miles from us.

In a kindly tone, someone explained to Ricky, "Quakers no more Christian than Catholics, son."

"What other options are there?" someone else asked.

Dr. Vaughan said, "Don't they have a dog?" with a deep, soft laugh.

My father snapped, "We aren't hurtin' anyone's dog."

Our beloved dog, Buddy, had died a year and a half ago of old age, and we were all still devastated, especially my father, who'd spent long evenings in his chair scratching Buddy's ears. Buddy was part collie and part something shorter, and he was the best dog in the world. After a pause my father added, "Maybe a few apes, but no dogs." The men chuckled. Though I saw the source of the humor and chuckled too, I did not believe my father or his friends would actually hurt anything—not a dog or a colored. My father didn't even go hunting; he didn't have a gun. His friends sometimes went hunting for ducks, and everyone went fishing. That was all. They talked tough to keep the coloreds in line but that was all.

Someone said, "Mighty nice pie."

Mr. Owens piped up, "We oughta think on it, take it up at our next meetin'."

"We don't wanna wait too long," someone else said. "Weather'll get cold."

"Not that long."

"Next month. We'll decide next month."

"No use waitin' till it's cold."

"No."

"We oughta think on it a bit."

The conversation rambled on. My father and Mr. Doyle complained about the lily-livered superintendent of schools, who was just waiting around for the federal government to tell him what to do. The governor was not much better—what were people thinking electing him? Someone asked about the new Reverend Swanson, where did he land on the issue of desegregation? My father didn't know; he'd never heard Swanson talk about it specifically. Mostly Swanson preached on the Gospels and brotherhood, in an analytic sort of way, my father said. Once he gave a peculiar sermon all about Martin Luther—peculiar because we weren't Lutherans—and every time Swanson said "Martin Luther" you couldn't help but think "Martin Luther King," but my father didn't read anything into that.

I thought of Reverend Swanson lying on his couch with a book, seeming remote from the world of politics. But then I thought of Langston Jones sitting at his kitchen table. The reverend obviously knew he was there. Then I thought of Ruth, leaning toward Langston and smiling, opening her home to that boy. Then I thought of Nat Turner.

As the men began to leave, I stayed sweating in the closet, the story of Nat Turner echoing in my mind. In my imagination, he looked just like Langston—tall, with a jaw sloped at a sharp angle. *Hundreds of white people slaughtered.* My stomach churned. I needed to know more. I'd feel better if I knew more: print on a page was always calming. I slipped from the closet into our family room, where our encyclopedia was packed onto the bottom shelf of the bookcase. It was the 1960 edition—as up-to-date as you could get. I read along the spines and extracted vol. 22: TEXTILE to VASC. I rested the weight of the book on my bare legs, the cover feeling textured, a little greasy, and flipped to "Turner." There were a couple of Turners in the encyclopedia. On page 628, I found "TURNER, NAT (1800–1831)":

...Negro leader of a slave insurrection in Virginia, known as the "Southampton insurrection." Having studied the Bible, Turner became a Baptist preacher of great influence among Negroes. In 1828 he told companions a voice from heaven had announced, "the last shall be first," which he interpreted to mean the slaves should seize power. On the night of Aug. 21, 1831, he and seven other slaves entered the home of his master, Joseph Travis, and murdered him and his family. Turner and his marauders then stole guns, horses, and liquor and invaded other houses, sparing no one. Recruits were added until the group numbered about 60. On Aug. 22, they were vanquished by a small force of hastily gathered whites. In all, 13 men, 18 women and 24 children had been butchered. Turner made a full confession. He was tried and hanged along with 19 accomplices. The insurrection led to stricter slave codes.

I let out a puff of air. That was it? "Turnip" had a longer entry than this. I added up the number of victims listed—fifty-five. Miss Cooke had said hundreds. At first I thought the encyclopedia was wrong, but of course Miss Cooke was more likely in error. I checked the index of my history book for "Nat Turner": *Tobacco; Tories; Traveler, General Lee's horse.* Under "N" I found *Negroes, first brought to Virginia; New Market, Battle of; Newport, Christopher.*

Then I recalled a book written by a retired school principal, the now ancient Worrell Bunkley, about the history of southeast Virginia. My father had brought home an autographed copy. I found it in our bookcase, a slim gray volume titled *One Hundred Years of Virginia History: Southampton, Warwick, & Isle of Wight Counties, 1760-1860.* My father said Mr. Bunkley was working on a sequel, *1861-1960,* but had gotten bogged down in the War Between the States. I took the book to my room, closed the door, and propped myself against my pillow.

The book didn't have an index or a table of contents. I had

to flip through page by page. It began with a chronicle of our local battles in the American Revolution, then moved through a tedious recounting of crops, weather patterns, who lived where, who married whom, who got elected to what. Here were all the Wallers, Cobbs, Pretlows, and Moreheads whose descendants surrounded us today. I was nodding off when I came to a section called "Evil in Sunny Southampton: Nat Turner's Insurrection." I straightened up:

Nat Turner, born October 2, 1800, was the property of carriage-maker Joseph Travers. By all accounts, Nat appeared to be intelligent, albeit mentally deranged. Taught to read at an early age, Nat read the Bible and began preaching to his fellow slaves, calling himself "The Prophet." Ignoring Bible verses that admonish slaves to obey their masters, Nat often repeated Matthew 20:16, *The first shall be last and the last shall be first.* On February 12, 1831, a shadow moved across the sun, which Nat took as a sign from God to kill white people. He spent months planning the brutal attack, which quickly failed.

On the night of August 21, Nat commenced his rampage with only a small group of slaves and free Negroes, apparently believing their numbers would increase as they went from farm to farm butchering white Christian families and liberating slaves. Nat's band of killers armed themselves with axes, hoes, razors, knives, and blunt objects. After imbibing alcoholic cider, they went to the home of Nat's master and hacked to death Travers, his wife, his infant son, and two young boys. The marauders then stole guns and traveled southeast, killing Salathiel Francis, the widow Reese and her son, Mrs. Elizabeth Turner and sister, an overseer, and others.

The killers then turned north, toward the widow Whitehead's farm. Their final destination was alleged to be the town of Jerusalem on the Nottoway River, Nat likely mistaking it for the town in the Bible. On the roadside, they slaughtered the widow Whitehead's son, a Methodist minister. Also butchered along the way was the Bryant family—Henry, his wife, child, and the wife's mother. At the Whitehead farm, the killers axed to death Caty Whitehead, three of her grown daughters, and an infant grandson. Nat spotted a fourth daughter, eighteen-year-old Margaret, attempting to flee. He pursued her, stabbed her with his sword, then smashed in her skull with a fence rail.

The marauders continued north but then wound south, west, and north again in a nonsensical route from house to house, leaving carnage in their wake. Victims included Nathaniel Francis's overseer and two children; John T. Barrow; George Vaughan; William Williams, his wife, and two boys; Mrs. John K. Williams and child; Mrs. Jacob Williams and three children; Edwin Drewry; Trajan Doyel; Mrs. Caswell Worrell and child; Mrs. Rebecca Vaughan, her niece, and her son; and Mrs. Levi Waller and ten children, who were found in a grisly pile of blood-soaked corpses on the Waller farm. In all, sixty-five white people were murdered. Many more would have died had it not been for the loyal slaves who protected their masters, hiding them or leading them to safety, thus showing gratitude for their masters' care.

The rampage ended at noon on August 22, when the killers encountered a white militia with twice the manpower and three companies of artillery. The murderous mob was easily vanquished. White retaliation was swift and vigorous. After the bloody rampage, roughly 120 Negroes were killed in Southampton County alone. Negroes who participated in the insurrection were decapitated, and their heads were mounted on posts at a crossroads.

After the insurrection, rumors circulated across the South that Negro hordes were swarming down highways. Terrified white people were forced to kill many Negroes, until a US general issued an order to cease. Hundreds of Negroes may have died in the aftermath of the Southampton insurrection, representing a significant loss of property for white families.

The insurrection resulted in new laws restricting Negroes from assembly and prohibiting all Negroes, enslaved or free, from receiving an education. Nat Turner's motive for initiating the bloody rampage was never established.

I closed the book and stared at the wall. Miss Cooke was right about one thing: a lot of the victims were children. But it was still unclear how many white people died. How could these sources contradict each other? And what did the author mean, Nat Turner's motive was never established? Wasn't that rather obvious? Until then, I hadn't given much thought to slavery, but it struck me now that no matter how well your master treated you, being enslaved probably seemed like a problem.

It was early for bed, but I put on my nightgown anyway, brushed my teeth, wound the alarm clock, and climbed under the sheet. I tried reading an old, dog-eared *Nancy Drew* from my closet shelf, but phrases kept intruding: *armed with axes, hoes, razors, knives...butchered...women and children...ten children... hacked to death...* I dropped *Nancy Drew* on the floor. *Murderous mob...carnage...a grisly pile of blood-soaked corpses.* Fears swarmed through me like wasps in my stomach, crawling up my throat and into my brain. *The first shall be last and the last shall be first.*

Shuddering, I pulled the sheet over my head, closed my eyes, and saw the image of a monster, blue-black, broad-chested, wild-eyed. I saw a muscled arm raising a sword, a massive hand gripping the hilt. A blade sliced through the small, tender body of a woman—Ruth Swanson; the hand seized a plank of wood, dark and splintered, swung it back, aimed.

My bedroom door slowly squealed open and I heard myself gasp. It was just Barb strolling in, oblivious to all the dangers. *Lovely young woman...head smashed with a fence rail....* I peeked over the edge of the sheet. She sat on her bed, glanced at me, and burst into a laugh. I'm sure I looked ridiculous.

Her rosy face and laughter sent a wave of reassurance over me. "Are you all right?" she said with big-sister sarcasm. Suddenly, I was: all was as usual, all was well. Barb was safe. We all were, I knew, because my father and the klavern protected us. My father, brave and wise, alert and primed, a leader of men. I imagined him standing stalwart in a firm-footed stance at the edge of our lawn, his sheer presence a repellent to the danger that hid in the blackness of night. I felt my body ease into a supple calm. My father was a savior, a savior of good people; and maybe someday, I could be too.

# 4

September rolled by as usual, holding the heat as though the season would never change, a stranger to the concept of autumn. Ricky played tennis. Barb got phone calls. The Swansons got a kitten—black and white like a penguin, with a lopsided splotch of black on his chin. I racked up As, which I proudly presented to Ruth, who never tired of praising me. I could tell, though, despite my A+, she was disappointed in my essay on my family's summer vacation, which concluded with me pledging to be more patient with my little brother. She said, "Next assignment, maybe you can find a fresh angle."

Our next assignment was about family heritage. We were to write about how our dirt-poor ancestors in England, Scotland, or Ireland bravely journeyed to America and prospered. What would be a fresh angle on that? I thought how my ancestors did not in fact prosper as much as other people's, but I didn't know why, and it didn't seem likely I could find out by Friday. At thirteen, I knew nothing about indentured servants in the New World, so I could not have realized my ancestors were likely among them. Anyway, Mrs. Beale would not have wanted a gloomy essay. The point of this assignment was for us to marvel at those spunky suffering people of old who'd struck out across the Atlantic, valiantly pursuing their dream of not dying in a famine, and to exude gratitude for having been born in America.

When I received an A+ on my history test, I had a double reason for showing it to Ruth Swanson: first to see her face brighten with pride, and second because a lot of the questions were about Nat Turner's insurrection. These questions were a little unfair, I thought, since Miss Cooke hadn't taught us the details of the insurrection—I only knew the answers because I'd obsessively read about it on my own. I'd gotten an extra credit point for knowing Nat Turner's master was named Travis, not Turner, and I'd even put that the name was spelled "Travers" in older records. Then again, most of our time in history class was spent not learning about anything in particular, but listening to Miss Cooke rant about John F. Kennedy and Martin Lucifer Coon.

Ruth read the test with glistening eyes and handed it back to me. "Congratulations again!"

"So, you know the story of Nat Turner?"

She said, "Yes, I do. Do you know the story of Emmett Till?"

I didn't, but I nodded anyway, not liking to appear stupid. I figured I'd look it up in the encyclopedia when I got home. I did look him up, but he wasn't there, so he must not have been that important. I read about tillage machinery instead.

I'd taken to leaving my high-scoring papers on the kitchen table for my father to see in the mornings. He rose early every day and was gone before any of us kids got up. One morning I found my summer vacation essay relocated to my spot at the table: he'd circled in red a misspelled word the teacher hadn't caught. The history test looked untouched, and he didn't say anything about it either, which felt worse than being corrected—no response. My mother saw me moping at the table and said, "Wait till he sees that first report card. He'll be so proud!"

"He will?" I couldn't help but say. Breakfast bowls rattled into the sink.

"He's proud of you now," she assured. "He just doesn't say much. Men are like that. They don't say much."

This seemed untrue. My father talked a lot—on and on and on at times—and his pride in Ricky's tennis accomplishments was always visible, as was the pleasure he took from Barb's beauty and Billy's funny little-boy antics. But I said, "Okay," anyway.

A week before my fourteenth birthday, my parents invited Jim Darden for Sunday dinner. He and Barb were now officially going steady. Jim and his family went to the Episcopal church, but that didn't bother my parents. He arrived in a blue Sunday suit brandishing a bouquet of hydrangeas, a "hostess gift," he said, for my mother. Patsy Beale had also been invited to provide lively conversation if needed. Patsy had become indispensable to Barb, who was increasingly nervous around Jim, unsure of what to say, worrying especially about her clothes, which were handmade or, at best, bought at Peebles, not from Thalhimers in Richmond or even Rices-Nachmans in Newport News. Usually Barb and Jim double-dated with Patsy and Warren, though Patsy and Warren weren't really dating.

My mother had splurged on a Darden ham. The table was laid with our good china, and as everyone took their seat my mother burbled, "Aren't the flowers *pretty!*" thus officially launching the superficial dinner conversation: weather, peanut crops, cars. Soon all talk narrowed to the topic of Jim: What had Jim done over the summer? How were Jim's classes going? How were Jim's folks? Was Jim planning to attend William & Mary like his father? So absorbed was everyone in the life and times of Jim Darden, Patsy's conversational skills were barely needed. During one brief pause, she mentioned volunteering as a candy striper at the hospital, which I thought was far more interesting than Jim's sailboat, but the talk was quickly reclaimed by male voices.

At one point my father said to Jim, "Did you know that the Russians' Sputnik launch nearly failed? A part malfunctioned, so the thrust was unbalanced. Fuel regulator in the booster failed too, fifteen seconds after the launch."

Jim was mute.

Ricky joined in: "Traveled at 18,000 miles per hour—that's 8,100 miles per second." He knew this only because our father had quizzed us on it.

"One *thousand*, four *hundred*, and *forty*," my father added. "Number of orbits around the Earth, before it burned up on re-entry."

I realized they were attempting to impress Jim with their

knowledge of scientific facts, which struck me as kind of pitiful.

Then, suddenly, I was angry. Couldn't Patsy have been allowed a few more minutes of airtime? Why were Ricky's rotely memorized facts more important than Patsy's stories about the hospital? Why did men's conversations so often have a "No Girls Allowed" sign pinned to it? What made female voices so annoying to the male ear? I wanted to say something, to claim center stage for female voices everywhere, my impulse like an object hurtling toward the sun. I blurted, "Mrs. Swanson was really upset about that colored church in Birmingham, Alabama."

Poking at his collard greens, Billy asked, "What colored church?"

My mother commented, "Mrs. Swanson's health has been bad lately. She missed today's service."

Barb leaned toward Jim to murmur, "Mrs. Swanson has *MS*."

"She your new minister's wife?" Jim asked.

"Yes!" my mother exclaimed, as though he'd said something brilliant.

Patsy said, "Sometimes at the hospital I go down to the colored floor. Did y'all know they don't need anesthesia the way we do? Doctors can stitch up colored kids without any painkillers 'cause they don't feel pain the way we do. Their skin is thicker." After a beat, she added, "I feel sorry for those poor little colored girls in Alabama."

"What little colored girls?" Barb asked. Ricky shrugged.

My father was clearly needed to explain: "Bomb went off in a colored church in Birmingham. Four colored girls got killed."

My mother shook her head, and in the stretch of silence that followed, I could feel the topic slipping away, leaving a space for the men to step in and change the subject. I asserted myself: "Mrs. Swanson was crying the day after it happened, and then she was crying a week later too because the *Tidewater Times* didn't have any stories about it."

Ricky said, "Well, why would it? It's the *Tidewater Times*, not the *Birmingham Times*."

"Such a shame," Patsy muttered.

Suddenly Billy stopped fidgeting. "Why did a *bomb* go off?"

Jim Darden tilted toward Billy and said, with a smirk, "*Klan* planted it."

The way he said "Klan," clipped and abrupt and sneering, made us all pause. Hands stopped cutting, mouths stopped chewing. I remembered his scoffing expression the day the Klan marched down Main Street.

My father offered, "Men feel desperate these days. Country's goin' to hell."

Jim said, "Buncha hillbillies and rednecks hardly gonna help that," and he laughed, high-pitched and horsey, like a whinny.

Slowly, everyone resumed eating. I thought how my father, having grown up in the mountains and now living in the swampy lowlands, could be considered both a hillbilly *and* a redneck. He looked distracted. The very next night, I knew, the Klan was meeting to talk over the cross-burning at the Quakers' house. My mother shook her head ambiguously. Patsy gazed at her plate, and Barb grew fretful, her thin penciled eyebrows rising and falling and squirreling together. Finally my mother asked, "Jim, do you like peach cobbler?"

He did, which was a good thing, she said, because that's what we had for dessert. Everyone laughed.

After dinner the girls cleared and the men went outside to mill around the property. Barb and my mother ran bowls from the table into the kitchen, while Patsy and I stood at the trash can scraping plates. Patsy smiled at me and in a quiet voice said, "I hear you're really smart in school this year."

"What? Did Barb say that?"

"Barb and Ricky both do. They say, 'Willa's the brains of the family.'" Her smile widened. "They're jealous. Don't tell them I told you."

"I won't." I wanted to grab her and hug her. Then I wanted to run outside and race around the yard and whoop with joy.

Patsy whispered, "Maybe you can help me out with somethin'."

"Sure!" I'd doing anything for her now.

"Keep an eye on Jim Darden. I don't trust him. Don't let him be alone in the house with Barb."

"Why not?" I whispered back, but I knew why not. A young adolescent who reads voraciously finds a lot of interesting material when the librarian is loitering in the restroom. I'd found an ancient copy of *Womanhood and Marriage* stuffed on a back shelf, which explained how virile man and passive woman fit together. And romance novels by Janet Lambert and Rosamond du Jardin were plentiful.

Patsy said, "I don't like his attitude."

"I'll keep a watch on him," I replied and beamed, happy to belong to her conspiracy.

All day the next day I was a helium balloon: *Willa's the brains of the family*. I couldn't wait to tell Ruth. But when I got to the Swansons', no one answered the back door. Through the screen I could hear water running in the kitchen sink, so I poked my head inside. "Hello?"

"Hello," replied a tense baritone—Langston's voice. I walked in. He was standing at the sink, washing dishes. I paused at the kitchen door and watched his dark forearm rise from the pool of suds, his large hand gripping a bowl, rotating it meticulously under the faucet to rinse off the soap. I'd never seen a boy wash dishes before, but of course colored men did in restaurants.

"What are you doin'?" I asked.

"Cleanin' up."

"I can see that. Why?"

"Reverend don't know how."

At first I was silent, trying to grasp his meaning. Then: "Where is Mrs. Swanson?" my voice sounding alarmed and a little accusing.

"She at the hospital. They took her last night. She havin' a flare-up."

"Oh," I said, and the reverend roamed into the kitchen, looking dazed and wobbly on his long deer legs.

"Willa. Good," he said, not looking at me. He was extra

disheveled today, one side of his hair lumping up, and he was hunched over, as though looking for something on the floor. He said, "I'm going back to the hospital." He bumbled around the kitchen and into the family room. "Car keys," he said to himself.

"When'll you be back?" I asked, which made him straighten up to his full height and squint into a corner of the ceiling.

"Oh," he said. "I don't know. Can you stay? Can you and Langston get the girls supper?"

"*I* can do that," I said quickly—to remind him he couldn't possibly leave me and his daughters alone with a colored boy.

Close to my ear, Langston sighed, "I said I could stay."

"Yes, yes, both of you, good. Ruthie would like that. She'd like that."

My throat hardened. But before I could gather my thoughts into an objection, he was shambling out the back door. "Home around eight, I guess," he said and left. *Left.* Left me and his two young daughters alone with this colored boy four years older than me, half a foot taller than me, and far stronger. *The last shall be first.* I trailed after the reverend, across the backyard, trying to think of what to say to keep him here. I watched him fold his legs into his car and drive off.

Inside, Langston was at the sink again, submerging a plate.

"Where are the girls?" I barked at him.

"Out front, playin' with a hula hoop."

I ran to the living room window. Indeed, there was a hula hoop, flat on the ground, Julie and Annette sitting inside it, as though it were a perfectly round island. They'd picked some yellow dandelions and were marching them around in the grass. In the kitchen behind me, pots clanked, and I realized I'd better keep an eye on Langston—he might steal something. I slunk again to the kitchen door and peered at his back, at the ridges of his shoulder blades beneath the worn white cotton of his shirt. Without turning he said, "You could help."

He held up a limp towel, and I was compelled to walk up beside him. I took the towel.

"I don't know where they go," I said, meaning the dishes.

"You such a *smart* girl. Figure it out."

In silence he handed me dripping dishes, and I ran the rag over them. I had to open all the cupboards to find where the plates went, and seeing all of Ruth's things—the plastic tumblers with the green diamond pattern, her blue-and-yellow ice cream bowls, a shapely green glass vase—swamped me with sadness. Because there was no one else to ask, I asked Langston, "Did the reverend say what happened?"

His response was almost gentle. "Yesterday Ms. Swanson feelin' so bad she couldn't get out of bed for church. But after the reverend and the girls left, she got up and made Sunday dinner for them, had the whole thing cooked by the time they got back, he said—nice roast chicken and potatoes. She got it all on the table, then she just sat there, he said, not eatin'. He asked her what's wrong, and she said she had no appetite. After they finished she started clearin' the table and she fell, broke a few dishes. She couldn't get herself up, he said, but didn't want his help neither. She just sat there cryin'. Reverend called it a *cryin' jag*. He didn't know what to do, so he took the girls next door to Ms. Poole's and took Ms. Swanson to the hospital and they said she need to rest, so she there, restin'."

"They said it was a flare-up of the MS?"

"I don't think anyone really knows." Langston began scrubbing at a pan, leaning his weight into it, scraping at it with angry, vicious little movements.

"The girls must've been scared," I said. "Seein' their mama like that."

Langston looked right at me, pinned his dark eyes to mine, full of incredulity and disdain. "I 'spec they was."

"You don't have to stay," I snapped.

"I said I would."

"I can get the girls supper." Though in fact I wasn't sure I could, having been so recalcitrant to my mother's attempts to teach me.

"I told the reverend I would stay and I *am* stayin'." He turned away and continued his aggressive scrubbing. I shoved the last of the plates into a cabinet and slipped outside to see the girls.

"Willa!" Julie squealed.

"Wumma!" said Annette.

I sat down in the pine needles, outside their hula-hoop island, and listened as Julie explained their game. The two taller dandelions were the parents, and the two shorter ones were the kids, and they were on a picnic.

"I'm sorry your mama had to go in the hospital," I said.

"Mommy needs to *rest*," Julie said with the authority of a practicing physician. I wondered if all Ruth was doing there was lying in a bed. Didn't they have treatments for MS? Or maybe they weren't keeping her there for MS; maybe they had her there because she'd been crying out of control. Ladies making a big fuss were considered an emergency.

I said, "You know, they find cures for diseases all the time. Someday we'll wake up and we'll hear on the radio, 'Doctors have found a cure for MS!'"

"Wumma, when is Mommy coming home?"

"I don't know. Soon. Not today." I added, "I miss her too. Your mama's a good person."

A good *person*, I thought, because "good woman" was not quite the right label for Ruth. Unlike my mother, Ruth seemed to extend beyond the boundaries of her family life. Maybe my mother had been contained inside those borders so long, she'd shrunk herself to fit. If she ever once had a desire to exist outside of my father's house, she must have given it up. Complete dependence requires total compliance. It must be exhausting, I realized, to always feel beholden, to live every moment trying to be in the good graces of someone else.

I rose from the pine needles and said, "Y'all wanna see what you're *supposed* to do with a hula hoop?" They nodded. They were the most docile children I'd ever encountered. I stepped into the hoop and whirled it sideways, knocking it hard against my hips, spinning it faster and faster. I was pretty good at it. The girls applauded and leaped up and wanted to do it too. I laughed. "You aren't tall enough!" So instead they leaped as high as they could, which in Annette's case was hardly a few inches, and we were all giggling and tumbling to the ground when Langston appeared on the front step wielding a butcher knife. I screamed.

With a long, annoyed stare, he said, "I'm makin' supper, Willa. Think you can help?"

The girls followed me inside and settled onto the family room floor with their coloring books and crayons, and again I stood in the kitchen doorway examining Langston's back. Sure enough, he was doing something there with a chunk of meat and a couple of potatoes. Whatever he was doing was far fancier than I would have done. His head turned slowly until his profile appeared: he seemed always aware of where I was.

He said, "You really just gonna stand there?"

"What are you makin'?"

"Pork." He had a hunk of it on a big wooden board. He raised the butcher knife and with a whack hacked off a slice of it. Then he whacked off another, and another. I jumped with every thud until he put the knife down.

"How do you know how to cook?" I asked.

He chuckled, almost natural sounding. "My mama never had a daughter, so she make her sons cook."

"Oh," I said. If my mother had had only sons, I thought, she would've just worked double time, waiting on them all. Of course, things were different in colored families.

"You gonna help?" he asked in the exasperated tone of my mother.

"Yes," I replied, indignant. I set the dining room table— three places for me, Julie, and Annette. Then I was planted in the door again, watching as Langston patted flour onto the slices of pork, put them in an iron skillet, plopped half a stick of butter into the center of the pan, crinkled aluminum foil over the top, and slid the pan into the oven. Then he turned and presented me with a tiny knife.

"Can you peel potatoes?"

"Of course I can." I took the knife and looked at it. Probably Ruth had a proper vegetable peeler somewhere, but I was suddenly too proud to scrounge in the drawers for it. I watched as Langston opened the refrigerator and peered in. He opened the freezer door, pulled out a box of frozen peas, gave it a quizzical look, and put it back. He moved a few milk bottles around on a shelf and retrieved a turnip. He found three small apples, too, and returned to the counter, looking pleased with himself. I was still standing with the tiny knife in one hand and an unpeeled potato in the other.

"You waitin' for the Rapture?"

I began peeling. It was surprisingly difficult with the little knife. The blade bumped over the irregular surface, occasionally launching itself off the potato, sending a slice of it into the air. Langston snickered. "Your mama never teach you how to cook?"

"She keeps tryin'," I replied. Then, somehow, my voice got away from me. "But I refuse to learn because I'm not gonna spend my whole life cooking for some man. I'm gonna have a career. I'm gonna be a newspaper reporter—a war correspondent—and travel around the world and write important articles and be famous someday. I'm gonna be on the cover of *Life* magazine."

This was the most I'd ever said to Langston. In fact, he was simply a bystander: this was a speech I didn't get to make anymore, since Becky was no longer my friend. It struck me that if I didn't say these words out loud, my plan might not happen—the words might sink into a bog in my brain and be lost. I peeked at Langston's face, tipped toward me now, looking startled and impressed. A stripe of light ran down his broad brown nose. He smiled a natural kind of smile and asked, "You tell your mama all that?"

"Yeah."

"What she say?"

"That if I don't learn to cook, my future husband will starve."

"Aw," he said, still smiling. "She don't listen."

"No, she doesn't!" I said, suddenly excited. Someone understood! "Or she doesn't believe me. She says I'll meet someone and change my mind."

"Yeah," he murmured. He wrapped the apples in foil and slid them onto the rack in the oven. "But you wanna do somethin' big with your life."

"Exactly!"

He picked up a potato, found another small knife, and pushed the blade smoothly along, just under the skin, sacrificing none of the meat beneath it. I said, generously, "You could be a cook at a restaurant."

He chuckled. "That what you think I should be?"

"I don't know." I heard my voice sounding irritated. I'd been trying to give him a compliment.

"Naw, I'm gonna be an engineer."

"Oh."

I was trying to recall if I'd ever seen a colored train engineer, when he added in a sly tone, "A *aerospace* engineer. I'm gonna design rockets, maybe go up in space myself one day." My body stiffened, which he must have noticed, because he said with spit in his voice, "I wanna do somethin' big with my life, too."

My mind became a tangle of thoughts. Was he making fun of me? He could never be an aerospace engineer—that was like Julie and Annette thinking they could do the hula hoop, ignorant of their limitations. Was he mocking me? Was he saying my being a reporter was as ludicrous as him being an aerospace engineer? Was he trying to humiliate me?

"I'm *serious*," I said.

"*I'm* serious," he said. His eyes squeezed into angry slits. His hand reached out toward me, like a big slow paw. I froze. He snatched the potato from me and said, "I can finish here. You go play with the girls. You good at that."

This was another insult, of course, but I was relieved to go. I took the girls into their parents' bedroom, where they had a telephone extension. I called my mother to say I'd be home late that night. I wanted to tell her the colored lawn-mower boy was here too, and I was scared, and I wasn't sure what to do, but she rushed me off the phone—Jim Darden was supposed to call. When she hung up, I wanted to cry.

The girls were under the bed, giggling; the kitten was hiding there. Their laughter and an occasional tormented "me-ew" began to calm me. I sat quietly, taking long breaths, and eventually Langston's voice called down the hall, "Supper on!"

The girls and I sat at the dining room table, where Langston had laid a platter of pork, potatoes, and apples. I dished a bit for each of us, and we ate. The pork, I couldn't help but notice, was much tastier than my mother's, not dry at all. From the kitchen came the sounds of Langston eating—a fork against a plate, a slurping from a cup.

Julie asked, "Willa, do you like Langston?"

The noises from the kitchen stopped.

I replied, "Well, I don't know."

"Does he like you?" she persisted, and I gazed at her.

"Probably not," I said.

"Why not?"

"Sometimes people just don't like each other. That's all." I resumed eating, turning my eyes from Julie, though I knew she was still looking at me. What else could I say? I didn't want to frighten them. Anyway, how could little children understand?

Then we heard something weird, like a high-pitched squeal. We looked around and heard it again—a distant, squeaky cry. It sounded like it was coming from above. We heard it a third time, and a fourth—it was definitely coming from above our heads.

Julie shrieked, "Mr. Softy's in the ceiling!" We gazed up.

"Maybe he's in the attic," I said.

"He sounds scared!" Julie whimpered, which made Annette whimper too.

"No, no, he's fine," I said, wavering, the mournful me-ew reverberating. The cat actually did sound distressed. "Well," I said, "I'll go up in the attic and look for him." But in fact, he sounded closer than the attic, like he was in a pipe in the wall.

The mewing intensified, truly alarmed now, and Annette began to weep.

From the living room Langston's voice boomed. "I see him!"

We ran in and looked up: somehow the cat had gotten onto the top of the Swansons' enormous bookcase and, crowded by the books, was teetering at the edge.

"How did he get up there?" I said.

"Cats are smart," Langston proclaimed, which irritated me half to death. Apparently, he was an expert on cats as well as cooking and human psychology and aerospace engineering. I reached for the kitten, but I was short, my hands nowhere near him. The kitten grew more agitated, puffing out and crouching and twitching. The circular black markings around his eyes amplified their look of terror. Langston reached up. He could touch the top of the bookcase, but even stretching, he couldn't quite get hold of the cat. Julie began a jumping frenzy.

"I'll get a chair." I headed toward the kitchen, but Langston said, "Here," and grabbed Julie under her arms. He raised her up, his black hands enormous on her sides.

"Put her down!" I yelled.

He shot me a hate-filled look. "I'm not gonna drop her."

Was that my concern? "Just—" I yelled. Just what? What was my concern? *Just don't hurt her!* I wanted to scream. *Don't hurt her!*

Julie got her hands around the kitten's belly, and Langston lowered them both carefully to the floor. Mr. Softy scampered down the hall and the girls ran after him, leaving me to stand awkwardly with Langston. His eyes locked on mine again, black and hostile. When I started down the hall after the girls, I heard him grunt—guttural, bestial. I followed the girls to their parents' room, where Julie was once again trying to scoop the cat out from under the bed. I closed the door and locked it.

On the floor beneath the open window I sat waiting for the sound of Reverend Swanson's car. After an eternity, it came. Then came the reverend's voice from the family room, thanking Langston, emphasizing how happy Ruth was that both Langston and I were looking after the girls. I heard the sound of Langston leaving and again the reverend's voice calling out, "Bye-bye!" jovial and utterly clueless.

Full of fury, my body couldn't keep still. I rode my bike fast, standing up on the pedals, rocking my weight, the bumps sending shocks up my legs. The sun had dissolved into a plum-colored sky; the air was tepid. I knew where they'd be meeting.

My father was right: Northerners were completely ignorant of the dangers of living alongside coloreds. Ignorant, and unwilling to listen. Northerners calling us racist, coming down to meddle in our business. My father was right: too many people in Kingsfield didn't understand the urgency of our situation. We had to do something *now* to stop these Northerners from forcing their ways on us. Northerners, in their idiocy, wanted us to *integrate*. My father was always right. Northerners had no concept of what these coons would do if we loosened our grip. They'd steal, vandalize, rampage across the countryside, kill. Innocent little girls would be at risk. *In a grisly pile of blood-soaked corpses.* It wasn't that I hated Northerners; I didn't hate Ruth and Matthew Swanson. They just didn't know, and they refused to be educated on the issue. What can you do when someone isn't listening? You raise your voice; you scream. You put on hoods and march. You burn crosses.

I rode past the high school, across the football field to the edge of town, where Main Street morphed into US-58 and the houses gave way to cornfields. By the time I reached Old Bridge Road, the sky was dark charcoal, starless, but ahead I could see a man in overalls with a flashlight waving a car onto a dirt path through the field. I leaped off my bike, tucked it between two cornstalks, and crept along the corn row parallel to the path of the car.

I had no coherent plan. I had energy and a bolus of feeling. Frustration washed around inside me at a near-boil. Probably I thought my tenacity and the strength of my devotion to my father's cause would persuade him to accept me into his secret world. I thought there'd be a music-swelling moment when he realized I was as brave and smart and worthy as any boy. I'd burst onto the scene with the shocking tale of the Swansons leaving me and their young girls alone in the house with a belligerent uppity seventeen-year-old colored boy who'd wielded a knife at me. My emotional recounting would rile up the whole crowd, even the resistant ones, and we'd all ride off together to burn a cross in the yard of those Quakers' house, returning flush with righteous victory. I wanted to inspire them. I wanted not only to ride with them, but to lead them.

It never occurred to me that the Klan might, in fact, ride off to confront the Swansons or nab Langston. How could I be so unaware? In my hazy understanding, the Klan brandished power through abstractions—they marched, burned crosses, used nasty language. Sometimes Klansmen broke windows, but that didn't seem so bad to me either, the drama of it far exceeding any real harm done. Like all children, I was growing up siloed in my parents' culture; I lacked enough knowledge to realize what could have happened.

Now, in near-darkness, I slunk along the cornstalks, expecting to come upon a clearing. I listened for voices, but my own rustling and crackling over the parchment leaves were deafening. Every small movement produced a crunch among the cardboard stalks. I stepped on a downed ear of corn, rock hard, which caused a miniature explosion of dry foliage. I paused, listened, crunched; paused, listened, crunched.

At last, through the stalks, I saw a line of parked cars and heard voices—casual, chatty, jokey picnic voices. Someone was talking about a football game over in Suffolk. Someone else made a comment about the coach at that high school. And then I heard a sharp crackle in the cornstalks behind me.

My arms tensed against my sides. Several moments passed. Motionless, I listened. Suddenly there came a rapid succession of crunches, as though someone was sprinting toward me. I dropped to the ground and wedged myself between stalks. I imagined it was Langston after me—Langston, leading a horde of wild Black boys—armed with hatchets and knives. But the crackle of feet through the stalks wasn't loud enough to be a whole group, and before I could formulate a different fear, I saw a flickering through the stalks, ghostly and shapeless. A beam of light blinded me, and a hand grabbed my wrist.

"What the hell?" a voice said, muffled in its hood. It sounded like Dr. Vaughan. I said nothing as he pulled me from the cornstalks. He marched me around the cars and into the clearing, where a dozen hooded Klansmen stood conversing in small groups.

"Look what I found!" bellowed Dr. Vaughan. "A little spy!"

Someone said, "Isn't that your daughter, Dick?"

All the hoods rotated toward me; two dozen sets of eyeholes pointed at my face. A familiar voice yelled, "Damn it, Willa!" and a figure billowed toward me. "What *the hell* you doin' here!"

I couldn't help but lean away, still in the grip of Dr. Vaughan. "I..."

"*You?* You *what?* What? *What?*" His arms thrashed in their flapping sleeves.

"I—I have something to tell you."

"Get in the car, Willa! Damn!" he shrieked, and Dr. Vaughan held my arm out for him to seize. "We don't have time for you! Come on, Ricky."

Another hooded figure drifted toward me, and the three of us marched along the row of cars. Behind us, voices chuckled. My father wouldn't have liked that: he had a low tolerance for anyone laughing at him, or who seemed to be laughing at him.

We jerked to a stop next to the outline of our car and my father yanked open the back door and shoved me in. He pulled off his hood and threw off his robe, fumbling in his pocket for the car key. Ricky copied my father's gestures in slow-motion—hood off, robe off, garments shoveled in back with me. My father hurled himself onto the front seat and ground the key into the ignition. Ricky jumped in next to him. Backward down the path we flew, my father's burning-up face looking past me out the rear window. We rolled onto the street, and he shifted gears.

"My bike is here," I said.

"I don't care where your goddam bike is! What are *you* doing here?"

I forced myself to breathe, in and out. "I—I had somethin' to say."

"Well, no one cares what you have to say! You think you got somethin' to say we don't already know? Who do you think you are?"

"I—"

"You have no business bein' here! You understand that? No business. Where'd you get such a high opinion of yourself? Your mama's a good, humble Christian woman, happy to serve."

"I just—" A gulp of air stuck in my throat; I had to heave it out. "I just wanted—"

"You think we got any use for you? A dumb little girl? *Who do you think you are?* You supposed to stay at home with your mama."

I screamed, "But I wanna be with you!" It was a cry from the heart, a ripping open of my chest.

"*You* want, *you* want. Doesn't matter what *you* want, Willa. *I'm* the one in charge. All that matters is what *I* want. You understand that? That means *I* say what you do, not *you* say what you do. Got that?"

I didn't answer. He went on: "*I* say you stay home, *you* stay home. Doesn't matter what *you* want. *You* obey *me*, got it?"

"Something hap—"

"Shut up! I say *shut up, you* shut up."

I looked at Ricky, who remained mute, his shoulders and arms clenched tight. His head was set at an angle, turned toward my father, his lips curled open in a nervous uncertainty.

The silence seemed to agitate my father as much as my voice did. He repeated: "*I'm* the one in charge. You got that?"

This sounded like an invitation to speak. "I just wanted—"

"I said *shut up!*"

His hand flew off the steering wheel, backward over the seat, and struck my face, smashing the tip of my nose and lip against my teeth. It stung and throbbed and I dropped down behind the seat and pulled the bundle of Klan garb on top of me. A cry exploded from my mouth. I couldn't help the tears.

Otherwise, the car was dead silent. We swung around a few more turns, stopped and started. Eventually I heard the familiar crackle of our driveway. My father turned off the engine, and everyone sat until my father's voice emerged again. "Go on in, Ricky."

I heard the passenger door open and close and footsteps scuffle away. I stayed on the floor. My father coughed—a throat-clearing—and as he spoke, his voice grew calmer, softened by regret or guilt or both. "Now, Willa. You go inside." His tone was almost tender. He'd never hit me or any of us before, and I think he'd surprised himself, maybe believing he wasn't capable of it. "Now, you go inside, and you get yourself a Coke, and you think about what I said."

I reached up slowly and pulled the door handle, pushed on the door, and rolled out with no sound. Then I bolted across the lawn. Through the door and up the stairs I raced, covering my nose and mouth. I knew I was not to tell anyone about this. I didn't want to anyway. This was my own private shame. In my room I lay down, lifted my palm from my face: there was no blood. I cupped my hand over my nose and mouth again until the throbbing subsided. What my father said was true, of course: there was nothing I could say that these men didn't already know. Had I thought I was going to rush in and rally the Klan to action? Who did I think I was? I was just a girl in elementary school; I was a nothing. Everyone was right: I had too high an opinion of myself. I overestimated my ability. I needed to be humbler, like my mama. I cried, and fell asleep, and did not dream.

The next morning, I woke with a sadness that filled every crevice of my interior. I was a bucket of packed mud, heavy and bleak. This, I thought, is how I would feel from now on. But deeper down, there was another sensation—a nudge, a jostling, a seed attempting to sprout, a stem pushing up through that dense dirt. This feeling was not familiar, not comfortable, not even nameable at the time: it was a pang of hatred for my father. Soon it would sprout, jet up, shake itself free of the dirt, and blossom into a fire-red fury for this man, whose love had never been within my reach.

# 5

The next afternoon I walked the three miles to retrieve my bike from the cornstalks. I didn't want to ask anyone for a ride. It seemed too personal, this mission to reclaim my means of independence, my mobility, my freedom. The bike was fine, of course, but the first thing I did after lifting it from the ground was apologize to it—the poor thing, left alone overnight in a field abandoned.

Two days later, Ruth was home from the hospital, proclaiming in a shrill voice that she was completely recovered now. I sensed a new layer of sadness under her placid face. I told her she looked fine, though she didn't really, and we resumed our routine: Tuesdays and Wednesdays were all mine, with Langston doing his odd jobs in Franklin those days. Mondays and Thursdays, I had to endure his presence. Sadly, my fourteenth birthday—October 10th, 1963—fell on a Thursday, but Ruth made the time all about me, with cupcakes and the girls singing a giggly rendition of "Happy Birthday." She made Langston say "Happy Birthday, Willa" twice, because the first time he did not sound enthusiastic enough. She gave me a copy of *Wuthering Heights* by Emily Brontë. "It's one of my favorites, very *romantic*," she said with a wink, adding, "It's a high school book," which put an idea in my brain: I could seek out more high school books and get a head start.

My mother also bought me a book for my birthday, the *Better Homes & Gardens Pies and Cakes* cookbook. She smiled as I pried open the anemic pink wrap. "I know you don't like cooking," she said. "I thought you might enjoy baking!"

I saw no distinction between the two, but my father, nodding, said, "Good thinking, Trudy!" apparently considering it genius.

On Saturday she and I baked him an apple pie. Politely I read out the ingredients, paid attention to her tips, and stood beside

her as she slid the pie into the oven. A while later I was the one
to pull it out. That evening she told my father, "Willa baked
you a pie!" wanting to improve the relationship between us. She
never knew precisely what had happened, only that I'd made a
pest of myself and my father had to scold me hard. Everyone,
even Billy, sensed a change: I'd grown quiet at the supper table,
and my father's demeanor toward me had shifted—he was awkward and timid, occasionally blurting out weird compliments.
Once he said my hair looked pretty, when it looked just the
same as it always did. Another time he said my shirt was very
stylish. He could not stop raving about the pie.

"Willa," he proclaimed, "you're a *good cook*," dragging out the
"ouh" in both words. This was intended as high praise. I tried
to feel pleased, but my father's compliments only underscored
the fact that he had no idea who I was.

But I had not given up on proving myself to him. My academic achievements would show I was smart like him, or at
least not stupid. The first report card came in mid-November.
I burrowed into my studies, re-reading textbook chapters,
taking notes, doing the optional math problems at the end of
the chapter, and practicing typing so I could get a corrected
version of my essays in by the deadlines. My teachers actually
worried I was working too hard. They told me to go to the
school Halloween party, so I did—I went with my entourage
of misfit friends, whom I'd grown fond of. Joe Pedicini dressed
up as a huge marshmallow. At one point he pretended to trip
and bounced himself off the cafeteria wall. I laughed all night.
Florence Whipple came as Tippi Hedren from *The Birds*, with
thickened catsup streaking down her face and a realistic fake
bird attached to one shoulder by the beak. Florence really was a
little strange. Sue Bates was a ghost with a sheet over her head,
which even she knew was not very imaginative, but it hid her
acne, and she felt more comfortable that way. I'd assembled
a Batman costume for myself and spent the evening feeling
surprisingly free, the outside of me a bit closer to what I felt
like on the inside.

November arrived with its drizzling days, the temperature dipping below 50 at night. I finished *Wuthering Heights* and sought out other high school books to read. I asked the dreamy Mr. Marcus if he could lend me a ninth-grade math book. He hesitated, his face drooping, and suggested I read ahead in English or history, which would be easier than math. He gave me the name of his friend at the high school who taught history and would be happy to lend me books. So even the wonderful Mr. Marcus, with his youth and progressive ideas about education, assumed that girls were unlikely to be good at math, even when they were.

The following Monday, I had a chance to seek out Mr. Marcus's friend, my mother having sent me on an after-school errand to the high school. Barb had forgotten her enormous peacock bow, part of a costume needed for the dress rehearsal of *Oklahoma*, in which she'd been cast as the romantic lead, unsurprisingly. I had to stuff the bow in my locker all day, and I'd be late to the Swansons'.

I'd been at the high school before, of course, but never all by myself. The place was colossal, with distant ceilings and white-tiled walls and gray-tiled floors as far as the eye could see. I wandered past towering double doors, a case of trophies, a room full of band instruments—glossy gold horns big and small mounted on the walls and hanging from the ceiling. Maybe in high school they'd let me play the trumpet, even though it was a boy's instrument; I so hated the flute. I came to a row of portrait-sized photographs hung high: the faces of past principals in gray tones, humorless men glowering down in disappointment at whatever teenager happened to be glancing up. At the end of the row was Mr. Councill, the current principal, looking more up to date with his slim lapels and friendlier eyes.

First I sought out Mr. Marcus's friend, a Miss Jones, in the history department office. Miss Jones, it turned out, was why Mr. Marcus had come to Kingsfield. They'd met at the teacher's college in Lynchburg, and Miss Jones, a Tidewater native, wanted to come home. She was tall with strawberry hair and sapphire eyes and a tiny round waist, and I could see why men would follow her around the state. She handed me two books about Thomas Jefferson and grinned. Forty-five seconds later I was on my way, carrying my binder and books and the giant bow.

The auditorium was down a long, wide, clattering staircase. I was to take the bow to the "green room." I followed the sound of raucous teen voices and opened a door—indeed, the room was green—but my sister was not among the throng of kids.

"Anyone seen Barb?" I yelled in.

"Try the auditorium," a boy yelled back.

"Last row," a girl shouted out, and a volcano of laughter erupted.

I went around to the front of the auditorium and pulled on one of the heavy doors. Beyond it, the theater was dark. I left the door open a crack, poked my face in, and spotted two forms at the far end of the back row. One was the unmistakable ponytailed Barb; the other, of course, Jim Darden. I'd seen necking before. I wasn't ignorant or shocked. But Jim was all over Barb, his body pressing hers back across the armrest, which must have been digging hard into her side. Who knew where his hands were. She began to emit noises: a jagged puff of air, a strained giggle, a tentative cry. I stood stone still. These were not joyful sounds. She huffed out his name and something that sounded like "no," but he didn't stop. I yanked open the door, flooding the center aisle with light, and hollered, "Barb?"

There was a rustle. "Who's there?" her voice responded. "Willa?"

"Mama sent me. You forgot your bow." I stood in the bright, wide door frame, holding the bow above my head.

"Oh!" she said. "Thank you!"

For a moment no one moved.

I said, "They need you in the green room."

"Oh." She rose, smoothed her skirt, walked toward me.

I held the door for her and she hesitated, glancing over her shoulder. Jim Darden was silent. Were they pretending he wasn't there? Barb walked through the door, and I let it slam shut on him. I smiled to think of him there, sitting alone in the dark. Barb and I didn't speak. Her face was blank, closed. At the green room door, she said "thank you" again and grabbed the bow. She went inside, and once I saw her safely subsumed into the troupe, I raced away.

Then I couldn't find the exit. I turned one corner after another after another. Cobwebs of discomfort clung to me: I was lost. I went up a half staircase, through a common area, down a longer staircase. I passed the gymnasium and a row of classrooms and a teachers' lounge. My unease morphed into panic—where was I? The corridors lengthened ahead of me; at the end of every hallway was another hallway running off in a new direction, exit-less. I was moving, but I was stuck. I turned yet another corner and, at last, spotted the front entrance. I started toward it, then stopped: just past the entrance was the main office, and there, in its open doorway, lolled my father, chatting with a group of students. I stared.

His face seemed different, less creased, less sunken. His eyebrows were not tensed into a knob over his nose. He seemed broader, his shoulders looser. He talked and talked, but his lips never lost their smile. I realized, slowly, he looked *happy*. I caught snippets of phrases—he was telling that muskrat story, and the students were spellbound, all faces turned delightedly toward him. No one looked bored or obligated to stand there. They surrounded him like adoring fans.

I kept watching. This was some different version of my father, some public version, his voice deeper, his hands full of energy. This was not the man I sat with every night at the supper table. The man I knew was perpetually irritated, forcing his face into a grin, pushing himself to respond when my mother spoke. The man I knew was so deeply angry he had to hide himself inside a white hood. This man was someone else entirely—this main-office Dick McCoy.

Abruptly he turned and saw me lurking there. I froze. But he called out, "Willa!" as though he was glad to see me. "Come on over!" He waved; I hesitated. "Come meet my star students!" I walked toward them. "Kids, this is my other daughter, Willa."

They said hello. They were the older brothers and sisters and cousins of my classmates—Brownes and Pretlows and Cobbs. Firmly in his public persona, my father bellowed, "They stopped by to tell me Cathy's good news!" The girl who must have been Cathy beamed. "She's just been accepted to VCU! Goin' to be a *nurse*! Smart gal!" His hand could not help reaching out to pat her shoulder. She was stately, with a miniature nose and wide mouth. I didn't know why I felt so agitated. He said, "Willa's in the eighth grade." Everyone nodded as though that were interesting.

Then a female voice came singing from the office behind my father, "Mr. McCoy-oy! Danny Holland's mother on line two."

The students dispersed. He entered the office; I hung around in the doorway. He leaned against the secretary's desk, phone to ear, face gleaming with authority as he informed Danny's mother of Danny's shenanigans. As I watched him, I realized gradually, the secretary was watching me. When I looked at her, she looked away.

I didn't know her. She must have replaced the ancient Mrs. Hines. This new lady was maybe thirty-five, stuffed into a satiny blouse. Her skin was bad—her cheeks and forehead pocked and bumpy—but she wore sparkly blue eye shadow that flashed when she blinked, and she had thick blue-black hair styled like Jackie Kennedy's. My father said a reassuring goodbye to Danny's mother and hung up the phone. "Willa, this is Mrs. Wallace. She commutes all the way from Franklin every morning!" He seemed amazed by this, though Franklin was only eight miles away. "Doris, this is my other daughter, Willa."

"I heard," said Mrs. Wallace. Her lips were very thin and bright orangey-red.

"Hello," I said, and my father emitted an odd slow laugh, a kind of Santa Claus ho ho ho.

Apparently stuck in his public persona, he boomed, "We'd be lost without Doris! She runs the school! Knows where everything is, types like a whiz, got all this *technology* down pat—*line two, line three*—ho ho! Doris is one smart lady!"

Mute, I nodded. So much praise heaped on all these random people.

"I am pleased to meet you, Wil-*la*," Mrs. Wallace said in a way that made me think she didn't mean it. I took a step back.

"Well, see ya at home!" my father thundered. Why was he talking so loud? I nodded again, took another step back, and bolted.

Outside, I shuddered, zipped my jacket up to my throat, retrieved my bike from the brown grass, and pedaled as fast as I could across the football field, onto the narrow road through the woods. This was the shortcut to the Swansons', and I wanted to get there as fast as I could—back to something that felt familiar. The high school was too big and twisted and full of unsettling surprises. I didn't like it at all. I couldn't imagine going to school there. I pumped hard through the gravel. I didn't like Mrs. Wallace, the way she sat slathered with makeup, inert at her desk as my father praised her for working hard. I rode as fast as I could.

By the time I got to Ruth's, I was roiling, without understanding why. Everything just felt wrong. Ruth and Langston sat at the kitchen table chattering away, which only magnified my irritation. Had they even noticed I was an hour late? I could have not shown up at all and they wouldn't have thought of me once.

"Hello, Willa," Ruth cooed, as though everything was fine.

Langston turned into a statue, face tucked down. I supposed I'd spoiled his heart-to-heart with Ruth. I hated that he was here today. If he hadn't been, I could have told Ruth about Barb and Jim and how strange my father was at the high school, but now everything had to sink into the bottom of my brain and fester wordlessly. All I ever wanted was to speak and be heard. Why did I feel so upset? I slammed my books on the table.

After a surprised pause, Ruth asked, "Would you like a Coke?"

"No." I sat.

She continued, "Langston was just telling me some good news—his mother received a big teaching award! The 'Esteemed Negro Educator of Hampton Roads' award, from the *Virginian-Pilot*. Isn't that wonderful?"

Several moments slogged by before I spoke: "Well, my *daddy* is the assistant principal of Kingsfield High and that's a very important job. Everybody loves him there. My *daddy* has a master's degree and his students get into very important universities. My *daddy* is so esteemed he'll get promoted to principal any day now. Or maybe next year."

Ruth blinked at me. "It's not a competition, Willa."

"I *know*," I said. She got me a Coke. Then she got me a chocolate chip cookie, and they were silent until I ate the whole thing.

Ruth purred to Langston, "Tell your mama I said congratulations." She leaned forward, set her forearms on the pink laminate tabletop, and asked me, "What do we have today?"

I produced my latest A+ essay and said, "Thank you."

She was the one teaching me how to do commas correctly, and this time I'd even used a semicolon, which had drawn public praise from Mrs. Beale. Ruth took the paper from me: "Oh yes. This is the one about your ancestors coming to America to be free." To Langston she said, "I bet they don't give this assignment at the Negro school."

Langston snickered, and I boiled. It wasn't my fault Langston's ancestors were slaves. It was also not the fault of my particular ancestors, either, who'd gotten stuck scraping out a living on little farms in western Virginia, just as they'd done in Scotland. Ruth's comment wasn't fair. She asked me, "What's the next assignment?"

Miserably I said, "What we want to be doin' in ten years. We're supposed to imagine ourselves in 1973. I don't know what she wants."

Ruth replied, "Aren't you supposed to say what you want?"

"I could say I want to be an English teacher."

"That's not what you want. Why wouldn't you write what you want?"

I could feel Langston's dark eyes on me. He said, "She afraid no one gonna take her seriously."

"No, I'm not." Yes, I was, but there was more to it than that. I'd heard the other girls talking: they were writing about being married and decorating their homes. Claudia Holland had herself as a Virginia state senator's wife, living in a mansion. Tammie Hines was writing about her first baby, whom she'd already named Christopher. Donna Bowman was describing her wedding, which was rumored to include Johnny Cobb, the cutest boy in eighth grade. Mrs. Beale would wonder why I didn't want those things. What was wrong with those things? Nothing, those things were normal. Who did I think I was, imagining I could have some big career? I didn't want Mrs. Beale to think I thought too highly of myself. What was wrong with me?

A nasal melancholy voice called from the living room, "Ru-uth?" It was the reverend, home with a head cold.

"Be right back," she said and wobbled away to see to his needs. Langston poked his face at me and locked me in a menacing stare.

"*What?*" I said.

In a vicious whisper he said, "*Your* daddy. *Your* daddy. I know all about *your* daddy."

"No, you don't. You don't know anything about my daddy."

"I know more'n you do."

"What're you talkin' about? What do you mean?"

"I seen him. I seen him places."

"You did not. You don't know anything." How could he have known it was my father inside one of the hoods? He couldn't have, not for sure. "You only know what people tell you," I said, and he laughed a deep, vengeful sort of laugh.

"I know what my own eyes seen."

"Quit talkin' about my daddy!"

Ruth appeared. "What's going on here?"

Neither of us spoke. Langston opened his chemistry book and pretended to look at a chart, and I tugged a piece of loose-leaf paper from my binder and wrote glumly across the top, "Where I'll Be in '73."

Suddenly Ruth's voice dropped to an annoyed alto, a tone she'd never used on us before: "Listen, maybe you two aren't going to be best friends, but you can at least be polite to each other. Do you think you can do that for me?"

We must have looked stricken, gazing up like guilty five-year-olds caught with a broken cookie jar. I'm sure our mouths were hanging open, our chins on the verge of quivering. She sighed and walked to the stove, dragging her left foot, and turned the heat on under a teapot. "Willa," she said, sounding defeated. "The girls are starting to bother their dad. Could you go read to them for a while?"

"Sure." I rose, re-stacked my books, and left the room, squinting at the side of Langston's long face, knowing he could feel my sharp eyes on him.

In Julie's blue-walled room at the end of the hall, the world shifted back to normal. There were puzzles and Lincoln Logs and books. I sat on the floor and even volunteered to read *The Little Engine That Could*. Their eyes grew huge with gratitude, and a calm spread through me. I'd come to appreciate children, I realized: their honesty, their consistency. Julie and Annette were always Julie and Annette—children didn't have a dozen versions of themselves. They didn't have mean secrets, and they didn't have hidden desires that would rise up like a hedge of water on the horizon, growing ever larger as it roared toward you. I read and reread, "I *think* I can, I *think* I can," until the light in the windows drained away.

The next morning, all the little puddles of distress lingering inside me evaporated: report card day had arrived, and I'd succeeded—I'd gotten straight As. Suddenly I was a star at school. My teachers lavished praise on me, my classmates in awe. Even Becky Campbell said congratulations. The only other straight-A student in the eighth grade was the freakishly smart Jimmy Morehead, who'd never gotten anything below an A in his whole life. After a two-hour celebration with Ruth and the girls—and no Langston—I soared home, my perfect report card zipped into my jacket, against my heart.

"Your dad's delayed at work again," my mother said, sliding a chicken back into the oven to keep it warm.

I stood in the center of the kitchen, my arm extended toward the sky, holding the card like the Olympic torch.

"I knew you could do it," she said, bent over the open oven door, her slippery brown hair falling out of its clip. The cuffs of her dress—the green and blue floral one—dropped forward over her stick-thin wrists, and the fabric hung down from her chest. I watched her, as though seeing her for the first time. She closed the oven door and stood up into her permanent slouch. Then she smiled at me. She looked tired.

Billy began to leap around the kitchen, so impressed was he by my accomplishment. He pretended to be knocked back at the sight of my report card, yelling "Boing! Boing!"—the sound of his eyes popping out of his skull.

"*Billy,*" Barb said, which meant *Shut up and sit down.* She was seated at the table, leafing through a copy of *Ingenue,* pausing at an article titled, "Romantic Holiday Hairdos." Abruptly she stood and strode into the living room. I pranced after her swinging ponytail. "Did you see? Did you see?" I sang, waving the card at her back. I paused to admire it again, opening the stiff beige bi-fold, gazing at the tower of As hand-printed neatly in the first column of tiny boxes. Math, science... When I looked up, Barb was scowling. She wrapped her hand firmly around my wrist and said, "Come upstairs. I want to talk to you."

In our room she shut the door and turned the key in the lock. But she didn't look angry; she looked mortified. She stood flushed and faintly trembling. I sat on my bed.

Trying to sound accusing, but sounding mostly scared, she said, "How much did you see yesterday? In the auditorium?"

I thought about this. "I saw Jim push you backward." And

I saw her pull down her skirt when she rose, but I was too embarrassed to say it.

"That's it? That's all?"

"Yeah."

She exhaled and sat on her bed, across from me. "Please don't tell on me. Not Mama. Not even Patsy, okay?"

"Patsy's worried about you."

"I know. She thinks Jim is just *using* me, and next fall he'll go off to college and find some rich deb and forget me."

I did not say I thought Patsy had a good point.

"Promise you won't tell."

"Okay," I said.

"Say it. Even Patsy."

"I promise I won't tell, even Patsy."

She grinned and gave my shoulder a grateful sisterly squeeze. She tapped on my report card, still clutched in my hand, and said, "You did good," with no trace of sarcasm. Then she started to leave.

"But, Barb?"

She paused. "Yeah?"

"Well, whatever it was that was happening"—and I did not want to think too much about it—"seemed like you didn't really like it."

She returned to her bed and sat, frowning at the backs of her hands. "I'm just nervous about it."

*It?* I must have looked startled, or horrified, because she coughed and leaned away from me. I blurted, "Well then, don't do it."

Her shoulders hardened, and the sting returned to her tone. "It's not that easy, Willa."

"It's not?"

"*He* wants to, and I want to make him happy, and he won't be happy if I keep sayin' no."

"You *keep* sayin' no?"

She didn't respond. I continued in an increasing whine. "So, one of you is gonna end up unhappy, and it has to be you?"

"I don't want to *displease* him. What kinda woman would I be?"

"You *aren't* a woman! You're *barely sixteen!*"

"Well, Jim wants a woman, so I'm gonna have to be a woman, because I want Jim."

"Why?"

"Why? God, Willa. He's *Jim Darden!*"

"So you have to do somethin' you don't want to do, to make him happy."

She seemed to think about this. "What matters is *he's* happy," she concluded, and a look of suspicion skulked along her face. "You sayin' I should put my *own* wishes ahead of his? Willa, that's just selfish. Haven't you learned anything in church? Good Christian women are supposed to serve others."

"But—" I stopped. I didn't want to drive her further into the cave of what she'd always been told. I tried to tamp down the emotion in my voice. "Barb. What if you end up, you know? Aren't you worried, you might, you know. Get in trouble?"

She tipped toward me and half whispered, "No. It's okay now. There's a *pill*."

"A *pill*?"

"Cindy told me. A girl takes this pill and she won't...you know. Cindy's gonna get one for me. Her sister in college has a friend who has some."

"Oh."

"Everything's okay. I know what I'm doing. Everything's fine. As long as you don't tell on me." Her azure eyes grew wide and her chin dropped. "Okay?"

I gave her a reluctant nod.

"Good. Now come on. I just heard Daddy. Let's go show him your report card." She gave me another shoulder squeeze, and we went down together. But at the bottom of the staircase, Barb turned toward the kitchen.

I dashed into the living room. Barely out of his overcoat, my father was already examining Billy's report card, alternately nodding and grimacing. Billy stood next to him, twitching; Ricky was draped across the arms of a wing chair. "Here's mine!" I hollered, flapping it at him.

"Now, now, let's finish lookin' at one before we start lookin' at another one," he replied.

Ricky smirked. I waited. All of a sudden my father was taking an extra-long time to inspect Billy's report card. "Citizenship, B; well, that's good, son," he drawled. I waited. "Penmanship, C." He chortled. "When I was your age, Billy, even *I* couldn't read my own chicken scratch." Billy fidgeted. How long could one man take to look at a little kid's report card? "Okay." My father finally handed the card back to him, laid his hand briefly on the top of Billy's head and said, "You'll do better next time. Go tell your mama she can sign it." Off Billy went.

"All right now." My father took the card from my bouncing hand. I jumped up once, squealed, and waited for my father's stiff face to transform, to melt with astonishment and admiration and pride. He began to nod, eyebrows raised.

From the chair, Ricky drawled, "What? What's she got?"

My father didn't reply. He said to me, in his regular voice, "Well, that's *good*, Willa." And he passed the card to Ricky, whose face scrunched into a hateful look as though I'd done something to thwart him. My father said, "What d'you think, Ricky?" Why was he asking Ricky?

"Pretty good," Ricky croaked and handed the card back to my father, who looked at it again.

"Mm, hm," he said. "*Very* good, Willa, *very* good. I'm glad to see this 'cause next year it's high school for you and that's when the *real* work begins. Right, Ricky?"

"Yes, sir."

"In high school," my father continued, "the work gets *tough*. So you be careful not to go restin' on your laurels. The hard stuff's comin'."

"Okay," I said, reclaiming the report card.

"Don't let me catch you braggin' about this. Don't go tootin' your own horn."

"No, sir." I walked into the kitchen. My head was numb as I

set the table and carried bowls of food in with my mother and Barb. I took my seat. I heard the squeak of Billy's chair beside me, the sound of serving spoons in bowls. I saw my hand dish corn onto my plate. My father started the pop quiz: "Question one. Name the three parts of a battery."

I heard Billy's voice: "Cathode..." and Ricky's: "Anode..."

*Electrolyte*, I did not say. I couldn't summon the breath to speak.

That was it. All my studying and rereading, all my rewriting of essays. A crusty piece of pork appeared on my plate. Ricky was talking about buying Mr. Parker's old car with the money he'd saved working for Dr. Vaughan over the summer. Mr. Parker wanted him to have it, Ricky said, and was dropping the price just for him. My mother made chirpy noises. My father wondered aloud if Uncle Pete and Aunt Irene and the boys would be coming from Danville for Thanksgiving, and my mother said she didn't know—she'd sent a note but hadn't heard back yet. She could make a quick call after dinner if my father wanted her to. Long-distance? He didn't know about that. If they were coming we'd need extra chairs, he reminded her, and what about that tenth plate in our set of good china? That tenth plate had a chip in the rim. My mother assured him she'd have that plate at her place and turn the damaged part toward herself. What were the Dardens doing for Thanksgiving this year? Barb didn't know.

Eventually, my thoughts started to move again in my head. It's all right, I told myself. It's all right. This was going to take time, that was all. What did it mean—*one* report card? I had to show my father this wasn't a fluke, but an ongoing achievement. This was not a one-time thing; this was something I had to build, over time. For all my father knew, my current teachers were easy graders. Maybe they were. Earning my father's respect, becoming someone my father could genuinely admire— *that* required a building up. This year was laying the foundation, I told myself. In high school I'd construct the walls, nail down the roof, plaster and paper and furnish every room, and when

I was finished, I'd have an edifice so formidable that everyone would see it—no one could miss it—and it would be discussed, praised. Noticed. That was my plan now. I promised myself I would not deviate, no matter what.

Thinking this way helped me feel better, though I would not have been able to articulate why. Now I understand: it was better to take all the responsibility on myself than to imagine that my father's love and respect might be unattainable forever.

# 6

A week later Ricky bought Mr. Parker's car. I'd never seen my brother so gleeful. The car was ridiculous—a '56 DeSoto Adventurer, two-tone like a saddle shoe, with gold anodized trim and a tiny clock in the center of its sprawling skinny steering wheel. Ricky drove like a maniac. He'd had his license for a few years but hadn't gotten much practice, my father reluctant to lend his beloved Super 88 to an amateur. Nevertheless, Ricky acted like an expert, overconfident, flying backward out of our driveway like our dad did, rear wheels treacherously close to the ditch. I knew because now every day I was packed into the car with my siblings to go to school, and every day in the back seat with Billy I pressed my face to the cold window and watched the tire careen toward our deadly ditch. My mother watched us from the house, and at supper she'd admonish Ricky. "Now you be cautious, be cautious with that car. You slow down and be cautious."

Every evening she repeated this until my father barked, "Lay off, Trudy. You tryin' to turn him into a *girl*?"

One afternoon in Miss Cooke's history class, a week before Thanksgiving, our school principal burst in and shouted that President Kennedy was dead. He'd been shot  shot in the head—in Dallas, Texas. Miss Cooke threw her arms into the air and shouted, "Hallelujah!" which brought cheers from most of the boys and some of the girls too.

Immediately I thought of Ruth. She'd be devastated.

After the wild ride home from school in the DeSoto, I took my bike to the Swansons'. The reverend answered the door. Ruth was on the couch, red-eyed, a daughter tucked under each arm, the kitten curled like a black-and-white shrimp in her lap.

"Is she okay?" I whispered to the reverend, who whispered

back, "Better, better," then blurted, "She blames the South. She says she wants to vomit all over the South."

"Willa," Ruth squeaked and with the tips of her fingers motioned me over. I snuggled next to Julie, and the reverend squirmed in beside Annette, and the five of us sat there in silence, the TV off, Ruth's arms reaching far enough to embrace us all.

That Sunday Reverend Swanson preached a sermon about brotherly love and John F. Kennedy and civil rights, and the next morning a copy of *The Fiery Cross* appeared on the Swansons' front step, rubber-banded around a brick. I discovered the paper on her kitchen counter: the "Official Organ Of The United Klans of America." Of course I recognized it. It was a couple of months old, the issue with the Statue of Liberty on the cover. I remembered that issue because inside was the list of officers just elected at the Klonvokation and my father had pored over the names, memorizing them. The outgoing Imperial Wizard wrote his last editorial on federally forced race-mixing, signing it, as always, *Yours for God and Country.*

Ruth caught me looking at it and said, "I'm still trying to figure out what racism has to do with God," but with a laugh in her voice, inexplicably cheerful. Possibly that was the day she and the reverend started talking about moving back up North.

Thanksgiving was a few days later. Uncle Pete and Aunt Irene and their two grown sons came. The ladies cooked and the men sat chatting about politics: newly inaugurated President Johnson was needling Congress about that civil rights bill. In the fading light of our living room—none of the men thinking to turn on a lamp—Uncle Pete, Ricky, and the cousins nodded along with whatever my father said. "Kennedy's assassination may not've been such a good thing after all," my father groaned. "LBJ gettin' all high and mighty over that damn bill."

"That's right," Uncle Pete said.

"That's right," Cousin Wally said.

At dinner, the adults said how grateful they were to be in America instead of one of those awful Communist countries, and we kids were challenged with listing them: the Soviet Union, Poland, Czechoslovakia. Was Finland one of them? Crammed full of turkey and gratitude, our guests left before sunset.

Through that weekend and into December, the air jittered with tension. The Klan had extra meetings; my father was rarely home. Everyone seemed restless, on the verge of taking some action, no one knowing what that might be. I felt it too, this amorphous urge to rise up and do something.

One group of Kingsfield businessmen, also members of the Sons of Confederate Veterans, wanted to erect a Confederate monument in Triangle Park. Peanut mogul Henry Morehead was quoted in the *Tidewater Times*: "It's high time we get it up, a monument to honor the brave men who fought to defend our freedoms." Suffolk had a monument. Norfolk and Portsmouth had monuments. Why couldn't we? Everyone heartily agreed we should commission a statue of Robert E. Lee, intrepid Virginian and general, but there was disparity over whether his horse should be included. In an ideal world, said one *Tidewater Times* editorial, we'd have both Lee and Traveller, but Triangle Park was small; perhaps Lee's ceremonial sword would suffice. By the following week, there was a flood of support for Lee and his sword, though everyone concurred the horse would be missed.

Another letter to the editor, signed only "Concerned Clergymen," objected to the monument altogether. This letter urged us to consider that monuments to the Confederacy raised the specter of slavery, which would be offensive to some Virginians. At first we didn't understand what "Virginians" the authors meant. Then we realized they meant coloreds. My father huffed around the house for an entire evening.

The monument was commissioned, and soon after, on the coldest night of the season, a cross burned on the front lawn of the Quakers' house.

The days grew darker. I'd taken to walking the six blocks from school to the Swansons', forgoing the crazy ride with Ricky. A week before Christmas, the temperature plummeted to below freezing, but I walked anyway, bare-legged, my toes miserably cold inside the noses of my shoes. Ruth greeted me with hot chocolate and a blanket.

"Couldn't your brother drop you off in his car?" she asked on the third day of the cold snap.

"I'd rather walk."

On Wednesday—a Langston-free day—we sat poring over sentence diagrams in my *Warriner's English Grammar*, which Ruth insisted I needed to understand. I was working through an especially long sentence when the phone rang.

"Hello?" Ruth said, then, after several moments, "Oh, dear! Oh no! Yes, yes, we can go—Matthew left the car today…no, Regina, please, it's no trouble at all…of course you're worried. I'm worried too. We'll leave right away."

In the next instant, Ruth was pulling coats out of the closet and calling the girls: we were all driving to Franklin to pick up Langston. That was his mother on the phone. His car wouldn't start in the cold, and he was stranded.

"I can stay here with the girls," I said.

She sighed. "Please hurry. I don't want him alone out there after dark."

Already the sky was the color of wet asphalt. She bundled Annette into a fat coat and pulled a knit cap over her downy head. Julie got herself zipped up, and we piled into the Swansons' car. I sat in the back, the girls on either side of me. We drove along narrow roads, past fields, in and out of woods. It felt like the drive was taking forever. I could have been finishing my homework, and instead I was on a rescue mission for a damn colored boy. I began to fume. When we reached the outskirts of Franklin, Ruth pulled over, clicked on the dome light, and retrieved the map from the glove box. She crinkled it one way and the other and turned to me. "Can you navigate?"

"Yes." I was a gifted map reader.

"See where we are now?"

"Yes." My *yes's* sounded formal and cold.

"We need South and Delk."

I directed her. Five minutes later we came upon Langston on

the street corner, shivering in a nylon jacket. He heaved open the front passenger door. "Thank you, Ms. Swanson, thank you." His hands trembled with cold.

"What are you wearing?" Ruth shrieked. "You people don't know how to function in the cold!"

"I'm sorry, yeah. Thank you." He shut the door.

"I didn't want you out here alone."

"Thank you." He shuddered, shaking the cold off himself and around the car. He glanced into the back seat. "Hello, girls."

"Hi, Lankin!" Annette chirped.

He glowered at me, then said to Julie: "How's lil Miss Softy doin'?"

"It's *Mr.* Softy," Julie corrected, indignant. Annette giggled. I remained quiet, staring at his long profile. He had on some kind of cap, like a beret, with a button in the center.

Ruth asked, "So what happened? Dead battery?"

"Ye-ah, ye-ah, most likely. My dad and his friend gonna come out tomorrow and take a look. Thank you again for comin' all this way." Langston turned again to flash a smile at the girls but not me. His hostility was like a heater blasting me.

I said, "My family has two cars now." My voice rose and fell in a taunt.

Ruth explained. "Her brother just bought a car."

"Well, ain't that somethin'," he said, his tone thick with sarcasm. Flashing through shadows, the back of his neck was a shiny solid brown.

I said, "My sister's datin' Jim Darden. He drives a brand-new Chrysler convertible."

"Well, well," Langston said.

In the rearview mirror, Ruth's eyes widened at me, but I kept on: "And my daddy has a brand-new Olds Super 88. Almost brand new. It's silver."

After a pause, Ruth said, "What a lot about cars."

Langston said, "I know your daddy's car."

"You do not know my daddy's car."

"I seen it enough times."

He was starting in on me again. Couldn't Ruth hear it? This boy was pugnacious. This boy was uppity. But she didn't say anything, just drove along, keeping her eyes on the road, her shoulders curled forward. So I said, in a voice bent to sound sweet and genuine, "Langston, how're you gonna be an aerospace engineer when you can't even fix your own car?"

Ruth turned on the radio, loud. We sat through the screeching falsetto, "Walk like a man…" then a commercial for Forbes Furniture. Langston lunged at the dashboard and turned down the volume—very aggressive, I thought—and said, "Ms. Swanson, I'm so sorry, but could we make a quick stop?"

"A quick stop?"

"*Real* quick. I told Ms. Wallace I could check her garage door today. She in a fit, worryin' she might get stuck in her garage."

"Who?"

"Ms. Wallace. I do lots of work on her property on account of her husband bein' a trucker and hardly ever home."

"Do I know a Mrs. Wallace?" Ruth asked no one.

"She the secretary at Kingsfield High. Willa's *daddy* know her."

I said, "That's right. My daddy knows just about everyone."

"Okay, well, is it far?"

It wasn't. He directed her around a few corners and soon we arrived at a small ranch house on a street parallel to the train tracks. The windows were dark except for one at the far end, where a pulled shade vaguely glowed. "Is she home?" Ruth asked.

"Don't matter, I just have to check it. Pull up in the driveway and leave the headlights on so I can see."

We rolled up the slight slope and Ruth shifted into park, leaving the motor running and the headlights pointed at the garage door. Langston jumped out—leaped out—couldn't wait to get out—and ran around the side of the garage to peer through a window. Then he ran back, his face in a wild smile in the glare of the headlights.

"What is he *doin'*?" I complained.

He bent down, gripped the garage door handle, and yanked it upward. Smoothly the panels scrolled up, and our headlights illuminated the interior of the garage.

"Hey, look!" I burbled. "That car's just like my daddy's!"

Ruth leaned forward and said dreamily, "Oh yeah?"

"Wow, it's almost identical." I leaned forward, too, draped my arms over the front seatback and examined the rear of the car: the small round taillights like deep-set eyes, the sleek strip of chrome outlining the top of the bumper. "Hey!" I went on idiotically. "Even the license plate number is the same! Are people allowed to have the same license plate number?"

I turned to look at Ruth and was startled by her expression: a deep frown twisting into a look of disgust. She pulled the gearshift into reverse and we flew backward, into the street, leaving Langston standing in front of the garage. His face popped open in alarm. He yanked the garage door down and ran toward us. I looked at the house again. In the room at the end the dimly lit shade shimmered, lifted a little on one side so an eye could peek out.

In the car, Langston was buoyant with joy. "*Ain't* that funny, Willa? Your *daddy's* car in that lady's garage? *What* could *that* be about?"

"Langston," Ruth snapped, her voice oozing with disappointment. Instantly he shut up, and his shoulders began to contract.

My body dropped backward. Annette climbed into my lap, and I rubbed my cheek against the rough contours of her cap. Ruth said to me, "I'll drop you off at home first, sweetie," her eyes in the rearview mirror searching for my face. "Then I'll take Langston home. He and I can have a little chat on the way." She flashed him a terrifying smile.

"Okay." I hugged Annette tight against me, her warmth and weight on my chest pressing back the pain. I tried to wonder, Why was my father at Mrs. Wallace's house? My skin tightened. I tried thinking he was there to work. That he'd stopped by for some file, some piece of paper, and put his car in the garage to keep it safe from the cold. He'd given her a ride home, maybe, because her car wouldn't start in the cold, and she invited him in for a cup of hot tea. Maybe the room at the end of the house was like a den, not a bedroom, and her overhead light was burned out, so it was dim. My brain contorted with possible explanations.

Ruth turned the radio on again: *"Please, please me..."* Trees swished by. Another commercial for Forbes Furniture blared. The ride home went on and on, and halfway there I had the sense of anesthesia wearing off. My chest was throbbing. My father was at Doris Wallace's house in the dark, his car hidden in her garage, and I wasn't stupid, I wasn't a little kid, I knew what it meant, I knew what he was doing there. I knew. I kept trying not to know but I did and my eyes fogged over. He was cheating on my mother. He was having an affair, *an affair* with his secretary. My breathing stopped, and I began to suffocate. Would he leave us? Was he planning to run off with Doris Wallace? Francine Gray's father had done that—fallen in love with some dumb lady at work and moved to California with her and that was the last they'd seen of him. The pounding in my chest became a stabbing, and I hung on to Annette. If he said he was leaving, I thought, we could beg him to stay. We could do that—all of us—we could *beg* him, get down on our knees and *beg*, and then how could he go? The new Katy Dee song came on the radio: *Darling please, hear my plea, I would die if you left me, darling please, hear my cry, without your love...I'll surely die...*

Ruth shut it off, and we rode in silence for a while. Then Annette started to sing the alphabet song. Julie joined in. When they got to Z, they began again. Ruth said, "Girls. Let's just be quiet," her voice soaked with sadness.

We rolled up the back driveway of my house. All our windows were bright and full of activity: Billy's head bobbled in the family room, TV flickering. Ricky's form moved from window to window. There in the kitchen, of course, was my mother, the outlines of her arms reaching up.

Ruth turned to me. "I'll see you tomorrow." Her voice

gentle. "I was thinking, enough with the grammar. Let's bake Christmas cookies."

Feebly, I replied, "I don't like to cook."

"Oh, that's right. I'm sorry, I forgot. Would you like to decorate the cookies with the girls? Frosting and sprinkles!"

"Sure." I peeled Annette off my lap, slid across the seat, and opened the door. When I turned to say goodbye, Ruth's eyes were enormous with gloom. In the cold I stood and watched them drive away, Langston like a rag doll on the seat next to Ruth, his head hanging.

The first person I encountered in my house was Billy, cross-legged on the family room floor, six inches from the TV screen. *My Three Sons* was on, blasting its raucous laugh track. I marched over and wrenched the knob as hard as I could to turn the thing off.

"Hey!" Billy whined. "What're ya doin'?"

"You watch too much TV! That's why you're so stupid! Go read a damn book!"

"Ma-maaaaa!"

My mother appeared, dish towel in hand. Billy howled, "Willa said a bad word!"

"I did not." I glared at him. He looked utterly confused.

He whimpered, "Well, she turned off the TV."

My mother snapped, "You two behave. We have company."

I followed her into the kitchen. I heard Barb and Ricky and their friends in the living room, playing records. My mother said, "There are burgers on the dining room table," and buzzed around the kitchen, taking things out of cupboards, putting things back into cupboards, taking things out of the refrigerator, putting things back into the refrigerator. I tried seeing her from a different perspective, as though she were not my mother but a stranger I might encounter on the street. I saw a tired, aging woman, who looked deprived. Her dress—the navy-blue floral one, her very best at-home dress—drooped on her insubstantial frame. I thought of Doris Wallace nearly bursting from her blouse. I thought of Doris Wallace's shiny black hair sprayed into a perfect curve around her jaw. My mother's hair was loose, flat, the color of dust.

"Mama, you should get your hair cut and styled. Maybe dye it black."

"What?"

"Or blond. You should go to the beauty parlor more often, not just for a special occasion. You should go every week like the other ladies do."

"You know I don't like spendin' money on those things."

"You should. Wouldn't it make Daddy proud? You were so beautiful in your wedding pictures. Barb gets her good looks from you."

My mother paused in her endless trajectory around the kitchen. "Well, thank you. Get yourself some supper."

"I'm not hungry. Where's Daddy?"

"One of his meetings."

"He's been havin' a lot of those meetings."

"You know how things are."

"Why isn't Ricky with him? Ricky's sittin' in the living room."

"Well, I don't know."

"Isn't that a little strange? Ricky sittin' right there in the living room?"

"What are you talkin' about, Willa?" She ran water into the sink and filled it with soap.

"You and Barb could go together to the beauty parlor— you'd enjoy that. Afterward she could take you shopping at Peeble's for new outfits."

"New outfits?" she sputtered at me. "Why would I spend money on store-bought clothes for myself?"

"So you could look nicer."

She didn't respond, and I watched her slouch over the sink, eyes vacant, fingers pincered together. She was like some mindless animal, ignorant and vulnerable, inviting abuse.

A viciousness surged inside me. "You look terrible, Mama. Your clothes are awful. You always look old and ragged and you're too skinny! You're constantly cooking, why don't you *eat* more? Why don't you stop running around waiting on Daddy for one minute and take care of *yourself?*"

"Willa!" Her voice emerged breathy, sounding trapped in a box.

I kept at her: "I'm just sayin' the truth. Don't you ever look in the mirror?"

"That's enough." She turned away and pawed at a stack of grimy plates. One by one they slipped beneath the surface of the suds and wafted to the bottom, dirtying the water. I started to walk away but stopped and stared at her back, at the lines of her shoulders and scapulae like chicken bones beneath the limp fabric. I thought she might turn around and say something, but she didn't. I thought I might say something else—something softer—but I didn't. Instead I rolled into the living room like Sherman's army on its path of destruction.

Patsy stood beside the record player, a forty-five raised to show everyone, her thumb through the center hole, her fingertips careful along the edge. "WGH is playin' them all the time!" she wailed. The boys snickered. Ricky sat in a wing chair, Warren Bunch on the floor, Jim Darden on the couch smoking his cigarettes. Patsy turned to me. "Willa, what do you think of the Beatles? That new band?"

Ricky drawled, "Oh yeah, let's get *Willa's* opinion."

He could not have predicted my reaction. I exploded. "What's wrong with my opinion?" I lurched toward him, hardening every muscle. "What's wrong with it? Why do you think your opinion is better than mine? You're not better than I am, Ricky. You're not smarter than I am. You don't know *anything*. None of you know *anything!*"

Dumbfounded faces gawked at me. It took Ricky a moment to regain his composure. When he did he said coolly, "Watch out, world, it's *that* time of the month!"

Warren shrieked out a laugh. Jim grinned, nodded, then— and this is what sent me over the edge—he rolled his eyes. I turned my fury on him.

"Everyone's right about you!" I shouted. It was probably the first time I'd ever spoken to him directly. "You're just a rich snob and you don't love my sister, you're just *takin' advantage* of her. You're just tryin' to get up her skirt!" Someone gasped. "You're just a lyin' cheat, aren't you? *Aren't you?*"

The grin remained stuck to his face, his chin slowly descending, his rodent eyes rounding out. From the floor Warren Bunch said, "Gaw, McCoy. Your other sister's a mental case."

A hand gripped my shoulder from behind and an arm across my back propelled me toward the staircase. It was my mother, explaining in a bizarre singsong. "I'm sorry, kids! Willa's not feeling well today. Up we go." She forced me up the stairs, into my room, and deposited me on my bed.

"Willa. Get into bed."

"It's too early—"

"Sometimes a girl needs extra rest."

"Mama—"

"I'll bring you some soup."

"Mama, somethin's wrong."

"Nothin's wrong. Get into your nightgown. I'll be back in a minute."

I did what she said. I pulled on my winter nightgown and I ate the soup, Campbell's Chicken Noodle. I turned off the ceiling light and slunk under my covers and through the window I watched the night.

Eventually I heard my father's car roll up the driveway, and I heard his voice downstairs, greeting Jim and Warren and the others, placing his drink order with my mother. Talking and walking around as though everything were normal.

Alone in the dark, I thought, Husbands are supposed to be faithful to their wives. They promise it, in public ceremonies. They give their word; they make a pledge; everyone expects it. It says it in the Bible. My father had betrayed my mother—he'd betrayed us all, making us think one thing when another thing was true. I shut my eyes and tried to sleep, but I hurt too much. Part of me felt ripped out—I could feel the torn spot, ragged and sore and wet. It kept tearing until my heart was ripped into long useless shreds. I couldn't sleep. Even after the room grew dark and Barb was in her bed dozing off, I lay awake, buried alive in the night.

By dawn, I was exhausted, still devastated, but I'd formed a plan: I would have a talk with my father. I would simply sit down with him and have a rational adult conversation about this terrible situation. I would say just the right words, and he would listen, and he would understand the problem, and something would shift. There'd be resolutions, epiphanies. He'd repent; he'd quit seeing Doris Wallace. He wouldn't leave us. He would not move to Franklin or California or anywhere else. I'd have a heart-to-heart with him like kids on TV did with their dads, which always turned out well. I could do this. I could put everything right.

Looking back, I see my repeated attempts to be heard—all those times I thought, *This time, this time my words will matter*—as a kind of hopeful push toward self-preservation. How many times had I tried to raise my voice with no success? But I had to believe I was moving toward agency, and each step on that path brought a small awakening, carrying me toward the revelation of my father's true character.

The speech I planned was magnificent. I would begin with calm facts, informing him I'd discovered where he was last night. I imagined his face: surprised, worried, then contrite, tipping forward with shame. He'd be unable to look me in the eye. His head would shake achingly. Maybe he'd say, "It was just a terrible mistake." Or, he'd be speechless, and I would say, "I know it was just a terrible mistake. You're a *good* man." And then I'd say, "You have to ask Mama for forgiveness. That's the only way. She'll be upset at first but you know she'll forgive you—she's devoted to you. Then, you can take her on a trip"— because in the movies, couples having problems reunited and went on trips—"and when you come back, everything will be back to normal. Mama's a *good woman*, isn't she? What kind of a woman is Doris Wallace? Going after someone else's husband! And isn't she married too? To a trucker? She isn't a good woman at all!"

He would see the logic in this; he would agree. How could he not?

Then I'd say, "Daddy, I know you love Mama. She's a hard worker and she does everything you say, and now she has to forgive you for this terrible thing. Don't you think you should treat her better? Maybe she'd like to go out more often, you know, get out of the kitchen sometimes. Maybe she could have a hobby. Maybe she'd like to get a part-time job so she won't worry so much about money. Lots of women have jobs—" Doris Wallace, for instance, "—and maybe we could let a colored woman into the house to do the cleaning."

I imagined him nodding, a trace of sadness in his eyes. I wasn't sure how the speech would end. I pictured myself standing up and him rising with me, then reaching out, his hand extending, wobbling toward me, perhaps to pull me into a hug.

I told Mama that morning my cramps were too bad for me to go to school, which she readily believed. I stayed in bed until ten o'clock, eating the dry toast she brought. I waited until the vacuum roared on, then I snuck out of the house and rode my bike to the high school.

It was so close to Christmas vacation, the corridors were chaotic, full of festive crowds on their way to some special assembly, kids decorating lockers, teachers setting up a nativity scene on a table outside the cafeteria. Someone had taped a glossy red bow on the forehead of the most malicious-looking past principal. Laughter reverberated. Cool and detached, I walked toward the main office. I hesitated, realizing I'd see Doris Wallace, then forced myself through the outer office door. She was there, idle at her desk, staring into space with her gaudy eyes and pockmarked face. Today she was stuffed into a nubby red turtleneck sweater with short sleeves. Her arms were full of freckles. I stared at her.

"Yes?" she eventually said. "You need somethin'?"

She didn't remember me. She thought I was a student here. Boldly I replied, "I'm here to see my father, Dick McCoy."

"Oh," she said. "Let me see if he's in." She lifted her phone handset and pushed a button. What an idiot. She'd know whether he was "in"—his office was two feet away from her desk. "Hello," her voice dripped into the phone. "Your daughter is here to see you."

The inner office door flung open and my father stepped out, smiling—of course, he would have thought I was Barb. At the sight of me, his expression morphed into a surprised frown. "I thought you were home sick."

"I feel better," I said, and added with a tremor, "May I speak to you?"

He looked around, as though searching for some reason why I couldn't. Then he shrugged—a weird gesture I hadn't anticipated. As I followed him into his office, my confidence evaporated. Somehow I managed to close the door behind me.

"What's goin' on, Willa? You don't look good."

Suddenly, stupidly, my eyes began to tear up. I plummeted into the visitor's chair. He sat on the opposite side of his vast oak desktop and peered at me. "You okay?"

"No," I bleated and heaved air into my lungs. I breathed out slowly and was able to say, "I know where you really were last night."

He made a show of being surprised. "Where I *really* was last night? I was home last night, Willa."

"I mean, before you were home."

"Before I was home? You know we've been havin' extra meetings."

"Yes, I know, but that's not where you were."

Again, the show of surprise—his neck elongating, his eyes growing wide. "That's not where I was? Where do you think I was, Willa?"

"I saw, your car, in her garage."

"You saw my car in *her* garage? Whose garage, Willa?"

I wished he would stop saying my name, and I wished he'd

stop speaking in questions, turning up the end syllables incredulously, as though I were crazy. I blurted, "Doris Wallace!"

Eyes expanding, neck stretching: "How could you see a car
in a closed garage, Willa? You're not making any sense."

"I *know* you were *there*!"

"Where?"

"At *Doris Wallace's house*. You parked your car in her garage!"

"Well, sometimes I do stop by there to deliver documents,
but why would I park my car in her garage, Willa?"

"Because you didn't want anyone to know you were there!"

"Why would I want that?" Now his neck was as long as a
giraffe's, and his eyes were about to spring out of his head.
With each sentence, the pitch of his voice rose; now he was
squeaking like he'd been inhaling helium.

"Because," I began, but he'd trapped me—he'd talked me
into a corner. How was I supposed to phrase this? I tried to
put the words together in my brain, but the harder I tried, the
harder it became. *You're, you're...*

"Does your mama know you're here?"

"No."

"Did you ride here on your bike?"

"Yes."

"Well then, you get right back on that bike and ride home.
I'm callin' your mama now. She'll be mad as hell you came here
on that bike when you're supposed to be sick in your bed. Did
you *lie* about being sick, Willa? Did you *lie* to your mama?"

"No!" I whimpered and cried, cried like a five-year-old. I
closed my eyes and heard him emit a dramatic sigh.

"You want Mrs. Wallace to drive you home?"

"*No.*"

"Then you had better pull yourself together and get back
home and quit cryin' like a baby and quit sayin' crazy things. I
don't even know what you're sayin'."

"You *do too*!" I shrieked and stood up and looked down at
him. He looked right back at me, his eyes blank, his mouth
open in righteous indignation, his face and posture and silence

proclaiming his innocence. "Stop it!" I shrieked again and stomped my foot.

He punched at the intercom. "Doris, could you step in for a minute?"

She hurried in, obliged to take many tiny steps in her too-tight skirt, lurching in her high heels. "Yes?" she said, feigning concern.

"Could you take my daughter to the girls' room until she calms down?"

I screamed, "I'm not goin' anywhere with her!"

"Willa." He stood. "You're actin' crazy. Go home and do what your mama tells you to do. Go on. Go home. I'm callin' her now. Go on. Go."

I ran from the office, down the corridor, and out the front door. I grabbed my bike and rode through the gravel, in and out of woods, past the Swansons', across yards. A cold wind stung my cheeks, poured its burning ice down the front of my jacket, but I barely noticed. I had only one thought in my head: I hated him. *I hated him.* All those years I'd tried to please him, working so hard for his love and respect, longing to be like him, to *be* him—and now I loathed him. I detested him. My arteries coursed with rivers of fire. He was a liar and a cheat and a fake and I reviled him. The wind froze my face, but underneath I burned. *I despised him.* Fury blazed in my skull, a crematorium incinerating every bit of bone and viscera that were the old Willa, the girl who'd once longed for her father's love. That Willa was gone; in her place was rage incarnate.

I turned onto my street. My mother was on our front lawn, coatless and shivering, watching for me. She shrieked when she saw me, pulled me off my bike, and bustled me inside.

"What on earth!" she cried. "I went up to check on you and you were gone! I looked in every room in the house! I ran up and down the block!"

She shook my coat off me and sat me down in a kitchen chair, laying her palms on my cheeks, then placing the back of her hand across my forehead.

Then she stepped back, her face contoured with worry. "What has gotten *into* you?"

"Mama," I said, still panting. She fetched me a glass of orange juice.

"I was worried!"

"I have somethin' to tell you."

"All right, I'm listening," but she was standing at the sink, her fingers twisting themselves in a dish rag.

How could I say this? "What if, all this time, someone was tellin' you one thing but doin' another thing. Like, what if I was sayin' I was at the Swansons', but really I wasn't there, what if really I was sneakin' off, to *meet* someone?"

The dish rag dropped from her hands. She pulled a chair around the side of the table and sat opposite me, our eyes on the same level. "Is that why you're actin' so strange?" she said, her frown softening. "You have a boyfriend?" Then her face began to shine.

"I meant, no, no, I meant—"

"Is that why you went runnin' off to the high school? To see a boy?"

"Mama, that was like an analogy—"

"Willa." She smiled. It was the same saccharine smile as when I got my period for the first time and she said I was *growing up*. "Are you in love?"

I fell silent.

I don't recall consciously forming the idea. I remember only my desire to punish my father. I wanted him hurt; I wanted him tormented. I wanted him to lie awake all night suffering and feeling powerless to achieve what he most desired. And what did my father desire most? What drove him? I thought of him sitting at the dinner table, bitter, festering with hatred and fears. What he wanted most was status, to feel himself above everyone else. What he feared most was humiliation, being pushed down. He especially hated anyone trying to come up from beneath him to get a hold of something he thought was his—a promotion, a title, a daughter.

"Yes, Mama," I said. "I'm in love."

"Oh, Willa. He goes to Kingsfield High?"

"No, no, he doesn't."

"Well, thank goodness. He's in your grade." She nodded knowingly. "Is it Johnny Cobb? He's so cute."

"No, it's not *Johnny Cobb*." How annoying. Had she been sitting around picking out future boyfriends for me? "The boy I love is not in my grade."

"A seventh grader? Well, that's okay."

"No, Mama. He doesn't go to my school either."

"What do you mean? Where else would he go?"

"Trackton."

She stared. After a moment she said, "Trackton's the *colored* high school, honey," as though I'd made a simple mistake, misspoken. Another moment passed.

"That's right." I gazed at my hands in a pretense of shyness. "That's right, Mama. I'm in love with a colored boy. Don't tell Daddy."

# 7

My mother told him immediately, in an earnest alarmed whisper, as soon as he returned home that evening. She met him at the front door and pulled him aside. From around the corner I could hear her urgent murmur, then a hush. And then, I heard him chuckle.

"C'mon, Trudy," he said. "She's makin' that up. She's tryin' to get attention." He didn't believe it!

"Do you think so?" my mother's voice responded, thick with doubt and optimism.

His reply was a scold. "You gotta get that girl under control, Trudy. She's *your* responsibility. I can't have her showin' up at my place of employment sayin' all kinds of crazy things."

"What was she sayin'?"

"Hardly matters. Important thing is *you* gotta get her under control."

In the silence that followed, I imagined my mother's face: eyes darting worriedly, upper teeth chomping her lower lip. "You're right, Dick."

Yes, yes, Dick was always right. Why was she compelled to say it out loud on a daily basis? Why did he need to hear it all the time? Man of the house, head of the family, the great and irreproachable Dick McCoy. Why did he need constant validation? And he didn't even believe me! My hatred for him nearly choked me.

Over the next several days, my mother kept me close, filling my hours with little feminine chores. She made me hem Billy's shepherd costume for the children's pageant at church, which I did badly, even after she showed me how for the third time. Then we were busy-busy baking Christmas cookies and cakes, delivering them around town, making tree ornaments out of pinecones and cotton balls, and delivering those around town too, wrapping gifts, scrubbing the oven, dusting off the tops of board-game boxes, polishing silverware, washing and refilling the holiday salt and pepper shakers.

But all these mindless tasks left my brain free to contemplate and revise my plan. Okay, so my father didn't believe me. The problem was, I couldn't just *say* I was in love with a colored boy: I had to *show evidence* of it. Actions spoke louder than words. But what actions? I couldn't possibly touch a colored boy. Then I thought, actions may be more powerful than words, but neither words nor actions were as potent as suspicion. Suspicion prompted everyone to look for evidence, to prove they were right, and because they were looking, they saw it everywhere, whether or not it was there. I could get a rumor going—Dick McCoy's daughter involved with a colored boy—and the slightest of actions would lead people to conclude it was true. It would be doubly easy, I realized, because this was something everyone was already inclined to believe: let the colored boys too close to the white girls, and look what happens.

I just needed to name the object of my desire. Who could it be but Langston? My parents didn't know about his regular attendance at the Swansons', but they could find out. The Swansons' neighbors would have seen him coming and going; maybe some church members knew. Beyond this, I had to plan: how could I contrive to be seen with Langston, or in the vicinity of Langston, to make people talk?

If it occurred to me my plan would put Langston in danger, it didn't deter me. I still didn't think of him as a real, three-dimensional person, as fully human. Coloreds had always been in the background of our lives, like cardboard cut-outs. So it was easy to think of Langston as a flat character in my drama, when I thought of him at all. Mostly my thoughts were dominated by one thing: how to skewer my father. What kind of Klansman had a daughter running around with a jigaboo? He'd lose the Klan's respect. He'd never be elected Exalted Cyclops. What kind of man couldn't control a fourteen-year-old girl? He'd

lose *everyone's* respect. People would talk about him behind his
back; people would ridicule him. He'd never be promoted to
principal. He'd never be anyone in this town.

He might even leave—he and Doris Wallace could vanish
together in the night. I'd been so afraid of this, but now I could
see the benefits of life without him: no more insufferable family
dinners, no more soul-withering contempt and condescension.
My mother would get a job, like Fran Gray's mom, and she'd
have more important things to do than fuss over the house
cleaning. Ricky would graduate from high school in May and
leave for college in August, and wouldn't it be nice, I began to
think, to be rid of him too—to be rid of all the men—released
at last from all the female fawning, the continuous anxiety over
how men felt.

After Christmas, when the holiday clean-up was accomplished and my mother ran out of tasks to assign me, my idle-
ness worried her. She asked me what book I was reading, as
though it might be something smutty. Once, when I got off
the phone with Sue Bates, she snapped, "Who were you talking
to?" I could tell the notion of me in love with a colored boy still
rankled in her mind. My father may have been too busy with his
job and extracurricular activities to remember this possibility.
My mother had endless time to fret.

On New Year's Day I called Joe Pedicini on the kitchen
phone to wish him a happy 1964, holding the handset a short
distance from my ear, so my mother could hear the male voice
on the other end of the line. All through supper I caught
her casting glances at me, her forehead wavy with impending
doom. The rest of the family was oblivious—Billy donning his
new cowboy hat; Barb puckering her Coty-extra-red lips; Ricky
flashing around the new gaudy-faced Geneva Sport watch on
his wrist. My father's small, mean eyes concentrated on the
food on his plate, the side of his fork digging into a lump of
meatloaf, occasionally striking the porcelain underneath with a
screech.

The next day, Sunday, my mother was peculiarly eager to

rush us to church, not simply herding us with her usual efficiency, but in a near-panic. She wanted to go early for coffee
and donuts, she said. My father was clearly irritated by this; he
could have slept an extra twenty minutes. In the car on the way,
he complained about the cold and the potholes on Pitchkettle
Road, and she twisted toward him, hyper-alert to his mood and
patting his shoulder. *There there, there there.*

In the Fellowship Hall, we hung our coats on the rolling
metal rack and helped ourselves to donuts—glazed or pow-
dered sugar. My mother parked us kids at one of the long tables
and drifted over to where Ruth sat with a collection of ancient
ladies. My father roamed to the other side of the room, where
there were men, including Dr. Vaughan and a new Klan recruit.
The Swansons likely had no idea that members of their flock
were also members of the Klan. How would the topic come
up?

I didn't eat my donut. I watched my mother hover weirdly by
the big tank of coffee, near Ruth, waiting to catch her attention.
So this was why she wanted to come early. I rose and slunk over
to Ruth's table.

"Hi, Willa!" Ruth sang out and strained toward me, probably
wishing to escape from the old ladies. "Happy new year!" She
stood up. "Excuse me, ladies," and with an empty coffee cup,
she lurched toward the urn. I stuck by her side.

"Well, good morning, Ruth," my mother said with a surprised tone, as though she had not in fact been lying in wait. She
shot me a suspicious squint.

"Good morning, Trudy. How are you?" Ruth drizzled coffee
into her cup.

"We're fine, fine, just fine. How's Willa been gettin' along at
your place?"

"Oh, fine, fine, just fine." Ruth's grin tilted. She picked up
a packet of sugar and shook it around. Side by side, the two
women made an odd pair—my mother tall and knobby in a
loose beige dress, her face permanently browned by the sun;
Ruth short and neatly tucked into a fitted coral jacket and

matching skirt, face and hair an iridescent shade of pale. Ruth said, "The girls just love her."

"They do?" My mother did not need to sound so surprised. I spotted the girls in the far corner with the little Beale children, apparently having a jumping contest. Julie and Annette flopped up and down in matching green plaid dresses. My mother stepped closer to Ruth, away from me, and lowered her voice: "No *problems?*"

"What do you mean?"

"With Willa. Has she seemed...upset? Irrational? A little strange?"

I peered around my mother's shoulder; Ruth's face was poker-still. What must she be feeling? She knew my father was cheating on my mother, and that my mother didn't know. "Well," Ruth bleated, and I half-shouted, "I'm comin' over to-morrow, right? After school?"

"Of course!" Ruth replied. "I could use your help taking the tree down. Julie and Annette are good at taking the balls off the bottom, but then there's the whole rest of it! Matthew doesn't want me climbing ladders anymore, and I can't reach the top of the tree from down here!" She laughed at herself.

I asked, "Will Langston be there? He's tall." How clever was that? I'd worked him seamlessly into the conversation. I was a genius.

"Langston?" my mother sputtered. "Who is Langston? You don't mean that colored boy? Why would he be there?"

Nonchalant, a little dreamy, Ruth said, "Oh yeah, sometimes Langston comes over to help me too—thank you for recom-mending him, Trudy. He's a very polite young man. Oh, Mrs. Bowers! Excuse me, Trudy, so nice chatting," and she lurched away toward another group of ancient ladies.

My mother scowled at me. I smiled: it was a perfect smile. It was a guilty-trying-to-look-innocent-while-in-fact-guiltless smile. I could have won an Academy Award.

Her face turned to granite. "How often is that boy over at the Swansons'?"

Suddenly I spotted a flaw in my plan. I didn't want to be barred from going to the Swansons'. I stammered, "Not that much, I don't know. Just every now and then. Not very often." My alarm, which was genuine, worked in my favor—I sounded like a nervous girl protecting her boyfriend.

"Huh," she said, and her jumpy eyes searched the crowd for my father. But he was across the room with important men, leaning in with a grave expression, engrossed in significant matters. You could tell because his charcoal suit jacket swung open aggressively. My mother's concerns would have to wait until after church, and then until after Sunday dinner, and then until after whatever absorbed him this afternoon. By that time her worries would sound flimsy, the particulars of the conversation forgotten, the force of her emotion thinned. Some tone would creep into her voice that would make him dismiss her: I'd witnessed it a thousand times. She'd sound girlishly uncertain of her facts, and the bottom of his face would pull to one side and he'd say, simply, "Trudy." That would be the end of the conversation, and still my father wouldn't believe I had any association with a colored boy.

I would have to spread the seed farther and wider.

That night, hunkered under my blanket, I watched Barb in her bed on the other side of the nightstand, propped against a pillow, reading *Ethan Frome*. I listened to the pages turn. When at last she closed the book, clicked off our lamp, and rustled herself under her covers, I whispered loudly, "Barb? Are you awake?"

"Nope. I'm fast asleep."

"Ha ha." My eyes strained to see the lines of our furniture, the spires of my footboard. I lifted myself onto an elbow and began to see her more clearly: her head sunk into a pillow, the shapely sweep of her hip ascending from her waist. "Can I ask you something?"

"Maybe. What?"

"Are you *in love* with Jim Darden?"

For a while she didn't budge, and I began to think she was refusing to answer, or pretending to be asleep. Then came her high-pitched reply: "Well, *of course* I am!"

"You are?"

"Of course! Why wouldn't I be?"

"How do you know you are? What does it feel like?"

I could not have cared less about her love of Jim Darden. This was my sneaky way of launching the conversation

"Um…" Silence. Poor Barb. Putting her thoughts into words was not her strong suit. Of course, she was rarely asked to. She was so good at being pretty and pleasant; nothing more was required of her. What happens to a person's thoughts when she seldom, if ever, gets to articulate them? "Uhhh…" Then: "It feels like, I want him to think about me, and ask me out for Saturday night, and I want him to think I'm *classy*. That's the word he uses, 'classy.' I want to be what he likes."

"Oh." I felt a surge of disappointment. Was that what love felt like? I profoundly hoped not. I watched the contours of my sister grow clearer, her shoulder sloped forward, her hand curved loosely at the edge of the mattress. "Is that all?"

"No, that's not *all*," she said, as though I were the dumbest kid on planet Earth. "It feels like, I want him to think I'm special."

"Do you think he's special?"

"Of course."

"Why?"

"How can you even ask that? He's from such an important family."

"He's special because his family is rich?"

She groaned. "Not just that they're rich, it's…the family *name*. They're important people in the town. You know all this."

"So by that logic everyone is in love with Jim Darden."

"What? That makes no sense."

"Barb, I thought love was, like, you can't *bear* to be parted from him, and you just want to wrap your arms around him and squeeze him all the time, and when he glances your way, you feel all bubbly inside."

"Yeah. That's right."

I'd gotten myself off track. This series of questions was supposed to be an on-ramp to my soulful confession of love for Langston. But now I felt a genuine need to understand. Some deep instinct, some atavistic impulse, drove me to get this clarified; even then, on some level, I realized the importance of getting love right. I continued, "And you want to stay up all night talkin' to him on the phone. Time *flies* when you're talkin' because you're so interested in each other, in what the other person believes in, and dreams about."

She paused for a long moment and replied, matter-of-fact, "I think that's probably overrated."

"What about mutual respect? Mutual respect and admiration? You listen to him and you think, *Wow*, he is so smart, and he is such a good person. And he thinks you are too! He respects and admires *you too*."

"I don't know, for Pete's sake. Why are you askin' me all this now?"

There it was: a perfect set-up, so natural, so organic. I swallowed and said in my most sincere voice, "Because I'm in love too."

Barb's legs kicked around under the covers. "Oh my Lord, Willa, you are not. You got a crush on some boy, that's all."

This genuinely irritated me. "So *you* can be in love but I can't?"

"Okay then, who are you in love with? That fatso Joe Pedicini?"

"Hey, don't call him 'fatso'!" I snapped. "No, he's just my friend."

"All right then, who? Who, who, who? Who could it be? Let me guess. Johnny Cobb, the cutest boy in eighth grade."

"No."

"Stevie Hedgepeth."

"No."

"Then who?"

"I can't tell you who."

"Uh-huh. That's because he doesn't exist."

"Does so."

"Does not."

"Does so."

"Then tell me."

"I can't. If people knew, they'd be upset."

"Oh, I see, yours is a *forbidden* love," she said in her melodramatic movie voice.

"Well." I paused. "Yes, it is."

"You're in love with that handsome math teacher, Mr. Marcus."

I took a minute to think about this: I was a little in love with Mr. Marcus, but I was a gawky fourteen-year-old, and even if I were his age I doubted I could compete with the flaming-haired Miss Jones. I said, "No," in a tone that invited her to guess again.

"Warren Bunch."

"*No*. You'll *never* guess it."

"Willa," she said, feigning exhaustion. But I could tell she'd grown a little curious. "Do I know him?"

"You've seen him around. You know who he is."

A long silence ensued, her form motionless, her breathing protracted. "Well, I give up. Who is it? Not Reverend Swanson."

"No! God, Barb! What a weird guess!"

"If you don't tell me, I will have to conclude you're makin' it all up."

"Okay." I inhaled; I exhaled. "It's...Langston Jones."

The silence was so thick, it pressed on my ears. From far away came a croaking, or a quacking, or the barking of a little yippy dog. In a slow voice, Barb said, "Langston Jones. Langston Jones. That colored boy who comes over to mow our lawn. You're in love with the colored lawn-mower."

"Yes," I whispered wistfully.

She snorted. "Willa, *why* are you so peculiar? *How* is it we're related? Why on earth would you say you're in love with a colored?"

"Because I am."

"You are not. You're makin' up stories to get everyone upset and get attention."

I snorted in return, my indignation complete and real. Of course, she was right, absolutely right: I was making it up. It was funny how genuinely offended you could be by the truth about yourself.

She continued: "You're jealous of all the attention I'm get-tin' because *I* have Jim. You have *always* been jealous of me. I never knew anyone as jealous of their sister as you. There's a term for that—sibling rivalry!" she said triumphantly. "That's what you have."

My head pounded. "I am not jealous of you and Jim Darden. *Jim Darden.* 'Oh, Jim, I love you so. You're a real jerk who just wants to get into my panties but I'm so stupid I love you anyway.' Your problem is you think the world revolves around you—"

"*You're* the one thinks the world revolves around you, Willa McCoy. Willa *I'm-so-smart-I-got-all-As-on-my-report-card.* You think that makes you better than everyone else. You know what you are? An *egomaniac.*" What a lot of terminology for Barb, and so late at night. "Egomaniac!" she shrieked and slammed herself onto her other side, facing the wall and away from me.

"*Egomaniac!*" I screamed at her back, not knowing if I was calling her one, too, or making fun of her use of the word.

From down the hall my mother's tired voice called out, "Girls!"

I lay quiet. A shadow oozed across the wall. I rolled onto my back and looked up at our ceiling, at the network of interlock-ing cracks in the plaster. Two summers ago, Barb and I realized the cracks formed the shapes of states. "Look!" she'd giggled, pointing straight up. "That one's Georgia!"

"There's North Carolina," I squealed, and we both laughed. Barb's was a musical, contagious laugh.

Now I rolled onto my stomach, furious. Maybe she was right that I was making it up, but I wasn't making it up to get attention. What a juvenile motivation. Everyone thought I was a little kid, but I wasn't, and my motivation was far more adult: vengeance. I no longer wanted my father's attention; I wanted his suffering. I wanted payment for years of neglect. What was more adult than being the one to decide and mete out punishment?

Across the room, Barb's breathing syncopated into a dainty snore. She thought of me as a useless child, but I had in fact accomplished my goal: this piece of appalling social news— that I was in love with a colored boy—would remain in her head, even though she didn't believe it now. It would cycle through her thoughts until it became a possibility, and with a little evidence, it would grow into a suspicion. She'd tell Patsy, and Patsy would spill it to her mother, and her mother would leak it around town. I had succeeded in advancing my plan.

Yes, my plan was horrifying. It was dangerous, reckless, reprehensible. Did I understand this at the age of fourteen, in 1964? I don't recall, or maybe I don't wish to, not wanting to reopen the floodgates on my shame. I did not yet know the story of Emmett Till. *To Kill a Mockingbird* was published in 1960, but it was not a book taught in our schools, nor had I read it. Had I somehow absorbed the message that white women are free to use Black men for their own purposes, with no need to consider the consequences? Was I unforgivably ignorant, or had I tapped into a fetid underground pool of racism? I believe it was both. What we're capable of not realizing is as vast as the world beneath an ocean's surface.

School resumed the next day. Everyone paraded up the corridor in new sweaters and skirts. My former best friend, Becky Campbell, wore a glimmering silver bracelet that slid up her forearm as she raised her hand to answer questions in class. I studied her compliant profile, her domesticated hair, and thought how different things were for us now. I would have loved to tell her about my father and feel her arm across my shoulder while I cried.

After school I went to the Swansons'. It was the first time I'd gone since Langston's triumphant reveal of my father's car in

Doris Wallace's garage. The girls greeted me at the door, holding the stuffed animals their grandparents had sent them for Christmas: a silky lamb for Annette, a plush penguin for Julie. I spied Langston at the kitchen table. His shoulders were rounded forward, his wrists crossed in his lap, his expression molded in hard dark clay. With eyebrows raised, he peered sheepishly at me, an apprehensive statue.

Of course this was Ruth's doing. She'd planted some kind of conscience in that head of his. I wanted to kick him in the shin. I forgot I was pretending to be in love with him. At the sink, Ruth sang out, "All righty! Everyone's here. Let's tackle that tree!"

We trooped into the living room. Unlike our tree, the Swansons' was not slathered in tinsel. This would make it easier to un-decorate. At my house, we had to rewrap the tinsel around its original square of cardboard and be careful not to break any of the strands or tangle them, because that would be wasteful. It took forever.

Ruth sat on the couch amidst a pile of shoeboxes, each labeled in bold marker: Glass, Antique, Unbreakable, Wood, Balls. Each ornament belonged to a category with its own box. I began to wonder, What if you had a wood ornament that was also antique and unbreakable? What if you had a Christmas-tree ball that was also glass? Once they were sealed up in a box labeled with one word, their array of qualities would be obscured. I looked closely at each ornament. Almost all defied easy categorization. I wondered how we'd determine which feature takes precedence over others. We'd have to come up with a system, I thought, which would be kind of random but seem reasonable to all. Next to Ruth's feet stood a large cardboard box marked "Tree Lights," from which two fuzzy triangular ears emerged.

The girls pulled the unbreakables from the lower branches and pranced them over to their mom, who put them into boxes. Langston stood beside me, too close, in my opinion, and reached up to extract the gold angel from the top of the tree. I watched his fingers encircle the angel's waist, tug at it gingerly, and lift it down with great care. He gazed at it; it gazed back at him. Its eyes, I thought, were sorrowful. "This *beautiful*," he said, apparently to me. "Never seen nothin' like it before. You?"

"No." I had to answer, because he'd asked me a direct question.

"Wow. I bet it a Scandinavian thing."

Why was he talking to me? I shrugged.

"Look how the lace go along the top of the wings."

"Uh-huh."

Then I realized: he was trying to be nice to me. He was attempting to engage me in a friendly exchange. Did he feel *sorry* for me? Surprisingly, I didn't get angry; instead, I felt myself soften toward him. Maybe I could deeply despise only one person at a time, and now that person was my father. Or maybe my defenses had been shattered, and this was my new self in the world beyond my home: soft-boiled, a layer of pride peeled away, vulnerable.

Ruth reached toward Langston, took the angel, and swaddled it in tissue paper. The girls had already abandoned their task, now in fits of giggles, hunkering below the flaps of the lights box and dangling unbreakable ornaments over the edge until a little white paw darted up to smack them. I pulled decorations from the midsection of the tree: a slender blue wooden horse, delicate red snowflakes, a heart-shaped ornament in blue and red with "God Jul" in white script across it. Ruth saw me studying it.

"*Gode Ye-ill*," she pronounced. "Merry Christmas in Swedish."

"Oh!" I'd heard words in French and German before, but never Swedish.

"You speak Swedish?" Langston asked, sounding equally amazed.

"Yup! I say, *Gode Ye-ill*." And she laughed.

"Have you been to Sweden?" I asked.

"Oh, heavens no. We can't even afford a trip home for a

belated Christmas." She glanced around, looking disoriented, as though she wasn't sure how she'd gotten here. "I still have relatives in Sweden, though. My grandfather immigrated to Minnesota when he was twenty."

I said, "I always wondered, if you're gonna move away from Sweden for somewhere else, why wouldn't you pick somewhere *warmer?*"

She laughed. "Good question! I don't know. Think how hard it is to make such a big move. Maybe you'd look for somewhere that feels familiar. Somewhere you'd feel like you belong." Langston and I kept at our work, unhooking ornaments from branches, and Ruth went on: "My grandpa went to St. Paul and found a nice Swedish girl to marry, and they got a farm under the Homestead Act, about fifty miles west of the city."

"You grow up on a farm?" Langston asked.

"No, the farm went to the eldest son, not my father. I grew up in St. Paul." She added proudly, "My father is a pharmacist. Saved enough money to put all three daughters through college."

I detached a flat wooden goose from a branch and passed it to Ruth to crinkle up in paper. The branches were still supple, but the needles pricked my fingers and wrists, my hands now covered with invisible scrapes.

Ruth went on: "But my father brought scandal on his family when he married my mother. Want to know why?"

"Why?" we both said.

"My mother was…*Norwegian.* A mixed marriage!"

I was confused by this, but Langston chuckled, saying, "How'd they get along bein' so *different?*" which made Ruth laugh. It was easy to make Ruth laugh she laughed even when someone was just hoping to be funny. She made everyone feel witty and smart. Langston's voice grew serious. "He a good man? Your daddy?"

My eyes shot up, but his expression was sincere. He wanted to hear that Ruth's father was good to his family.

"Oh my, yes," she replied. "Salt of the earth, loyal, true-blue. I was lucky. You don't get to pick your parents."

"No, ma'am, no, indeed you don't."

I was disentangling a string from a branch, unthreading it from a clump of needles. The ornament was a ball wrapped in flaxen angel hair, and some strands had come loose. The more I tried to free it, the worse it got, and eventually I was yanking on the thing, rattling the entire branch. Ruth said, "It's not the children's fault if the parents make mistakes."

"You got that right, and nobody get to *pick* their parents."

"I'm standin' right here," I bellowed, and with a vicious yank got the decoration off the branch. By the time I handed it to Ruth, it was a mess of loose hair.

Langston walked to the couch and sat down beside Ruth. Then he folded his hands in his lap, and Ruth folded her hands in her lap, too, and they lifted their chins at the same angle to point their faces at me. There it was: pity. Their eyes exuded it.

Some people believe that pity is an expression of kindness or love, when in fact it is a vehicle for condescension, making its object feel small. Generally, I could not tolerate it. But on this occasion, coming from these two people, the pity felt different. This time it was not for a botched piano recital or a party I hadn't been invited to. This was an occasion full of consequence, and somewhere inside I sensed the impact of what had happened: my life's path had been altered, diverted through a dark wood. Now I was headed toward a future of distrusting men, failed relationships, years of disappointment. Pity was a reasonable response to my situation. Ruth said, "Langston has something to say to you."

"Okay." I stared at Langston's stone-still face. A millennium passed.

He said, "I am sorry."

"For what?"

Apparently this response had not been anticipated. He turned toward Ruth for guidance. She didn't speak, her eyebrows sunk deep into the crevice above her nose.

"For, for—"

He didn't even know what for! I hardened into an aggressive

posture, one foot forward, head cocked. Finally he belted out. "For makin' you find out! For wantin' you to find out and feel bad! Not your fault your daddy like he is." He stopped, but his face was still animated. He had a bundle of mean things to say about my father, I could tell. How much did Langston know?

Ruth prodded, "And you were going to say something else to Willa too."

He sighed. "I hope you can forgive me."

"*And...*" insisted Ruth.

Langston sank, shrinking to half his height. "*And*, I hope you and me can be friends. I would like for you and me to be friends."

That's when I remembered I was pretending to be in love with him. I nearly gasped. This was perfect. Now Langston was beholden to me; he'd feel compelled to suffer my presence, my schemes to be seen with him. The glee in my voice must have confused them both. "Okay!" I tried to push my face into a frown and contain my tone. "Okay, Langston. I will forgive you. If you insist. And from now on, you and me are friends."

Ruth clapped, her snow-white face glowing, and Langston let go of a sigh. Together he and I unstrung the tree lights. I went for the broom, and he waddled the tree out the back door. Then he and Ruth taped the ornament boxes shut, and I, grinning, swept the chaos of shed pine needles into a neat and manageable pile.

## 8

To my astonishment, Langston was true to his word. The days we were together at Ruth's, he was genuinely friendly, greeting me with a jolly hello as though pleased to see me. He'd ask how my day was going, and when I answered he'd listen and nod or shake his head at the appropriate moments. His brother Sammy was Billy's age, and one afternoon Langston asked what Billy liked to do. I had to think about it. "He definitely does not like goin' to school." Langston and Ruth leaned toward me, so I kept going: "In spring he'll be back to playin' softball, but now he mostly watches TV and plays cowboys and Indians with the neighbor boys."

Langston said, "Sammy do that too!"

I'd never imagined a colored cowboy before, but I stopped myself from saying that out loud, which must have been some kind of progress for me. I reflected that light-skinned colored boys would make more convincing Indians than Billy and his pasty friends. Ruth rose to take our empty cups to the sink and returned to her seat with a weary grin.

"You need anything, Ruth?" Langston said. "You let me know, okay?"

"I'm *fine*." She turned to me. "What's your next essay assignment?"

As I explained it, I could barely contain my irritation. Mrs. Beale had discovered a new technique for writing—the five-paragraph essay—invented by *college professors*, she'd said. We were supposed to write a persuasive essay in exactly *five* paragraphs giving *three* reasons to support our *thesis*. Even worse, the topic was, Would you rather live in the South or the North? It was phrased like we had a choice, but really we didn't. This was just more adult fakery. Here's what any of us knew about the North: it was cold, it had lots of big noisy cities, and they hated us. None of us could think of one positive thing about it, all our knowledge being a vague compilation of adults' stereotypes. On the contrary, it was easy to think of three positive things about the South, because that's where we lived.

With her chin perched on her knuckles, Ruth asked, "So what are you going to write?"

I let out a puff of air. I was so tired of trying to please my teachers. First you had to try to get into their brains to figure out what they wanted, then you had to work and work to give it to them, while all the time pretending it was what you wanted.

I proclaimed, "I'm gonna say the North."

Ruth let out a whoop.

"But I don't know anything about the North!" I said.

She grinned. "If only you had someone sitting right here who could tell you all about it."

Langston shook his head. "Minnesota not what Ms. Beale mean by 'the North.'"

"What?"

I said, "He's right. She means New York City, or Boston, or Philadelphia." She meant all those silly little states sitting atop the elegant peak of Virginia. Minnesota was more like the West, or Canada, or the moon.

"Oh," Ruth said. "I've never been to those cities."

"*Daisy* has," Langston said, inflating with the opportunity to say her name aloud. "Daisy used to live in DC," he said, as if he hadn't told us this a million times. "And she got an uncle in Philly. Her mama used to take her up every summer. Daisy know all about Philly. She can tell you." His eyes were all a-twinkle.

Ruth raved, "Oh, let's have her come over! She can tell us all about it!"

"No," I said, seized by an idea. "I mean, there's not time—the paper's due Thursday!" This was a lie. "I'll have to talk to her right away. I can go over to Trackton tomorrow and meet y'all when school lets out, okay?"

Langston's face dropped. "What?"

"I can go over to Trackton tomorrow, okay?"

"You gonna come to the colored school. Stand outside the colored school."

"Sure! Yeah!" I smiled at Ruth, who said, "Why not?"

Of course, there were a million reasons why not. A young white girl roaming around the colored side of town? When the sun was about to set? Hanging around outside the colored high school? Waiting for a *colored boy*? But Langston did not seem able to articulate these problems in a polite way to someone like Ruth Swanson—an outsider, a kindhearted woman whose view of humanity was overly rosy, which he may have wanted to protect. To Langston I said happily, "Where should we meet?"

His eyes began to dance, landing finally on Ruth's face with a plea for help. "I don' know about this, Willa."

"Oh, please, please?" I bounced in my seat. "Isn't there one of Mr. Priddy's drugstores across from Trackton?" Priddy's enthusiasm for the Klan did not prevent him from selling to coloreds. "We can meet there!" Though Priddy himself would not be in that store, his assistant manager would eagerly report anything out of the ordinary, like a white girl who looked like Dick McCoy's daughter walking down the street with a colored boy. "Okay? *Please?*"

"Please what?" Julie galloped in, drawn to the familiar sound of beseeching.

Ruth bent toward her. "Willa wants to meet Langston at his school tomorrow. Isn't that nice?"

"Uh-huh," Julie replied, her robin's-egg eyes drifting to Langston's face.

Then Annette was in the room, too, singing, "Lankin, Lankin, Lankin…"

"Please, Langston?"

The stereophonic female pleading must have been hard for him to resist. But in the end, he may have felt he didn't really have a choice. "Okay," he said, his voice cracking.

❧

The colored high school was the old county high school for whites, constructed in a long-past decade when school buildings were designed to look menacing. Its once-ruddy brick was worn now and gaping where mortar had chipped away, made dim by a film of industrial grit from the paper mill and the ham processing plants. The building looked unclean, as we imagined the people inside did too. It sat on a small grassless square of land across a cracked street from a row of shabby storefronts. There was a barbershop, a used furniture store, a place boarded up, a diner, and Mr. Priddy's drugstore for coloreds.

I peered through its grimy windows at racks crowded with old-looking merchandise. Fortunately, the day was mild enough for me to stay outside, next to its droopy screen door. I felt achingly awkward, self-conscious, pulling my crocheted hat down over my white-girl hair and forehead, drawing looks anyway, from a colored man walking into the barbershop and two colored women inside the drugstore. I waited. I'd gotten there too quickly, even without my bike, too eager not to miss the final bell. I watched the school, its symmetrical banks of windows, the front door tucked inside a columned portico that must have once been painted white. I tried to imagine the interior and pictured dingy corridors, tattered and blank.

When the bell sounded—more of a honking than a ringing—I jumped. A moment later the main door flung open and colored kids poured out, jabbing at each other, singing, shrieking with laughter, yelling out names—noisy, just as my father had always said; these colored kids are *hyper-charged*, he'd say—it was dangerous, all that energy. I tried to straighten myself and appear nonchalant. But they came at me in a wave: packs of boys shoving, clumps of girls swinging across the street, shouting over heads at other clumps of girls. *Uncivilized*, my father always said. Easily distracted. They needed *remedial training*, he'd said, just to *sit still* in a *seat*—disgusting, subhuman.

But now that I hated my father, I felt allowed to question what he'd always said. Why was noise "uncivilized"? Did "civilized" mean everyone but him had to keep quiet?

Still, the torrent of black faces lodged a wood block of fear in my chest and parched my throat. One group of girls stared at me as they passed, then burst out laughing. The boys who saw me stopped talking to eyeball me, and the image of Margaret Whitehead's crushed skull appeared in my mind. I shoved my hands into my coat pockets to hide their trembling. I shrank against the drugstore wall.

No one spoke to me. They passed by, glancing, staring, smirking, or not. In my memory the hordes kept coming, though there could not have been as many as it seemed; the sidewalk was tight and the street narrow—the space would have filled up readily. Self-conscious and burning with dread, I turned my face and squinted at something imaginary in the distance. "What *she* doin' here?" I heard someone say, and I thought of slipping away, along the wall of the drugstore and around the corner, then running back to the white side of town. I could do that. I drew in a stream of cool air. What was I doing there again? I was too obvious, too anomalous—I should run away, that's what I should do, and I got ready to.

Then I saw Langston coming toward me.

"Langston!" I called out, buoyant with relief, and it struck me: I was no longer afraid of him. I waved at him uncontrollably and he looked embarrassed, gave me a furtive nod, then pretended he hadn't seen me. By his side was a slender girl with a wistful face, pastel brown. She wore a cloth coat, cerulean, with gigantic matching buttons. She carried a small box of a purse with shiny gold clasps, her delicate hand in a loose grip around its handle. Langston was carrying her books, or else he had an exceedingly large amount of homework.

They inched toward me, exuding apprehension, letting the crowd around them thin. Langston stopped at the curb rather than stepping up onto the sidewalk beside me, and he kept himself turned as though he was not actually speaking to me. His tone, though, was genial. "Hi, Willa. This Daisy."

"Hello," she said in a deep, confident, suspicious tone. Her hair was smoothed back from her forehead and tied in a fat bun at the nape of her neck. She had earrings—big glittery squares. She was short, rising only to Langston's shoulder. She was shorter than me.

"Hi," I said, and we all just stood there.

Eventually Langston said, sounding befuddled, "You got your questions?"

"Oh yeah. Yeah. It's for a school assignment," I said eagerly to Daisy, though of course, Langston would have explained. "I need to know three things about Philadelphia." The word felt furry in my mouth, coming out as "Philadel-TH-ia."

"Okay." She smiled slightly with glossy teeth.

Then I remembered to step away from the drugstore wall and take off my hat—the better to be identified by Mr. Priddy's drugstore manager and anyone else who might be inclined to spread the word.

"Can we walk?" I said. Walking would increase our chances of being seen. "I don't want to be too late to the Swansons'."

I knew Langston wouldn't question this, but he swayed and turned, agitated. He scanned the street and the storefronts to see who was watching. Daisy stepped up next to me, positioning herself between me and Langston. I supposed this made sense—she was the one I was interviewing—but I needed to be seen walking beside Langston. I didn't see how I could maneuver myself. I'd used up most of my brain cells simply standing outside of the high school. The three of us walked down the sidewalk, Langston half in the street, and I explained the assignment to Daisy. She asked, "Why you wanna write about livin' up North?"

"To make people mad," I said, and she laughed, the sound like fluttering wings. I looked at her. Her eyes were wide-set ovals, caramel; the lines of her cheeks were soft, rounded. I found myself thinking she was kind of pretty. Langston was gazing at her with such adoration I thought his head might fly off his neck. Was she *that* pretty? I looked at her again, but she was talking, and I needed to be paying attention. "...people in the park," she was saying. "Lots be goin' on there. You can make lotta new friends in Philly." Her voice was thick cream pooling in my brain. "You can get all over the city on the bus. Anywhere you want. Downtown, museums—"

"Oh, what museums?"

She listed them, and I listened to the voice, so smooth and soothing, intelligent, sure of itself. If I listened to it forever, I thought, I'd never feel anxious again. No wonder Langston liked this girl. Was she a singer? She must have been.

"Where we goin'?" Langston blurted. We'd stepped off the sidewalk and turned up a dirt side street. The more we walked, the more jittery he got, his shoulders rising and tensing, his eyes darting.

Daisy replied, "I was walkin' toward my house."

"You goin' that way, Willa?" His voice sounded strangled.

"For a little ways." I peered around Daisy to smile at him. We were passing the unpainted facades of wood houses, a line of them sharing walls and raised up on a rickety platform so they wouldn't flood when the street did.

Daisy went on about Philadelphia: a person could get a good job there. Her uncle was a mailman, and he and his wife and their little boys lived in a brick row house in Point Breeze. "And," she added, "my opinion is, it's a little easier to be Black there."

*Black*, she'd said, not colored, not even Negro. This meant something, I could tell. I glanced at her and discovered she'd been looking at me, her caramel irises rolled toward me, showing the bright whites of her eyes, large and gently curved. She had beautiful eyeballs, I thought; then, What a weird thing to think.

She said, "Don't you need to be writin' this down?"

"I have an excellent memory. Anyway, I only have to remember three things: buses, museums, jobs. Got it." I smiled at the thought of explaining in my paper that colored men could get good jobs as mailmen. "This the way to your house, Daisy?" We were heading north toward Main Street, where there'd be traffic—white people on their way to Emporia. "You live north of Main?"

Now they were both looking at me, suspicion creeping back into their expressions. Langston said, "You comin' the whole way, Willa? Gonna stay to supper?"

Daisy laughed. I giggled nervously.

"No, but I'll walk with y'all to Main," as though this would make them happy. Silence descended. We plowed on toward the intersection together, all awkward and stiff. This wouldn't do, I realized. Ahead of us, a car swished past. I'd wanted to be seen chatting happily with Langston, not Daisy. I scrambled in my brain for something to say. We were half a block from Main. Unnaturally loud, I asked Daisy, "You ever meet Ruth Swanson?"

"No," she replied. "I have not had that pleasure."

"Langston," I yelled over her head. "You should bring her some afternoon!" This was good—clearly I was engaged in conversation with the boy. Main was only a few feet ahead of us. I said, "We could have a party! With the girls, and Mr. Softy! I could bring cookies and party hats and we could play games, like, like…" I was smiling, craning my neck, gazing dreamily at Langston. "Pin the tail on the donkey! Bobbing for apples! Or no, maybe the girls are too little for that—"

We were almost there. Quietly, Daisy asked Langston, "Who is Mr. Softy?"

At the intersection, we all paused, and Langston said, "It a cat."

A car passed. Together we crossed the street. There I stopped, which had the effect of making them stop too. Cars were headed our way, swooshing up from behind us, and I began a new sentence. "Daisy," I said, elongating her name. "I just want to say thank you," I was talking in slow-motion, "very much, for helpin' me with this paper, and for providing me with all this—*interesting* information, about Philadelphia—" Two more cars passed.

She said, "I don't think it was that much."

"Oh no! No!" I lurched toward Langston. "I didn't know anything at all, so it was great, I have so much now. Like all those museums. I can easily fill up a paragraph with their names. My paper's already one-fifth written! And the buses! That was *interesting*." I'm sure they thought I was insane. Langston reached for Daisy's elbow, intending to lead her away. I took another step toward him. "Thank you for letting me come, Langston." You'd think he'd invited me to a royal ball. He nodded.

Daisy intoned, "Well, goodbye."

Over her shoulder, I saw, turning onto Main a block east of us, a '57 red Ford pickup—a truck I knew well. It belonged to Gene Buck, a roofer from Smithfield who never missed a Klan meeting. The truck swayed and huffed, then accelerated with a rattle. Gene Buck had a clear view of me, Daisy, and Langston.

"Okay!" I smiled and giggled and stepped closer to Langston. "Then I'll see you later at Ruth's!" I kept my eyes fixed on Langston.

"Okay." He and Daisy spun in unison and walked fast up the next ragged block, toward where the coloreds' houses got a little nicer.

"Bye bye!" I hollered and waved at their backs. They didn't turn or respond, but the truck slowed down, wafted toward the curb, and stopped.

Mr. Buck's pointy face frowned at me through his window, which he commenced cranking down in irregular jerks. "Willa McCoy?" he asked, as though I could be someone else. He had a tall forehead with a small disc of black hair at the very top, his eyes and nose and mouth all crowded together into the bottom half of his face. "What you doin' out here?"

"Walkin' home."

His idling engine sputtered, loose and tubercular; the dark rim of his brow sank lower over his murky eyes. "This part a town ain't on your way home."

I didn't speak. I felt genuinely caught, guilty, deserving of punishment. He said, "What you doin' out here with them coons?"

"Schoolwork," I said. "I have a paper for school. So I was

talking to them." For some reason I added, "I'm gonna be a newspaper reporter."

Mr. Buck's shoulders vibrated along with his engine. "Paper for school 'bout what?"

"Philadelphia." His eyes bore into me, and I lost all control of what came out of my mouth. "You know, the Liberty Bell. Benjamin Franklin." Apparently I knew more about Philadelphia than I'd realized. "I have to write a paper about Benjamin Franklin, I mean, the Liberty Bell, and that girl saw it once, the Liberty Bell, so I was askin' her about it. It has a crack."

His face tipped forward, his forehead growing longer. "Get in. I'll drive you home."

"No, thank you. I'm goin' to Reverend Swanson's house. I like to walk. Isn't it a nice day?"

His head rotated away from me until he faced his windshield again. His hand levitated to the gear shift. But once more his possum eyes turned back toward me and he said, "You behave yourself, girl. You know you shouldna be over this way by yourself. What would your daddy say?"

"I don't know," I replied boldly, adding, "He might be mad." I smiled broadly, my eyes laughing at him, which made him sneer and crank up his window hard. I sauntered away, victorious.

That evening, the phone rang during supper. This rarely happened. My mother leaped to answer it—the sound irritated my father. The rest of us sat listening to her pleasant voice: "I'm so sorry, he's eating his supper right now. May I please take a message?"

She returned with a square of paper and handed it to my father, which doubled his irritation: first the phone had rung, and now he was obliged to take a piece of paper from his wife. She sat without a sound. We all knew that complete silence was needed when Daddy's irritation exceeded a certain level, and we were all expert at knowing when that was. But that night Patsy was over to study for an algebra test with Barb, and she had not internalized our unwritten rules. She resumed her tales of candy-striping at Kingsfield Hospital: "Anyway, we all agreed we're lucky to be livin' in these incredible times, with these other medical marvels! The polio vaccine!" No one was interrupting her tonight; no one was really listening.

My father asked my mother, "What does he want?"

"I don't know, he didn't say." My mother stared at her food as though she didn't recognize it.

Patsy continued, "Dr. Peters said I could come see him take X-rays, I'm so excited! *X-rays*—it's like we're livin' in the future! Pretty soon we'll all have flyin' cars! I like to think if you took X-rays of people's heads you could see their thoughts." She laughed, and when no one else did, she added, "I know it doesn't work that way, but aren't we lucky to be livin' in these times! The polio vaccine, antibiotics—"

My father cut in. "What people don't understand is these new antibiotics are spawning *superbugs*. *Superbugs* evolving to resist those same antibiotics. That's what people don't understand. Whole new race of deadly *superbugs*."

"That's right," Ricky said, and we all, including Patsy, finished supper in silence.

After supper the boys ambled into the family room to watch TV and the girls began the clearing ritual, table to kitchen and back again in a line like marching ants. My father had gone upstairs to use the extension to return his phone call, and all was in order—bowls and glasses and serving spoons and plates—until we heard his footsteps thundering back down the stairs. "Trudy!" He barreled into the kitchen. "Trudy!"

She gasped. "What is it?"

"Tell me one thing, Trudy. What is your responsibility in this family?" His voice simmered with contempt, and everyone froze: my mother at the sink, Barb holding a plate to scrape over the trash can, Patsy and I inside the kitchen door with dirty silverware and a serving bowl. Even the boys in the adjoining room went rigid, stretched up like prairie dogs peering into the kitchen.

"What?" My mother shut off the faucet and turned toward him.

His voice dipped to a snarl. "Are you or are you not responsible for looking after these children?"

"What happened, Dick?"

His red-fisted hand, raised at the angle of a Hitler salute, waggled the phone message at her. "Do you know why Gene Buck called?"

"He didn't say."

"*He didn't say,*" my father mocked.

I believe we were all waiting to be dismissed from the room, expecting my mother to instruct, "Girls, go upstairs," but she didn't, and we stood as still as we could, sapped of volition. My father continued, "I'll tell you what he said. He saw Willa not *two hours ago* hangin' around the colored side of town!"

Barb's face flashed toward me, lit with astonishment and realization. Patsy's expression was more curiosity than shock, but still incredulous. My mother's voice rose an octave: "She was at the Swansons' two hours ago."

"Oh, that so? That so, Trudy? She in two places at one time? She *magical?* She practicin' *witchcraft?* She wavin' a magic wand? Flyin' around on a broomstick?"

"She was *supposed* to be at the Swansons'—"

"Well, she was *not* and you had *no* idea, did you? You have no idea what goes on in this house. You have no idea about anything, do you?" He was yelling full volume now: "Here you got a girl sneakin' around with *coons* and you're too damn stupid to know about it! You need your IQ tested, Trudy? You an imbecile? You a low-grade moron? You know what you are, Trudy? Useless!"

Patsy gasped. Barb's eyes brimmed with tears. Suddenly I wondered, Why was he screaming at her and not me? I was standing right there, wholly visible. But he kept at her, stabbing her with insults, slicing layers off her self-esteem.

"Maybe you don't care if your daughter runs around with coons. Maybe you're a goddam secret coon-lover, that it? Like that Jackie Kennedy and all those big-shot Northern liberals think they're better'n we are? That it? Huh? That it? Or maybe you're just too *goddam lazy* to keep track of your own kids."

My mother's head nodded forward, too heavy to keep upright. Down went her face until it was parallel to the floor. I looked at the spot she must be seeing—a square of linoleum with the pattern worn off. I heard her whisper, "I'm sorry."

"You're *sorry*. You're *sorry*. What kinda wife *are* you?"

At that, my head snapped up. I looked directly at him, stiffened, and in my loudest voice said, "I guess she's not a very good wife, huh, Daddy? *Poor man* with a useless wife. What's a poor man like that to do?"

He reeled toward me. I'd never seen such a look on anyone's face, ever before in my life. Contorted, compressed, his eyes blazed with contempt, piercing me with a white-hot hate. His expression punched the breath out of me. His lips mashed together until the lower one burst out, his chin thrust toward me. His arms muscled up at his sides. I waited for him to punch me. He might as well have—he'd already shattered me with his pure loathing. And yet I had nothing to show for it—no bruise, no welt, no crimson scars, no marks to signal others. All the evil that pools inside families should at least break the skin.

Barb and Patsy had wilted, and my mother's face, rising slowly, was ground to a red pulp. Did she know? I could have told her then, her and everyone else. I could have shouted out, "Daddy's having an affair with Doris Wallace!" I said nothing. Maybe I'd used up all my courage for the day, or my willingness to inflict harm.

My father twisted back toward my mother and jabbed at the air between them. "You get this girl in line, Trudy. That's my final word." Then he stormed from the house, slamming the screen door, the car door, revving his engine, squealing away. So he'd gotten what he wanted: a legitimate reason to leave. Now he was free to drive around in the dark, justified in finding some comfort there.

# 9

For nearly a month, I was imprisoned in my house. Ricky and Barb served as guards, ferrying me to school and back, ensuring no unauthorized stops occurred. Of course they were furious. Ricky lost valuable tennis time driving me. Some days he refused to do it, and Barb was stuck walking me. She was also tasked with monitoring me inside the house to ensure I didn't sneak out—poor Barb! Prom with Jim Darden was a mere two months away and she wanted a store-bought dress, which would require many shopping ventures to Norfolk and Newport News, and here she was shackled to me. She barely spoke to me. But my mother was terrified I'd escape. As an extra measure of security, she had Ricky attach my bike to the fence with an anchor chain and a padlock. Then she told him to hide the key. Sometimes I pressed my face against the window and gazed at it.

My mother had phoned Ruth to say she needed me at home for a week to help with spring cleaning. I cleared out the hall closet, then my closet, then the kitchen junk drawer, where I found the metal egg slicer no one had seen in years. At the end of the week, my mother phoned Ruth again to say she needed me for a while longer, and she put me on Green Stamp duty. I sat at the kitchen table pressing sheets of S&H green stamps onto a soaked orange sponge, then affixing them to their corresponding pages, smoothing them flat with the palm of my hand. Glue leached onto my fingers and couldn't be washed off. I had to let it dry and pick at it all evening. By the end of the week we had enough completed books for the Corningware Electromatic Percolator.

I tried telling my mother I needed Mrs. Swanson's help with my English homework, because we'd begun studying poetry. My mother didn't believe I needed help, but I did—my attitude was atrocious. When Mrs. Beale explained, in a tone of mystical reverence, "Poets say *one* thing but *mean* another," I was infuriated. Why couldn't they just say what they meant? Why did everyone have to hide and disguise and distort? I was living in a fun house hall of mirrors. We read a Robert Frost poem about a boy who sawed off his hand. Gross! Why was that in a poem? Then there was "After Apple-Picking," about a woodchuck and a guy who got tired of apple-picking, which Mrs. Beale said was a metaphor for death. Everything was a metaphor for death. None of us understood any of it, because what did eighth graders know about death? We read poems and waited for Mrs. Beale to tell us what they meant. I grew suspicious that she was making stuff up. Although I did kind of like "The Road Not Taken," with the way leading on to way, it wasn't clear if going on the path less traveled was a good idea or not, and when I asked Mrs. Beale in class, she got off on a tangent about how all the poets in our anthology were Northerners and there ought to be Southern poets in the book too.

My mother said, "You don't need Mrs. Swanson. Your daddy can help you with the poetry."

"Mama, he's a *science* teacher."

"He's a very smart man who knows about everything. He can certainly explain eighth-grade poetry."

Thankfully, my father was rarely there. He'd come home for supper and leave right after—there was so much work at the school, he kept saying, and so many meetings. It was true the Klan was meeting more often. They were *strategizing*, I'd heard my father explain to Ricky. They'd already managed to oust a pro-integration teacher from Southampton High in Emporia—fired on grounds of moral turpitude—and they were looking for dirt on our district's superintendent, who went around talking like school integration was inevitable. I had no doubt my father spearheaded these efforts. There were other incidents, too: trash dumped on coloreds' doorsteps, cars stalking coloreds on the street. Rocks were hurled against the window of the colored barbershop, and the glass shattered. Rumor was the barber's teenaged son had disrespected Mr. Browne's son, who was five, and Mr. Browne and Mr. Doyle and the Parker boys spent a wild night throwing rocks on the colored side of town, a reminder of who was in charge.

At the end of my second week of confinement, I overheard my mother telling Ruth on the phone I had a bad cold and needed to stay home another week. All these excuses—my mother unable to simply state I wasn't allowed to go there anymore, too afraid of offending the reverend's wife. My mother could not bear other people's disapproval; she lost sleep, fretted all day, fawned over the displeased person to regain favor. It was horrible to watch. I overheard her say, "I'm sorry, Ruth, her laryngitis is so bad she can't even talk on the phone."

Midway through my third week of captivity, I realized it might never end. This would be my life forevermore. I grew somber. I took to watching TV after school with Billy: reruns of *Mister Ed*, the talking horse. One day after the show I called Florence to tell her about it and had the most annoying conversation I'd ever had in my life: "I don't *know* how Mr. Ed is able to talk, he just *is*." The next day I tried calling Sue Bates, who was just as shy on the phone as in person. I would have called Joe Pedicini, but he didn't like to "gab" on the phone.

Mrs. Beale returned our essays on the North versus the South and I got an A minus, the minus because she hadn't seen how job opportunities for coloreds were relevant to my "argument." I longed to show Ruth. She'd laugh—I could hear the fluttering sound of it in my head—and I'd laugh too, and so would Langston. But now I was trapped forever in my oppressive childhood home. The dogwoods in our yard bloomed. Softball season began. On *Mister Ed*, Wilbur grew a mustache, which his wife didn't like, and Mister Ed wanted a shower installed in the barn. Now on the way home from school every afternoon I'd wonder, What was Mister Ed up to today?

One day, during the fourth week of my captivity, I trudged through the back door and heard a familiar voice from the living room. Along with my mother's languid Southern murmur were the clipped Northern assertions of Ruth Swanson. I ran, and there she was, in a wide yellow skirt overflowing our gloomy couch—a patch of sunshine in my sepia house.

"Willa!" she sang out, setting down her glass of sweet tea. "So good to see you!" The lopsided grin spread into a smile that engulfed her face.

I raced to the couch to hug her and sit beside her, which made my mother's face pinch into startled disappointment. My mother, wearing a dark green sack of a dress, sat stiff in a wing chair. I asked Ruth, "Where are Julie and Annette?"

"Oh, I left them with another sitter." She winked.

"How are they?"

"They're fine. They miss you!"

"They do?" I jerked forward in excitement.

My mother broke in. "Mrs. Swanson was inquiring when you'd be able to come back, and I was explaining about your bad health." Her face grew rigid and flushed: there was obviously nothing wrong with my health.

"Trudy," Ruth cooed and leaned toward her. "I wouldn't blame you if you felt you needed to keep Willa home because of…the *incident*." My mother cocked her head, feigning puzzlement, forcing Ruth to say out loud, "The day Willa went over to Trackton High. I think you must be furious with me, and I don't blame you one bit."

"Oh no! No, no!" my mother blathered. "I would never be furious with *you*, Ruth. It's Willa we're furious at."

"But I am to blame!" Ruth proclaimed. "Willa is a good girl. It was *my* fault, *all my fault*. I encouraged her to go over to that colored high school to do research for her paper." Breathily she added, "I really didn't understand, you know. Coming from the North, we're not used to the situation here with the coloreds, and I didn't understand. It was stupid of me." Then her voice softened, her pitch deep with sincerity. "I didn't stop to think, of the danger. Of course, it was much too dangerous for her to go over there." My mother shifted and exhaled. Ruth said, "I am so sorry, Trudy, and I can promise you it will never happen again. I'll keep Willa safe at my house from now on." She smiled, but my mother squirmed and looked at her hands, her fingers knitted together on her crossed knee.

"I don't know," she said. "I would have to check with my husband."

"Oh, of *course* you would! I just pray the answer is yes. The girls do miss Willa, and she is so helpful to me around the house."

"She is?"

"Yes, she is! She washes the dishes, which is so helpful because standing at the sink for a long time is hard for me now. She helps me bake cookies."

Suddenly my mother was animated. "She's baking?"

"Oh yes! Next time we'd better send some of those delicious cookies home with you, right, Willa? They're—" and she hesitated, thinking up a cookie type, "—rosettes. Swedish cookies. Yum. *And* we were going to start making some play clothes for the girls!"

At this, my mother hardened: Ruth had gone too far. My mother's head tilted, the side of her face caught momentarily in a dusty sunbeam, her chalky skin soaked in gray bath water. "She's *sewing?*"

I pounded my heels on the floor. "Aw, Mrs. Swanson, do I *have to*? You said maybe, not for sure." This was the right move. My mother smirked knowingly at Ruth, whose eyes slid toward me, smiling but serious too.

"Please," she said to me. "It's gotten hard for me to stand to pin the patterns and cut the cloth. I can do the sitting work—that's not a problem. But, Willa, I need you to do the standing up." Real tears glinted in her eyes.

"Oh," my mother said. "Well."

A funereal silence passed. This was a serious dilemma for my mother. Here was the pastor's wife, a woman with little children and a crippling illness, tearfully asking for help. Yet a good Christian woman obeyed her husband, and she knew he'd say no. I examined my mother's shadow-washed face, tilted and twisting over the predicament. I began to understand that her commitment to being a good Christian wife was infused with practical concerns: she had no place to be but here, no money of her own. I realized, too, she was afraid of my father, and that fear pulled the binds tighter. "Well."

I burst out, "All this is because of my father! He's the one wants to keep me trapped in the house and not have a life of my own!"

"Willa!" my mother scolded. "We don't speak badly of your father! He just wants to make sure you're safe."

Ruth interjected, "Yes, yes! We all want Willa to be safe! How about if every day she calls you as soon as she gets to my house, and when Matthew comes home at suppertime, he can run her home in the car so she's not walking by herself after dark—you know, with, all these *coloreds*." The last phrase came out laughably awkward, but my mother didn't seem to notice.

I said, "Mama! Ricky and Barb would be so happy. Ricky could get more practice time and Barb could go shopping for her prom dress." Wildly I added, "Jim Darden!"

My mother began to nod.

I went on. "Anyway, Daddy's so busy these days he probably wouldn't even notice. Every evening he's gone out of the house. You wouldn't even have to tell him." Instantly I regretted saying this. Surely my mother would never withhold information from my father—that was the kind of thing a conniving, scheming, *bad* woman would do. *Bad* women try to get the upper hand, to siphon authority away from their husbands.

I waited for her admonition, but instead she said, "That's true. He's hardly ever here anymore." Her eyes registered a look of defeat that had nothing to do with me or Ruth. "All right," she said. "You can go back."

Ruth clapped her hands, and I let out a whoop of joy.

The next day, Julie and Annette greeted me with squeals and hugs, then skipped me down the hall to their parents' room to phone my mother.

Ruth called after me. "Come to the kitchen when you're done, we have a surprise for you!"

A surprise! For me! Cookies, I thought. Or maybe cupcakes! Devil's food cupcakes with deep swirls of chocolate frosting. In Ruth's bedroom I listened to my home phone ring and ring. The girls ran off and came back, Julie carrying Mr. Softy.

"He's big!" I said, and finally my mother picked up. "I'm at the Swansons', I'm fine, bye." I hung up and we traveled in a happy herd down the hall to the kitchen.

The surprise, sadly, was not cupcakes or cookies. It was Daisy—Langston's Daisy—sitting in my spot at the table.

"Oh," I said.

Langston was in his usual place, Ruth in hers. The Swansons kept their kitchen table pushed against the wall; there were only three spots for adults to sit comfortably. Ruth said, "Daisy's been coming these days with Langston!" and pulled over the step stool so I could squeeze in at the corner. I sat, my head much lower than everyone else's.

"How are you, Willa?" said Daisy in her creamy voice, looking directly at me with her beautiful eyeballs. Annette climbed into her lap. Langston was arched toward Daisy in a relaxed slouch, his face glowing.

Ruth said, "We've been discussing where Langston will go to college in the fall."

"Oh," I said, and did not ask where colored people went to college.

"Somewhere not too far away," Langston said, "and where Daisy want to go in a year."

I did not say, *Daisy's* going to college *too?*

Daisy replied, "And I was tellin' Langston, once again, *that* should not be the main criterion."

*Criterion?* How'd she know a word like that?

To me, Ruth said, "I thought Florida A & M looked good, but he didn't even apply there."

"Too far," Langston said.

"In the wrong direction," Daisy added.

Still to me, Ruth said, "Morgan State in Baltimore, Wilber-force in Ohio—"

Langston winced. "Too far, too far—*Ohio?*"

Daisy said, "I suggested a few schools in Pennsylvania and guess what he said."

"Too far?" I replied.

"Nothin' wrong with Virginia State," Langston pronounced. "And if Hampton was good enough for Booker Washington, it good enough for me."

Daisy said, "It's gotta be Howard," adding, for my benefit, "that's in DC."

"How many colored colleges are there?" I blurted.

Ruth looked embarrassed. "There are plenty, all outstanding institutions."

"Mostly in the South," Daisy complained.

"Yeah," Langston snickered. "Like we be goin' to Alabama."

Daisy said, "Howard is where *I* want to go."

Annette squirmed off Daisy's lap and pranced away after the cat. Langston reached out and took Daisy's hand, stroked the side of it with his thumb, communicating something, something personal, spiritual, transcendental.

At last I said, "You gonna be a rocket scientist too, Daisy?" in a tone not completely kind.

Ruth interjected, "Daisy wants to be a lawyer, and run for public office someday!"

I really couldn't help it: my mouth dropped open. This was more ludicrous than Langston being a NASA engineer. *Public office?* She wasn't just colored, she was a girl. *A lawyer?* We only had one lawyer in town, but I'd seen plenty on TV; lawyers were all middle-aged white men in suits.

"Remember," Ruth said to me patiently. "Daisy grew up in Washington, DC."

"Ye-ah," I replied.

"I know what you're thinking," Daisy said, but nodding, un-offended. "Elected officials are all white men. That's true, but that's the *problem.* All our laws are made by white men who put themselves first because they believe they are superior to the rest of us. So *their* interests are represented but *ours* are not, and that's why we need to make a change. A democracy is supposed to be for *all* the people, not just a privileged few."

Good grief. She already had a campaign speech. Langston's smile was so huge it was causing his body to rock back and forth. Any moment he might fall off his chair. A confusion crept through my brain, and I asked him, "You okay with that plan?" Given his boundless enthusiasm for this girl, I'd assumed he dreamed of marrying her and having babies.

"Sure!" he crowed. His eyes bounced to my face, which must have still looked puzzled. He explained, "I'm gonna finish college and get a job, then a year later Daisy finish, and with me workin' I can pay for her to go straight to law school." In a whisper he added, "Hopefully after the weddin'."

Daisy's expression crinkled with embarrassment and joy. "Let's not get ahead of ourselves, Langston." Her hand floated up in an elegant backward wave and she giggled, and he giggled, and I thought I might throw up. I leaned back on my stool and looked hard at Langston. The steep angles of his face had softened, his posture loose; he was completely unaware of himself, wholly absorbed in Daisy. I imagined Barb telling Jim Darden she wanted to be a lawyer. He'd bust out laughing, along with Ricky and Warren Bunch. I thought of the times I'd told people I wanted to be a newspaper reporter. The men tittered and said nothing, and the ladies winced and wondered aloud what my future husband would have to say about that. And here was Langston, not only *not* laughing but working out how to help her achieve her goal. I stared at him, and a weighty loneliness pressed down on me. I found myself thinking Daisy was lucky.

Ruth said, "All three of you have such marvelous plans! Here's Willa, wanting to be a journalist!"

Daisy's eyes blinked shut in a momentary smirk. Then Langston said, "Yeah, Willa, when Daisy become the first female Negro senator from Virginia, you can come interview her!"

"Oh boy."

"I can't wait to read it," Ruth said to me and took my hand and squeezed it.

Then, abruptly, Langston and Daisy had to leave. They were cooking supper tonight for Langston's mother, cooking *together*, Daisy emphasized, *to-gether*. *To too two gether*. I did not say that once Langston and I had cooked together, or point out that Langston had been coming here for months and sitting at this table with me, and in fact this kitchen and this house and the entire town had existed before Daisy arrived in it.

Everyone stood and Langston helped Daisy on with her jacket as though she had two broken arms. I watched her sleek, elegant hands descend from the sleeves and waft up to fasten a button. I watched her face tilt upward to smile at Langston and her body swivel toward the door. Then the lovebirds fluttered away, down the step and across the grass to the sidewalk, and I was not aware that my face was pressed to the window watching them. Gradually I felt it—my forehead mashed against the glass, my jaw clenched.

When I turned, I found Ruth right behind me, regarding me quizzically. She said, "Daisy is a remarkable young woman." Then she reached both arms out and pulled me into a hug. I could feel all the bones in her shoulders and back. She held on to me. "I'm so glad you're back!" She squeezed once more and let go, leaving the hug imprinted on my body. "I *was* sorry for what happened," she said. "I should've realized how dangerous it was." I felt momentarily gratified, until she added, "Not for you, for Langston. I should've told you not to go. I just wasn't thinking that day. You know the story of Emmett Till."

"No," I replied, though the name sounded familiar. "I know the story of Nat Turner."

"I'll tell you another time."

Julie and Annette were sprawled on the floor a few feet from us, drawing pictures of cats with crayons. "And I *am* gonna make you sew!" Ruth took my hand and together we sat on the floor next to the girls, who insisted we draw cats too. I drew a red cat, because that was the only color left in the box. Ruth plucked the black crayon out of their pile and drew perfect likenesses of Mr. Softy—first curled into a nap, then stretching into an arch, then leaping with his front legs raised in a sign of victory.

As arranged, Reverend Swanson drove me home at the end of the afternoon. He was a nice enough man, a little weird, his gangly arms and legs not quite under his control. He asked me about school and my favorite subject and if I liked to play a sport and then I was home.

During supper I found myself studying Barb, observing how her hair, styled in a fashionable flip now, brushed her shoulders, how the corners of her mouth remained in a permanent slight upturn. She held her fork as though barely touching it; she tilted her head invitingly when she smiled. Like my mother, she made a big show of listening when my father talked. For some reason that night he was telling us about the Jamestown colony's original fort, which had been built five-sided because of how the land was formed, and which was under water now, lost to erosion. Ricky and Billy were allowed to look bored; the women and girls were not. Of course this irritated me, but a distant part of my brain was taking note: *Look interested in what the man is saying.* Why was it doing that?

After dinner I went upstairs to stare at myself in the bathroom mirror. My face was too long, the distance between the bottom of my nose and the top of my lips too vast. My nose had a hump in it, like a camel's back. In fact, didn't my whole face resemble a camel's? My hair was just brown. It lightened in the summer but never achieved blond. Fortunately, my complexion was okay—nowhere near as bad as poor Sue Bates's, which was always erupted into a lunar landscape and smelling of isopropyl alcohol. However, I did sometimes discover a hard zit growing in the crevice of my chin, and if I left my cheek resting in the palm of my hand too long, a nasty red splotch would blossom on the fleshy part under my eye—awful, horrible. I thought of Daisy's smooth light-cocoa skin. Did colored girls break out? What a *remarkable young lady. Running* for *public office. Daisy.* The sound of her name in Langston's voice vibrated in my skull. What a dumb name, *Daisy.* Why not Hyacinth or Chrysanthemum? Mrs. Chrysanthemum Jones running for Congress, standing at a lectern, her tiny zit-free chin uplifted.

But what was I doing standing at the bathroom mirror? I had poetry to read and worksheets to complete. In my room I dug through my binder for the mimeographed sheets and hauled the literature anthology to my bed. Walt Whitman: *Forests at the bottom of the sea... Sluggish existences...* The words sounded in my skull, but my brain was not bothering to attach meanings to them. *Daisy,* my thoughts kept thinking. Daisy in my chair at the Swansons' table, chatting with Ruth, so confident, speaking in a tone that assumed people would listen. How had she grown so sure of herself? *Passions there, wars, pursuits, tribes, sight in those ocean-depths...*

Daisy had this advantage over me. How was that possible?

And what was I doing, obsessing over Daisy, being jealous of a colored girl? This made no sense. I could see how colored boys might think she was cute. But she couldn't possibly be as smart as I was. *Breathing that thick-breathing air, as so many do...* And why was I wasting energy on these comparisons instead of paying attention to the text? *The change onward from ours to that of beings who walk other spheres.*

At least now the poem was over. I picked up the mimeograph, pressed it against my nose, and took a long drag. Its sweetly chemical smell had gone. I read the first fuzzy-inked question: "1. What is this poem about?" *Death,* I wrote—it seemed a safe guess. "2. Who is speaking in this poem?" What? Wasn't it the poet? Did I have to read it *again?*

I left the question blank and went on to the next poem. Emily Dickinson. *The heart asks Pleasure—first— / And then—Excuse from Pain— / And then—those little Anodynes...* I had to stop and look up "anodynes." I bet Daisy would've had to stop to look up "anodynes" too. No way Daisy was smarter than me, though Langston probably thought she was, gazing at her like she was some kind of miracle out of the Bible, a divine being, heaven incarnate. I bet Daisy did not know the word "incarnate."

Anodynes were painkillers. *That deaden suffering— / And then—to go to sleep— / And then—if it should be / The will of its Inquisitor / The liberty to die.* On the worksheet I wrote the poem was about death. *The heart asks pleasure first.* That was certainly true for Langston, all gooey and moony over Daisy, Daisy sitting in my chair like I didn't exist. *Cooking together.* My mind raced to the evening Langston and I cooked together, at the kitchen counter, side by side, me trying to peel a potato without a potato peeler and watching his expert hand with a tiny knife stroking the skin off the potato he held, the blade skimming off the rough surface, his hand so careful to preserve the interior, to avoid causing it injury.

What was I reading? *And then excuse from pain.* On the worksheet I wrote that the speaker was probably some poor girl whose heart got broken. Maybe the boy loved someone else, I wrote, then rambled on miserably: Maybe the speaker was a lady whose husband didn't love her anymore. Maybe she finds out he's having an affair with another woman. Maybe he goes off and leaves her. I closed the anthology and stuffed the worksheet pages back into my binder and put on my nightgown and got into bed and couldn't sleep.

The bedroom door squeaked open and Barb came tiptoeing in. She clicked on the lamp, turned, and found me staring at her. She jumped. "What is *wrong* with you?"

"Everything."

"Well, that's a true fact." She unbuttoned her shirt, wiggled out of her skirt, and stood in her new matching underwear: pink long-leg panties with garters clipped on, and a bra with concentric stitching that rounded out her boobs, making them look like two pink dart boards.

"Barb?"

"Yeah?"

"Do you think when Jim Darden goes off to college, he might find another girlfriend?"

She turned away from me to unhook her bra and slip modestly into her nightgown. "Why would you bring that up?"

"I don't know. Just popped into my head. It happens sometimes and it doesn't matter how nice the girlfriend is. I mean, it's not about how nice you are to him or how beautiful. Sometimes he just wants something else. Can a girl *make* a boy love her if he just doesn't?"

"Go to sleep." She climbed under her blanket and switched off the lamp. I tried closing my eyes. *The heart asks pleasure first, and then excuse from pain.* I thought of my mother, and I thought of Barb, both of them exerting so much effort to keep a man's love, working so hard to be agreeable and undemanding, vigilantly silent.

Then I thought of Daisy, so effortless, speaking out loud whatever came into her mind and being loved anyway—or maybe even because of it.

Finally my mind slowed down, and I slid into an image-filled sleep. I dreamed that Langston, Daisy, and I were walking along a dust-filled street, and I was bubbling on about my future plans, brimming with confidence, determined and courageous, my arms swinging free, my body unrestricted. Langston and Daisy strode alongside me, listening, rapt. Then Daisy was gone. Langston and I were alone, strolling, laughing, talking. And then Langston was reaching for my hand, catching it midswing, gently pushing his fingers through mine, his radiant gaze now on me. A jolt of thrill shot through me, and when I woke the next day, I felt luminous.

# 10

Once, when I was much younger, I visited Virginia Beach with my former best friend, Becky Campbell, and she and I went on a hunt for the most beautiful shell. We crept along the strand, searching for edges nudged through the dark sand. We each chose one. On the drive home in her parents' car, sitting on towels so our legs wouldn't stick to the vinyl, squinting into the blast of air that roared through the open windows, jiggling our encrusted feet, we pulled our shells from our pockets and examined them, stroked and admired them, then silently slid them back into our shorts. I pulled mine out again and again: it was pearl-pink, delicate and strong, so smooth it was soft. I couldn't resist this secret treasure, exquisitely personal.

The dream was like that shell. I pulled it from my memory time after time to examine and admire it—Langston's wide smile, Langston's fingers threading through mine, his grip tightening, reassuring. Attaching. I was thrilled and embarrassed by it and there was no one to tell, not even Ruth. Being alone with the knowledge of the dream magnified its intensity, and some nights I could barely sleep. On the days when Langston was at the Swansons', I studied his hands, the backs creased with bone, fingers long, the nails bright pale squares against dark skin. On the days when Daisy came with Langston, I sat at the table for several morose minutes, then took the girls outside to play.

It was ironic, I thought, how my goal had flipped: no longer did I want to be seen publicly with Langston. Instead, I longed to be with him in private, to have secret encounters. I imagined us crossing paths coincidentally: I'd be riding my bike, he'd be driving back from Franklin, and there we'd be, alone together. Langston had no idea all this was going on in my head. He'd been unaware I was pretending to be in love with him, and now he had no idea I truly was. He must have thought I was just a weirdo. My head was so full of him—*Langston*, I thought, admiring the sounds in his name—there was little space for thoughts of my father. My big plan to humiliate him had evaporated. My fury toward him dispersed to the far edges of my mind. I wish it had stayed there. I suppose it was bound to condense and pour down on me again.

Easter came. Even in church I thought of Langston, mixing my dream with reality, recalling Langston's listening face, his forward slouch, the smooth brown skin of his neck shiny beneath his ear. I was sitting with Julie and Annette so Ruth could sing in the choir. My own family, across the aisle and one row ahead of me, was an image of piety: starched and straight and serious in dark suits and peach dresses, my mother and Barb in pillbox hats and white gloves. I too wore a peach dress and white gloves—somehow I'd escaped the hat. Reverend Swanson preached about mankind's sins, which Jesus had died for. Erect at the lectern, towering above us, the reverend posed questions: "What *were* the sins that Jesus died for?" he said, in an uncharacteristically sharp-edged tone. "Taking the Lord's name in vain? Stealing an egg from a henhouse? Coveting a neighbor's *cow*? Were *these* the sins that required the agonizing death of the son of God?"

I wasn't sure where he was going with this. I was pretty sure all those things were in the Ten Commandments.

Then he boomed, "Above all, Jesus told us, we must love one another—love one another!—*love* even the lowliest among us. Jesus taught us we are a brotherhood—the brotherhood of man—*all* of us, no matter the color of our skin!"

It being Easter, all the church members were present, including the Klan—Jerry Owens and his cousin Henry Jones, Chuck Doyle, the Parkers, Mr. Cobb the car salesman—all with their pleasant-faced wives and leaden-eyed children. Mr. Cobb sat directly across from me with an expression purposefully blank, his eyes forgetting to blink. Finally he let go of a throaty cough. On the other side of the sanctuary sat a row of Parkers, identical frowns on their square faces. Four rows ahead of them, Mr. Doyle blew his nose dramatically.

After the service, the handshaking at the door seemed perfunctory, possibly even rude. In the car on the way home neither of my parents spoke, and at Easter dinner, my father delivered a treatise on molecules and atoms.

I meant to ask Ruth whether anyone had complained about the sermon, but I kept forgetting. Days went by, my brain preoccupied. Was I hoping that somehow Langston and Daisy would break up and he'd begin to gaze longingly at me? This seemed unlikely. *Daisy*, I thought. Daisy and her boundless confidence. The thing about Daisy's self-assurance was how real it felt, steady and calm; it wasn't the phony boisterous confidence I heard from boys in my class—it wasn't just a bunch of noise. When she said she was going to be a lawyer, anyone could see she would be.

A worry coagulated in my brain.

It took until Thursday for me to put words to my anxiety. "Ruth?" I said.

"Yes?"

We were in her family room, me on the floor with the girls in a sea of Lincoln Logs, Ruth on the couch, tugging a needle and thread through butter-colored cotton.

I said, "No one believes I'm really gonna be a newspaper reporter. Like Daisy, she doesn't think I will."

"I don't know about that." Her eyes remained fixed on the thread that trailed behind the rising needle.

I said, "Thing is, I'm not sure about it either. I know how to *talk* about being a newspaper reporter, but how do I actually get to *be* one? I don't know. I don't even know how to find out." Her hand paused over the cloth and she looked at me. She understood. I asked, "Could you show me how?"

"Oh, Willa. *I* don't know." Her eyes fluttered to the side. I recognized the hesitation and the gesture—I'd seen it often in my mother and sister—that polite, feminine reluctance to feel good enough.

I said, "You help me write those dumb essays for school. You could help me write an article for the newspaper."

Her face drooped. "That's a different kind of writing altogether."

"Yeah, but we *read* the newspaper. Can't we just look at the articles and kind of figure it out from there?"

"Well, yeah." She shifted. "I suppose we could give it a try."

"Please?"

"Tell you what. You write something over the summer, and I'll help you with grammar and punctuation and whatever else I can see to do. It's a good idea. Write something over the summer and then when school starts in fall, you'll have something to submit right away!"

"Oh."

She meant I could write for the school newspaper. I'd been thinking of the real newspaper. Of course she'd assume I'd write for a kid's publication—I was a kid. But I'd seen plenty of issues of *The Kingsfield High Times*, smudgy sheets crammed with articles about football and tennis and upcoming dances and the Keyettes. I said, "I wanted to write about something important."

"Well, sure!" She resumed her sewing, one side of her mouth upturned. "What's something important?"

I thought for a moment, then half-yelled, "Integration! I could write about that Supreme Court case everyone's still all upset about."

Her smile expanded. "That's a great idea. You could interview kids your own age—see what they think about it."

"I could interview Langston!" I said wildly and felt bubbly-headed, having spoken his name aloud.

"Langston," she parroted, but her eyebrows slid together.

"And some other colored kids too!" I said, because it seemed required, even though it probably meant interviewing Daisy.

Ruth drew the needle upward, her expression murky. "I don't want you getting in trouble again. I don't want trouble for anyone."

"You worry too much."

"You aren't allowed to go to Trackton," she said.

"I know. I won't. I'll get Langston and his friends to meet me somewhere else, in the woods or someplace no one'll spot us."

Her worrying eyes settled on me again. "Willa, as soon as anyone reads the article they'll know you've been talking to Negroes."

This was true, and the problem seemed insurmountable until I had a brilliant idea. "I'll use a pseudonym! I'll be, I'll be... Walter! Walter...*Swenson*!"

The gloom in her eyes dissolved. "Maybe not *Swenson*."

"Okay then, Walter...Jones!"

"That's Langston's last name."

"That's everyone's last name, except for the Beales'." I turned to Julie and advanced my hand for a shake. "Hello, I'm Walter Jones. Walter A. Jones. Nice to meet you." In fits of giggles, both girls shook my hand.

Ruth said, "And how is Walter A. Jones going to submit an article to the school paper when he's not a student enrolled at the school?"

I seized an unclaimed Lincoln Log and began spinning it on the tile floor. "Maybe I won't submit it to the *Kingsfield High Times*. Maybe I'll send it to the *Tidewater Times*."

"Oh, sweetie. They'd never publish an article like that. They hardly covered Kennedy's assassination."

Of course, she was right again. I recalled a lengthy editorial about integration in the *Tidewater Times*, listing all the reasons why the idea was nonsensical. The main reason was the fact that coloreds didn't have the intellectual capability of white children. How could teachers possibly teach students with such wide-ranging abilities? Coloreds in our schools would drag down the quality of education, and then how could we compete with the Soviets? There'd have to be special classes created for the coloreds—whole tracks of classes—which would separate coloreds and whites anyway, so why not leave things as they were? Another dilemma was how to control the coloreds, especially the boys. It wasn't feasible to expect teachers to keep those boys contained. How could a demure, small-statured white lady fend off a horde of coloreds? Policemen would have to be stationed in schools to maintain order, and there goes another nickel out of the taxpayer's pocket.

I kept spinning my Lincoln Log. Round and round it went with no purpose. When I glanced up, Ruth was gazing at me sympathetically. A few more moments drifted by, and she said, "But you know who might? The *Virginian-Pilot*, in Norfolk."

"What?"

"They've taken a stand in *favor* of integration."

"Yeah?"

"Yeah. Maybe they'd publish an article like that." She set her sewing on the table beside her and leaned forward, her eyes iridescent. "It's worth a try. We could mail the article to them, say you're a stringer. Walter A. Jones, freelance journalist. I'll write a cover letter. I'll get Matthew to sign it so the signature looks like a man's."

"Yes!"

"Let's do it!" she sang out, so jubilant the sewing slid off her lap.

We made a plan. On Saturday—the day after tomorrow—my mother would be gone with Barb and Patsy to shop for prom dresses. I'd ask for my bike back; I'd been good for weeks. I'd ride out Main Street through the fields and meet Langston and his friends by the Nottoway River under the railroad bridge, where the dense woods met a small patch of beach. Ruth wrote down Langston's phone number for me—Liberty 4-4193. I would call him that evening and explain the plan. My excitement over the article merged with a fizzy anticipation of talking to Langston on the telephone.

"Tell him to bring lots of friends," she said. "Get as many interviews as you can—the more, the better. No one will see, right? It's a dense wood?"

"Yes," I assured her.

Then Ruth realized she should be the one to call Langston

that evening. I might be overheard, and she would definitely be more influential. She was right. I gave her back the piece of paper with Langston's number on it and smiled. Of course, I'd already memorized it. *Liberty 44193*.

But the night before the rendezvous on the Nottoway River, a swarm of worries began to buzz in my brain. Langston told Ruth he'd try to bring friends, and I flashed back to the mob of colored kids pouring from the doors of Trackton, surging toward me, my throat parched and petrifying. Who would Langston bring? Those tough-looking boys with pitch-black skin?

Nat Turner and his murderous rebels never made it across the Nottoway River, though they'd intended to: they'd planned to take the town of Jerusalem on the other side. I thought of the wild circuitous path they took across the landscape, invading farms, killing entire families, beating young women to death with fence posts. A hundred and thirty years later, some of those houses still stood abandoned. Jerusalem was named Courtland now, but it was the same place, and tomorrow I'd be going there secretly to meet a bunch of colored boys. I reminded myself that Langston would be there: I didn't need to be afraid. Most likely, Daisy would be there, too, and she'd keep all the boys on their best behavior, like confident girls do.

When I woke the next morning, my trepidations returned. What if Daisy wasn't there and it was just me and a group of colored boys? In my head I heard my father's words in my own voice: colored boys can't control themselves; colored boys get out of hand. I looked at myself hard in the mirror—skinny, mousy-headed, unremarkable. Lacking courage, devoid of confidence. How did girls grow up to be strong? Not just beautiful and pleasing and agreeable: *strong*. How did they speak out with no hesitation, take action despite their fears? Maybe they just kept pushing forward. That was my best guess, so that's what I did.

I dressed and went downstairs. My mother had said I could

have my bike back, but she'd already gone—off with Barb early, eager for department stores and lunch at a restaurant—and the key to the padlock was nowhere in sight. Ricky, I discovered, was also gone. Only my father and Billy were home, throwing the softball in the backyard. I shouted at Billy, "Mama said I could have my bike back. Where's the key?"

Billy shrugged with leaping arms and shoulders. "Ricky put it somewhere." My father squinted his mean eyes at me.

For a moment I stood in our backyard, feeling the air cool with spring, the grass yellow-green and soft underfoot, and I thought, this is a sign from God. It's a sign that I shouldn't go. Then I remembered I didn't believe in signs from God. It was just my cowardly self resurfacing, looking for a way out. I'd always thought of cowardice as weakness, but the coward in me had a damn sharp elbow, pushing to the front of the line. Billy suggested, in my mother's helpful tone, "Could you take Barb's bike?"

My father snapped, "Not without her permission," and, turning to squint at me again, demanded to know, "Where you goin' in such a hurry this morning, young lady?"

My muscles tightened. "To Florence's. We got…a project for school."

"Well, you can *walk* there, can't you? You need a bike to go *half* a *mile*?"

"No, sir," I said, and I could see what he was thinking: stupid *girl. Stupid* girl. Willa, *not that bright.* Needing a bike to go *half a mile.* His voice in my head was distinct and loud: *She's not that bright.* I turned and walked away.

Then, with my notebook clutched to my chest, I started to run. My feet pounded dirt, gravel, asphalt, and my head pounded too. My father had no tolerance for stupidity, especially in girls, but he liked it even less when girls were smart. He'd never wanted me to be capable and intelligent—that would puncture his soft ego. What he wanted was to make a big show of annoyance at ladies' ineptitude, to rest in his assumption of superiority over half the human race. He *wanted* to laugh affectionately

at Barb and roll his eyes at my mother and strut away. I ran until
my side ached. He *wanted* me to fail. But I'd show him. I slowed
to a jog and walked a while.

Courtland was nearly four miles away. The most direct route
on foot was along the railroad tracks, so I turned and crunched
along in the gravel by the rusting ties. I would've had plenty of
time to ride my bike; now I'd be late. How long would Langston
and his friends wait? My breath caught and I began to jog again.
If I stood them up today, they wouldn't waste their time on me
again. Suddenly my whole being hinged on writing this article.
If I didn't, I'd never be a newspaper reporter; I'd be a nothing;
I'd fail and I'd be a failure forever, and then my father would
be right. I ran alongside a dense patch of pines, woods striped
with morning light and thin knotty trunks. Abruptly the woods
ended, and the landscape opened to a field, massive and plowed
into long gray beds newly planted with peanuts. The sky above
it was big as the field and cluttered with ashen lumps, clouds
rolling across, picking up speed: it was going to rain. I ran past
the field, past a rusty silo, and dipped onto a path that diverged
from the tracks. Clusters of hickory trees, poplars, and sweet-
gums leaned overhead. I crossed Flaggy Run and came at last to
the intersection of Main and Meherrin.

Courtland was a smaller version of Kingsfield, with low,
flat buildings and houses scattered at random. I passed a coin
laundry and an auto shop across a gravel parking lot dented
with puddles. I walked the last infinite stretch of road, which
narrowed, tucked inside swaying treetops, marshy ground falling away in clumps on either side. By the time I crossed the
Nottoway Bridge, I was nearly half an hour late. I climbed over
the guardrail, plowed down through the tall grasses and into
the woods, crunched through the branches, and burst onto the
beach in a red-faced pant. Langston was sitting in the sand,
reading a book, alone.

"I knew it," I wailed. "Everyone else left!" He stared at me.
What a wild and sweaty fright I must have looked.

"Naw," he replied, calmly. "No one else came."

My body dropped onto the sand beside him. "What?"

"I tried, Willa. Called 'em again this mornin'. They all—how can I say this—*declined* the invitation."

"Why?"

"Everybody know who your daddy is. My friend Burt thought maybe it a trick."

"They don't trust me."

"They don't know you."

I heaved in a huge breath. "Where's Daisy?"

"Daisy a busy person."

"Daisy doesn't like me!" I lamented.

Sounding confused, he said, "She like you okay. She just busy."

"*You're* busy. You got all those jobs over in Franklin. *You're* here."

"Ruth ask me specially to come." He looked at me, and suddenly I realized: we were alone together. For the first time, ever, Langston and I sat side by side, holding each other's gaze. A rush went through me, like carbonation up my throat and into my brain. Then, I began to feel calm. His eyes were set wide, not large but shaped like almonds. I began to giggle. Mortifying. In a tone gentle and friendly, he said, "So?"

"So?"

"So? What you wanna ask me?"

"Oh." I giggled again—how annoying—and opened my notebook. The shadows of branches overhead shimmered on the bright page, and I glanced up. The sky was full of cool sun, strips of ashy cloud gliding past. It wasn't going to rain after all. I looked at Langston and smiled idiotically.

"You okay?" he said.

"Yeah." I was tingling. "Just winded."

"Take your time."

I tried clearing my throat and elongating my torso and assuming a professional air. "Okay, yes. All right. First question. I know you're about to graduate from Trackton, but tell me, why do you wish you could have gone to the white school instead?"

He blinked at me. "That what I wish?"

"What?"

He rocked sideways. "That what white people think? We all just dyin' to go to school with y'all?"

"Well, well, yeah. That's what *Brown versus the Board of Education* was about, right?" I sounded so smart—like I knew about *law*. "Colored families want their kids to go to white schools, right?"

"You think we all want the same thing? The whole Negro race goin' round thinkin' with one brain?"

"Well, no. I mean, I don't know. I never really thought about it. Why wouldn't you wanna go to the white schools? The buildings are so much nicer."

"True."

A breeze rose and rumpled the sides of my hair.

He said, "But school's more than a building. The thought of bein' with white people all day long make me feel kinda tense."

"Tense?"

"That surprise you? When I'm around white people, I gotta keep in my place. I can't say what I really think. I gotta be careful not to sound too smart. Or worse, too confident—or white folks get testy."

"Oh." I studied the side of his steep-angled jaw. "I kinda know what you mean."

"People want the world to be like they think it is. Nobody want a surprise, like a smart colored boy. White teachers *assume* we not as smart as white kids."

"Well, yeah, that's true." Like my father.

"So then what? Then you be sneakin' around tryin' to learn stuff. I'm lucky 'cause my mama's a teacher. Not all kids have mamas went to school to be teachers."

"True."

"So I don't know. It a good thing for us to go to school with y'all? I don't know. Maybe Daisy would tell you all the pros and cons. I think more like a scientist. I wonder, what happens to a human brain that keeps gettin' shut down, that keeps gettin' discouraged from thinkin'?"

"I don't know."

"Maybe it get weak, like a muscle you don't ever use. Maybe it start to starve to death 'cause it not gettin' the proper nutrition. Maybe part of it just goes to sleep. I worry about that. Would Black children be treated right at the white school? They be treated with respect?"

I was horrified. I'd never even thought of that before. Who would treat the colored kids with respect at Kingsfield High? Ricky and his friends? Mr. Doyle, revered football coach and Klansman? My father?

"You think integration is a bad idea?" I asked.

He shook his head noncommittally. "Like I said, I don't know. You supposed to be writin' this down?"

"Oh!" I started writing frantically. I had more questions: Did he think colored teachers would get jobs at the integrated schools? No, he didn't see that happening at all. Did he think colored boys and white boys would play on teams together? He doubted that. Did he think colored kids and white kids would be all right using the same bathrooms? What about the water fountains? He kept shaking his head, seeing trouble brewing any way you looked at it. Was there anything he wanted to add? Not really.

Then for a while we sat in silence, staring at the river, calm and colorless today, the trees along the banks duplicated upside down in its surface. Upstream, the hefty lower limbs of maples sagged into the water. I said, "Did you know 'Nottoway' was the name of an Indian tribe?"

He looked askance and snickered. "Yeah. That why we got 'Indian Town Road' and 'Indian Woods.'"

"Oh, yeah." My face eased into a smile—not an idiotic one, just regular.

Langston began to fidget. Clearly the interview was over, but I didn't want him to leave. So I asked him what his little brother was up to these days. As we talked, the breeze kicked up, eventually whipping itself into a wind. In the corner of the sky a green-gray blob oozed toward us, spreading and sinking toward the treetops. "Here come the rain," he said, and I said, "Oh no, I had to walk here!"

"You *walked*? Why'd you do that?"

I started explaining, then. "It's a long story. Please can you give me a ride back?"

"Nnnnnn…"

"Please? I'll duck down if I see a car, and you can drop me at Benns Church Street—no one will see."

"How many favors I gotta do for you today?" he moaned, but in a tone more teasing than annoyed.

"I'm sorry, I really am."

"Okay, come on."

He went ahead of me through the woods, holding branches out of my way, checking behind him to make sure I was okay—but with concern, not with the irritated look of my father when burdened with asking my mother, "You okay, Trudy?" Langston had parked a ways up, just off Meherrin, so for a quarter mile we walked along the road side by side, me at a trot to keep up. He kept his eyes on the bend in the road ahead of us, alert too for the sounds of a vehicle approaching from behind, poised to leap back into the woods if need be. My head was full of the dream. I watched his right hand swing toward me; I imagined the feel of it locking onto mine. My brain was so giddy I could think of nothing to say. I imagined his face turning, eyes jubilant, lingering on me. But then we were at his car—an ancient Hudson with rust gobbling up the doors. I climbed in, and he climbed in, and the sky cracked open, releasing buckets of rain. We laughed at the same time. Soon the car was cloaked in steam, and we were safe, invisible, cocooned in this space together.

Suddenly I was self-conscious—clunky, too young, too white. He turned the key in the ignition and the engine sputtered to a start. He pulled the gear shift and the car bounced forward, suspension-less, across dirt that was fast becoming mud. He made a U-turn across the macadam toward Kingsfield. The wipers labored over the windshield, not quite working, and from the rear came a persistent quiet roar. When I looked at him, he mumbled, "Car need some work," and I smiled, comfortable again.

Down the road we rattled in our private capsule, hitting bumps. Each time we hit one our bodies flew up nearly off the seat and I squealed with laughter, and he laughed too—it felt like a carnival ride. I inflated with excitement: there I was, riding wildly down the street with a Negro boy in a falling-apart car in the rain. It was an adventure, an affirmation of a world beyond Kingsfield, a liberation. But then a car appeared in the distance, coming toward us. He yelled, "Get down!" laying his hand on my head and gingerly pushing. His hand was warm and firm and comforting. I wriggled under the dashboard, where the car was louder and bumpier, the rust having eaten a hole in the floor, and the ride got wilder. I bounced and bonked my head on the underside of the dashboard and laughed to hysteria.

"You okay down there?" Langston's voice came from above. "You crazy, Willa!"

"It smells like feet!"

"What you expect it to smell like? A flower garden?"

This was the funniest thing I'd ever heard in my life, and I folded up with laughter, gulps of air banging against my ribs.

"Here come the car, now be quiet," he whispered.

"He can't *hear* me!"

"Shh, shh, just keep control of yourself, Willa, you losin' your mind! Oh, great, that man just went by lookin' in my car and here I be talkin' to myself like some crazy old Sambo, just ridin' down the road havin' a conversation with myself."

I laughed harder. My jaw began to hurt. I wrapped my arms around my folded legs and jostled along, eye-level with Langston's knee. I thought of reaching out to poke it, and then that was all I could think of, which made me laugh more. Too soon we reached Benns Church Street. He pulled to the side, peered in every direction, and whispered, "Okay, it safe." The downpour had slowed to a dribble, but I pretended to hesitate because of the rain. I just didn't want to leave.

"Thank you," I said.

"Okay, okay." His worried eyes flew left and right. His fingertips began tapping the wheel.

"Thank you, for *everything*."

"Okay, okay."

"We did it! No one saw us."

"Uh-huh. Bye, bye, now; bye, bye."

"Bye, Langston."

From under the dashboard I reached up, pulled the door handle, and rolled out. Then I bolted into the trees and paused to watch the Hudson rumble away. I stood, pelted by occasional fat raindrops, and watched until I couldn't see him anymore. I stood in a soggy silence, letting myself brim over with him. Then I picked my way through the sparse woods, cutting through to High Street, and walked toward home. His laughter rang in my head. *You crazy, Willa,* the first two words stressed hard—*you crazy*—the syllables of my name melting into the natural softness of his voice. *Willa,* he said. *Willa.*

I was still smiling, replaying scenes, inhabiting those moments, when I opened the front door of my house. The hinges squeaked as though asking a question. I stepped inside, pushed the door closed behind me, and turned. There in my living room sat the entire membership of the Warwick County Ku Klux Klan.

My father lolled in his chair like a monarch on a throne and pronounced, "Good. Willa's here. She can get us our tea."

I hugged my notebook and began to slink away.

"Willa!" he called.

I halted.

"You hear me? Sweet tea. Where's your mama?"

"Shoppin' in Newport News with Barb and Patsy. She told you two nights ago."

"Oh yeah. Bring in your mama's sugar cookies too."

The couch was packed with Klansmen, short and tall, wide and narrow, in plaid or solid blue or green shirts, sleeves hanging loose at their elbows. An overflow of men sat on dining room chairs and kitchen chairs that Ricky must have dragged in. Dr. Vaughan sat in the rocker with his legs crossed the way men's legs do—the ankle over the opposite knee, making an open triangle, claiming additional space. Ricky was perched on the kitchen stool by the dining room doorway, and Billy, for some reason, was there too, wiggling on the floor by Ricky's feet.

"Willa!" My father's voice came sharp and demeaning, showing off for his friends. I went to the kitchen, set my notebook on the counter, and pulled our glass pitcher from the refrigerator. I'd have to make more tea. I poured out four glasses, put them on our silver-handled tray, and carried it to the living room.

"They'll never pass it," Jerry Owens was saying, and Henry Jones concurred, "They do, no Southerner'll ever vote Democrat again."

"It'll pass," my father replied with unwavering authority.

In his usual panic, Chuck Doyle exclaimed, "Can't we do *somethin'*?"

"Coons with *rights*," Mr. Priddy murmured, then wailed, "It'll be the death of our nation!"

Bob Browne, a middle manager at Kingsfield Ham and great admirer of drugstore emperor Mr. Priddy, nodded in furious agreement.

Dr. Vaughan leaned forward. "We gotta hit back hard, but we gotta be savvy about it."

My father said, "Number one priority, send Lou Waller packin'." Lou Waller was the superintendent who thought integrating the schools might be okay after all.

Gary Johnson asked my father, "You put in your application to the school board yet?"

My father nodded and the men emitted a muted cheer. Then my father glared at me—me loitering with an empty tray in my hands. I scurried off to mix up more tea, which I didn't really know how to do, but I didn't care; I did it fast and filled more glasses and raced back. It was too hard to hear from the kitchen.

"—nothin'," Gene Buck was saying. "Man's a saint."

"No one's a saint," Dr. Vaughan jeered.

"I'm tellin' ya, I couldn't find nothin'," Gene Buck whined.

"Don't need to be true," Bob Browne said. "Well placed rumor'd do it."

"Good thinkin', Bob," Mr. Priddy said, and Bob beamed.

"What if he's havin' an extramarital affair?" my father cackled. I swiveled toward him. Of course he'd think of that. But he did not look at me or acknowledge my presence.

Emboldened, Bob Browne tilted forward, his hands dangling between his wide-spread knees. "What if he's havin' an extramarital affair with a *colored girl?*"

A circle of admiring nods ensued. Dr. Vaughan actually rubbed his palms together, smiling his thin pointy teeth. "Perfect!" he replied. "We let it slip to our wives and they'll spread the rumor all over the county."

Men chuckled.

"What colored girl?" Mr. Owens seemed confused, or concerned.

I watched Mr. Priddy's eyes roll to one side. He said, "How about that uppity bitch moved down from DC?"

"Who's that?"

Men shook their heads.

"Daisy somethin'," Gene Buck said. "I seen her walkin' home from Trackton, swingin' her hips, checkin' me out in my truck."

I wanted to laugh at him, but I was paralyzed.

Mr. Owens said, "A high school girl? Ain't that kinda young for Lou?"

"Naw," Gene Buck said. "Them girls start young. Can't help themselves."

My father affirmed, "That's a true fact. Coloreds got an *underdeveloped* sense of morality. They can't tell right from wrong. They got poor impulse control."

"Still—"

"I like it," Mr. Priddy said. "It's a good idea."

Chuck Doyle seemed worried. "So the school board gets

wind of these rumors and they hire Dick instead of Waller. Then what? That gonna stop the Commies and coons from takin' over our country?"

"Chuck's right," Mr. Cobb said. "We gotta do more'n that."

"We will," Dr. Vaughan pronounced, nodding and smirking, full of secrets.

Agitated, my father said, "Where're those cookies, Willa?"

I startled. I was so completely invisible to these men, I'd forgotten I could be seen. I trotted to the kitchen, as though eager to obey my father, and ran back with Mama's ceramic hen jar and a handful of rose-embroidered napkins. Around the room I went offering cookies, staring into eyes that didn't look back.

Gary Johnson said, "Did you know some of them jigaboos graduatin' from Trackton are goin' to college in the fall?"

"Seven of 'em," my father added, demonstrating the value of precision.

Henry Jones said, "That happens every year—a handful of 'em go off to those colored colleges."

"Not this many," my father replied apocalyptically.

"So what?" Jerry Owens said. "They go off and we never see 'em again. Good riddance. Let some big city have 'em. That's a good thing."

A silence stretched across the room like a rubber band about to pop, which it did when my father barked, "You don't get it, do you, Jerry?"

Jerry Owens fidgeted on our kitchen chair. "I get it, I get it. Okay. So what's there to do about it?"

Dr. Vaughan and my father exchanged a clandestine nod. My father said, "We march the morning of their graduation. Then we attack. There'll be plenty of parties that night over in coon town."

Chuck Doyle said, "Break some windows!" Being the football coach, he got excited at the thought of throwing things.

"No feds gonna tell us what to do," Mr. Priddy said, and Gary Johnson smacked his palms together, as though catching a gnat, and yelled, "States' rights! We got a *Constitutional right* to do whatever we want!" My father seemed irritated, perhaps because the history teacher had made the point he'd wanted to make. Bob Browne was about to speak again when we heard the car in the driveway and exuberant female voices approaching the front door. The men fell silent, waiting for the entrance, for the obligatory niceties, then to be left alone again.

Barb swept in holding aloft a gown encased in plastic on a hanger, and everyone but Ricky and Billy smiled. Yes, yes, this is what the fight was for—a lovely young girl in a new dress. The gown was such a pale yellow it looked white, the bodice covered in lace, the straight skirt satin. If it weren't for the wide ocher sash and bow at the waist, it could have been a wedding dress. Patsy entered next, empty-handed, and my mother stepped in last, smiling at first, then aghast at the crowd in her living room. "Dick! I didn't know y'all had a meeting today!"

"No? I told you about it two nights ago."

"You *did*?" She rushed to set down her purse and peel off her jacket. "I am so sorry, gentlemen! Do you need anything?"

"Some decent tea'd be nice," my father said, and my mother fled to the kitchen.

Dr. Vaughan spoke, "That's a mighty pretty dress, Barbie. You goin' to the prom?"

"Yes, sir. I'm goin' with Jim Darden," she replied, melodiously elongating his name, and all the men hummed and clicked and clucked and gazed at her, avuncular and lascivious. Barb turned and flapped the dress at me. "Did you see, Willa?"

Visible again, my role as server ended, now I'd be expected to leave. I nodded. She pivoted back toward the group and said, "It's so nice to see y'all. Please excuse us now." So poised, so alluring yet pure, going off with a flourish, ascending the stairs with grandeur, leaving the men with foggy distracted smiles. Patsy trailed behind her.

I left too, before my father could command me. Out through our back door and into the yard I went. The clouds were pale shreds now, lingering. I walked to edge of the lawn and stared into the ditch that demarcated our property. The skinny moat teemed with leaves and twigs and drowned bugs in its deep crevice, trickling with rainwater. I walked the length of the trench to the chain-link fence, where my bike still stood padlocked, handlebars speckled with rain.

Of course, I thought of Langston. Was his mother planning a graduation party for him? Would she be cooking and baking and setting up a table in their little front yard? Were aunts and uncles driving up from North Carolina? Joking and happy on the long ride, graduation gifts piled in the back seat? Was Langston's father planning a brief speech, crafting phrases to express his pride, anticipating his eyes misting over with joy? Daisy would be there, in a bright lavender sleeveless dress, arms glowing brown against the fabric, her chin upturned, her lips fixed in a subtle, delighted smile.

Then a car would creep up, and another, close behind, then another. The party guests would turn and see the slow-moving caravan of white-hooded apparitions, vacant eye holes pointed at the celebration. The Klan didn't need to throw rocks. Just the sight of them would be enough to destroy this family's happiness. But the car windows would jerk down anyway and stones would hurtle toward the party. People would shriek and flee into the house—confused little children, men with hands raised to protect their wives. And Langston would remember this day for the rest of his life, his academic accomplishment forever fused with feelings of terror. Left with no way to seek justice or expel that pain from his body, he would have to absorb it. The indignity would sink and spread and muddy his heart.

I swept the water off the seat of my bike, leaned against the metal bar of our chain-link fence, and made a decision. It would take more courage than I'd been able to muster in myself so far, but with Ruth's support, and the image of Langston's gorgeous face in my mind, I would try. Instead of an article about school integration for the *Virginian-Pilot*, I decided, I would write an exposé: I'd write about the terrorist intentions of the Warwick County Ku Klux Klan.

# 11

Walter A. Jones and his devoted editor, R. Swanson, worked diligently on their article about Klan activity in Warwick County. I'd never seen Ruth so buoyant, exhilarated by our mission. It was my idea to start the article with the rock-throwing incident at the Negro barbershop, to set a scary scene that would *hook* the reader. "Hook" was a term I'd learned in English class. Ruth talked Langston into bringing the barber to her house one evening for an interview, after dark. It was all very undercover. My inner spy was elated. Reverend Swanson was out at a meeting of the church finance committee; the girls were asleep in their beds. Langston rapped once on the back door, like a secret agent.

At first the man sat stiff and suspicious on Ruth's couch, but gradually his shoulders settled and he ate a piece of sponge cake. Then he described the incident: the sound of the idling car—sputtering, rattling—that brought him out from the back room that night. He'd been closing up, sweeping one last time and putting away his barber's tools; he'd been about to turn out the lights. But the idling drew his curiosity, and as he approached his front window, something struck it. Instinctively, he ducked. He wondered if someone had shot a gun at him. Then another object struck the glass, this time shattering it. Still crouching, he watched the car labor away, and he recalled thinking how moronic it was for these men to be hiding inside hoods—everyone knew Chuck Doyle's car.

In a hushed tone Ruth asked, "What did the police say?"

We all stared at her. Eventually she asked, "Did you call the police?"

"No, ma'am," the barber replied. "I put up a board across the window to keep the bugs out. Got a piece of glass comin' from Norfolk."

"Oh."

The next day I wrote the opening for our article—two entire pages packed with suspense, mystery, fright, and trepidation. I described the barber hunkering fearfully on the barbershop floor, with waves of sweat pouring copiously down his trembling facial muscles. I described the car engine growling demonically in the shadowy street and eerie crickets chirping in the nocturnal darkness. Ruth read it with sinking eyebrows, and when she finished she picked up a pencil and deleted all the adverbs. Then she crossed out the adjectives. Then she sighed and rose and wobbled into the family room to get her newly arrived copy of *Life* magazine.

"Okay," she said, all business and efficiency. She turned to an article and showed me how the "lede"—that's what it was called—was chock-full of basic information: the wheres, whats, whos, and hows all crammed into that first sentence. In fact, the whole paragraph was just one sentence.

"Mrs. Beale told us a paragraph has to be five sentences!" I cried and lost all respect for Mrs. Beale.

Ruth and I rewrote the first paragraph together. It did sound more like the lede in the magazine, but secretly I preferred my version. We continued writing until we had the whole article done. After the first paragraph, it seemed to pour out of us— the nighttime meetings in the cornfield, the plans to disrupt Negro graduation parties, the veiled rage of the Klansmen toward anyone who was not like them.

Sitting in Ruth's kitchen, waiting while she went down the hall to check on the girls, I wondered: What kind of person needs everyone else to be exactly like him? Why did a person need to see himself mirrored in everybody around him—the color of his skin, the texture of his hair, his thoughts and beliefs—all reflected back every way he turned? It had to be someone who felt so weak inside he needed constant reassurance, who felt so afraid in the world he needed to imagine himself replicated into a sizable tribe. My father, who had once seemed so strong to me, was, in reality, a fearful, fragile man.

In our article, Ruth and I did not name names, but we gave an approximate number of men involved and emphasized that they came from many walks of life, including "the professions." We spent a few more days polishing the sentences and getting the commas in the right places, and then Ruth wrote a cover letter, and the reverend signed "Walter A. Jones" in a masculine hand, and we mailed it to the *Virginian-Pilot*.

In the meantime, Lou Waller abruptly resigned as superintendent of the Warwick County Schools, withdrawing his application for reappointment. Apparently he had a sudden longing to spend more time with his wife on her family farm in South Carolina. I asked Langston if he'd heard any rumors about Lou Waller and a colored girl, but he hadn't. Magnanimously I said, "If you do hear anything, don't believe it. It's a lie."

So my father became one of two finalists for the superintendent job. His lone rival was a man from Richmond. There was talk among the teachers about the value of "new blood." To make matters worse, the man from Richmond was also a *blue* blood—one of a half dozen sons of a wealthy peanut farmer descended from an actual First Family. My father fretted over this genuine Virginia gentleman wooing the members of our rural, rinky-dink school board. Though the board was stocked with our own landed gentry—Dardens and Morehcads—they were a definite notch below First Families. My father didn't know what to do. He bought a new suit and shoes and tried entertaining. He hosted luncheons at the country club for school board members and their wives, and for three weeks my mother lived in a panic, frantically accessorizing her Easter dress, borrowing dresses and hats from Patsy's aunt.

I couldn't stand the thought of my father being promoted. I couldn't bear the thought of him bursting into the house with his good news, calling us all over to flutter around him and buzz with admiration. I pictured my mother's bright, adoring face pressed against his, him sucking in all her light. I wanted him to suffer as many disappointments as he'd inflicted on me. Now that I'd abandoned the scheme of ruining his reputation by pretending to be involved with a colored boy, I needed a different plan.

Had I thought logically about it, I would have realized my father would never get that superintendent job. But my unformed adolescent brain was obsessed with action, and generally oblivious to the concept of consequences—I had to *do something* to ruin his chances. I had to be an active participant in his downfall. Unwittingly, my former best friend Becky Campbell put an idea in my head.

With less than a month before school let out for summer, Becky's new friends dumped her. Apparently, she was not clique worthy after all. At lunch now she sat alone at the end of a table of seventh graders, earnestly reading a book, her hair slowly morphing back to its natural wild state. Two tables away sat Donna Bowman and her gang, making a show of looking over and laughing at her, wallowing in the pubescent thrill of destruction.

One day, Joe Pedicini asked me, "You want to invite her over?" Florence Whipple and Sue Bates, fearing they might be expendable, scrunched their eyebrows at me. Did I want Becky back? I had to think about this. What I really wanted was to travel back in time and ride bikes with her and climb trees and eat peanuts and plan our futures. Too much had changed. How could I ever trust her again?

"Maybe tomorrow," I replied.

Then it occurred to me: Becky, daughter of the town photographer, may have access to something I could use. Polaroid had invented a new model that printed a picture all by itself immediately after you took it. You didn't have to bring the film to the drugstore to get it developed. I'd seen the ad in the Sears catalogue. My busy brain jumped into hyperdrive: What if I could get my hands on a camera like that? What if I rode my bike over to Franklin while my father was paying a visit to Mrs. Doris Wallace and snapped a few photos? What if I then put the photos in an anonymous brown envelope and mailed them to the offices of the school board? I could end his bid for superintendent. I could snuff out his greatest ambition. The blue blood from Richmond would be hired, and, I reasoned, Kingsfield would inch closer to desegregation—to the aristo cratic mind, there would not be much difference between the coloreds and us white small-town hicks.

The next day at lunch I paused beside Becky, who was already seated pathetically with her book, and invited her to join us. A smile overwhelmed her face, and she followed me. I pulled out a chair for her, next to my usual spot, and Florence looked a little devastated, but I grinned at her and she was happy again, peeling the wax paper from her tuna sandwich with the crusts hacked off. Beside her sat mute Sue, who'd taken to covering her acne with a thick layer of taupe pancake make-up, slathered only to edge of her jaw, a shocking contrast to the goose-white skin of her neck. Joe was on his way over with his tray stacked with food. He caught my eye and made a show of tilting the tray back and forth, pretending it was so heavy he was about to drop it. The plates slid riotously from edge to edge; his roll wheeled toward the lip of the tray. I laughed so hard my jaw ached. He sat on the other side of Becky, and when everyone was settled, their food organized, I asked Becky what was new. Her parents had promised her a puppy, she said, a beagle dog like Snoopy.

"What will you name him?" I asked, not caring at all.

"I don't know!" She was so excited. "Maybe Snooky."

"Snooky's good," Joe said, and I nodded, though I thought it lacked all traces of imagination.

I watched her take a bite of bologna sandwich and asked, "How's your dad's photography business?"

"Fine."

"You know what I saw in the Sears catalog? A Polaroid cam-era that prints pictures instantly all by itself. Did you know there was a camera like that?"

"Sure. My dad got one last year."

"Really?"

Florence and Sue listened wide-eyed, munching slowly, continuously—like horses. Joe was scooping mashed potatoes into his mouth.

"Yeah," Becky said.

"I bet he doesn't let you touch it."

"Sure he does. He lets me use all his cameras; you know that."

In earnest Florence commented, "It must be *complicated*."

"*Yeah*," Sue added, succeeding in saying something.

"Not really," Becky replied.

"Do you *really* know how to use it?" I prodded.

"Of course I do. I've been working cameras since I was six years old. You know that."

Sensing how I wanted to conversation to go, Florence said, "Yeah, but can you work this new one?"

Through a mouthful of Salisbury steak, Joe spoke: "She keeps *sayin'* she can."

Becky turned to me. "Come to the shop and I'll show you. I'll take your picture. It's really neat."

"Maybe. I'm pretty busy these days."

The conversation paused as we all took bites. Then Becky said, "You could all come over and I could take a picture of everyone. A group picture."

"That sounds fun!" Florence exclaimed.

I took another bite of my cheese sandwich, so Becky would have to wait for my response. Finally I said, "We're all goin' to Virginia Beach after school lets out next month."

"My mom's drivin' us!" Florence said.

I turned to Joe. "You're goin', right?"

He nodded, and I smiled at everyone in turn: Joe, Sue, Florence. Then I took another bite.

"Well," Becky said. "If I went along, I could bring the camera and take everyone's picture at the beach."

"Oh boy!" Sue bubbled.

I said, "Your father would never let you take that new camera to the beach."

"Of course he would. He trusts me. I'm basically his assistant. You know that."

"Would he let you show me how to use it?"

Florence interjected, "I bet he wouldn't."

Becky was irritated now, shooting Florence an annoyed glance. "Sure he would."

"You'd let me take a picture with it?" I pursued.

"Sure."

"Is it heavy?" I asked. "Does it make loud noises? Would it fit in my purse?"

Even Florence looked startled by this, but after a moment Becky replied, "What, that purse there? Sure."

I smiled. "Okay, let's all go to the beach! That'll be so much fun."

I spent the afternoon thinking the plan through. I did not intend to steal the camera—that would be cruel—but I was willing to let Becky and her father spend a miserable few days believing it was lost at the beach: the tide sweeping it out to sea, sand kicked over it by running feet. And then it would turn up again somehow—how? I worked on that dilemma through English class. If Mrs. Beale said anything important, I missed it. I could say I'd wrapped it in a towel for safekeeping and forgot about it, and the towel went into the hamper. Or I could sneak over to Becky's at night and slide it into the lilacs by their front step.

The bell rang and I traveled with the crowd to Miss Cooke's class. It would be easy enough to ride my bike to Doris Wallace's house, but how would I take the pictures? I'd need to climb up on something to see into her windows. Were there bushes alongside her house? I tried to recall. We all settled into our seats, and Miss Cooke started her rambling monologue—something about George Washington—and my train of thought ran off onto another track.

You'd think that, after beginning the school year with the War Between the States, we'd have moved forward in time, learned a thing or two about World War I and World War II. Instead, we'd gone backwards, through westward expansion and the savage Indian attacks, through spunky Andrew Jackson and the War of 1812, and now, yet again, I was studying the American Revolution. For the sake of my A, I dutifully memorized names and dates—Cowpens, January 1781; Yorktown, October 1781—but I could barely stand it. Miss Cooke adored the founding fathers. Her favorite, predictably, was George Washington. Miss Cooke was not someone who thought outside the box. She spoke of the Constitution the way people spoke of the Bible—as a sacred text demanding complete obedience. To deviate from or question it would be heretical. I wondered why the same people who worshipped the founding fathers also despised the government, which was, after all, what the founding fathers had founded. Of course, in Miss Cooke's mind, the whole plan had been corrupted. Today she was explaining how our remarkable forefathers had the wisdom to allow only white, propertied men to vote. Yet *here we were*, she said ominously, letting all *sorts* into the "voting pool," which of course made us all envision a swimming pool, where no one wanted colored people.

I thought of raising my hand to ask if she meant women shouldn't have gotten the vote, but before I could, surprisingly, the coif-headed Claudia Holland asked the question. Miss Cooke considered it with great seriousness, then said, "Only people of a certain level of intelligence and moral aptitude should have the vote. The problem now is too many stupid people votin'. Bunch of lazy illiterates, ignorant lazy criminals castin' votes."

Johnny Cobb raised his hand. "You mean coloreds, don't you, Miss Cooke? Like Nat Turner."

This was a game Johnny and his friends had begun several months ago—reminding Miss Cooke of Nat Turner. Inevitably she flew off on a hysterical tangent, and the boys loved to watch the tirade: the chin flab waggling wildly, the bottom of her dress undulating from side to side with increasing speed, her skin flamed to a bizarre shade of fuchsia. Off she went now, reiterating Nat Turner's brutal acts—all the stabbing and bashing and hacking and beheading of innocent Christians and babies. Each time she told the story, there were more babies.

You'd think the only inhabitants of Southampton County at the time were babies toddling around the countryside in fluffy white Christening gowns. Johnny and his friends tried to hide their snickers; the rest of us slumped in boredom. If no one stopped her, she'd go on for the rest of the class period. I raised my hand.

"Yes?" She'd grown tired of acknowledging me. She preferred to call on boys, whom she expected to be important someday.

I asked, "Do you know the story of Emmett Till? What was that about?"

"Emmett *Till*?" she said with revulsion. Faces swiveled toward me; no one else knew the story either.

"*Tull*? Emmett something. Do you know that story?"

"Of course I know it. Why're you askin'?"

"Because I don't know it. I was just curious."

Faces turned back to Miss Cooke, who emitted a noisy breath. "Emmett Till was a thug from Chicago. That's the kind of coons they got in big cities, *thugs*. Fourteen years old, he goes down to Mississippi to make obscene advances toward a white lady."

I said, "Why'd he go to Mississippi to do that? Aren't there white ladies in Chicago?"

Someone behind me giggled. Miss Cooke was not amused. "Maybe he was used to gettin' *away* with it up there in that big city, but down in Mis-sippi the men caught that boy and brought him to justice. That boy was a big dangerous brute and the men *feared for their lives*, so they killed him." Here Miss Cooke's voice dipped to a contemptuous murmur: "Then, his *mama* took *pictures* of him in his coffin. Imagine. What kind of mama does such a thing? The coloreds don't care about their children like we do. *Pictures. Pictures* of your own dead child in his coffin. *Disgusting.*" She jabbed a stubby finger at me. "The only reason you ever heard that boy's name is because of those pictures and the Jew media. Jew newspapers got a hold of those pictures and *published* them. Disgusting."

Debbie Beale pushed a shaky hand into the air. "Emmett Till *murdered* that white lady? Did he bash in her head?"

"No," Miss Cooke snapped. "But you girls remember, some things are *worse* than death." A dark silence followed, which she let fester. My breath rolled down my throat like a slow fiery rock. I glanced around. Half the girls were ashen, but the rest, including all the boys, wore a confused look of terror on their faces. Whether my classmates understood or not, everyone looked frightened.

As so often happened lately, I got angry. Why was Miss Cooke trying to make us feel afraid? What was the point of that? So far, none of us had been hacked to death—or "worse"—by wild marauding Negroes. Why was it so important to make us all scared of Black people? I knew I couldn't ask this, but I needed to say something, so I raised my hand again.

"Yes?"

"Is the *Tidewater Times* a Jew newspaper?"

She snorted. "Of course not. We have a proper Southern paper."

"What about the *Suffolk Star*? Is that a Jew newspaper?"

"No."

"What about the *Virginian-Pilot*?"

"That's enough."

"Okay, but I really want to know if the *Virginian-Pilot* is a Jew newspaper."

"No, it is not."

"Are they called Jew newspapers because they're written *by* Jews, or *for* Jews?"

She did not reply. She lifted her chin and lumbered to the other side of the room and resumed her praise of the founding fathers.

When I arrived at the Swansons', Julie and Annette greeted me alone. On the other side of the screen door, their grainy faces were solemn.

"Hey!" I stepped inside. The family room floor was strewn

with crayons and pencils and half-drawn cats. "Where's your mommy?"

They gazed up with sad cartoon eyes.

"What's the matter?" I asked.

Julie's tone was stoic, like a broadcaster on the evening news reporting an unfortunate incident: "Mommy's been in bed all day crying. She fell again last night and dropped the dishes and she's been in bed crying all day."

Annette burst into tears. Julie draped an arm over her shoulder and said in a tiny maternal voice, "It's okay, Net-Net, it's okay." She ran an open hand down the length of her little sister's hair, which filled it with static electricity. "Want a Coke?" Julie asked, and Annette's cry softened. Hand in hand the girls marched toward the refrigerator. I rushed down the hall.

Ruth's door was open a crack, undoubtedly so she could hear the girls; I pressed on it and whispered, "Are you awake?" The lamps were off and the shades were pulled, but the sun behind the fabric was strong enough to bathe the room in amber.

"Oh," she replied, her face turned away. "Is it that late already?" She made such a small lump on the bed, like the lowest of sand dunes, lying on her side with her head sunk into a pillow.

"May I come in?"

"Of course." She rolled onto her back and patted the empty side of the bed. I sat. Her face was mottled and swollen from crying.

I asked, "What happened?"

"Mm." She heaved in a shaky breath. "My legs are getting worse. Last night I was clearing the table and nearly stepped on the cat and I couldn't regain my balance and *bam, crash*. We're running out of plates." I grinned, but she began to cry again, in soft, slow gulps. "So, Matthew said I shouldn't carry the dishes anymore. Then Matthew said he was going to buy me a cane—a cane! I'm twenty-eight years old! A cane! He tried to make a joke of it, said he'd get one with a parrot head like Mary Poppins's umbrella, but I think he was annoyed with me. I don't blame him. A minister needs a wife who can *do* things, like church bazaars, vacation Bible school, and at least take care of his children."

"The girls are fine." I reached across the bed and patted her shoulder. "They're drawing. They have Cokes."

"I've been lying here all day thinking, Why am I a minister's wife in the first place? Is that what I wanted to be? I didn't know what it'd be like—these ladies with their secret opinions of me, all this pressure to be perfect. I just can't do it. I can't be everyone's role model. Sometimes, sometimes I get so mad at these judgy old ladies with their hats and their casseroles, talking about nothing, nothing and more nothing, and I want to scream! Then I think, how unkind of me! I think, is God punishing me for these unkind thoughts? Why did *I* get MS? And doesn't God have more important things to do than zap me for unkind thoughts? I do love Matthew, I do, really, but why did I get married so young? I could've gotten a job for a few years, shared an apartment with another girl. All day long I've been lying here thinking, What happened to my life? I used to read great works of literature. I used to have real friends. We laughed all the time—what were we laughing about? I don't remember! We'd go swimming in the lake and run along the shoreline. I was a fast runner. I always wanted to race my friends because I always won. Ha! Now look at me. It's like my life is already over."

She reached out and pulled me down next to her in a hug alongside her body. She squeezed me tight, like a daughter. My head found a hollow along her clavicle to nestle in.

She said, "Listen, sweetie. *You* figure out what kind of life you want, and then, no matter what, *do not* let yourself get talk-ed out of it. Don't let other people put reasons in your head for why you shouldn't do exactly what you want. Okay?"

"Okay."

She snuggled close to me. "Tell me, what do you want to do with your life?"

"Well, I want to be a newspaper reporter."

"Yes. What else? What else do you want to do?"

"Travel."

"Good!"

"And live in different places—not here."

"Good."

"Most of all," I went on, with mounting fervor. "Most of all, I want to be somebody *important*. I want to be an *important person* and prove everyone wrong—everyone who ever underestimated me, who thought I was stupid or incapable of doing things. I'm gonna *show* them. They're all gonna *eat my dust*."

She was silent. For several moments we lay listening to ourselves breathe. Then she said, "That sounds like something your father would want."

"What? No, it doesn't." I was mortified. How could she say such a thing? I was nothing like my father and thank goodness! I was struck by this change in me: all my life I'd wanted to be like him; now hearing it, I felt profoundly insulted. Did Ruth really think I was? I said, "He's the main person I want to show up." My brain twisted into a knot, and I said, "I *do not* want to be like my father!"

"Okay." Ruth stroked my arm with the tips of her fingers. "You don't have to be. No one has to make the same mistakes their parents do." The room dimmed, the windows filling up with clouds. She said, "I should get up. I should start supper."

"I could call Langston. Maybe he can come over and we can cook for y'all. I'll call Langston," I repeated so I could say his name again. *Liberty 44193*.

She squeezed me again. "You are a sweetheart. It makes me so happy you've become friends with him. See? Already you're not like your father." She pushed herself into a sitting position. "I'll be okay." But she kept sitting, her hand remaining draped over the edge of the bed, as though unsure whether it could propel her upward. I wanted her to be happy again; I wanted to hear her praise me again.

I said, "I tricked Miss Cooke into telling us about Emmett Till today. I'm sure she got it all wrong. She told us Emmett Till's mama took pictures of him in his coffin to give to the newspapers. That can't be true."

Ruth twisted toward me. "That is true. His mother wanted the world to see how badly he'd been beaten."

"She *did* that?"

"She did."

"Miss Cooke said he attacked a white lady. Is that true too?"

"He whistled at her."

"He *whistled*? Well, that was stupid! Why on earth did he do that? Didn't he know better?"

"People do stupid things all the time. They aren't executed for them. If everyone who ever did a stupid thing was executed for it, there wouldn't be anyone left on the planet." She rose. "We don't execute white men for whistling at white women, do we?"

"No." But that was different. Why was that different? I worked it around in my head. Because white boys aren't as dangerous and violent as colored boys? That's what people like Miss Cooke wanted me to think. Because white men were supposed to get white women? I thought of Jim Darden pushing himself on top of my sister. She hadn't wanted that, but somehow his doing it seemed normal and not really wrong.

Ruth stood up and took a few steps to look at herself in the mirror. She moved with a deliberate, heartbreaking slowness. She smoothed her hair, her little cap sleeves, her sides with hands anxious for everything to be normal.

"Are you okay?" I asked.

She fastened her eyes on me and forced her lips into the crooked smile. "I'll be fine."

I worried about her all the way home. Even the girls could see her little upbeat comments were faked. But once inside our back door, I heard my father's angry voice coming from above: he must have been talking on the upstairs extension. I crept up a few steps until I could hear: "I'm tellin' you, he doesn't get it—him and his dimwit cousin. Who else could it be?"

Then my mother called, "Willa! For Pete's sake, come give me a hand." She was in one of her kitchen frenzies, which meant company. I leaned over the railing to see who else was there—Barb and Ricky's gang were all in the living room, and on a school night, which could only mean one thing: Jim Darden.

In the kitchen, my mother was speaking into the open oven. "This was a bad idea." She pulled out a Chef Boyardee pizza. Pizza was an exotic treat at our house; making it for a Darden was a daredevil choice.

"Clear the kitchen table!" she cried out.

I turned, and there on the table was a copy of the Norfolk *Virginian-Pilot*. I stared. Its front pages were peeled back, its interior revealed, and below the fold was a block of text under a modest-sized headline: "Klan Activity in Warwick County." Byline: "Walter A. Jones."

I snatched it and ran upstairs.

*"Willa!"*

I shoved the paper under my mattress, but I knew it had already been seen. I padded down the hall and hovered outside my parents' room. My father's voice, cooler now, said, "I understand what you're sayin'. I know they won't like it, 'specially Doyle." There was a pause. "We don't know that, but if nothin' happens, we prove the article wrong. We make this Walter Jones and the *Pilot* look stupid. We show 'em all is well down here in Warwick County." There was another pause, and my father laughed, deep and slow. "Yup, nothin' but happy darkies here."

Pressed against the wall, I realized, gradually, what it all meant: the Klan was canceling their attacks on the coloreds' graduation parties. They were canceling—canceling because of the article, *my* article. We'd won. *I'd won.* The breath in my lungs turned to helium. I was ten feet tall, immense, a master, a superhero, a god. I couldn't wait to call Ruth—but I'd have to wait until the phone was free. I galloped downstairs, wanting to tell everyone about my victory. Of course I couldn't. But I imagined myself bounding in and singing out, "See? My words do matter! *I* matter!" *I*, I concluded, was all-powerful.

Somehow, I thought my win was permanent, that the Klan would now cease terrorizing Black people once and for all.

I found my mother in the kitchen sawing doggedly at the pizza pie with a butter knife. "Lord!" she exclaimed to no one and yanked open the sharp-knife drawer. She seized the turkey-carving knife and waved it over the pizza. "Run in and tell 'em just another minute."

"Okay!" I bounced into the living room and delivered the message with an exuberant authority.

"Don't you look like the cat who ate the canary," Patsy said, poised again by the record player, herself looking luminous.

"School's almost out," I replied, and Warren Bunch, who was wandering around the room, punched his fist into the air and cried, "Forever!" Like Ricky, he'd graduate at the end of the year.

Jim Darden sat with a cigarette sagging from his lipless mouth, an arm stretched along the back of the couch, a grinning Barb tucked into his armpit. Cindy Poole sat in the rocker looking bored, and Ricky slouched in our father's chair. Patsy said, "I'm happy, too, Willa. Guess what! They offered me a *payin'* job this summer at the hospital! A dollar fifteen an hour!"

"That's great!"

Barb remarked, "You'd think she'd been elected Queen Azalea."

Ricky and Warren chuckled in sync. A 45 dropped onto the turntable. *Love me do...* Now apparently approving of the Beatles, Warren began rapping out the drumbeat on the back of my father's chair, next to Ricky's head, and Patsy wiggled her bottom a few times. Joyously she told me, "And I decided, when I graduate next year, I'm goin' to nursing school. I'm gonna be a nurse!" She was so thrilled with the plan—to say it out loud, to make a commitment, to know her future. Her square face radiated dreamy joy. No one but me paid attention to her, and there I was, pumped up with my own sense of accomplishment, tingling with agency, ready to push the world off its axis. I said, "Or you could go to medical school and be a doctor!"

She smiled, surprised and embarrassed.

Ricky said, "Gaw, Willa, you have to be *really smart* to be a doctor."

"Patsy is really smart," I said.

"She's smart for a girl."

"She's smart for anyone," I barked back.

Warren said, "Oh Lord. Look out, y'all—Willa's goin' mental again."

I said to Ricky, "You don't think girls are smart enough to be doctors?"

Unexpectedly, the languid Cindy Poole came to life: "Mrs. Parker told my mama there's a lady doctor comin' to the peninsula."

"Oh, please."

"It's true," Cynthia said.

"See?" I said. "Girls are smart enough to be doctors."

Jim Darden joined the discussion to correct me: "That's *one. One.*"

Another 45 dropped onto the turntable, and Connie Francis belted out, *Where the boys are...*

"I'd never go see a *lady* doctor," Warren said.

Cindy straightened her back. "Mrs. Parker said this lady doctor graduated first in her class from Johns Hopkins."

Ricky's spitting voice emerged, "Oh, I get it. I would definitely not want to see *her.*" Warren laughed and started to snort like a hog, which prompted Ricky to oink in a high pitch, simulating a lady hog. Jim snickered.

Patsy jumped in. "You don't know she's ugly. You don't know anything about her. And you know what? So what if she is ugly!"

This caused Ricky and Warren to shriek hysterically. Jim gently shook his grinning face, and in a teasing voice, Barb asked him, "What, you don't think a lady could be a good doctor?"

The grin widened as he began to explain. "A doctor has to have a level head. He has to be...*levelheaded,* to consider all the symptoms and make a diagnosis. He has to stay cool and... *rational.*"

"Exactly," Warren said. "Girls are too emotional. They don't think straight. They get all mad over nothing."

Patsy snapped, "What do you mean?"

Ricky hooted and pointed at her. "Just like that! See? Just like that!"

Cindy said, "We get mad when y'all insult us!"

I was impressed, but the boys completely ignored this comment and filled the next several moments with lingering guffaws. Jim continued his instruction of Barb, apparently having thought of another word: "*Logical.* A doctor has to be *logical*, to make *rational* decisions. Men are more logical than girls—that's a scientific fact."

And there it was: the rationalization of privilege, the tyranny of self-aggrandizement. With enough hubris and intentional ignorance, you could mobilize entire academic disciplines to justify your oppression of half the human race. Another 45 dropped. Little Peggy March sang, *I will follow him...*

No longer was I bathing in carbonated joy. Fury surged through me in waves, gushed down every blood vessel in my body. My newly empowered self was not inclined to inhibit it. My voice rose on a crest and wildly, recklessly crashed out of me: "You boys think you know everything! You just wait and see. We are *not* inferior to you, and we're gonna fight for our civil rights just like the Negroes are fighting for theirs, because we are *just as good as you.*"

In the confused silence that followed, plates were heard rattling on the dining room table behind me.

"Pizza!" chirped my mother.

No one moved.

She pattered up beside me. "Well! What're y'all talkin' about, everyone lookin' so *serious.*" As she said this, she pushed her face down into a pretend, childish scowl.

Barb sighed. "Apparently Willa is gonna organize a girls' march on Washington. Like the coloreds."

"What?" my mother squeaked.

Warren let out a laugh again, big and loose and full of spit. "I can see it now—The Girls' March on Washington!"

In a female falsetto, Ricky said, "*Ow, ow, my feet hurt!*"

Warren continued, even shriller, *"These new shoes are killin' me! Can you bring the car around?"*

"Stop!" I yelled, and my mother clucked at me, "C'mon, Willa, they're *joking*. Where's your sense of humor? Y'all come on now and tell me how this pizza turned out!" She clapped and everyone rose and began to file past me, all attempting a nonchalant saunter to hide their unease.

Patsy paused and asked softly, "Mrs. McCoy? Do you have any more of that dietetic Dr. Pepper?"

"Let's check," my mother cooed, and they went together into the kitchen.

I started to follow when a hard grip on my arm stopped me. "Ouch!"

It was Ricky. I looked up into his face. His once-blue eyes, I realized, had matured into a dense gray, the color of pond water. There was a darkness beneath the surface, the shadow of something that doesn't seek daylight. I repeated, "Ouch."

He whispered, "What the hell you think you're doin'?"

"What?"

"Talkin' about *Negroes* and their *rights*. You listen to me, you little bitch. No member of this family's gonna go around talkin' like that."

I swallowed. Something heavy oozed down my throat.

He hissed, *"You hear me?* You keep your goddamn mouth shut about coons and their rights; you keep your goddamn mouth shut, period. You remember your place."

He released my arm and grinned and strolled into the dining room as though he'd said nothing to me. Around the table everyone stood happily tearing goocy slices off the pizza, tipping their heads back, like baby birds, so strings of cheese could dangle into their open mouths.

"Willa!" my mother's voice called. "Run to the garage please and get a few bottles of that dietetic Dr. Pepper!"

I went out the back door. For a long while I stood and watched the sky grow from violet to purple to plum. Soon, I knew, my mother's exasperated voice would holler for me to hurry up. What was I doing? What was I doing out there? Why wasn't I doing what was expected of me? Hurry, hurry—someone had a desire, this is what women are for—to ensure no one was thirsty or hungry or uncomfortable or aggravated. But for a long moment now a strange calm was pooling in the center of me, and I stood in a pocket of silence, feeling the air thick with movement.

# 12

Two weeks later we were liberated from school. As usual, I felt relief and confusion: the routine I'd had for nearly a year—the rooms I'd inhabited, the teachers whose voices echoed in my head—were abruptly gone from my life, forever. The dreamy Mr. Marcus signed my yearbook: *Good luck in the future to a great student!* I stopped by Mrs. Beale's classroom to say goodbye, and she told me to consider going to college to be an English teacher. Lots of women teach even after they're married, she said, until the babies come. I did not stop in Miss Cooke's room, but I caught sight of her, in a swinging orange floral tent dress, lumbering away down the hall. How many more years until she retired?

Once last time, I tromped down the locker-lined corridor, pausing at the exit to look back. I struggled to picture myself next year at Kingsfield High. I worried, imagining myself in its cavernous spaces, its labyrinthine halls. I needn't have bothered: I would never be a student at Kingsfield High School. By the end of August, I'd be far away, exiled for the ruination of my family.

With school out, Ruth wanted me to come over for whole afternoons. She'd never fully recovered from her last flare-up, her walking now a lurching from one handhold to the next—countertop, chair back, sofa back, wall. On my first full afternoon with her and the girls, we drove to the Kingsfield Public Library and looked for medical books with information about treating MS. The librarian, another Miss Beale, suggested we try Norfolk. On the car ride back, windows down, all Ruth said was, "Here comes the heat."

Trackton High had its graduation ceremony, and a few days later we celebrated at the Swansons'. Ruth baked an angel food cake. I made Langston a card, with a mortarboard cut from

black construction paper and taped to a tiny spring inside so it
would jump up and dance when the card was opened. He and
Ruth raved about the cleverness of it. Then he described his
graduation party at his house, a joyous occasion with relatives
from North Carolina and Suffolk, free of trouble.

Ricky's graduation had not yet occurred. My father, as a
candidate for school superintendent, wanted to host a big party.
My mother worried about what that meant: were we to have
crepe paper, flowers, a banner? She could paint a banner. Did
we have to buy invitations at a store? No matter what kind of
party we threw, she complained to me one morning, it wouldn't
compare to the Dardens'. And when would she find time to
sew Barb new dresses for both? I stood next to her in the kitch-
en, looking at our Traveler's Insurance wall calendar. Marked in
a square, the end of June was the school board meeting to elect
the new superintendent. Fortunately, my beach trip with my
friends and Becky Campbell and the Polaroid was set for Friday.

Florence's mother drove. We left early enough for her to park
near the Miller & Rhoads, where she intended to spend the day
shopping in the air conditioning. She gave Florence a dollar to
treat us to hamburgers for lunch and sent us off toward the
surf. Towels tucked under our arms, beach bags slung on our
shoulders, we sloughed through the deep, pale dry sand toward
the darker stripe along the ocean's edge.

No one but me could decide where to spread our towels.
Florence and Sue claimed the spots on either side of me, leaving the outside to Becky, who was being painfully nice to Sue,
complimenting her on her new polka-dotted swimsuit, which I
thought looked odd. It was new but homemade—I recognized
the Butterick pattern—with gargantuan blue polka dots, one
of them misplaced, swallowing up the left side of her butt.
Becky's new swimsuit was clearly store-bought: a sunny yellow
two-piece with bottoms that dipped just below her belly button
and a daring scoop-necked top that rode up under her small
ridge of breasts. She had a matching yellow beach bag with an

orange anchor on it. Her parents must have bought her these items to impress her potential new friends, which was kind of pathetic, but I didn't give it much thought, preoccupied as I was with how to kidnap the camera.

We did the usual morning beach things: walked up the concrete boardwalk toward the tall hotels, walked back, sat squinting on our towels. We burrowed our toes under the sand, sculpting tawny miniature mountain ranges. I closed my eyes and listened to the splat of feet running in the surf. Seagulls screeched out the agonies of their existence. I opened my eyes and saw the beach glitter with shells and clumps of seaweed.

"Are we goin' in?" Florence asked me.

"Sure," I said but hung back, feeling an unexplained pinch of sadness. The others barreled toward the water and smacked into the surf. I stood watching the tide erase the pockmarks of their footprints, the sand washed back into a sleek band. In the distance, past the breakers, blond heads and tanned shoulders bounced in the water. The waves folded and tumbled onto themselves, a line of shadow splashing into a foamy clatter. I felt puny. At the water's edge, the tide bubbled over my feet, cold. It withdrew, taking the sand out from under my heels, my feet sinking fast into the shifting surface, soaked granules molding to the precise shapes of my toes. I waded in, pushed through the waves, swam out toward my friends. We kicked and splashed and bobbed around. We shrieked when a jelly-fish appeared, dangling underwater near our thighs. Joe was so embarrassed by us. He was intrepid, sloshing right over to the jellyfish and swishing water at it.

Back on the beach, Florence said, "Once, my sister stepped on a jellyfish." This initiated a tedious conversation about past stings and bites and scrapes and allergic reactions and a par-ticularly gruesome broken toenail. Then we went to lunch. We sat in our sandy wet suits and ate burgers, thin and soggy with grease. The fries weren't bad. We balled up our wrappers and Becky pulled the Polaroid from her bag.

I blurted, "Can I try it?" She smiled and sat beside me.

She was right—the camera wasn't hard to use. You just opened the case, pulled out the front like an accordion, then adjusted the aperture, clicked open the shutter, and pushed a button on top to take a picture. Then you pulled the film out of the side, firmly but gently, and after a couple of hours you peeled off the outer layer and there was the picture—we could barely believe how fast the process was. By mid-afternoon, we had our photo: everyone but me crammed together on one side of the metal-weave table, faces in grays and darker grays, grinning or blinking.

At the end of the afternoon, on the tired ride home, I made sure Becky sat up front with Florence and her mother, leaving me in back with Joe and Sue and everyone's bags. It was easy to pretend I was rustling around in my beach bag when in fact I was rifling through Becky's. I slipped the camera from her bag into mine.

I still cringe when I recall it. I'd grown and changed so much that year, yet somehow I could not foresee the obvious conse-quences of an expensive new camera gone missing. Minutes after Florence's mother dropped me home, the phone began to ring: Becky in tears, Becky inconsolable. Had I seen the camera? Did I know where it could be? Her pleading, helpless voice sounded like her six-year-old voice, and I collapsed inside. But I didn't confess. I said I'd seen her put the camera in her bag after lunch. That was true. That wasn't a lie. I suggested it may have fallen out of her bag in Florence's car. That wasn't a lie, either—that could have happened.

An hour later she called again. It wasn't in Florence's car. It wasn't anywhere. Again she was crying. I heard the frantic voice of her father in the background and remembered what a nice man he was, a big bear of a guy with a beard and a sparkly smile. I heard her mother in the background trying to soothe them. I burned with guilt. I said I'd go look again through my stuff and call if I found it. I hung up abruptly and looked around the kitchen in a muddle: I saw a pot on the stove, a spatula, a paper bag of peapods on the table. But I needed to stay strong; I had a good plan. All I had to do was wait to catch my father on his way to Franklin again—it would be a few days at the most—then I'd go to Florence's house and magnanimously offer to search her car again and with my eagle eyesight I would spot the camera. It would be returned; I'd even be kind of a hero. It was an excellent plan.

The next morning, Becky called again. Had I found it? "No," I said weakly, and again she began to cry. *Be strong,* I told myself. *Be steady, be cold-hearted. Think of how she broke your heart last year.* I said, "I'll look again," and hung up.

All morning I hung around the house under a black cloud of guilt. I wouldn't have the distraction of the Swansons that afternoon—the reverend was taking his family on a picnic. There was nothing to do but read and imagine Becky crying. Just before supper, she called again, and my mother talked to her mother, and our entire meal was spent discussing this awful misfortune. Poor Mr. Campbell, what a loss, poor Becky, poor Mrs. Campbell, poor everyone. What could have happened to it? I didn't know, I didn't know—I had to lie over and over. Billy bet it got washed out to sea. Ricky speculated some coons stole it. Barb and my mother nodded at the plausibility of all these scenarios. My father seemed distracted, disengaged, uncaring. I imagined Becky's dad, so much nicer than mine, sinking into their couch, his face heavy with suffering. Then, abruptly, I thought of Ruth, and how disappointed she'd be in me if she knew what I'd done.

So after supper I grabbed my beach bag, the camera still in it, and got on my bike. Sunset was not for another hour, but the sky was dim, piled with gray. What would I say to Becky and her parents when I returned the camera? I pedaled, full of dread. I considered telling them the entire truth: My father was a horrible man who was having an affair and I just wanted to get evidence to show the world and I was sorry. I was truly sorry. Perhaps they'd be overcome with sympathy for me, forgive me, and Becky would be my best friend again.

Or maybe they'd call the police. I slowed but kept going,

down Old Sedley Road past the high school, onto Third toward
Main. The stoplights swung somberly overhead, turned yellow.
Then one more car sped through: it was our car. It was my
father, driving in the direction of Franklin.

I didn't hesitate. This was my chance. I turned onto Main,
pumped hard, forgot all about Becky and her family's misery. I
rode out of town through the cornfields into a patch of pine
and birch, alongside a split-rail fence. Franklin was nearly eight
miles away but that was okay, I figured—he needed time to get
all settled in with Doris Wallace before I got there. Main Street
became Route 58, a paved two-lane highway with an amber
stripe fading from the middle. The ditches along this stretch of
58 were shallow, dipping gracefully into fields. I passed scattered
clapboard houses, mailboxes teetering on posts. Against the
lifeless sky, the tops of trees were suddenly tugged by a wind.
A car swooshed by, then two more, then a flatbed truck piled
with skinny logs, heading toward our paper mill. Finally in the
distance appeared the red-brick Hunterdale Church, marking
the place to turn. I soared onto Hunterdale Road. Fading into
twilight were clumps of willows and dogwood, crepe myrtles
about to bloom. By the time I found Doris Wallace's street, the
mountain range of clouds in the sky had solidified into a leaden
ceiling.

Her house was up a few blocks on the right. I'd never forget
it. I got closer, hopped off my bike, wheeled it soundlessly into
her side yard, and laid it in the grass beside her driveway. I crept
around the end of the house, then dug the camera from my
bag. I opened its case and gingerly extended its accordion front.
All set.

I looked down the length of the house to where the bedrooms would be. Gauzy curtains tousled in dark open windows,
and I felt queasy. I wanted to catch them in a telltale embrace
but I didn't want to...*see* anything. The thought of that was
revolting. The window nearest to me was lighted, also open, its
rustling curtains patterned with cartoon hens in red and blue—
this must have been the kitchen. A shadow passed behind the

curtains, the shape of a person walking. I approached. Once a master spy, always a master spy. The windows of Doris Wallace's tacky little house were low enough to see into without the need to climb on anything. I crouched, pressed myself against the brick, slid toward the hen curtains, and slowly raised my head to eye-level.

It was a tiny kitchen. The walls were a putrid pink, the refrigerator even older than ours, short and white with a small, rounded head. On the table was a lamp with a shade shaped like an Easter bonnet. Next to it sat my father, drinking a beer. I'd never in my life seen my father drink a beer. But he did not look happy. From across the room came the exaggerated figure of Doris Wallace stuffed into tight blue pants and a fluffy white short-sleeved sweater, the V neckline like an arrowhead pointing to the deep, freckled crack between her breasts. She was bringing bowls of nuts to the table for my father. She was telling him, "*You know* how everyone admires you…" She hurried back to the counter to assemble a plate of cookies, fussing with fancy napkins—she was like my mother, waiting on him, praising him. Why couldn't he just stay with my mother? Doris Wallace continued, "I *know* you'll get that job, I can feel it in my bones, I can! Would you like another beer, Dicky?" *Dicky?* What an idiot. She hovered over him with an eager face, then began to pet his hair, which must have felt greasy. When he didn't respond, she made a pouty smile at him, which he didn't see. Then she wedged herself onto his lap, between his chest and the edge of the table. He wrapped his arms around her, and she began to peck at his forehead with little kisses—pecking, like one of her curtain hens. This, I realized, was the perfect scene. I raised the camera, centered them in the frame, and *click click, flash.*

"What was that?" Doris said. "Did you see somethin'?"

My father laughed at her. "You're seein' things."

I ducked down. I had to pull the photo from the camera, a process unnecessarily noisy. I heard her vapid voice say, "What was *that?*" and him laugh at her again. I tucked the photo into my bag and rose once more. He was kissing her on the mouth, which was gross, but I captured it. *Click. Click, flash.*

My father's face whipped back, turned, and looked straight at me. Our eyes locked. Doris saw me too and screeched and leaped up from his lap. "Who is that?" she cried.

"It's Willa!" My father knocked his chair back and barreled toward the window. I jumped away, dropped the camera, and lost valuable time scrambling after it, wiping it off, closing it up, wiggling it in through the drawstring opening of my beach bag. By then my father's footsteps were crashing around the side of the house.

I started to run. I knew I could outrun him—I was fast, and he was old. I kept going at top speed, tearing through neighbors' yards and hurtling over a hedge. "Willa! Willa!"—his scream shrinking behind me. When I came to a stand of pines, I felt safe enough to stop. I hid in the trees, panting, watching.

It was dark now, the air dense with a chilled humidity. I saw no movement. I waited, motionless, until I heard the sound of a car engine. Then I saw the outline of our car rolling backward out of Doris's garage and down the driveway—he was leaving! I'd chased him away! The car backed cautiously, uncharacteristically, onto the street. Then, suddenly, the engine gunned and the tires squealed and the car lurched forward. Something crunched under its wheels—he'd run over something. The car stopped, accelerated backwards, and there was another crunch. What was he doing? Back and forth it went—roar, squeal, crunch, roar, squeal, crunch. It sounded like metal crushed against asphalt.

Neighbors emerged from their houses. One man walked to the edge of his yard and yelled at our car. For a moment it idled, then it raced away, down the block and around the corner. I slunk out of hiding. The neighbor stepped into the road and with both hands lifted something from the pavement. I squinted to see it—large and limp, a flat murky form. Slowly my brain admitted it knew what this was: it was the mangled corpse of my bike. Silhouetted in the grainy cone of a streetlamp, the seat was detached and dangling, the basket crushed, wheel rims bent.

I think I screamed. My father had destroyed my bike—my independence, my propulsion, my freedom, my bliss. The neighbor left it at the curb and went back inside his house, and I ran toward it, over grass and gardens and driveways. On the curb, I sat down beside it, rested my hand on its bent rim, and started to sob. Then it started to rain. The concrete sky cracked open; rivers of water poured down. Before long I was soaked.

There was nothing to do but start walking. I thought of my beach towel, still in my bag, and of wrapping it around myself. I ducked under an oak and pulled the drawstring open. There, loose inside, was the camera, so sleek and expensive looking. I wrapped the towel around the camera instead of myself and tucked it deep into the folds for extra protection. Then I saw, at the bottom of the bag, a silver clasp catching light from a streetlamp—my coin purse, which still contained my emergency dime. I needed to find a pay phone.

I walked. Rain streaked across the streetlamp globes and hit my arms at a slant, dull needles on my skin. I walked south, toward downtown Franklin. The fronts of my pants were sopping, clammy, sticking to the fronts of my legs. I pushed myself forward. My clothes and limbs and heart dragged me down. I was utterly, thoroughly alone. But I was used to feeling this way: other people never seemed to see me, not for who I was. I walked. Even my own family—especially my own family—carried a preconception of who I was, their expectations rooted in hazy generalizations about girls. The only person who came close to understanding me was Ruth. At least she knew I was an individual to be understood. To everyone else, I was an appendage of someone—Barb's sister, Dick and Trudy's other daughter. Who was I? I walked, and my mind began to repeat, in a kind of chant: I'm *me*, I'm *me*, *I am me*. A sensation inflated inside me, a kind of power—a feeling of permanence, a palpable self-awareness.

Through the rain I pushed, stronger now, past squat, dark

houses and deep, narrow ditches and dirt paths that led into woods. I trusted myself to keep going. I would not sit down in the road and give up. *I am me.* I walked until I came to an intersection, and down the cross-street I spotted the preternatural glow of an Esso sign looming over a filling station. I ran, splattering through mud and puddles. Where there was a gas station, there was a phone booth. It stood near the street, under the sign.

Inside it, I was bathed in neon light, shuddering as I pulled out my dime. The logical person to call, of course, was Ruth. But she'd gotten nervous about driving at night, when her legs were extra tired; if I called Ruth, she'd send the reverend, and he really was a little weird. I told myself this loudly—yeah, he was pretty weird—and my thoughts continued along this path, rationalizing, until I convinced myself to call who I wanted to call all along. Liberty 4-4193. Langston's phone began to ring, three, four… *Please be there.*

"Hello?" It was his voice, soft and distant but close against my ear. I almost started to cry again; I was exhausted and soaked and cold. But I swallowed hard and told him I was stranded, I was drenched, I couldn't get home, I had no one else to call. He said he'd come. He knew the Esso station where I was. Twenty-five minutes, tops.

I stayed inside the glass booth, even after the rain stopped. There were people inside the filling-station building—an older guy and a younger guy and a lady. After a few minutes they gathered at the plate-glass window to peer at me. A car pulled up to the pump, and the younger guy ambled out to fill the tank, exchanging a friendly word with the driver, who also began to peer at me. I saw myself from their perspective: a stranger in their phone booth, a girl, after dark, by herself. Finally, the lady came strolling out of the station, across the lot toward me, and stood on the other side of the phone-booth door until I creaked it open.

"You all right?" she asked.

"Yeah, yeah, just waitin' on a ride."

"Where you from?"

"Kingsfield." And then, because I felt like such a stranger in that moment, so exposed, so upset and soaked and alone, I added, "I'm Dick McCoy's daughter," affirming that I belonged somewhere.

"You want a Coke?"

"No, ma'am. I'm fine. Just waitin' on a ride."

"Okay," she said doubtfully. "Well, you be safe out here."

"Yes, ma'am."

She went away, but back inside the station she and the men loitered at the window to study me further. When Langston rumbled up in his Hudson and I got in, I saw their expressions spring from curiosity to surprise, then to suspicion, then disgust.

What I saw next—or might have seen next—still haunts me, usually on nights I can't sleep, when I wake at three in the morning and my brain starts listing everything I've done wrong in my life: every mistake, every flaw, every instance of poor judgment. As I climbed into Langston's car that night, I glanced back at the people behind the gas station window. They were still watching me. Did they realize the driver of the car was a colored boy? Did the woman press a phone receiver to her ear, and pitch forward to dial?

"What you doin' out here, anyway?" Langston frowned, but not angrily.

I closed the door and blew my nose on my beach bag. He shifted and maneuvered onto the street, his eyes darting toward me, then back to the road. As we drove, I told him everything, in backward order: my father destroying my bike, my spying on him, my taking the camera. I told him everything because he listened so well, with a tilted head and expression fluctuating with every new incriminating detail. "Aw, Willa," he kept saying.

"I know!" I bellowed. "I oughtn't to have done any of it! It was a terrible plan! Why did I ever think it was clever? Why am I still this stupid?"

"Now, wait, don't be too hard on yourself. Your father the one who shoulda known better. Sneakin' around and cheatin' on your mama."

"She'll be so mad at me!" I cried again, the sound high-pitched and helpless.

The car slowed and Langston gave me a worried look, the side of his face so smooth, catching the glow of a streetlamp; his neck long and sleek, emerging from the collar of his jacket; his chin steeply chiseled, casting shadows. He was so handsome I stopped crying and began to hiccup.

He crooned, "Willa, everything'll be okay." I watched him stop his hand from reaching out to comfort me with a pat. "I know it feels like everything blowin' up right now, but it'll settle."

"You think so?"

He nodded with a cheerful assurance. "I do. You and I have a bright future." He smiled, and my skull lit up with fireworks. Of course he meant he and I had bright *separate* futures, but it sounded for a moment like he meant together.

"Yeah?" I said.

"Less'n two months, I'm off to college." He beamed. The thought of him gone made my sternum ache. "You will too when the time come, and you gonna succeed, I know you will. You *will* be a newspaper reporter like you want."

"You really think so?"

"Yes, I do. You a smart girl, Willa."

"Thank you." I did not stop my hand from reaching toward his, which was resting on the seat between us, and for a moment my hand was touching the side of his fingers. He gave my hand a quick squeeze and whipped his away, clutching the wheel two-handed now. For a while we rattled along without speaking. I felt myself sitting next to him, felt a kind of electric serenity, and I closed my eyes to revel in the feel of it.

When I opened them, there were headlights in the rearview mirror. They appeared out of nowhere, riding up fast behind us. Instinctively I turned to see if I knew the car.

"What the—" I said. "It musta come out of the field."

"*Get down.*"

It was too late. The car had come up behind us so fast, it was already close enough for its occupants to see us, and for us to see them: four pale bobbling heads, four pairs of eager eyes on me. I turned slowly. "It's Chuck Doyle's car. Gene Buck and the Parker boys with him."

Langston's gaze kept flashing to the rearview mirror. We were silent. He accelerated, and Doyle's car began to recede behind us. I turned and watched them falling further behind.

"We're okay!" I sang out, but Langston was still tense, and suddenly Doyle's car began gaining on us again.

"They playin' with us."

It came faster, as though it intended to rear-end us. I screamed, "*Go go go!*" and ducked down.

Langston shouted, "Stay up! Stay up like nothin' wrong!"

I flew up and sat erect as a statue, staring ahead, barely breathing. Chuck Doyle's car rolled up alongside us, and I allowed myself a glance. All four ghoulish faces swiveled to gawk at us. Gene Buck was in the passenger seat, his face gleeful and full of righteous anger. In the back seat the Parkers were tipped forward to stare, their eyes lost in the shadow of their massive brows. Then Doyle's car sped up, swung into the lane in front of us, and slowed down.

"Pass 'em, pass 'em!" I shouted, but the road was curving into a dense patch of trees, and we could not see if anyone was coming from the opposite direction. Doyle's car kept slowing; we kept slowing. "Turn around!" I screeched.

"*How? Where?*"

We were flanked by woods and mud. Doyle's car drifted to a stop, blocking both lanes, forcing us to stop too. Langston threw the gearshift into reverse and the engine heaved, but when we turned to look behind us, the Parkers were already there, broad and grinning in the rear window. Langston said, "Follow my lead."

"What?"

On the other side of Langston's window appeared the long, puckering face of Gene Buck. He rapped his knuckles on the glass. Langston cranked his window down halfway. "Yes, suh?" he said, exaggerating the accent.

Gene Buck reached over the top of the window, across Langston, turned off the ignition, tugged the keys out, and put them into his own pocket. His face leaned toward the glass and smiled at me. "I told y'all. It's Willa McCoy."

Chuck Doyle appeared beside Gene Buck and spent a moment looking back and forth from me to Langston. To me he said, "What you doin' out here at night with this eight ball?"

"I had an accident on my bike," I said too loudly. "In the rain. I fell in the mud and Langston was just drivin' by and he—Langston mows our lawn. He witnessed the accident."

"He *witnessed* the *accident*." Chuck Doyle yanked open the door and yelled at Langston, "Get out! Put your hands on your head!"

"Yes, suh; yes, suh." Langston got out, so compliant. I'd forgotten he could morph into this character—this submissive, half-witted colored boy. I was furious he was forced to do it, just because these white men expected it, required it, demanded perpetual reassurance of their imagined superiority.

Doyle put his hands on his hips. "You got a driver's license, boy?"

I slid across into Langston's seat and barked, "Hey! You aren't the police!"

Langston whipped toward me. "*Shhhh.*" I eased back.

Gene Buck howled, "What's goin' on here?"

Doyle's grinning expression folded into contempt, and he said to Langston, "Gimme your license."

From his rear pocket, Langston pulled a wallet—it looked brand new, like genuine leather. It must have been a graduation present. I was surprised by it; the men looked incensed. Doyle took the wallet and opened it, pulled out the license, and threw the wallet to the ground. "Langston Jones," he read out.

Creeping around the back of the Hudson, one of the Parkers said, "Jones. Ain't that the name of that reporter wrote that story 'bout the Warwick County Klan? Put it in the newspaper?"

I couldn't help myself: "Half the county is named Jones."

Langston shot me another glare.

"Keep your hands on your head, boy!" Doyle barked and shoved Langston against the fender.

I heard the thud of his body, felt the car shudder, and I gasped, "Mr. Doyle! I am tellin' you the truth! My bike got wrecked, I needed a ride, Langston mows our lawn—he works for Reverend Swanson too!"

This did not impress him. He leaned into the dark interior of the car and strained toward me. "Do you know what happens to girls like you?"

"Girls like me?"

Suddenly Gene Buck was shoving Langston in front of the Hudson, through the stippled glow of the headlights. He knocked Langston down in the road, and I shrieked.

Doyle hollered at me, "Get out here."

I popped out of the car and thought of making a run for it. But where to? We were halfway between Franklin and Kingsfield; the Swansons' house was miles away. Everything was miles away. I stood between the car and the ditch, helpless and useless, and Gene Buck kicked Langston in the leg. I let out a scream, which only made things worse. One of the Parkers stomped over to join in the kicking. This real violence was not like TV violence. This real violence was clumsy, noisy, disparate, inexact. The Parker boy swung his work boot at Langston's shoulder, grazing it with the sole; Langston huffed and rolled, but their attacks pursued him, off the pavement and into the mud. I clenched my entire body, realizing my reactions were provoking these men. But nothing I did or didn't do helped—the attack continued until Chuck Doyle stood over Langston and asked, "Where you goin' with this white girl?"

"Nowhere, suh. I's jus' droppin' her off home an' then I's jus' goin' home to my mama, tha's all. I's jus' gittin' home, gotta git home now, suh."

"Oh, you gotta get home?" Doyle bleated. "You got places to be? People to see? You *important*, boy? You got *rights*? That it? You gonna tell me about your *rights*?"

One of the Parkers shrieked like a hyena. "We got us a coon with *rights*!"

Then Chuck Doyle kicked Langston hard, and I screeched, "Stop! It's my fault. Mr. Doyle!" He paused and stared at me and I continued, "I *made* him, it was me. I *made* him give me a ride and I promise I'll never do it again. I promise, I promise, I'll be good, let him go! He didn't do anything wrong, really, it was *me*." My voice was wet, and suddenly sheets of tears were cascading down my cheeks. All eyes turned on me, shiny with hateful delight.

"Yeah?" Doyle said. "You gonna be a good girl now? Do what your daddy tells you to do?"

"Yes, sir! Yes, sir!"

Laughter erupted, more hyena shrieks. One of the Parkers knocked past me and I fell into the mud. I watched as the four men formed a circle around Langston, whispering, snickering. I pushed myself up from the ground but hesitated—I hesitated—my confused thoughts and fears assembling a wall between me and these persecutors. What could I do? I was just a girl— what could I do? I stood useless, immobile, incapable, hollowed out, thinking of nothing, doing nothing. If I screamed, no one would hear. If I screamed, would they beat me too?

We were saved by sheer luck. Up the road came a pair of headlights, fast at first, then slowing, then crawling up alongside us. Doyle and Gene Buck and the Parkers paused and stared as the car rolled to a stop—they all would have recognized it. The passenger window hummed down magically, and the driver leaned across the seat.

"Willa?" It was Jim Darden, looking puzzled. "Coach Doyle? What y'all doin' out here?"

The circle of men parted, revealing Langston on the ground, wet with mud and heaving, but sitting up now. Jim Darden asked, "What's goin' on here?" sounding mildly annoyed. The men formed a line, mute, standing at a kind of military-style attention.

I cried out, "I crashed my bike and Langston was givin' me a ride home. Langston mows people's lawns."

"Okay," Jim said, glowering at Gene Buck, "and what are these fine gentlemen doin' here?"

No one spoke. Langston pushed himself up from the ground, hobbled toward us, found his wallet in the mud, and managed to climb into his car. Jim Darden's eyes tracked him the whole way. Seated behind the wheel, Langston said to Jim Darden, "They helpin' me find my keys." Abruptly Gene Buck handed the keys back to Langston. To no one, Langston said, "I just wanna go home."

Jim Darden's voice rang out, "Good idea. You oughta get on home. Willa, come with me, I'll drop you off. You look like a drowned rat."

I ran to Langston's car first to get my bag. Neither of us spoke. I waited until Langston was safe behind his closed, locked door before I got into Jim Darden's car. Doyle and Gene Buck and the Parkers had no other option but to return to their vehicle. Jim Darden pulled in behind Doyle's car, in front of Langston, and we proceeded in an awkward parade to the edge of Kingsfield. Doyle turned right, Langston turned left, and Jim drove straight ahead.

He said nothing. The radio was on, but so low we hardly heard it. When he pulled up to my house he asked, "Okay now?"

"Yes, thank you."

He smiled liplessly. "Good. Now go get yourself fixed up. Make yourself presentable." As I scrambled out of his car, he winked at me.

Inside, my house felt abandoned. The family room was empty— no Billy in front of the TV. The living room was vacant too, and a cold silence attached to the walls. I stood at the bottom of the stairs and heard movement above. There was another sound, closer, coming from the kitchen, which I couldn't identify—a low moan, a whimpering. Then came a series of staccato sobs.

I walked to the kitchen and stood in the door. Neither of my parents acknowledged me. My mother was seated at the table, shelling peas. Chaotic piles of peapods were strewn across the tabletop. Her hands worked methodically, unhurried, cracking open the pods and pouring the fat round contents into our stainless-steel bowl. Her face wore no expression. After her fingers birthed the peas, she dropped the husks right onto the floor. I'd never seen her so untidy. By her foot was a haphazard graveyard of gutted pods.

My father was the one crying.

He said to her, "Please, say something. Say you forgive me." He paused to sob some more, his face contorted into hard red balls of cheek and forehead, eyes disappearing in shame. "All these years all I ever wanted was to be a good family man. Twenty-one years, Trudy. Twenty-one years. I don't know how it happened. It happened so fast. I won't see her anymore, I promise you, I promise you that. Say somethin', Trudy. I'll fire her tomorrow and never see her again. Help me out here, darlin'. Say you forgive me. All these years, you and the kids, all these years, all I ever wanted was to take care of you and the kids and provide a nice home. Didn't I do that? Wasn't I a good provider?" Another cascade of sobs, almost silent, shook him. "You and the kids, you're all I ever wanted."

Her hands still working, my mother finally said, "No, it wasn't." Her voice was flat, factual. "You wanted to be superintendent of the school district. You wanted to be an important man in town."

Brightening at the sound of her voice, he said, "But that was all for *you*, for *you*, and the children, to provide a better life for you and the *children*."

Her hands paused for a moment, and her eyes widened. Then she resumed shelling. Silence. Eagerly my father waited for a response that didn't come. What was he anticipating? Gratitude?

"Twenty-one years," he wheezed. "I been a *good husband* and father, and just this once, just this *one time*—I don't know how it happened!" His eyes yawned open: he genuinely did not seem to know. "Please, darlin'. Say you forgive me. I know you have the heart for it, you're a *good* Christian woman. Don't I always say that? I do. I say my wife is a role model for all women!"

Still she said nothing, and his hopeful expression slid into a look of panic. "*That* woman can't hold a candle to you! She isn't one iota the woman you are. You, you're a saint, Trudy, you are a Christian saint."

"Then why did you do it?"

Encouraged again, he belted, "I don't know! It was like, a madness came over me, a sickness. A *sickness* came over me, like the flu! All those times you took care of me when I had the flu, remember? You're a saint, a saint! I am a lucky man, that's what I am. Trudy, I will never see that woman again, I promise you that. I don't know what came over me." His head shook in sympathy for himself. "It was like a *sickness*. That's the only way I can explain it."

"You did it because you thought you had a right to. A right to…extra women. You think you have a right to do whatever you feel like doin' even if it hurts someone else."

"No!" he gasped. "How can you say that! Trudy! All these years! You know me, I'm a *good* man, but, *that woman*! It was that woman! You see the way she dresses? She…she must've had designs on me from the start. She wasn't happy with her husband, so…so, she wanted someone else's!" Despite his genuine misery, he sounded proud of himself for thinking up this line of defense. "Who knows! Maybe she's been goin' around stealin' husbands for years!" This possibility took him aback. "And there I was havin' a moment of weakness, and she got her hooks into me. That's what happened!" He paused, enthralled by his story. "I see it now!" He tilted his head, as though looking at it. "Oh, Trudy! I was weak! Man is weak. Weak!"

He lunged at her across the dwindling pile of pods, apparently to grasp onto her, but she pulled away, slid back in her chair, rose and got a tumbler out of the cupboard. Then she took the pitcher from the refrigerator and poured a drink, not for him, but for herself—Cherry Kool-Aid mixed up by Barb and Patsy the morning I went to the beach, a lifetime ago. She downed half the glass and stepped toward me and said, "Go get into some dry clothes, honey. I don't want you catchin' cold."

"Okay," I said. My mother had known I was there all along; my father still did not look at me. He'd stopped crying but still sat, small and guilty, on the other side of the big silver bowl. I said to my mother, "My bike is gone."

She pulled me into a one-armed hug. "I know," she whispered. "Try not to feel too sad. We'll get you a new bike, brand new, what do you think? You and I'll go together and pick one out for you."

Her gaze caught mine, her eyes swimming in tears and blinking fast, and I nodded and nodded in childish enthusiasm. I even said, "Okay, Mommy."

She released me, and I walked to the bottom of the staircase. My father's voice resumed its frantic droning apology, its pleas for forgiveness. I dragged myself up the steps and down the hall, my legs full of lead. She would, I thought. She would forgive him, eventually. Enough time would pass, and she'd forgive him. I was certain. Life keeps moving ahead, with the weight of a freight train, faster or slower but always forward, the contents of its boxcars growing old, rotting, dying, or already dead.

# 13

In a mid-morning glare I woke thinking of Langston, his hand quaking as he passed my bag to me. "You okay?" I'd whispered, and he'd looked away. How many times had they kicked him? In my head I summarized what I'd seen, as though testifying: Gene Buck was the one who'd shoved Langston to the ground. Then he kicked him, with the Parkers egging him on. Chuck Doyle drove the car. I'd seen them all clearly. Yes, I was sure. The scene replayed in my head again and again, concluding with Langston back in his car, crooked over the steering wheel, his hand shaking, his face turned away in pain or shame or both. I hadn't wanted to leave him, but Jim Darden's car was idling and everyone seemed stuck in time; only my leaving would restart the clock and allow Langston to escape.

Eventually my mother called upstairs. "Willa, get up!"

"Comin'!" I got up, dressed, went downstairs.

The house was empty, everyone gone to play tennis or softball or to shop at the fabric store. There was no sign of my father. My mother said, "I phoned the Campbells about the camera."

I flinched. "What did you say?"

"Only that we found it." She handed me a bowl of Crispy Critters and stood against the counter looking disappointed in everything. I ate, the noise of my crunching amplified by the stillness and loneliness of the room. When I finished, she and I walked to the Campbells' with the camera. The sky was cloudless, aquamarine, the air breezeless, gathering heat. I tried to look around and feel my feet on the ground and not die of dread. Mrs. Campbell answered the door. She and her husband did not call the police, but they stared at me speechless with wide hostile eyes, incredulous and, I think, repulsed. Becky, who was not even there, was clearly not going to be my best friend again. My mother kept apologizing without explaining, wallowing in contrition. She just couldn't imagine how it happened, she blubbered over and over, without ever identifying what "it" was. On the silent walk home I kept wanting to say something to her—something comforting and wise—but of course I had nothing.

At home my mother washed cereal bowls, and I crept up to my parents' room to call Langston on the extension. I must've let his phone ring twenty times. Was he in the hospital? I began dialing Ruth, who may have heard from his mother, when a crisp double knock sounded at our back door. I lingered at the top of the stairs as my mother swung it open. A familiar, resolute voice inquired, "Hello, is Willa at home?"

It was Daisy. I thumped down the steps. She stood on the other side of the door screen, as though in a picture frame, the sky deepened now to provide a vivid cobalt backdrop for her. She wore a prim aquamarine dress, looking her Sunday best. Had she dressed up to pay a visit to our house? Or was she just always a fashion plate? I was in shorts and a rumpled shirt, and I couldn't recall if I'd brushed my hair.

"Hello, Willa," she said in a voice as neat and contained as her appearance. "May I have a word?"

I looked at my mother, who was looking at me. "This is Daisy," I said. "Langston's girlfriend."

"Oh." My mother turned toward Daisy and after a pause asked, "Would you like to come inside?"

I stepped back. This was the first time I'd ever seen a colored person enter our house. My mother repeated, "Come in, please," and led Daisy into our living room, then actually invited her to sit on our couch. I must have looked surprised, because Daisy glared at me with large eyes full of hostility and discomfort. But she sat. She had a large canvas purse with a clasp adorned with an enormous daisy. How cute. She placed the bag gingerly on the cushion beside her. My mother and I sat facing her, my mother pitched toward her as though eager to hear what she'd come to say. Daisy cleared her throat. Then she cleared it again. Her mental image of this scene would not have included my mother.

I said, "Is Langston okay?"

"Yes," she replied stiffly. "Bruises and swelling."

My mother's pleasant, puzzled face nodded and frowned in concern. Then Daisy began her prepared speech: "What I came to say, Willa, is, I would like to know why you felt it necessary to call *my* boyfriend to come pick you up in another town."

I didn't speak. I didn't think I was supposed to. But my mother offered a reply: "I don't think she has a boyfriend of her own." She turned to me. "Do you?" She was completely serious. A silence buzzed by, and she said to Daisy, "Would you like some sweet tea?" Outside a dog barked, and somewhere far away, a car backfired.

"No, thank you, ma'am." We sat through another long mute moment until finally, from her huge purse, Daisy withdrew a magazine. *JET* was printed across the front in olive green letters. Against an olive background posed an Italian-looking girl in a skimpy swimsuit. Daisy said to us both, "Are you familiar with this publication?"

"Yes," my mother said. *Jet* was a magazine for coloreds. I recalled my father moaning once, "They got their own *magazine*." But this issue seemed old. I squinted to see the date on it—1955, nine years ago. Carefully Daisy opened it, turned pages with slow slender fingers, and said, "I thought it was important for Willa to see this." She smoothed open the magazine, then extended it toward me like a serving tray. My mother craned to see. The headline ran across two pages in red capital letters: *Nation Horrified by Murder of Kidnaped Chicago Youth.* My first thought, oddly, was, Shouldn't *kidnaped* have two *p*'s in it? What was that rule again?

Daisy said, "See the photo?"

"What, this one?" The picture on the first page showed a pudgy colored boy with his mama, both well dressed and pleasant-faced. The boy smiled contentedly. The roundness of his face reminded me of Joe Pedicini's. "You mean this little boy?"

Daisy replied, "He was fourteen years old in that picture." Whether she knew that was my age, too, I didn't know.

My mother sat with her head cocked, trying to see the page. "What is all this about?"

"Oh, this is just something I brought over for Willa to take a look." Daisy's voice was sharp but still melodious, like chords on a piano rolling down the keyboard. "There are more pictures, Willa. Turn the page."

I did and found myself looking at a photo of a rock. A bit of scraggly foliage was attached to the top of it. The rock was positioned inside the collar of a crisp white shirt. I tried to make sense of it. I studied the image, turned it slightly, leaned toward the page, and then I saw. The object in the photo was not a rock; it was a face—an old man's horribly deformed face, grotesquely swollen and pinched, chinless, eyes engulfed in hard, blackened flesh. Worse, on the opposite page was a full-sized photo of this face from a different angle, weird squares of light illuminating the unnatural planes of his cheeks, his lips like two wide strips of Play-Doh, loosely attached. My stomach roiled. His forehead was crinkled and crushed. I could make out the nose—the nose somehow was intact. It was obvious, especially in the page-sized photo, that the man was dead. I was revolted, but I kept looking at the photo until, abruptly, I understood: this was the face of the little boy from the previous picture. I said, "This is Emmet Till."

"Yes," Daisy said in triumph, as though she'd won a game. "I wanted you to see what can happen to a colored boy who appears to be interested in a white girl."

My mother rose and stretched to take the magazine from me and, without really looking at it, returned to her chair, shaking her head heavily. "Oh yes. I recall this. What a terrible thing. Shocking, shocking." My mother spoke with genuine sympathy, looking away, passing the magazine back to Daisy. "That was a long time ago. When was that? In the '40s?"

"It was 1955," Daisy replied authoritatively. "Not even ten

years ago, Mrs. McCoy."

My mother shook her head some more and clicked her tongue. "It is shocking how some people behave."

"Yes, ma'am, it is."

Then my mother smiled at Daisy. "You must feel very fortunate."

"Ma'am?"

"Fortunate, to be livin' here instead of some uncivilized place like Mississippi."

Daisy gazed at her. Slowly my mother placed one hand over the other in her lap, uncrossed and re-crossed her legs. A millennium passed. At last she said, "Daisy, I hope you're not implyin' that somethin' like that could happen *here*. Kingsfield is not some backward town in the deep South. *Virginians* have always been above such things."

Daisy appeared to be listening politely, then blurted, "You do know your husband's in the Klan."

My mother's faint eyebrows leaped up: how embarrassing. People were not supposed to blurt out such things. "You're not from around here, are you? I can tell by your accent."

I said, "She's from DC."

My mother nodded knowingly and explained, "Well, here in Tidewater we have men's organizations who help to keep the law and order. We don't like trouble here. We live peaceably here with the coloreds. Sometimes outsiders come in tryin' to stir up trouble, which we don't abide. Our men's organizations keep an eye on what's goin' on. They keep the peace, and they protect their families." She waved her hand toward the magazine. "*Our* men would never do such an awful thing." Then, "Do you understand?"

I kept my eyes on my mother. She'd spoken with such certainty, thinking she was helpfully correcting Daisy's misconceptions. Then I realized, not only did I used to believe what my mother just said, but I still kind of did, even after last night—surely *our* men weren't capable of that level of brutality. *Our men*—I'd known them all my life. We greeted them on the street, in stores, at church. They came to our house for supper with their wives and their children. Surely *they* were better than those coarse men in the deep South.

I'd understood that my father and his friends went around harassing Negroes. I understood now that it was despicable. But last night was an aberration: Doyle and Buck and the Parkers lost control of themselves. Probably they'd been drinking. I'd seen boys get into fistfights; eventually they quit. Doyle and Buck and the Parkers would have quit, even if Jim Darden had not appeared when he did. Surely they would have quit. I believed this, with my whole heart—they would not have *killed* Langston. Right? The sunlight grew harsh through the narrow opening in our drapes. Suddenly, I felt frightened.

"*Mama*," I said, hearing my voice wobble, attempting to convey volumes of meaning in two soft syllables.

My mother glanced from me to Daisy, her lips tightening into an irritated smile. She said to Daisy, "I think you've upset my daughter."

Intrepid, Daisy replied, "Mrs. McCoy, I am trying to make Willa *understand* that—"

"Willa is extremely smart." My mother was angry now, her smile a straight line across her taut face. "I'm sure there's nothin' you can tell her she doesn't already know." Daisy's luminescent eyes rolled toward me.

I had a sense of squirming in my chair, my legs pulling up, my body rocking. Quietly I said, "I get it, I get it."

My mother stood and stepped forward to loom over Daisy. "I'll show you out now."

Daisy rose, lifting her bag with one smooth motion, slipping its strap over her shoulder, laying a long-fingered hand on its clasp. I didn't stand up.

She said to me, "Because of the incident last night, Langston's family has decided he needs to leave for college earlier than originally planned." Her voice grew shrill with misery. "*Six weeks* earlier than we expected."

I said nothing. My mother corralled Daisy toward the back

door. I heard her say, "Goodbye now," and yank the screen door shut and hook the lock. I sat. Langston was leaving—soon. I heard my mother's footsteps march back into the living room and stop in front of me. I looked up.

"Listen," she said. "It doesn't matter what kinda trouble you're in. If you *ever* get stranded again, for whatever reason—*whatever* reason—you call *me*. Okay? You call *me*. I won't yell at you, whatever mess you're in. I want you safe. Hear me? I'll come get you, or I'll send Ricky. You don't call anyone else but me, you hear?"

"Yes," I squeaked. "You won't send Daddy?"

"No, not Daddy. I won't send Daddy. Okay?"

"Okay."

"I wanna hear you say it. Make a promise."

"I promise."

"You promise what?"

"I promise I'll call you if I get stranded somewhere again."

She went into the kitchen. I heard her sigh and open and close cabinet doors, run water in the sink. I remained curled into the chair, trying to not see the images of Emmett Till in my mind. I examined my hands, resting palms up in my lap. The crinkly skin was mottled with peach and pink and beige. I thought how people are not just one color. Langston's hands were many colors—the backs russet, the edges of his palms copper-tinged, the palms a dark beige. His shades of brown changed with the light. In shadow, his face was walnut; in direct sunlight, it brightened to caramel. I tried to keep Langston's face in my mind, but Emmett Till's faded in. Emmett Till's face, beaten to pitch. I thought of his proud, pretty mama smiling beside him, blissfully unaware of their fast-approaching fates.

Still, my thoughts insisted loudly, that would not happen here. My mother was right. My father and his friends weren't *murderous*. I thought of Emmett Till's swollen-shut eyes.

I'd seen other disturbing photographs: pictures of corpses in piles in Nazi concentration camps, pictures of the death camp survivors, their eyes huge in their shrunken heads. But that was nearly twenty years ago, in a different country. That kind of evil—*real* evil, Nazi evil—was something that existed someplace else, in a different kind of human—not here, not us.

Yet it was my father's friends who'd knocked Langston to the ground and kicked him, more than once. Daisy was right. I should never have called Langston for a ride. This was *my fault.* I'd put Langston in danger, and I'd done it before, walking with him and Daisy through the colored part of town. A crush of shame took my breath. I thought of Langston curled onto his bed, in pain, wincing, slow-moving, unable to go to his jobs. And now he was leaving his home six weeks earlier than he'd wanted to. Violence against a body disrupts the normal course of a life, dislodges expectations. What does it do to the mind? What are the long-term effects? Fear, distrust, and cynicism build up into the scar tissue that protects and deforms you. Langston was leaving. I had to accept my culpability for this.

I walked into the kitchen, where my mother was furiously rewashing all the clean pots and pans. "Mama," I said. "I'm goin' over to Ruth's."

She turned and settled her tired eyes on me. "You sure?"

"Yeah. I wanna tell her what happened. Everything."

"Don't be home late, Willa," she said, and began to dry.

Weeping at Ruth's kitchen table, I told her the whole story: the premeditated theft of the camera, taking the pictures, losing the bike, my desolate walk through the rain, my phone call to Langston, which was a mistake—such a mistake! I saw that now. I just thought, I just thought—I stopped short of telling her that I just wanted him to be the one who came for me, to rescue me, to carry me away from all that soggy misery. I did not say how much I wanted to see his face and hear his voice and ride along with him in his car. I told her I didn't know what I was thinking; I was a complete mess, and I did not have the presence of mind to realize the danger I was subjecting him to. This was true. I told her about the assault on Langston, sobbing and gasping through the details. I told her about the appearance of Daisy at my house, and the terrifying photos of Emmett Till.

And now Langston had to leave in two weeks and it was *my fault. Less* than two weeks. Tears dripped off my chin and onto my shirt. Ruth slid her chair next to mine and hugged me sideways.

"Oh, sweetie," she murmured, a little restrained, a little shocked. "How awful, how completely awful." Her voice melted into a soft sympathy, whispering, generous. "I'm sorry, so sorry for us all." She squeezed me hard and held me, her breath ruffling my hair. "Terrible things happen in this world, but we can heal. God will heal us. Have faith, sweetie. God heals our bodies and our souls." I couldn't stop crying. She rubbed circles into my back. "Everyone makes mistakes. Sometimes really bad ones. We just have to learn from them. Forgive yourself, but don't forget—learn."

For a long while we sat in silence. She brushed my matted hair from my face, and finally I stopped crying.

Annette came into the kitchen, her fist wadded around the leg of her pink stuffed lamb. "Mommy?" she said.

Ruth pulled her onto her lap, and Julie came in next, pinning her giant tragic eyes to my face. She climbed onto the unoccupied chair and knelt straight-backed, to be almost as tall as we were. To Ruth she said, "Is Willa sad because of us?"

"Shhh," Ruth whispered back. "I haven't told her yet."

"Told me what?"

Ruth's lips pressed together so hard they disappeared.

"What? What?"

"I'm sorry to tell you this now." Her voice low, dragging. "Matthew accepted a job in Albany, New York. He's given his notice. We're moving at the end of July."

The silence that followed was absolute: nothing rustled or hummed or chirped, inside or outside, anywhere in the world. Their faces were frozen in a desolate tableau.

I said, "Oh." Then, "Oh," again. Then, "You're leaving." They were all leaving.

"We'll miss you so much. But you know I'm not doing well here. Albany's a larger town, more doctors and hospitals."

Julie said, "And the schools are better too," though I could tell she was not supposed to parrot this opinion.

"You're leaving," I said.

"I'll write you every week! I'll call you on your birthday! You can call me too sometimes—*collect*. I told Matthew, I said there *will be* long-distance charges!" and she giggled, apparently proud of herself for this wifely victory, for asserting herself over the phone bill. I said nothing. "And you can come visit us next summer! I'll get it all worked out with your mom. You can come on the bus and stay for a whole week! See a new place! You'll like that."

In two weeks, Langston would be gone; in four weeks, the Swansons would be gone. All of them gone, and where would I be? Left behind, with nowhere to go but my own house, that shadowy, phony, frustrated place. Letters? Phone calls? She'd get too busy to write; long-distance would be too expensive. The bus ticket would turn out to cost too much; my mother wouldn't let me go alone. I would never see Ruth again. I would never see Langston again. I knew this as sure as I knew my own name.

"Hey," she said. "I'm really gonna need your help over the next few weeks, yours and Langston's, packing boxes and getting the place all cleaned up for the next minister's family. Moving is such hard work. Can I count on you?" She was trying to sound bright and cheerful and I wanted to yell at her, "Stop!" I wanted to shatter my Coke bottle against the wall.

I nodded.

"Good!" But today, she insisted, before all that work began, we should have a fun afternoon together. Julie pranced off to get Monopoly. They let me be the race car. The game went on and on. First Julie was ahead, then I was, then Julie again, then Annette, round and round we went, not buying too many properties or houses or hotels—no one was trying to win. We only wanted the game to continue.

When I got home, everyone was in their usual places, and the appearance of normalcy felt odd: Billy in front of the TV, Ricky and Barb and friends in the living room. My mother, of course, was in the kitchen. Crossing in front of the TV, I punched down one of the rabbit ears to make the picture fuzz up. "Hey!" Billy wailed.

I leaned against the kitchen doorframe and told my mother, "The Swansons are movin' away."

She paused, saucepan in hand. "I can't say I'm surprised."

"They're movin' to Albany, New York."

"It's too bad, honey, but I bet they'll be happier there. They must've felt they didn't belong here. They're so different."

"Does being different mean you don't belong?"

She ran water into the pan and set it on the burner. "People want to be with people they can relate to, people like themselves."

"Birds of a feather," I said miserably. "I *like* meeting different kinds of people."

"Well, sure, it's fun to chat with people from other places and different backgrounds, but we don't want to take up residence with them." She pulled a bag of frozen corn from the freezer. "It's human nature. It makes sense, doesn't it?"

"No."

"Now you're just bein' stubborn. The Swansons'll feel more comfortable up North."

"People feelin' comfortable. That's the most important thing in life, isn't it?"

She sighed, slow and aching, and I knew this conversation was over.

"Where's Daddy?"

"Upstairs. On the phone." She stirred the corn once with a languid hand, then laid the spoon on the counter and untied her apron. "I have to run to the Be-Lo. Patsy's over for dinner and we're out of dietetic Dr. Pepper." She looked around the kitchen, her face wan. "I am so tired."

"You don't have to go, Mama. Patsy won't mind drinkin' somethin' else, you know that."

"No!" she barked with startling conviction. "I'm a better hostess than that." She found her purse and headed toward the back door. "Keep dinner goin', please. Stir the corn and turn the chicken."

"Me?"

I watched her amble up the driveway, head hanging, and slide herself into the car. I watched the car inch backward, hesitate at the ditch, and roll away down the road. I turned to scrutinize the pan of frozen corn. Then I looked at the phone on the wall. Who was my father talking to?

I looked at the phone again, the black surface of the handset gleaming, enticing, inviting me to lift it up. I tiptoed over. My hand, seemingly by its own volition, reached up and rested on the smooth top of the phone. My other hand, apparently in cahoots with its mate, held down the receiver. I lifted the phone off the hook, then slowly, slowly released the receiver—you had to be gentle to avoid the "click" that alerted the other talker to the intrusion. I laid my palm over the mouthpiece and heard my father's exhausted voice: "…don't know."

The voice that replied was Dr. Vaughan's, distraught: "Parkers're mad as hell and I don't blame 'em. They had that uppity coon right there."

"I think we oughta hold off," my father replied.

"What's your reasoning, Dick?"

"Jim Darden was the one busted up the party last night."

"Yeah?"

"Dardens don't approve of the Klan, you know that."

"Yeah, so? When was that ever a factor?"

My father's voice hesitated. "Well, Jim's datin' Barb, and if we go too far, well…" Pause. "If our activities put him off, Trudy'd never forgive me."

Dr. Vaughan's response dripped with vitriol: "Your daughter's romantic interests dictatin' what we do now, Dick? Your wife got you wrapped around her little finger?"

"'Course not!'"

"Everybody besides you wants to go and get that coon."

"All right, all right, just hold on a minute, just, listen to this. I got a better plan."

"I'm listenin'."

"Civil Rights Act's back in the House. This time they're not gonna be able to filibuster."

"What, you really think that bill's gonna pass? You think Johnson's dumb enough to sign it? Democrats'd lose the South for generations."

"Johnson's dumb as a rock!" My father's voice rallied, energized by the chance to call someone stupid. "Hasn't got one brain cell in his head! Johnson'll sign it, and *that's* when we make our move. Show 'em nothin's changed. *Civil rights* means nothin'."

"You really think it's gonna pass."

There was a pause, then a throaty, "Country's goin' to hell, everything's outta control."

"Well, all right, but if that bill passes we move fast, no more discussion. Soon as it passes, we make an example of that boy."

"Okay," my father said. "He's easy enough to find. He's all over creation in that damn Hudson."

"This time," Dr. Vaughan's voice rose, "we don't just kick him around a little, we make him *disappear*, like they did in Mississippi. What d'ya think of that?"

I could hear my father inhale, exhale, inhale again. Then, "I like it."

"Willa!" Barb's voice was suddenly behind me. I pushed the receiver down as hurriedly as I dared and replaced the handset. "Where's Mama? The pan!" I turned—the corn water was boiling over. "Where is she? Did she leave *you* to cook for us?" Barb seized the spoon from the counter and gave the corn several vigorous stirs. I fled to my room and shut myself inside.

I sat on the edge of my bed and tried to think. I wanted to dive under the covers and never emerge. I wanted to crawl into the closet and hide for the rest of the decade. Instead, I made myself sit up straight. I turned toward the window, blasting with light. Who had disappeared in Mississippi? *Disappeared*. I tried to find some other meaning in my head to pin to this word, to what Dr. Vaughan was suggesting, but Emmett Till's bludgeoned face faded into my mind, and my stomach lurched. Were *our* men capable of murder?

I thought about our men, one at a time. Chuck Doyle was everyone's favorite football coach, corralling his players like a loving uncle, calling them all "champ" even when they lost, delirious with joy when they won; those boys loved him. Dr. Vaughan was everyone's eye doctor, his smiling grandpa face so reassuring behind that tiny flashlight, his tender fingers repositioning chins. The Parkers were basically two overgrown kids who loved joining in, wanting only to belong to a group—the Boy Scouts, the church youth group, the Klan—such good followers, enthusiastically failing to question. Even Gene Buck had a kinder aspect to him. Years ago he'd had a young wife from Roanoke and a horse named Junie, both of whom he adored. Both were beauties, gentle, slender, blond. But the wife left him, and a week later the horse died, and he'd sat all evening in our living room, red-eyed, while my mother ran to get him more sugar cookies. Were these men capable of killing another human being?

Then I realized that to my father and his friends, colored people were not human beings—they were animals. People kill animals all the time with no moral misgivings: hogs and chickens, vermin.

Long ago, at a dinner party at our house, my father and Dr. Vaughan had entertained our guests with stories of killing Japs during the war. I watched them both puff up in their chairs as their tales grew increasingly gruesome: Japs blown off a ridge, Japs blown into the sea, pieces of Japs floating on red waves. My father and Dr. Vaughan chuckled and crowed and the guests laughed too, the mood celebratory, everyone swelled up with patriotism and superiority, because these Japs were not people; they were subhumans bent on murdering us all. The same fear-laced adrenaline fueled their hatred of Black men too: it was the same wordless impulse to defend their tribe from another tribe, whose rituals and ways of speaking were unlike ours. Did it matter that we weren't fighting a declared war with the coloreds? That this threat was only imagined?

Surely my father and his friends felt this distinction. Abducting and killing someone would be cold-blooded murder, and surely they were not capable of that. They postured and blustered and inflated—that was all. I was certain of this. But I also knew it wasn't the whole truth. Maybe *our* men weren't cold-blooded killers, but they were inclined toward pride and fear, prone to feeling offended and losing control. I thought of Langston's gorgeous face turned to a charred mass of bruises and lumps. After the fact, our men would probably be surprised to find they'd beaten someone to death. After it was done, it would seem to them like an accident. Their collective conscience would assert itself, and their memories would alter their intent, along with the events, slightly at first, more radically with the retellings. They would blame Langston, the coloreds, the president, the government, the Jew media, anyone but themselves. Maybe some of them would suffer quiet pangs of remorse, and maybe some would truly repent—after it was over, after Langston was gone.

# 14

Together we made a plan—Ruth and Langston and me, Langston's parents, and even Daisy. Langston would have a suitcase ready to go if the Civil Rights Act passed before July 5th, the day he planned to leave for college. He'd have an envelope of money for bus fare. He could stay with a friend of Daisy's late mother in DC until his dormitory room at Howard was available. I was to continue in my role of spy, providing intelligence on the movement of the Klan. If they started to organize a meeting, I'd call Ruth, who would drive Langston to the bus station in Emporia, not in Kingsfield, where the Klan would check first. Ruth would take me and the girls along in the car too, speculating that my father's friends would be less likely to get violent in front of children. I thought Langston should hide under a blanket on the floor of the back seat.

In a fugue, Ruth said, "For Pete's sake, this is *America*."

The days edged by. Langston healed and came to Ruth's to help us pack for her move. Ruth was doing too much, making herself exhausted and rickety, and Langston and I had to tell her to sit while we worked. Langston ran to the grocery store for more boxes, and we started packing the books. "Smaller boxes for the books!" Ruth sang out miserably, relegated to the couch. Slowly all their belongings disappeared from shelves and cupboards and dresser tops.

At home, my mother was occupied sorting through Ricky's clothes in search of items that needed mending, preparing for his departure to Virginia Tech in August. She was unemotional about it, focused on all the mundane tasks to accomplish, her skin drawn thin over the bones of her face. Ricky, like Barb, was thinking only of the upcoming Fourth of July celebration in town. The Fourth being on a Saturday that year made the event feel extra festive. Barb and Patsy made themselves sundresses out of red and white gingham, and Barb found a blue nylon silky-looking sash to tie around her waist.

On the first day of July, my father got in his car and drove away. He didn't tell us why. He hadn't said much of anything lately, falling silent at the supper table after administering his quizzes, which had become cursory. In his last quiz, he asked us to name state capitals, which even Billy knew. Ricky and Barb must have sensed something was wrong, but they didn't know what I knew.

My father was gone all day and night; by suppertime of the next day, he still wasn't home. Billy asked, "Where's Daddy?"

My mother, focused on getting the beans passed to Patsy, said, "He's in Raleigh for a few days."

"What for?" Billy asked.

"He's applyin' for a job there."

Barb wailed, "Applyin' for a job? *Applyin' for a job?*" as though repeating the words might alter their meaning. Ricky's eyebrows disappeared into the fringe of his new Beatles hair. Barb shrieked, "You mean, we might move to *Raleigh?*"

My mother's reply was slow and matter-of-fact. "Well, I don't know if *we* will."

We waited for an explanation. She took another bite of fried chicken and stared at nothing. Billy's legs jittered, and when the waiting had condensed into a thick cloud above our heads, Ricky said, "What's *that* mean?"

My mother said, "Nothin's settled yet. Don't worry about it." She sawed open her biscuit, stretched for the butter, pretended not to notice Barb's intense gaze or Ricky's solemn frown. Billy channeled all his confused emotions into his kicking feet, which bumped the underside of the table. My mother murmured, "Billy."

Patsy said, "I went to Raleigh once with my aunt Arlene. We had a *great* time!"

The conversation halted again, and in this patch of silence,

I tried to figure out what I was thinking. From the commotion in my brain, my thoughts issued this statement: My father might leave us. He might really go. I'd dreamed of his absence; I'd actively wished for it. But now I found I could not truly imagine it. When you've lived with someone for as long as you can remember, you can't really envision life without him. You can't anticipate all the changes, big and small, all the gaps. If my father left us, there'd be a crater where he used to stand. I tried to identify what I was feeling: a heavy thumb pressing down on the top of my heart, a boot sinking into my soft interior. I'd come to hate my father, but that hatred, it turned out, was only a mirror image of all my yearning for his love and respect. My father still had a hold on me. Now he was the villain in my story, not the hero, but he was just as essential to the plot. What would my narrative be without him? My impulses, humming below the level of my thinking brain, would be untethered, driven toward anything that seemed to offer a sense of purpose. What would my desire go chasing after next?

The silence grew suffocating. Patsy attempted to restart the conversation: "Did y'all hear the Civil Rights Act passed today?"

My mother said, "That so?"

"Yup! President Johnson signed it."

Barb asked, "What is that, anyway?"

Ricky said, "A law makes coons think they got rights."

Billy kicked the table leg.

Patsy said, "Makes it illegal to discriminate against colored people. So colored people are allowed in with white people now, like in movie theaters. And schools have to be integrated."

"Wait," I said. "What?"

Barb asked, "Wasn't that already a law?"

"What did you say?" I asked Patsy. "The Civil Rights Act passed today?"

"Yeah, my mom saw it on the news before I came over."

"May I be excused?" I croaked. "I don't feel well."

"Okay, honey," my mother said.

In my parents' room, I dialed Ruth's number.

The reverend answered, "Hullo?"

"Hi, it's Willa. I need to talk to Ruth, it's *really important.*"

In a halting voice he said, "Ruth is resting just now. She's in bed with a headache."

"There's an extension right next to the bed."

"I think she's sleeping."

"*Please, please.*" I must have sounded hysterical.

Eventually, Ruth's drowsy voice came on the phone, "Hi, Willa."

"Did you hear the news?"

"Hmm? No, we didn't turn the news on tonight. I have such a headache."

"They passed the Civil Rights Act. Johnson signed it."

Her voice roused, "Oh! That's wonderful news!"

"But, Langston."

"Oh, Langston." Her voice faded, sounding confused.

"Ruth? What should we do?"

I heard her breathing, fast and uneven. There was a pause, a shuffling. I imagined her sitting up on the edge of her bed, resting her forehead in her hand. "What day is today?"

"It's Thursday, today's Thursday! He leaves Sunday. Two days!" It was both too long and too short.

"What is your father doing now?"

"He's not here!" I belted in relief. "He went to Raleigh!"

"When is he coming back?"

"I don't know!"

"Well, let's think about this. Would the Klan act without him? Or would they wait for him to come back?"

I thought about it. Dr. Vaughan was so adamant, the Parkers and Chuck Doyle and Gene Buck so angry. But they didn't know Langston was leaving Sunday. They'd assume there was more time. No one would make a pricey long-distance call to Raleigh, or from Raleigh.

I said, "They'd wait for him."

My certainty evaporated as soon as I said it. The image of Emmett Till's petrified head materialized in its place.

"Okay." She let out a loud breath. "Let me call Langston and talk it over with him and his folks." She sounded more awake now, but so tired. "I'll see you tomorrow, right?"

"Ruth." I didn't want to stop hearing her voice. But her phone clattered onto its cradle, and the line went dead. I sat on my parents' bed and stared at the blue-pinstripe walls. Yes, the Klan would wait for my father. Sometimes bunches of men rode around in cars and harassed coloreds when they happened to come across them, but for an organized event, they looked to my father to plan it. There'd be time. My father would come home and putter around and tell us facts about Raleigh. His brain would be occupied thinking up quizzes: Who was the city of Raleigh named after? Which great American president was born in Raleigh?

I told myself: There would be time.

The next morning, I walked through the sedentary block of heat to the parsonage. Langston was already there, elbows on the kitchen table, his shoulders hanging over them. His face was motionless, cemented into an expression of worried gloom. He was slick with sweat, the short sleeves of his bright white T-shirt clinging to the tops of his arms.

Ruth sat down shakily and I remembered to ask her, "How is your head feeling?"

"Better," she said, not convincingly, and grinned. "So we all talked it over, Langston's folks—"

"And Daisy," he added sorrowfully.

"Langston's folks want him to leave today, but Langston's being a little stubborn."

"Bad enough they runnin' me out six weeks early," he said. "I want my two more days with Daisy!"

"It's a risk," Ruth said, unhappily. "The compromise is he's going into hiding."

I interjected, "Like Anne Frank!"

He said, "Just no attic, please. It nasty up there."

Ruth continued, "He'll go straight home today at noon, park

his car behind his house, and stay inside till Sunday, when he'll leave as planned."

"No Fourth of July barbecue for me and Daisy," he mourned.

Ruth's head tilted. "Oh, you'll miss the picnic in Triangle Park."

Langston and I looked at each other: Ruth was still such a Northerner.

"We don't go to white folks' *picnics*, Ruth. We havin' our own barbecue, in our part of town."

"Oh, of course." Ruth continued the explanation: "Sunday he'll leave as planned. We'll drive him to the bus station in Emporia. It'll be the middle of the day—broad daylight. In the meantime we'll all be on the lookout for Klan activity." She smiled at me, and I straightened in a display of responsibility and competence. "For now," she said, "we're safe. We're safe and all together." I realized this was the last time we would all be together. Ruth smiled. "Let's not be sad." Langston and I forced grins onto our faces. "Let's tackle those cabinets!"

Langston climbed onto a chair to reach the highest ones. We'd already emptied and packed the contents. Now we had to pull up shelf paper and wipe down the wood. I stood at Langston's hip as he handed me wads of crackled-up paper, imprinted with tiny rose buds. Ruth sat at the table, her face paler than usual, small and elfin-round. We worked in silence until Ruth said, "Wanna know a secret about me?" Langston and I halted. Of course we did. "I…" and she paused for dramatic effect. "*I* have…*ESP. I* can tell the *future*."

"Oh," I said. "We thought you were serious."

"I am serious!" she protested.

Langston asked, "You learn some of that voodoo magic up there in Minnesota?"

She laughed. "You know *nothing* of the sleazy back alleys of St. Paul."

"Okay," he said. "Tell me my future."

She leaned over the table, eyes closed, fingertips resting

against her temples in a demonstration of mystical concentration. She began to hum as though entering a trance. Langston and I chuckled. In a ghosty voice she said, "Langston Jones, you will soon embark on a journey to a faraway destination."

In a loud whisper I said, "DC's not that far."

"For four long years you will toil, and you will emerge victorious, holding in your hands a magical piece of parchment that will lead you to a life of happiness and success!"

Langston rolled his eyes, tore up another strip of shelf paper, and handed it to me. Ruth emerged from her trance to grin at us. "Then what?" Langston asked, not really joking.

In her normal voice, she continued, "*Then*, you'll start another journey. You'll get a job. Not as good as you'd hoped, but it'll be a good start. Opportunities will come your way, because you'll work hard and treat other people with respect, because of who you are. You won't let obstacles throw you off your path. You'll work through the problems and keep going. I know this because that's what you do now, because in spite of all the ugliness in this world, you know you're a worthy person. Your parents taught you that. Jesus taught you that. Twenty-five years from now, you'll be an aerospace engineer at NASA."

Langston glowed, absorbing all her confidence, his head lowered in humble pride.

"And," she continued, "you will be married to Daisy, who will have a brilliant law career, and you'll have two beautiful children and live in Florida, in one of those adobe houses with a beige tile floor."

I laughed—I loved random details like that. Langston said, "Boy and a girl?"

"Two girls," she said without skipping a beat. "Named Ruth and Willa."

I let out a belly laugh, imagining Daisy stuck with a daughter named for me.

"Now me!" I said.

Again she inhaled dramatically, tapping her fingertips on her temples. She seemed to be concentrating hard, as though truly trying to work out my fate. "I see a rougher path ahead for Willa. I see some very hard times ahead."

What? Why would she say that? That wasn't fair.

"But," she continued, "Willa is the toughest of us all. She'll overcome, she'll persist. She will succeed, because she's strong enough and brave enough to make changes in herself. She'll be a journalist, but she'll feel its limitations after a while and do something different, something to make the world a better place, something far better than just being famous."

This was kind of confusing: I felt flattered and offended at the same time. Why wouldn't she just say I'd be a war correspondent for the *Washington Post* and travel to dangerous, thrilling, important places? That's what I wanted; she knew that. Was she actually attempting to predict my future?

Langston said, "Now I'll do Ruth!" Still standing on the kitchen chair, he squeezed his eyes shut and drilled his index fingers into his temples and made a whirring Martian spaceship sound. We laughed, and in a booming Wizard of Oz voice, he prophesied, "You will soon have a very clean kitchen! Then you and your family will travel to a distant city…in a vehicle…with wheels…"

"Ah!" Ruth roared. "Your powers are legion!"

He opened one eye and nodded at me, signaling it was my turn. I began to rock as though possessed by clairvoyant spirits. My eyes closed. I tried to mimic Langston's authoritative bellow, but managed only an alto shout: "Then, the cooling northern winds will blow magical breezes and you will be healed! Once again you will run joyfully along the lakeshore!"

My eyes sprang open, and I presented Ruth with an enormous smile. But this had not been the right thing to say. A despondent silence commenced. We listened to the soft rustle of the girls playing at the end of the hall, then to the crackle of Langston tearing up more shelf paper.

Ruth said, "I do think I'll feel better there."

Langston handed me the last wad and got down from the chair. "Tell us somethin' real we don't know about you."

"Somethin' funny," I begged, wanting to bring back her crooked grin.

"I can tell you something funny about my mother-in-law."

"Okay."

"Matthew—Reverend Swanson—was her first-born. A year later, she had another baby boy, whom she named Mark. So she got it into her head she'd have two more sons and name them Luke and John." Ruth giggled at the folly of this. "Two years after Mark, she had a girl, Terry. Then she had Mildred, then Jill. And the last time she was expecting, it turned out to be twins—both girls. She named them *Lucy* and *Joan!*" She exploded into laughter, loud and belly-sized, rolling on endlessly. Langston and I laughed politely until she stopped.

I said, "I was supposed to be a boy named William. That's why I'm named Willa. I was the back-up for Ricky."

"What do you mean?" Ruth's face was rosy.

"You know, like parents have another kid as a back-up in case somethin' happens to the first one."

"Oh, Willa, that's ghoulish," she said.

"But it's true, right? Langston's parents have two boys. You have Julie and Annette."

"Oh my goodness. Annette is not a substitute for Julie."

From the family room Julie called, "What?"

Ruth called back, "I said, come get some juice!"

The girls ran in for juice, then ran off to find Mr. Softy, and the reverend came home. He went immediately toward his wife to ask how her head was.

"Much better. A little achy. Not as bad as this morning. I think it's getting better."

The reverend eyed me and Langston. We were obviously there to help her, but it was equally obvious he wished we'd go away now. We finished fast and started to leave.

This could have been the last time I'd see Langston, but that didn't occur to me. I'd already imagined our goodbye scene a thousand times, and this was not it. I knew how it would play out: we'd be back at the bank of the Nottoway River, somehow, in our sandy alcove encased in rustling oaks. Langston's cop-per-bright face would tilt toward me, and I'd reach up, and we would hold each other; we would hug and rock each other, and Langston's almond-shaped eyes would be on mine in a deep and wordless gaze. So certain was I that this would occur, that when we left Ruth's, turning in different directions, I waved backward at him and hollered out a careless, "See ya!"

At supper that evening, my family was unusually lighthearted, giddy with freedom in my father's continued absence. Even without Patsy, who had a late shift at the hospital, we were talkative and playful, chasing the food around on our plates. Ricky tilted back in his chair, his arms swinging loose. At one point, as surrogate man of the house, he did embark on an ex-planation of how transistor radios were assembled, but then a cauliflower bounced into Billy's lap and everyone laughed. Barb and my mother bubbled excitedly about purses and shoes, and I was grinning, relaxed, knowing that as long as my father was gone, Langston was safe. It was July 3rd. In less than forty-eight hours, Langston would leave.

Then we heard our car rolling up the driveway.

We spent a slow moment listening, isolated from one anoth-er again, each in our own mental bell jar. We heard the engine turn off, the car door open and close, the trunk open and close, footsteps shuffling in gravel. Our back door wheezed open; a suitcase plunked onto the floor. Billy broke the silence: "Dad-dy's home!" and galloped to my father to hug his waist.

"Hey, buckaroo! *This* is a nice welcome." My father stood peering at us from across the living room. I left the table too, rushing my plate into the kitchen, clinging to my feelings of optimism. The Klan would not act tonight—it was too late to get everyone organized. They wouldn't act tomorrow—they wouldn't want to miss the town picnic in Triangle Park, the fireworks at the high school. They'd spend the Fourth lolling around with their families, and Langston would get away before they knew it. Right?

While my father grabbed a bite at the table, somber and silent, I crept upstairs and hid in my parents' closet. If my father were going to call Dr. Vaughan, he'd do it from his room. I pulled the door closed behind me and crawled over my father's shoes—rough tennis shoes and oily work shoes—brushing against the bottoms of his trousers. I accidentally kneeled on his shoehorn, carving a crescent into my knee. I wedged myself into the corner beside the stack of dusty hat boxes where my mother kept her sewing supplies—zippers, buttons, shoulder pads, scraps of cloth that might be useful someday. On my mother's side of the closet, I felt the swaying skirts of her house dresses, smelling of powder and sweat.

Suddenly my mother's voice was coming into the room, my father's in pursuit. I heard the suitcase heaved onto the bed. She'd be unpacking for him, sorting his laundry, putting away his shaving supplies, hanging up his ties and trousers and suit jacket. I pressed myself tighter into the corner. I heard her patter around the room, drawers open and shut. My father said, "It's a nice school. Money's not bad. They're anxious to get a science teacher in by September." His voice was tired, sheepish.

Hers was terse: "Private?"

"That's right. Chartered in '59 for the white families. Our kids could attend free of charge."

"Barb doesn't want to go anywhere. She's comin' up on her senior year."

"Barb makin' the family decisions now?"

"*Family* decisions?" My mother's voice rose with an aggressive breathiness I'd never heard before. "They're always just *your* decisions, Dick."

Silence followed. A drawer slammed shut.

My father's voice warbled: "Well, okay, Trudy. I'm not an unreasonable man. I'll take everyone's wishes into account."

"And Ricky," she said. "How can he come home from college to some strange house in a strange city? This is Ricky's home, he grew up here."

"Okay, okay."

"All of Billy's little friends are here. The only one who might benefit from a fresh start is Willa." More drawers opened. I heard the hamper slide across the floor and clothes plop in. My mother continued, almost belligerent: "You wanna know what I think?"

"Well, sure I do."

"I think you should take that job. You should go. The children and I will stay here."

"What?" He sounded genuinely confused.

"You go, we'll stay here."

"Well, how'd that work, Trudy?"

"You could rent a room down there. Plenty of places, I bet."

"A room?"

"You could come up sometimes, it's not that far. Come up for holidays."

"Holidays?"

The closet door opened and her hand reached in, dangling his neckties, looping them over a hook. She pushed the door not quite shut. "That's right," she said.

"I don't know about that, Trudy."

"Well, I don't know either, Dick."

"What don't you know?"

"I don't know."

"You don't know what you don't know?"

"Dick. I'm not happy."

"*Happy*? You're not *happy*? Christ, Trudy, who do you know that's *happy*? I'm not *happy*. You think life's about being *happy*? You been readin' articles in women's magazines? Nobody's *happy*, Trudy. Why aren't you happy?"

"I just, I'm just—"

"You're still mad about Doris Wallace, that's what you are. You're holdin' a grudge. I told you I wasn't gonna see her anymore and I didn't. She's gone. She's gone off somewhere, I don't even know where—all the furniture's gone from her house. I told you it's over. You holdin' a grudge? That what you're doin'?"

"No," she murmured, her voice straining. "It's..." Silence.
"It's what? What?"

"It's like the grudge is holdin' on to me."

I could hear him breathing, huffing, working his voice up to
a reply: "Well, well, *that's* not forgiveness, is it? You're supposed
to *forgive.*"

"Maybe I can't. Maybe I'm not capable of it. Maybe I'm not
such a good Christian woman after all."

I heard the suitcase whoosh shut, the latches click. My father's voice returned, meek again. "Honey, I don't want to live
anywhere without you and the kids. You're my wife. You and
the kids are my family. What's a family man gonna do without
his family?"

"I don't know. All I know is, I don't want to move down
there with you."

"Well, can we talk it over a little more? Maybe if you went
down there with me, next weekend—"

"Dick." She let out a noisy breath. "I feel like—"

"Like what? What?"

"Like, I need some *reason* to stay with you."

"A reason? What kind of a reason? A *reason?*" Silence. "Trudy, honey, what can I do to make this right? Tell me, what can
I do?"

"You can carry your own suitcase back up to the attic."

"Sure, sure. I can do that. I can do that. Anything else?"

More silence oozed through the room. Then I heard her
leave, her footsteps sweeping fast across the floor. I heard the
bedroom door close and him flop onto the bed, his weight
screeching the bedsprings. I did not hear him pick up the phone.
I heard him huff again and mutter and cuss. Then, perforating
the air was the sound of him crying. It was not the grandiose
weeping I'd seen the night he confessed to my mother; these
sobs were simple, rhythmic, helpless, high-pitched, wounded,
exposed.

Abruptly, it stopped. Time flowed by. Through the crack
in the door, I could see evening shadows pooling on the bare

floor. I couldn't stay there much longer—at some point my mother would try to account for me. I crawled over the shoes and peeked out at my father's motionless form on the bed. He lay on his back, nose pointed skyward. A moment later his mouth dropped open into a snore. The closet door moaned as I pushed on it, but I knew he wouldn't wake—the driving, the talking, all the emotion would have exhausted him. I slipped out.

I admit, I felt a little sorry for him. No one intends to destroy their own lives. What seems like a choice to people on the outside usually doesn't feel that way on the inside. You don't sit down one day and decide to be racked with insecurity, fear, paranoia, hatred, and bigotry. So the actions born of such feelings also don't feel like choices: they feel like reasonable responses, calls to rise up and bravely face challenges, displays of righteous convictions. The key to being a good person in the world, I thought, was being able to listen—to listen to other people's perspectives, and especially to your own inner self that urges you to pause, calm down, and reconsider; to change direction; to change yourself.

Of course, my father had never been a good listener.

# 15

My sleep that night roiled with nightmares. I dreamed I was alone in a field of wide black slippery rocks. The heat was suffocating, and I was struggling toward an old willow swaying in the distance, longing for its shade. But my feet felt glued to the ground, and when I looked down I saw the rocks were not rocks but human faces, twisted into screams—I was stepping on faces. I kept walking, dragging my feet across suffering faces, because I wanted the comfort of the tree. I could get there, I thought, if I did not look down, if I did not see what I was treading on, but I kept looking down, and when I looked up again the willow was farther away, at the top of a steep hill. Then I was scrambling up the side of the embankment, my hands gripping muddy roots, slipping. I looked down and saw I was at the top of our narrow ditch. The sun dropped from the sky, and the ditch widened into a grave. Barb was somewhere above me, calling down, "Willa, Willa!" Then, "Wake up!" Her hand shook me awake.

All morning the memory of the nightmare had me rattled and hyperalert. I'd risen early to keep an eye on my father. From behind my bedroom door, I saw him go into the bathroom, then heard the buzz of his electric razor—a much-admired Christmas gift from my mother, purchased excitedly before the facts of Doris Wallace emerged. I watched him return to his bedroom. I heard the closet door opening, a belt buckle rattling. Then he thumped down the stairs, with me in soundless pursuit.

He did not have his usual eggs and bacon for breakfast. My mother declared she was too busy preparing our Fourth of July picnic and handed him an orange plastic bowl of Cap'n Crunch. He sat wordless, chomping and slurping up milk. I hung around in the doorway. As long as he was nowhere near a phone, we were safe.

After breakfast he trailed after Billy to watch *The Jetsons* and *Casper*. Then Billy took him outside to show him his bucket of tadpoles. I spied through the window. My father stood morose and sweating next to his son, face hanging toward the mouth of the green plastic bucket. The phone rang, but it was only Florence Whipple, asking when I'd be at Triangle Park for the picnic, fretting over whether she'd be expected to play volleyball. She didn't deserve my impatient response, but I had more important things to do than assuage Florence's fear of sports. At noon my father and Billy ambled back inside, looking for lunch. My mother, absorbed in dicing potatoes and boiling eggs, had no time to stop and get it for them.

"Here's Willa," she said. "Maybe she'll make some cheese sandwiches." It was clear she did not really care about my father's lunch. Dejected again, he sat. I shrugged and pulled the Velveeta from the refrigerator. Barb traipsed in, rosy with holiday happiness, and my mother handed her stalks of celery and an onion to chop for the potato salad.

My father pricked up. "Celery and onion in the potato salad?"

My mother replied, "I'm makin' Marge Beale's recipe this time."

Marge Beale was Patsy's mother. My father referred to her as Large Marge, because of her weight, and often ridiculed her cooking—her soupy casseroles and charred pies at church potlucks—pointing out the irony of such a bad cook being so fat. He especially disliked her potato salad, which was full of celery chunks and onion bits and other impurities.

Incredulously he asked, "Why are you doin' that? The regular kind's better."

"Barb likes Marge's better," my mother replied.

"No, she doesn't."

Barb said, "Yeah, I do."

"Why would you like it better when it's not as good?"

My mother interjected, "It's a matter of *opinion*, Dick."

"What?" The concept seemed to baffle him. "Well, *I* like the regular kind better and so does Ricky and so does Billy."

My mother turned toward Billy. "Is that so?" Billy shrugged. Then she turned to me. "Which do you prefer?"

My father's eyes squinted into angry pinpricks. "What's goin' on here? The *ladies* in charge now?"

I said, "I like Mrs. Beale's," though I didn't really, and Barb kept chopping.

My mother dumped potato pieces into the boiling stew pot, and my father bellowed, "What about the fried chicken? You doin' that Marge's awful way too?"

My mother gave him no reply, none at all—no words or reassuring clicks or hums. This was notable. It was as though he'd said nothing, as though he wasn't even there. This was a form of neglect traditionally aimed at coloreds and unattractive women. I handed him a cheese sandwich on a pink plastic plate. He grabbed it off and took big dramatic bites. No one spoke. I listened to the thump of Billy's foot against the table leg and the thwack of Barb's knife on the cutting board. My mother cracked a hard-boiled egg on the countertop and began the arduous process of peeling it. I glanced at my father. He was finishing his sandwich, dabbing a napkin against the reddening skin of his face. The neglect of him stretched over several more minutes, no one attending to his possible needs or wishes. Then, fiercely, he said, "I have an important phone call to make," and marched upstairs.

I waited as long as I dared, then sprinted up after him. By the time I'd pressed myself against the wall outside his bedroom door, he was already on the phone: "Timin's perfect. Think about it—the *symbolism*. Fourth of July, the birth of the nation—*our* nation. It's still our nation and we're takin' it back."

I wondered, If it's still ours, why would we need to take it back?

His voice sped up. "People have to know who's in charge, that's the problem. Everyone tryin' to come up out of their place, gettin' the idea they can tell *us* what to do. That is *not* how this works. It's *us* tellin' them, not *them* telling us! Nation's goin' to ruin. Everyone talkin' about their *rights*." There was a pause, then: "Okay...good...yeah...I will." Pause. "See you then."

The phone smashed back onto its base and I darted into the bathroom. My father's footsteps stomped past, down the stairs and out the door. From my bedroom window I saw his car race backward out of the driveway—I thought for sure this time he'd end up in the ditch.

"Willa!" my mother called.

"Just a minute!" From my parents' room I dialed Ruth's number. We had to go—we had to go now. Ruth's phone rang, rang, rang. "Answer the phone!" I yelled into the phone. It rang some more. I hung up. But what if I'd dialed the wrong number? I dialed again. Four, five, six, seven…I hung up.

But maybe they were all just outside in the backyard and they'd been rushing to the phone right as I hung up. I called again. Seven, eight…by the tenth ring I realized I'd only wasted more time. I barreled downstairs. Thankfully, Patsy had arrived to take over my domestic duties. She stood smiling in the kitchen, wiping off our plastic picnic plates, arranging items in the basket.

"Mama!" I said. "I just remembered I have to go over to the Swansons'. I just remembered, okay?"

Patsy looked up. "Oh, Willa." Her hands paused, the damp towel stopped on the rim of a plate. "Ruth Swanson's back in the hospital."

"What? What?"

"Reverend Swanson brought her in last night. Doctor said she'd be all right, no need to worry. She just needs a few days of rest."

I felt my jaw drop. "A few days of rest?" I said, then shrieked, "*A few days of rest?*" They stared at me. "Is that all these doctors know how to say? Is that all they learn in medical school? *I* can say that 'she needs a few days of rest'—see! I can say that and I haven't even started high school yet!" One last time I screeched, "Rest!"

My mother stepped toward me to pat my shoulder. "She'll be okay, honey, everything'll be okay. You wanna go over to the hospital, find the reverend? Get him to fill you in? Everything'll be okay, honey." She patted, patted, patted. "You don't need to worry—"

I screamed, "Maybe I *want* to worry! Maybe everything will *not* be okay!" I gulped hard and heard my voice sounding tearful: "I don't have a bike."

In alarm, Barb said, "You can borrow mine."

"Go on," my mother said. "I'll wait here for you. You and I can meet everyone at Triangle Park later." She smiled, lips together, the edges of her mouth sinking into sallow folds.

So I hauled Barb's bike out of the garage. The bike was cumbersome and pink and didn't suit me at all—the seat was too high, the tire pressure low—but I climbed on and plowed up the driveway. I rode to the end of the block and turned south. But my anxieties grew noisy in my head: What was the use of going to the hospital? She couldn't leave to drive us to the bus depot. They wouldn't even let me in to her—I wasn't old enough. What were we going to do? Why didn't we have a back-up plan? The bus to DC left Emporia at 3:15 daily. What time was it now? It must have been nearly one o'clock. The drive to Emporia took half an hour at least—time was running out! But how would we get there? Worries flopped around like caught fish in my head. We'd have to risk taking his Hudson. I pictured Langston and me together, fleeing down the two-lane highway. I'd have to figure out how to drive it back—I could do that.

It did not occur to me that Reverend Swanson would have driven us to Emporia. Why not? Even now, I can't say. So many options hadn't occurred to me that day. Langston and I together loomed so large in my brain, we crowded out the image of anyone else. I could have taken Patsy into my confidence; she would have helped. I could have simply phoned Langston. But my mind was full of scenes of me rescuing him. I was a muddy mix of desire, guilt, hormones, shame, and self-aggrandizement—I'd put Langston in grave danger, but now I would rescue him! All in one afternoon I could atone and play savior and thrill at riding with him!

I've often imagined ways in which the day could have ended differently. I remind myself I was just a kid, and kids aren't able to see all the options: people can only choose from the choices they think they have. Or am I letting myself off too easy? Maybe there is no redemption in the end, only the memories of mistakes lodged like shrapnel in the chest.

I reached Main Street, and instead of turning east toward the hospital, I turned west, toward the colored part of town.

I rode to where the low brick ranch houses of white people gave way to rows of colored homes, places stuck together, sharing walls, their exteriors patched with discarded sign boards and plywood, a hodgepodge of color and texture. One place was patched with a piece of a Coca-Cola billboard, the worn red script still visible. I turned north, across Turkey Egg Creek, to where the colored homes were a little nicer—freestanding, built of clapboard that had been painted at some point, each with its own little yard and concrete step and porch. This was where the colored teachers and government office workers and the dentist lived. I pumped down the road. People were out on their porches seeking breezes, chatting with neighbors. Their conversations paused for a surprised moment as a white girl on a pink bike rode brazenly through their neighborhood, as though she knew where she was going. Langston's house was on a corner, near where the fields opened up. I knew because once I'd been in the car when Ruth drove him home.

It was a square house, once yellow, now a faded wheat. I dumped Barb's bike onto the front lawn and ran to the front door, which stood open. I peered through the screen into the shady interior and hesitated. From the back of the house his voice resounded, laughing, and another voice responded. I banged on the loose wood frame and the voices stopped.

I yelled in, "Langston?"

His silhouette appeared in a doorway across the main room, joined immediately, of course, by Daisy. Daisy was *tres chic* today in a sleeveless canary top and skinny, gray-checked pants.

How did someone of such tiny stature manage to fill the entire room? Suddenly I felt self-conscious standing on his porch. I pulled open the screen door, stepped in, and looked around. The balding couch, the sagging chairs, the lamps and photos in frames were all surprisingly like ours.

Langston spoke: "Willa? What you doin' here?"

I wanted to talk to him alone. That's how I'd imagined it, and there was so much to say. But Daisy, eyeballing me, was hardly leaving.

"We have to go *now*, but Ruth's in the hospital—"

"What?" he said. "She okay?"

"Yeah, yeah, she just needs to *rest*." I felt myself getting aggravated all over again. "But we gotta go *now*."

"*Go?*" he echoed, as though he had no idea what I was saying.

"To the bus depot, to Emporia—"

Daisy said to Langston, "She know somethin'," then accusingly to me, "What do you know?"

"I know a *lot* of things, Daisy," I couldn't help but say. "I know the Klan's meetin' right now and we gotta go!"

"I can't," Langston said.

"Why not?" I yelled.

"I...I..." He searched the room for the answer. "My parents. They in Suffolk with Sammy, at my uncle's."

Daisy laid a petite glossy hand on his forearm. "Langston, you heard what she said."

"But," he said, with nothing to follow.

"It's time," she whispered, and they wrapped their arms around each other, clung to each other, grasped at each other's arms and faces. Good grief.

"There's no time for this!" I yelled.

They released each other and sprang into action, as though they'd been having drills. Daisy ran to a drawer and pulled out the envelope of money. Langston pulled out a twenty and two fives and folded them into his wallet, then he scampered to the back of the house and returned with a suitcase, grabbed his keys from a table.

I said, "We ready?"

Daisy stiffened. "*We?*"

Langston's eyes jumped from Daisy to me.

"I'm comin' with you," I said, more of an announcement than a statement.

Daisy's reply was immediate. "Oh no, you are not."

I turned to Langston. "Please let me come. Please. I can keep a watch out behind the car. *Please,* let me do this." I was desperate, determined to assert my helpfulness whether it was wanted or not, to insert myself into a story that was his and Daisy's, which did not include me.

Daisy said, "May I remind you, Willa, *you* got Langston pulled over and beat up. Because *you* were in the car with him."

"I know," I cried. "But that was different. That was…" I wasn't sure what I would say next. "After dark, and…" I did not say *it looked romantic.* But this understanding hung in the air, weighty in the pouch of silence between us, making us all shift and break eye contact.

Daisy said to Langston, "I see no reason for this girl to come along. I can watch out the back for cars."

"But I know everyone's car! I can spot 'em a mile away!"

"Langston." Daisy's chin lowered along with her voice. "This girl only trying to ease her conscience."

Langston nodded. "Yeah, yeah." He turned to me. "Willa—"

"No, please—" And all at once, I realized it: "Langston, if the Klan catches you and Daisy, my father will be with them. I'd be a witness. I'd tell my mother, and she'd be shocked—she really, really doesn't understand. She'd be upset, and he doesn't want to lose her. Please, let me do this."

He and Daisy shared a long glance. She said to him, "Just so you know, I am *not* happy with any of this." Then she stormed around the room, snatching up snacks, grabbing her purse, shoving her tiny feet into tiny sandals. "Okay, let's go."

Daisy got to sit beside Langston, naturally. I climbed in back. Langston swung the Hudson around and paused in front of his house for a long last look, then accelerated toward Main Street.

When we turned onto Route 58, Langston said, "Okay, Willa, keep an eye out."

I turned and watched behind us, the road scrolling away, the sun shedding heat that glittered on the asphalt. I watched the fields, too, scrubby with patches of brown-yellow and yellow-green. The road was empty; still, we were silent, heaving with dread at what could happen. We drove for a mile, two miles, three. I was scared to take my eyes off the road, thinking in that instant something sinister could appear. We passed the Belco Motor Court with its orange sign: *Air conditioning!* Langston's voice rose, sonorous above the rumble and squeal of the engine: "When you take the car back," he said to Daisy, slow and sad, "will you wait for my parents, tell them what happened?"

"Of course."

"Tell them I'm sorry I didn't get a chance to say goodbye."

"Sure."

"Tell them I'll write soon as I get there."

"Okay."

"Tell them I love them. Will you do that?"

"I will, I will."

I tried to imagine sending such a message to my parents. Their response was easy to predict: my mother's face startled; my father's baffled. I'd certainly encountered families happier than my own: Becky Campbell and her parents spoke to each other in calm, purring voices. Once I'd met Joe Pedicini's dad, whose jovial face was lined from so much smiling and laughing. Other families, like Patsy's, were matter-of-fact but untroubled, free of that dragging sense of private frustration and hidden aggression. I imagined Langston's family around their dinner table, the father listening to the mother, the parents listening to the kids, no one in a perpetual state of correcting each other's behavior and ideas. I glanced at the side of Langston's face, at the steep line of his jaw, casting a thin triangle of shadow on his neck. I let myself imagine touching his cheek—I was close enough. Instead, I slumped against the seat, watched a turquoise Buick pass us from the opposite direction, and turned to resume my surveillance of the road behind us.

The turquoise Buick began to slow. It slowed to nearly a stop, then swung onto a dirt road through a field. I tensed, but it was gone. Was it gone? I thought, it's gone. A moment later, it reappeared, turning back onto the road and coming up behind us, picking up speed.

"Langston," I said. I didn't recognize this car.

Daisy turned to look over her shoulder and together we saw the car closing the gap between us. "Go faster," she whispered.

His eyes flicked in the rearview mirror. "I'm at the limit. Don't need the police on us too."

"I don't know the car," I said, but as it approached, I could make out two white men in the front seat. "I don't know them!"

The Buick came closer, closer. Daisy said, "Langston."

"We almost to Emporia."

I could see the driver clearly now, a young auburn-haired man, a stranger. I began to tremble. Undoubtedly my father and his friends had recruited men from surrounding towns, including Emporia—there was such fury over the Civil Rights bill. My father knew Langston's car: *all over creation in that damn Hudson.* In the passenger seat sat an older man, maybe the driver's father, and he was mountainous—broad and tall, filling up the entire space, his face puckered into a grimace. The driver looked angry, too, his eyes piercing the back of our car. The closer they got, the faster they went, flying up on our rear.

"Langston!" I screamed, and the car swerved up alongside us. Then it passed us, and at a safe distance merged back into our lane. We all saw the license plate at the same time: Connecticut. I belted out, "It's tourists! Who don't know where they're going!" We let out noisy breaths and bursts of laughter, all a bit too dramatic to be genuine.

But soon we reached the outskirts of Emporia. It was nearly three o'clock. We had fifteen minutes. "You know where the bus depot is, right?" Daisy asked.

"Yep."

"You think we better hurry?"

"Slow and steady," he said.

We rode in on East Atlantic, toward the center of town. Ahead on the horizon was a massive building, ornate in white and black, its façade a sweep of rounded archways. Pedestals rose into onion domes on either end. "H.T. Klugel" was stamped in stone across the top.

"What is that?" I asked.

Langston pitched forward to get a better look. "That the old sheet-metal factory."

"We're not *sightseeing*, Willa," Daisy intervened. "You watchin' out behind us?"

I turned again, and this is how I would always remember that drive through Emporia: buildings and trees and empty fields streaming away from me, me seeing everything five seconds after Langston and Daisy did.

The town was a larger version of Kingsfield, with more stores and diners, more intersections. On Main Street we were caught in a snarl of traffic and pedestrians—Emporians with picnic baskets. Stopped at a crosswalk, we were highly visible, and a few people glanced into the car, but then they went on their way. At one point the sheriff's car rolled by, but the man behind the wheel was focused on the crowd gathering in the park and took no note of us.

"It's 3:10!" I wheezed.

"Almost there," Langston said. We turned left onto Brunswick, and in the distance I spotted the outline of the Greyhound dog racing in the sky.

The Emporia bus depot consisted of an extended triangular roof attached to the front of a tiny diner and overhanging a parking lot. Langston pulled up behind the diner. The bus marked "Washington" was already idling in one of the diagonal slips. We sprinted toward the building, but at the front door saw a sign, "Whites Only"—the facility was not spacious enough for a colored waiting area too. But what were we supposed to do? If coloreds weren't allowed inside the waiting area, how were we supposed to walk through it to get a bus ticket? Here was the kind of dilemma I'd never had to face before, which Langston must have encountered regularly. And did the Civil Rights Act mean coloreds could go in now? Were Black people supposed to go inside and insist on their rights? Surely that wouldn't go over well. I paused. A few feet from the door was a wooden bench marked "Coloreds." Though outside, it was under the roof, protected from rain, which would have been deemed plenty good enough for the coloreds.

Langston flung open the door and walked in. Daisy ran alongside him; I trailed behind. Inside were a few metal tables and a long counter where a lady sold bus tickets and gum. A man sat at one of the tables, a newspaper unfurled before him, a cigarette between his lips. He was square-jawed, like the Parkers—a Parker uncle, maybe, an older cousin. As we passed, his eyes flicked up.

The woman at the counter was middle-aged with a puff of hair dyed the color of raspberries, her face freckled and blank. Langston said, "One-way ticket for Washington, DC, please, ma'am," and pulled out his new leathery wallet, from which he extracted a twenty-dollar bill. The woman stared and said nothing. She had no eyebrows, just two dramatic penciled arches over the stark ledge of her brow. Moments ticked by. What was she thinking? That this colored boy shouldn't have a twenty-dollar bill? She turned her sunken eyes on me, then slowly took his twenty, rang up the register, withdrew the change, and slowly, slowly, with the very tips of her fingers, slid it halfway across the counter. Lethargically she pulled out a flimsy piece of paper, carbons and copies attached. She flapped it onto the counter and began to write out the ticket laboriously, with unnecessary pauses, as though the bus were not already in its spot and leaving in two minutes. I glanced behind me. A brisk driver was climbing the steps of the bus and settling behind the wheel. I blurted, "The bus is about to leave!"

This made the woman stop altogether and lock a long cold

stare on me. "That's a good thing," she spoke for the first time. "Y'all don't need to wait." Finally she finished the ticket. Langston gathered it up with his change and nodded, "Thank you, ma'am," and we all ran for the door.

The bus was brand new, sleek and silver. Langston heaved his suitcase into the open side compartment and turned to Daisy. The romantic goodbye scene I'd been imagining, of course, belonged to Daisy—the warm rocking embrace, the promise of daily letters, the fast tender brush of lips. I was only part of the backdrop. Did he care for me too?

The driver called down "You comin' on the bus, boy?" and Langston released Daisy and hopped onto the first step.

Then he turned toward me. "You take care of yourself, Willa, you take good care," his face radiant with affection.

"Hey, Langston!" I said. "The bus looks like a rocket ship!"

His grin blossomed into a smile. Gorgeous. I watched him hand his ticket to the driver, and I watched his form move through the bus toward the back. The driver thundered down the steps again to close the luggage compartment, peered at me, and jogged back to his seat. Then the doors wheezed shut, the bus rolled backward, squealed to a stop, rolled forward, and accelerated. Langston's face remained in the rear window, beaming and nervous, excited and sad. He waved; we waved. The bus swung onto the street and as his face in the window grew smaller, his wave slowed, but Daisy and I, side by side, kept on, our hands in a frenzy until the bus turned a corner and vanished. Simultaneously, our hands dropped.

Daisy swiveled toward me and pinned me with a dead-eyed glare. "Now, I'm gonna talk, and you gonna listen. You got that?" I nodded. "Good. Okay. I don't ever want to see your pasty white face again. *Ever.* Got that? You are *not* invited to Langston's house when he home on vacation, you are *not* comin' over to hang around our neighborhood, and if I hear you been writin' to him, I will come over to your house and tell your mama. You understand me?"

I nodded.

She stomped toward the Hudson and climbed into the driver's seat. Defeated, I followed. But as I reached for the handle of the passenger door, she lunged across the bench seat and locked it. Then she cranked up the window. "Daisy!" I yelled. She stretched over the seat back to lock the rear doors too, and she started the engine. "Hey!" I kept pulling on the door handle. "Hey, come on! Let me in!" I heard the gear clunk into reverse, and the car backed up. "Daisy!" I trotted alongside it, banging on the passenger window. Her face rotated toward me, pinched with contempt. When she stopped at the parking lot exit, I ran around the front of the car and stood at her open window. "Daisy! Come on! Let me in."

"Goodbye, Willa."

"What? How am I supposed to get home?"

"Girl smart as you? I know you'll find a way."

"This isn't funny!"

"Am I laughing?" She shifted into drive.

"You *can't* leave me here—it's twenty miles back to Kingsfield! You *can't* just drive away!"

Probably there was a better way to phrase this. It sounded like a command, or a dare. She smiled. "I *can't?*" she sang out. Then she hit the gas, screeched across the parking lot, and roared away down the street.

I screamed. Then I screamed again. I stood like a fool in the middle of the parking lot, waiting for her to come back. She didn't. I stood listening to chirping birds, a distant whirring, the shrieks of children playing in the Emporia park.

Finally, I slogged toward the bus station and sat down on the coloreds' bench. It was mid afternoon. How long would it take to walk twenty miles? If I walked three miles an hour, it would take...*six and a half hours?* It would be dark before I got back; the highway was winding and narrow and lined with steep ditches. I'd fall in and break an ankle and be stuck there all night, and my mother would kill me.

Then I remembered my promise to her: if I ever got stranded again, I would call her. I did not want to call her. I should start walking and not lose another minute. I could run part of the way. Maybe it would only take five hours. I heard my breathing, heavy and irritated. An increasingly loud voice in my brain kept reminding me of my promise. I had to call her. I'd already spent my emergency dime; I had no money. Wouldn't the call be long-distance? I rose and crept back into the bus station. The man at the table was lighting another cigarette, his languid hand turning a newspaper page; the woman at the counter was inspecting her fingernails.

"Excuse me," I said in a humble voice. Her eyeballs rolled up. "May I borrow your phone?"

"Pay phone right behind you," she said and resumed the examination of her nails. The cherry-colored polish, I saw, was chipped along the edges.

I said, "I don't have a dime."

"Well, that ain't my problem."

"I know, I know, but I have to call my mama. I don't have a way to get home."

"Didn't you come in with them coons?"

I inhaled, not wanting to cry in front of this woman. "Yeah."

"Well," she replied, as though this settled the matter.

"They left, so now I don't have a way to get home."

"I ain't preventin' you from gettin' home."

"I live in Kingsfield."

Her eyes bore into me. "That'd be a *long-distance* call. You think you gonna make a *long-distance call* on *my* phone?"

My head drooped. The floor was a sea of tiny white octagonal tiles, each outlined in dirt. A wave of sorrow rose up through my chest and throat and swamped my brain, and I was about to burst into tears when behind me in a thick drawl a man said, "I got some change."

It was the man from the table. "Here you go." He held up a ruddy hand and poured three quarters and a nickel into my palm. "I do believe Kingsfield's long distance."

The woman scowled and he said, "Little girl's stranded, Eleanor. It'd be mighty un-Christian not to lend a hand."

"Thank you," I squeaked.

"Pay phone's right over here." He shepherded me toward it.
"Thank you."

He returned to his table and his newspaper and cigarettes,
and I rolled the first quarter into the slot. My mother answered
immediately. "It's getting so late! I was worried about you! How
is Mrs. Swanson?"

I had to tell her I was not at the Kingsfield Hospital. I had to
tell her I was at the bus depot in Emporia, and that I'd ridden
here in a car with Langston Jones and Daisy, that colored girl,
and that Daisy had driven off without me because she hated
me. Throughout my soliloquy, my mother kept gasping, finally
landing on a hoarse, "Willa McCoy."

"I promised I'd call you, remember? If I ever got stranded
again? I promised and see? I'm keepin' my promise, Mama.
Mama?" Pause. "Remember?"

"Yes. Yes. You did good." But now she'd have to walk over
to Triangle Park and find Ricky to come fetch me. It might take
a while.

"I can wait," I said, as though doing her a favor.

"You wait right there. Don't go wanderin' off."

"Yes, ma'am. No, ma'am."

I returned the extra two quarters and the nickel to the man at
the table, who smiled and nodded but said nothing, and I went
outside to sit on the bench and wait.

By late afternoon, the air had compressed into an anvil. Flies
landed on my skin. There were no buses idling now, and few
cars swept by the station. I stared at things: a trash can, a red-
and-yellow Sky Bar wrapper on the ground beside it, a crumbling brick storefront across the street. Over my head was the
long, skinny sign with "B-U-S" written vertically down it; suspended above was the cut-out image of the lean dog stretched
and running at full speed. Mid-air, seemingly detached from
anything, the dog flew, graceful, powerful, unbound, released,
and I imagined Langston in that shiny bus, soaring down the
highway, toward a life free of Kingsfield, free of me.

# 16

By the time Ricky's car pulled up, the sky was the color of dirty dishwater, the Great Dismal Swamp hovering overhead. The car screeched to a halt, and Barb got out to stomp toward me. I was struck by how beautiful she looked that evening, like a blast of sunshine in her bright dress, skirt flouncing, the cobalt sash cinched around her slim waist. The elegant straps of her alabaster sandals drew attention to her shapely legs. She was not happy. The perfect flip of hair on her shoulders bounced with fury as she marched toward me.

"*Why* are you here?" she demanded to know, fists on hips.

"Didn't Mama tell you?"

"Yes, she most certainly did."

Silence. "Why are *you* here?"

"Ricky's so mad, Mama made me come along to keep him in line so now both our fun is completely and utterly ruined."

That's why Barb was there. Ricky couldn't be expected to manage his anger on his own; he needed a soothing female at his side to pat down his wrath. Barb did not seem up for that role just now.

I said, "I'm sorry." I was so tired of saying this.

"Well, come on so we can at least get back for the fireworks." She grabbed my forearm and hauled me to the car. I scrambled into the back seat and curled myself into a ball, out of sight of Ricky's hate-drenched stare in the rearview mirror. Barb was barely in the car with her door shut when the car jerked backward and tore out of the lot.

Ricky yelled, "*Damn* you, Willa!"

"Calm down," Barb sighed.

"Damn you!" he yelled at me again. "Do you need your head examined?"

"Ricky," Barb repeated. "Calm down."

He jabbed a finger at her: "*You* don't tell me what to do. I got no patience for *sisters* right now."

She spat back, "Hey, I wouldn't have to be here at all if you'd've kept a lid on that hot head of yours! You're a *hot head!*"

"Shut up, Barbara."

She did. We careened through Emporia, Ricky grunting and yanking the wheel to the left and the right, racing us back toward Route 58. A wooly blanket of clouds descended over the rooftops, making the twilight darker than it should have been. The humidity was stupefying. Ricky and Barb had their windows down but still it was boiling, so I opened mine a crack, which only reminded Ricky of my presence. "*Damn* you, Willa."

"Calm, down, Ricky," Barb droned.

"I said *shut up.*"

This time she yelled back. "No, sir! I will *not* shut up! I will *express* my opinions any time I like!"

I was impressed by this. I slid across the seat to be behind her silky head. Ricky was preoccupied turning onto Route 58, so Barb continued: "You embarrassed me in front of *Jim Darden!* You made a *scene!* Throwin' your cup and stompin' around like a two-year-old and kickin' the picnic basket—God, I was mortified—"

"Don't you scold me!"

"I got hardly any time left with Jim Darden before he goes to college and how am I spendin' it? Stuck in this car with you."

"Not *my* fault we're stuck in this car. Blame that little coon lover in the back seat. Little coon-lover *cunt.*" He clearly relished the feel of these words, the alliteration, the relief of spewing out his hate. "Runnin' around like some goddam…"

Barb didn't respond. Briefly I dreamed she would defend me in her newfound voice—she'd launch into a monologue about love transcending the man-made rules of society—but she didn't. Her newfound voice would only be for herself. She muttered, "Six more weeks till he goes."

In his girlie voice, Ricky mocked, "*Jim Darden, Jim Darden.*"

My head dropped back. Eighteen more miles of this.

"You could at least speed up," Barb said, "so we don't miss the fireworks."

Ricky gunned the engine. Trees and fields flew past. Inside the car, we all faded to outlines. I watched Ricky's shoulders settle, then grow twitchy again. He muttered, "Daddy says there's a black sheep in every family. We sure got ours. Little *coon*-lover *cunt*."

Barb said nothing. She rolled her head against the seat back and dangled her arm out the window and continued to say nothing. Ricky started stealing quick glances at her, pursing his lips. I knew what he was thinking: Why wasn't she agreeing with him? Why wasn't she acknowledging him and assuring him he was right? He drove faster, and after a moment hollered at her, "You think it's okay she goes runnin' after that colored boy?"

"I didn't say that."

"You defendin' her?"

"I'm not defendin' her."

"Then I'm right. Say I'm right."

"I'm not sayin' anything."

"Then you're defendin' her."

"I didn't say I was defendin' her."

My face began to burn. Why was no one in my family ever on my side? It didn't matter anymore, I told myself. I was capable of standing up for myself. I lunged forward and grabbed the seat back: "I did not do anything wrong! All I did was go to the bus depot to say goodbye to a good friend!"

"A *good friend!*" Ricky said.

"Yes," I proclaimed. "A good friend, who I care about, and respect, because, he's a good person, he's...he's a way better person than *you!*"

Ricky's hand flew across the seat back at me, but I ducked it. "Ha! You can't get me."

"Shut up, Willa," he said.

"You can't shut me up and you can't stop me from likin' who I like. That Negro is a *hundred* times better than you!"

Again the hand flew back at me, and I swerved out of its

path. Down behind the seat I went, then popped back up like a whack-a-mole. "Ha, ha! You can't get me! You know I'm right. That's why you hate him so much, because you know it, you know he's better than you, you *know* it."

Ricky snorted and sputtered. "No way any coon's better'n me."

"He is! He's *kind,* and he's *considerate.* When're you ever kind and considerate? And not only that..." Suddenly I realized this was true. "He is *way* smarter than you, *way* smarter—that colored boy is *hundred times smarter* than you—"

This time the hand shot back to grab me. It got ahold of my collar but I yanked away and dropped onto the floor. He had to turn his body and stretch over the seat to find where I'd gone.

"C'mon, Ricky," Barb huffed but he kept swatting at me, his hand diving deeper and deeper down behind the seat to find me. I flattened myself onto the floorboards and the hand grew frantic, so strong was its need to slap me down. One more lunge and Ricky had me by the hair, snatching a handful and yanking me up by it. I smacked his hand but he wouldn't let go, and I screamed as loud as I could.

That's when we swerved. The car lurched to the right, bumped over a pile of dead branches or grasses or something that crackled. I saw both of Ricky's hands now back on the steering wheel, gripped tight, but the wheel was turning his hands—he had no control. I heard a sharp bang: the front tire dropping off the road, catching like a stubbed toe in the deep, narrow ditch. My stomach hurtled into my throat, and the car took flight.

Barb was shrieking, a cry of pure terror that crashed over me in waves. On and on it went, though it must have lasted only a few seconds. Time slowed to a near stop. I felt myself lift off the seat. I watched my arm suspend itself mid-air, my hand curve into a fist. Time was sinking through a sea of molasses. We were turning, tipping, and then I heard nothing—no sound at all, anywhere, the whole world packed tight in silence. *The world is gone,* I thought, and we hit the ground.

❧

A moment later, I was walking through the bright, vacant, high-ceilinged rooms of a grand house. I was in a group of people on a tour, led by Langston. His voice was soft and joyous, professorial. *In this room,* he was saying, opening one door after another, each space empty but aglow with tall blocks of sunshine. *In this room,* he kept saying. *In this room* what? I couldn't make it out. Each room held some possibility, some future, but untethered—it was all anticipation with nothing real to grasp. I couldn't concentrate. What was he saying? It was sound with no content, yet I was happy by his side, our hands brushing against each other. I turned to smile at the people behind me. My mother was there, and Patsy, and Joe Pedicini, Sue, Florence, and even Becky—everyone's face glossy and serene. From the corner of my eye I saw Billy jumping on a dark velvet sofa and realized the rooms were not vacant; they were full of furniture, straight-backed chairs and austere sideboards, antique, regal. I understood: This was not a place where I could live. This was a place for the privileged, for the favored few that stood center stage. I would never belong here. I sat, exhausted, on a wing chair upholstered in gold brocade. My head sank heavily into the cushion, and I grew aware of an ache. Somewhere in the house a kettle was whistling, and I asked Langston to please make it stop, it was hurting my head. The room grew dark, and I was alone.

The kettle whistled, stopped, then whistled again, the sound jolting, perforated. The room grew colder, a chill hovering, but I was not in a room, after all—I was outside, lying on a hard, smooth ground growing damp, and the keening was not a kettle but an owl, hooting high-pitched and sorrowful. Then it stopped. The right side of my skull throbbed, and now I felt a pain spreading in my leg. Ricky, I thought. Ricky must have smacked me with a board. Where did he get a board? "Ricky," I tried to say out loud. "That really hurt."

I wanted to get up off the ground but I couldn't make my limbs work. "Langston?" I called out, and he appeared in a crouch beside me, "It's okay, Willa. The tea's ready. I'll go get you some." In the distance was the sound of the kettle screeching. I saw him walk away, up a steep incline, and I raised my arm toward him and my hand hit something—a ceiling, a soft ceiling—I was inside again. But it wasn't a kettle. It wasn't an owl. It was some sort of creature that hooted and barked and screeched and concluded with a low raspy growl. Where was I? The pain in my head and my leg grew so intense I began to choke out little sobs; I tried to shift my weight off the hurt limb, but when I did, a hundred tiny knives punctured my shoulder.

I opened my eyes and saw I was in a narrow tunnel. The floor was metal and cold and the ceiling, only a foot above me, was padded. I tried to make sense of what I was seeing—lines, brown stripes, stitching, vinyl: the ceiling was a seat, a car seat. At the end of it was a pale opening, and I thought I should crawl toward it, but whenever I moved the knives sliced me—hundreds of them, thousands. I lay still. I was lying on knives. Why was I lying on knives? No, not knives—broken glass. Understanding dawned like a slow, watery, pink sunrise: I was lying on shards of glass. The rear window, shattered.

"Barb," my voice said, tentative. Louder: "Barbie?"

Carefully I stretched to look into what must have been the front seat. The top of Ricky's head was just touching the upside-down ceiling, his arm extended across it, his hand loose.

"Ricky?" I whispered, but he'd been knocked unconscious too. Louder: "Ricky? Ricky. Wake up."

I kept my head as still as I could and searched with my eyes for Barb. She was nowhere I could see, nowhere at all—she was somewhere outside. It was her voice I kept hearing, not a kettle or an owl: it was Barb, crying out.

As loud as I could, I yelled, "Barb!" A whimper responded, and my brain jolted into a stretch of clarity: she'd been thrown from the car.

"Ricky!" I said. "*Wake up.* You need to go for help." How far were we from Emporia? Ten miles? Courtland would be closer. The puddle spreading beneath my leg, I realized, was blood.

My voice gained strength: "Ricky!" I saw his hand twitch.

"I know you can hear me. Come on. I know you're still mad at me but I can't move and you need to go for help." He wouldn't respond. "I'm not kiddin' around, Ricky." Still nothing. As loud as I could I said, "Come on! I'm sorry I spoiled your Fourth of July!" I watched the back of his head, his hair in shiny pale brown tufts, shifting. Still he didn't speak. I shrieked. Rivulets of blood were snaking down my leg. "Ricky!"

Once, when I was four or five years old, I tagged along with Ricky and Barb and Patsy to scavenge for empty bottles on the construction site of the new high school, and I fell on a coil of wire and split open my shin. It was Ricky, skinny and gawky, who carried me all the way home. So little in his arms, I kept my tears back but gulped as I hugged his neck: "Ricky? Am I going to die?" "Naw," he whispered fast. "Naw, you're fine, you're fine," and then I was.

"Ricky," I tried once more. An airless silence settled over the car. I felt so cold. Why was I cold? It was July. I had a sense of dipping back into a dream, a room, a chair. I closed my eyes and felt the air in my lungs push at my chest. Was this what dying felt like? Ricky's voice said, "You're fine, you're fine," but it came from inside my head—outside there was nothing. I felt my body relax. Did I need to stay awake? I opened my eyes again and now I was in Ruth's house, sprawled on the cool tile floor with Julie and Annette. Julie was showing me a puzzle piece, crazily cut with knobs and wavy edges, a sunny shade of blue. Ruth was laughing, "You've got a piece of the sky!"

"Ruth," I said, but I woke again into the same nightmare, trapped in a car, on a pile of broken glass, Ricky hanging up-side-down. I looked again at his head barely touching the car ceiling. What was holding him in place? From faraway came a squealing. "Barb?" I called out. The squealing persisted, and gradually I realized it wasn't a human sound; it was continuous, rising—a siren! But it seemed fixed, trapped in the distance. It ended with a pop, and another squeal commenced, rising and falling and popping, followed by a soft explosion. Fireworks. Courtland had begun its show.

How long would it take for someone to find us? How long before someone drove by and happened to spot our wrecked car? How long until they reached the next town and located a phone and called the police? How long before my mother, standing in the dark in a crowded Triangle Park, realized we still weren't there? Would Jim Darden be missing Barb? Would Ricky's friends wonder where he was? It could be hours.

I drifted off again, this time with the sensation of floating, of rising and falling on sleepy waves, wafting out to sea. *You're fine*, Ricky's voice said; *you're fine*, said a voice in my head, and I knew I would be, as long as I kept drifting away, away. As long as I didn't come back.

Obviously, I came back. I woke in a harsh light, my eyes blinking achingly open. The sun screeched through the window, irradiating an unfamiliar room, everything in it a flat, sanitized white—curtains, walls, shelf, nightstand, metal bed frame. I rolled my head. Ruth was there, wrapped in a lavender robe, her head tilted back and eyes closed, slumped in a green-and-orange plaid chair. The chair was the only thing in the room with color. I imagined the hospital staff bringing it in to add a homey touch, realizing all this relentless white was unnatural.

"Ruth," I croaked. Her eyes sprang open.

"Hey!" she whispered and leaned toward me. "Hey!" Her hospital gown showed in the V between the lapels of her robe: she was still a patient here.

I asked, "How are you?" and a peculiar laugh escaped her.

"I'm fine, sweetie. I'm *fine*." Her hand squeezed mine. "Doing better than you, I'm afraid."

Was this another dream? The pressure of her touch felt real.

"*You*," she said with a forced cheer, "have suffered a concussion, *and* a badly broken leg, *and* a whole bunch of cuts and bruises. But you'll be fine, they said. Full recovery." Her smile stretched too wide, revealing clenched teeth. This was not Ruth's smile. This was a phony church lady smile.

In a cracking voice I asked, "Where's my mama?" But of

course, I knew: she'd be at Barb's bedside. My father would be at Ricky's. "See? I told you so. I'm an extra."

"Shhhhh, shhhhh." She looked genuinely confused, leaning over me, her powder-soft hand stroking the hair from my forehead. Her eyes were swollen, red. "I told them I'd stay with you," she whispered. "Your parents love you very much. I told them I'd stay in case you woke up. Your mama wanted to stay but they had to go."

"Go *where*?"

"Shhhh, shhhh, they had to go, they had to go, to the funeral home."

"Who died?" My mind projected images of grandmas and great-grandmas—all the ancient Mrs. Joneses and Beales.

Ruth kept stroking my hair, down its length to my shoulder, her touch speeding up and growing heavy. "Sweetheart," she said. "Ricky, Ricky was killed instantly."

"What?" Then, "No," simply to correct her. "He was knocked out. He was right there. He went to Courtland to get the police, that's how they found us."

Her snow-white face darkened. "When they pulled you from the wreck, you were unconscious—"

"I know, that's what I'm sayin'. Ricky was knocked unconscious, so he must be here somewhere."

"I'm sorry, Willa, I'm so sorry. Ricky's gone."

"No, that's not true, that's a mistake—" I kept repeating this, my brain insisting. But also in my mind was the image of him hanging upside-down, suspended. What was holding him in place? The steering wheel column, I thought, embedded in his chest. "I was just talking to him," I said again, because it couldn't be true, he couldn't be gone—how could he be *gone*? I let loose a wail, a terrible howling that filled the room until it got so big, it broke apart into staccato sobs.

Ruth's voice continued in a whisper. "I'm so sorry, so sorry." For a long while she was silent, stroking my arm. When my body grew exhausted from crying, I took a long breath and coughed out, "Does Barb know?" She'd be devastated.

Ruth's head nodded and nodded, and tears oozed from her eyes. I watched them dribble down her cheeks and collect along the edge of her jaw.

"Is she still in the hospital?" I asked, but Ruth couldn't seem to reply, and my mind raced to all the worst possibilities: Barb in a wheelchair, Barb's beautiful face crushed and deformed. Barb never able to smile again, never able to walk again. My heart began to thump hard. Ruth took my hand, her fingers fitful and twisting through mine. She said, "At first, they couldn't find her."

"She was outside the car! I could've told them! Why didn't they ask me?"

"They thought maybe she hadn't been in the car. Your mother said she was so mad having to go along, maybe she got out in Emporia and found a ride back with someone else."

"*No*, she was there, why didn't they ask me?"

"Your mama, she was convinced Barb had not been in the car. The ambulance brought you back to the hospital, and the police kept searching the crash site, but it was so dark..."

"I know, I know—"

"Finally, at dawn, they found her. She'd been thrown from the car, they think she must've crawled—"

"I could've *told them that.*"

"They radioed for the ambulance to come back right away and it came very fast, and they got her to the hospital, but, unfortunately—"

"Ruth."

"She died of internal injuries—"

From my throat came a sound I didn't recognize, there was no word for. My body split open, and the insides spilled out, viscera splayed across the sheet in lumps and puddles. I heard wailing, but it could not have come from me: I was a shell, emptied of life, sliding away, tumbling down the steep into the sea, plummeting to the murky bottom, and I heard screeching—it could not have been coming from me, because I was somewhere else, at the bottom of an ocean, washing around lifeless, washing up on a faraway shore, thrashed and battered against a jagged rock cliff. Someone was shrieking and footsteps were running and something was flapping and then there was a sensation—a jab in my arm—and mercifully, I broke free of consciousness.

In 1964, if you were in a car accident, you were kept in the hospital for weeks. You were confined supine and sedated through your brother's and sister's funeral. Cards and cups of flowers accumulated on the little shelf along the wall. You ate orange Jell-O. You read movie-star magazines because that's what the nurses assumed you, a teenage girl, would like. Sometimes a portable TV was rolled in and you could watch game shows and variety shows and late movies in shades of gray until the test pattern came droning on. You wondered whether you'd have a roommate, because there was another bed in the room, behind a curtain that clattered along a metal bar on metal rings, but there weren't that many kids who needed to be hospitalized, so you remained alone. You got lonely. Adults could visit, but not anyone under the age of eighteen. You could talk to your school friends on the oily black phone by your bed, but after a minute there was not much to say. Your mother came to visit, though she was very busy and could never stay long. Your father looked in twice.

The morning after the funerals, Patsy appeared in her uniform with a wheelchair, lifted me into it, and rode me down the elevator to the gift shop, where an excessively friendly lady gave us ice cream sandwiches for free. We went out the front door. Patsy parked me next to a bench, so she could sit too. Somehow the day was breezy and dry, more like spring than summer. Two passing nurses paused, also to be excessively friendly, and I realized this was pity kindness. Everyone knew. Everyone would know everything. Patsy and I ate our ice cream sandwiches, commented on the globules of cloud ambling along the sky. Then Patsy got up to throw away our wrappers, and when she returned she said, "The line of cars to the cemetery was so long you couldn't see the end of it. Went all the way up the street over the horizon. Everyone in the whole county must've been there. Except for Jim Darden."

"He wasn't there?"

"Nope. Dardens had their family vacation planned at their beach house in Nags Head and they didn't want a delay."

For a moment I couldn't speak. Barb had been hoping for an invitation to that beach house, optimistic she'd soon get the call. I said, "You were so right about him."

"I was so right." She paused. "The church was so full of flowers I thought I'd choke to death from the scent. They were beautiful."

"I'm glad."

"Reverend Swanson gave such a nice sermon." Here she had to struggle to stay calm, her eyes swampy. "He said how Ricky and Barb had joined the ranks of the angels, and would never again have to suffer life's burdens, and right now Ricky was in a great big park playin' fetch with your old dog Buddy—"

"He loved Buddy, so much."

"—and that beautiful as Barb was in this life, now she's even more beautiful in heaven, flyin' around with the angels." She blinked fast and hard. "He said Ricky and Barb had gone ahead of us, but soon enough we'd all be there together again in God's light." She pulled a hanky from her pocket and wiped her eyes. There was a crease in her forehead I'd never seen before, a new vertical fissure between her brows.

I said, "I hope Jim Darden gets stung by a million jellyfish."

"Ten million." She bent over and inserted an arm between me and the back of the wheelchair and gave me an awkward sideways hug, so tight it began to hurt, but I didn't pull away. I felt her warmth and the discomfort wrapped up together until it was over, and she wheeled me back to my room.

My most frequent visitor was Ruth, even after her discharge from the hospital. She left the reverend in charge of the girls and the packing and spent long afternoons with me, making me do crossword puzzles so my brain muscles wouldn't atrophy,

tacking up pictures drawn by Julie and Annette, bringing me
books and Cokes. She began to read *Moby Dick* aloud, assuring
me it was okay to skip the chapters on the whaling industry.
After a few weeks, she brought me a letter from Langston, sent
to her address. Gingerly I pried open the flap and pulled out the
single loose-leaf sheet of paper.

Dear Willa,

Ruth called after I got to DC and told me about the
accident. I wanted to write you sooner, but I didn't know
what to say. It was an awful thing that happened. I can't
imagine losing my brother or a sister, I don't even want to
try. I can't help think if it wasn't for me, this terrible thing
would not of happened. Ruth says not to think that way, an
accident is an accident, but I feel really bad about it.

I'm also writing to say thank you to you. If it wasn't
for you, something terrible might of happened to me and
Daisy that last day, if you didn't come over and say we had
to go. You made sure we were safe, riding along with us
and watching out. You did alot for me and I will not forget
you. At first I thought you were a big pain in the You Know
What, but now I think of you as a friend, and I will always
be grateful to you. Because here I am now safe and sound
and about to start college. I will remember you and you will
be one of the people I think of when I strive to do my best
to make my family and friends proud.

Your friend, Langston Jones

I burst into tears. I didn't know why. Ruth climbed into the
bed with me and held me and told me to cry as much as I
wanted. I said I didn't know why I was crying, and she said that
was okay, that was perfectly okay.

I composed a thousand responses to Langston in my head. I
never put one word on paper. This was not because of Daisy's
threat to tell my mother if I wrote; it was because a door had
slammed shut on a part of my life, and Langston was on the
other side of it.

Ruth would not talk about her impending move to Albany. The day approached anyway. I could hardly fathom another loss; my brain refused to think about it. Then, one morning at the end of July, Ruth and my mother appeared together in my hospital room, side by side, incongruous as usual, short and tall, pale and sun-browned, Ruth young, my mother aged two decades since the accident. My mother sat in the chair and Ruth perched at the foot of my bed, waiting for my mother to start the conversation.

My mother said, "Your father has come to a decision that's best for us all." She forced a smile, hollow-eyed. I looked at Ruth, who seemed nervous but excited too.

"What's goin' on?"

"We all agreed you should move up to Albany along with the Swansons. Your father will send support checks. You'll keep helpin' Ruth with the children and the chores. You'll go to high school there." As she spoke, her voice regained some of its old stamina; she began to sound like herself again, thinking through the details of a plan, dutifully executing my father's wishes. She continued, "If you want to go to college, your father will pay half, but you'll be expected to pay the other half. That's to teach you responsibility." She smiled.

It was clear she was no longer thinking of leaving him. A reason for staying had presented itself: she was needed to arrange for the relocation of our family shame. Being a good woman, she put her husband's needs over her own, even over her child's. My father needed me gone. He needed to be free of my troublemaking, and from a distance he could comfortably blame me for everything. He would be spared any residual culpability. He'd be able to reassert himself in the community despite the tragedy associated with him—perhaps even because of it.

I don't recall what I said. I don't recall what Ruth said, either, except it carried a cheerful tone. She was elated I'd be coming with them. I suppose part of me was glad too. But mostly I felt utterly abandoned. Now I was less than an extra. All those years

I'd worried that my father had never really loved me, and now I knew: he never really had. He never really had.

In the middle of August, I was discharged from the hospital. My mother loaded the car with boxes of my belongings—books and clothes and a few stuffed animals—and early the next morning she and I got into the car. As we backed arduously out of the driveway, Billy stood on the front porch in a droopy white T-shirt, blank-faced, soundless, watching us go.

We didn't say much on the drive to upstate New York. Mostly we dialed the radio up and down searching for a station. As we drove into Albany, we were awed—it was the most enormous metropolis we'd ever seen, though it was probably one one-thousandth the size of New York City. "Look at all the sidewalks!" I exclaimed. The streets had names like Roosevelt, Lincoln, and Kennedy. One was called Voorheesville. "How do you even pronounce that?" my mother asked the ether.

We rolled down roads where all the houses were stuck together, sharing walls and tiny yards. "Those are called *row houses*," my mother informed me, sounding like my father. "You see them in these big cities." There may have been a warble of trepidation in her voice, a belated concern for my well-being, but it didn't alter her actions.

The Swansons' new home sat beside their new church, both made of blond limestone and towering over the rest of the block. I spotted the girls waiting for us in the front yard. Behind them, Ruth sat on a porch swing, her face turned toward a cool breeze. She looked contented—more than I'd ever seen her in Kingsfield. Everyone hugged us with excited shrieks and led us inside to show us around.

This parsonage had three floors and five bedrooms, designed to accommodate whatever size family a pastor might have. It even had two bathrooms. Ruth admitted that all the stairs worried her, but Matthew had arranged for a church lady to do the heavy cleaning, after clarifying that his wife was in ill health, not simply lazy. My room was to be on the third floor. "Basically, you'll have the whole third floor to yourself," Ruth said, climbing the stairs ahead of us, both hands on the banister, pulling herself up.

My new room was twice the size of my old room—twice the size for half the number of occupants. In it stood a large pecan-colored dresser, a small bookcase, and a bed with no headboard, all donated by church people. The room felt cavernous and dim. I sat at the edge of the mattress and stared at the blank walls.

My mother said, "It's big."

"What do you think?" Ruth asked me.

"It's fine." My voice sounded small here. I could not imagine my voice ever expanding to fill this space, or that anything would be fine, ever again.

"We can change it," Ruth said, her tone deep with empathy. "We can paint it. What do you think of purple?"

I smiled, and my mother exclaimed, "Well!" clearly pleased.

She stayed the night in the guest room down the hall from me, and I woke in the morning knowing she was there, just down the hall, just like at home—at least in that moment, she was still there. I loved Ruth, but she wasn't my mother. I loved Julie and Annette, but I had no sisters. At breakfast, my mother praised Ruth's scrambled eggs and asked the reverend's advice on the best route home. Leaving, she was so absorbed in unfolding and refolding her Triple-A maps, she barely hugged me goodbye. She sat in the driver's seat smiling as she cranked down her window and called out thank you and bye now and drove away.

# 17

Thus began the rest of my life.

In high school, I did not join clubs or go to dances or make new friends. I became obsessed with history. I started by researching the Klan, needing to know everything: when and where and why it formed, who joined it, what it had done. I made myself read endless accounts of its brutality; I was shocked, ashamed, and sick over my own ignorance.

Then I researched slavery, the mistreatment of American Indians, the rise of fascism in Nazi Germany. All my hours were spent in the library, that musty capsule of silence where I could be alone and at ease. Walking through the stacks, dragging my fingertips across the nubby spines of books, I coped by trying to understand: How did educated people rationalize their atrocities against other races? How did ordinary people become monsters? What kind of monster was my father? What kind of monster was I? I stood at the wall-sized card catalog, crunching open its narrow wooden drawers, walking my fingers across the tops of cards, searching for answers. I read.

History in the North was different from history in the South. In the North, the War Between the States was called the Civil War, and it was assumed to be over slavery, not states' rights. Northerners appeared unfamiliar with the concept of the benevolent slave owner who took good care of his darkies. No one in the North suggested that slaves appreciated their masters' looking after them, as they, the darkies, were incapable of looking after themselves. In the North, Abraham Lincoln was revered, and people still mourned John F. Kennedy. History, apparently, depended on where you lived.

By the end of my first year of high school, my identity had unraveled. Who was I if I wasn't a Southerner? Who was I in a place where no one had ever heard of Dick McCoy? Inhabiting this unfamiliar landscape could have made me cling tighter to my Southern identity, driven me deeper into it. But I couldn't bear the depths of myself, where guilt and shame coagulated in fetid pools: I was to blame for Barb's and Ricky's deaths. I'd been the cause of Langston's beating. I'd endangered his life and Daisy's too. I had no choice but to eject myself from that Southern identity. Then I was no one, floating, belonging nowhere.

Looking back, I was probably clinically depressed. But in that era, depression was a thing diagnosed in bored housewives, not kids. If a girl was quiet and disengaged, she was judged to have a *bad personality*—to be shy or insecure, stupid or stuck up—and told to emulate girls with *good personalities*, who were bouncy, entertaining, and helpful. Ruth pulled me through the worst of my undiagnosed depression. Every afternoon she sat with me at the kitchen table and made me talk about my day. She didn't make me talk about my feelings if I didn't want to; she just made me talk. She was exactly what I needed, an amalgam of mother and big sister.

She kept up a correspondence with Langston and, with his permission, shared his letters with me. "Listen to this," she'd say and read aloud his funny descriptions of professors struggling with their slide projectors. "He's doing so well in college!" she summed up, to emphasize I had not destroyed him also.

But I could have. Even after I'd fallen in love with him—and I believe I genuinely had—I'd been selfish, not bothering to think beyond my own immediate desire. I wanted to be near him, no matter what. He was an *object* of my affection; I'd felt I had some right to him—a right to determine where he should be, when he should be with me. This was how my father regarded my mother—as a body he had a right to, a lesser being he had a say over. I'd felt a superiority over Langston, because I was white and he was Black.

He graduated from college the year I graduated from high school. That August, he married Daisy. I left for college. With my straight As and personal essay about the importance of overcoming racism, I earned a full scholarship to Washington University in St. Louis. I did not need my father's paltry contribution, nor his lessons in responsibility. In college, I blossomed. It was 1967, '68, '69—the whole world was waking up and wanting the same things I did: equal rights for women and Negroes, brotherly love. I fell in love with a skinny folk musician and we joined marches: at last, I got to march, to feel that warm swell of belonging. But I had to stay alert to my worst impulses. It was easy to get self-righteous. I'd befriended some of my Black classmates, and I noticed an urge to show off: Look how hip I am! Look how cool! Noisily cultivating the appearance of egalitarianism wasn't about social justice; it was about ego. I wanted to be a true friend and ally to people of color. I had a long way to go.

I still do. Continually I must check my motivations and assumptions. The roots of racism are deep and gnarled, sending up growths that require perpetual cutting back. Fears from my childhood still murmur through me in subterranean streams: *Look out for those coloreds, lock your car doors, clutch your purse. Do you know the story of Nat Turner?* What *was* the purpose of filling us with that amorphous fear?

After college, I managed to find a job at a newspaper, a St. Louis weekly. I was assigned human interest stories. It was the early '70s, and the country was roiling with racial tensions, riots, protests; we were on the eve of Watergate. Yet I wrote articles on charity galas, interviewed the wives of important men, and penned car-shopping tips for single gals. Basically, I was writing the *Women in the News* page, its name changed to "Features."

I got these assignments not just because I was a young woman, but because I was a young woman of a certain type: short, cute, curvy, with a slight Southern accent and mannerisms that suggested a lack of confidence. I did not lack confidence in general, but I did lack a particular kind—the Daisy kind—the assumption that people would listen when I spoke, that asserting my views was not futile. I wasn't good at advocating for myself; I was too affected by the judgments of men in charge.

In my head lived an apparition with a male voice dismissing my ideas before I could speak them out loud. The apparition had a male face, too, which regarded me with wincing annoyance. Gals who managed to get a foothold on the news staff were women who spoke in loud, knowledgeable city voices and demanded attention without apology, free of feminine hesitation. At first I thought these go-getters were just smarter than I was, a notion my apparition approved. Later I concluded they must have been raised by loving, bold, well-adjusted mothers and fathers, and I lost heart. I longed for change.

In 1976, I went back to Albany to seek Ruth's wisdom. By then the Swansons had moved to a one-story house to accommodate Ruth's wheelchair. We sat in the kitchen—at that same pink-topped table, which clashed horridly with the harvest gold and avocado appliances. Mr. Softy, now the size of an Egyptian pyramid, sat lethargic at his bowl. Julie was off at college, but Annette was clomping around the kitchen in platform shoes and bell-bottoms, her blond hair, pin-straight and waist-length, in a perpetual swish. She was wearing giant Elton John sunglasses in the house.

"Annette," Ruth sighed with the sound of a million little annoyances.

"What? I'm out the door." Annette sauntered out across the back porch. We watched her bounce into the driver's seat of the Swansons' Ford Monarch and roll away, then caught each other's gaze and laughed. A contented silence settled over us.

Finally, I said, "Do you remember that morning, when Langston and I were helping you pack, and you predicted I wouldn't be a journalist after all?"

"Hmm." She tilted her head. She didn't remember. Multiple sclerosis impairs memory and cognition: calcium deposits build up in the brain. But we'd been lucky. Ruth's disease had progressed slowly, and she was still herself despite the occasional memory lapse, despite the new, severely short haircut no one liked. Her eyes were bright, her grin tilted at the same angle. She said, "You're thinking of changing careers?"

"Journalism isn't what I thought it would be. There are important stories out there, but ninety-nine percent of what we do has to fit this formula of *shock* and *entertain*. It's all, look! A deadly house fire! Then, look! A funny duck! I feel like I'm not doing anything meaningful. But if I quit, is that giving up on my big dream?" Of course I thought of Langston, who'd just begun his career as an aerospace engineer at NASA. Daisy, now a lawyer, was expecting their first child.

Ruth said, "Some people outgrow their childhood dreams, people who work hard to change themselves, who try to be the best version of themselves, like you." She smiled.

"I want to do something to make the world a better place. Does that sound grandiose?"

"Not at all." She leaned toward me, inviting me to elaborate.

"So, you know I've always loved history. If you ask me, history is the most important subject to learn!"

"Okay."

"So, don't laugh. I'm thinking of being a history teacher."

She didn't laugh. She said, "Huh."

"But, I don't know. Teaching high school? Like my *father*?"

"Well, maybe you don't teach high school. Maybe you teach college. You go to graduate school and get a PhD and teach college."

"A PhD?" I echoed. My father's degree was only a master's. If I had a PhD, I would have surpassed him. I could not help thinking, *That'd show him!*

I started graduate school in Michigan, where I fell in love again, with a ginger-haired man earning a doctorate in English literature. We drank and talked and laughed and even moved in together. Three years later I was unsettled and depressed, clawing my way out of our tiny Ann Arbor apartment. I couldn't bear his assumption of authority over me, his corrections of my opinions, the expectation I would pick up his dirty socks and coins and matchbooks and pencil stubs dropped on the floor. He liked that I was smart, but he didn't want me thinking I was smarter than he was. We drank and screamed and threw things at each other. I moved out.

But on my own, I finished my dissertation in record time: "The Confluence of the Suffragist and Abolitionist Movements of the Mid-Nineteenth Century: The Historic Interconnectedness Between Racism and Sexism in the US." It was dry as dust, but it earned me my PhD and got me onto the job market. I applied for dozens of faculty positions, all over the country—even Idaho. I managed to get four interviews, and two job offers.

The first came from a small liberal arts college in the soft, idyllic hills of Maryland. The campus was cobblestoned and lushly landscaped, with clusters of colonial-columned red-brick buildings. On my campus tour, I was led past a grand stone fountain, a quaint clock tower, newly resurfaced tennis courts, a building named Darden Hall. The parking lot adjacent to the dormitories was full of brand-new Firebirds and Camaros, silver or candy-apple red. In the cafeteria I overheard two girls ridiculing another girl for wearing white shoes after Labor Day. In my interview with the history faculty—all middle-aged white men—the department chair glumly repeated what their dean had told them—"It's 1982, you have to hire a woman"—and coughed out a derisive laugh.

So I accepted the job at Malcolm X Community College, in the heart of Chicago. I still teach there, though I am past retirement age. My students are earnest, idealistic, anxious, and so easy to love. Most are the first in their families to attend college. They aren't all African-American; many are the daughters and sons of immigrants—Mexican, Puerto Rican, Polish, Lithuanian.

To be clear, I do not play the role of white savior to my students. "White savior" is a Northern concept—an attitude assumed by privileged white liberals who look down on the South and all its inhabitants. Chicago is the most segregated city in the nation. To this day, its public schools are not integrated. Racism is not a product of the South; it infests every longitude and latitude. Yet I have never felt a need to rescue my students, nor do I expect them to rescue me. We muddle through our work together, helping each other understand where we've come from and where we're going. Together we've witnessed so many resurgences of oppression: the backlash against the women's movement in the 1980s, rising income inequality, the mass incarceration of Black people. Wouldn't Miss Cooke be happy, I kept thinking: all the gorillas finally locked up in cages. I rant at my students: *Go to law school! Run for public office! Write the laws!* Some of them do. Ironically, I'm helping to inspire a new generation of Daisys.

We celebrated Barack Obama's election to president, but we knew this wasn't now a "post-racial" society. White supremacy still nudged its snout up from beneath the mud. In 2016, when a highly qualified woman running for president was defeated by an ill-qualified misogynist, I had to accept that the fight for human rights is not a war that can be won. It's a lifelong skirmish over lost ground, requiring stamina, humility, and a fierce hope that the arc of the moral universe really will bend toward justice.

In the summer of 2008, Ruth called to say my father had died of liver cancer. She'd seen an announcement in the Kingsfield church newsletter. There was a photo of him, she said. Would I like her to send it? No, thank you. Would I like to talk about it? Not really. Was I okay? Yes. Was I really? I tried to feel my feelings: sadness, anger, and relief that the world was now free of this man.

Ten years later, it was Julie who phoned with the news of my mother's passing. My brother Billy's wife had found her number and phoned her. "They wanted to make sure you knew," she said, her voice so like Ruth's.

"Mm," was all I could manage. I tried to say more, but my windpipe was punched in. I stood alone in my living room. My skin grew heavy on my bones. I'd spent decades angry at my mother, but I'd always imagined a reconciliation. I'd never doubted her love for me. I'd thought there'd be more time. Why did I think that? She was past ninety. I should have reached out when there was time. Time passed and I missed my chance.

Suddenly, all my old fury was gone, exploded into particles that hovered for a moment and floated away. A slow-moving bolus of grief moved up my esophagus.

"Willa?" Julie's voice in my ear.

I pulled in a breath, the air stabbing, my eyes swimming. But my living room was peaceful, still, usually full of sunshine, now shady with early twilight. On the wall was the shadow of roses in a vase on a slender mahogany table. I looked at it for a while—the shadow—then I looked at the fireplace mantel, which was lined with framed photos of me with friends and colleagues on trips. Some of my travels were for conferences; others were vacations.

"Willa?"

There I was in Berlin with Terry, in Helsinki with Arlene, in Vancouver with Mark. London; Venice; Edinburgh; Lyon; Valencia, Spain. Why did I think there'd be more time? My mother's voice was clear as birdsong in my head: *If you ever get stranded again...*

"Willa? The memorial service is in a few weeks. I have the details if you want to go."

"What?"

"You should think about going."

"*Going?*"

"Yeah."

"Oh, no, no."

"Might be interesting to see Kingsfield again. Might give you a sense of closure."

"Oh God, I couldn't go back there now. I wouldn't belong." But now the word was in my head: *Kingsfield.* "How's Ruth?"

"She's okay, zipping around the nursing home in her motorized chair. Reading, playing Scrabble. Come soon?"

"Definitely."

Later that night, in bed unable to sleep, I whispered to the air, "Mama, I'm sorry." It sounded like a prayer. I wanted to believe she could hear me. I thought of her face, narrow, worried; I thought of her hands, bone thin and chapped, reaching up, reaching in, stirring, pouring, chopping, shelling. I tried to sleep, but my eyes would not stay closed.

At midnight I texted Julie: *Email me the info, maybe I'll go.*

When I closed my eyes again, an image materialized, sudden and vivid. It was our old dining room, papered in faded greens, full of dark wood, shiny and marred. At the head of the table sat my father, frowning into his plate; beside him, my mother, in a fluster over the passing of bowls. Billy wriggled in his chair, feet jittering; Ricky sat at the foot of the table, loose-limbed. And there was Barb, turning toward Mama with a luminous smile, reaching out a lovely hand. All of them sitting, shouldering the weight of their unspoken fears and wants, shimmering in the glare of a shocking sun.

I was there too, thirteen years old, awkward, determined, restive, impatient, so eager for my chance to speak, near bursting with a desire to belong.

# EPILOGUE

## RETURN, 2018

The old man weeping at the lectern must have been my little brother, though I could see no trace of his lean boyhood face in this flab and pallor, nor could I hear the eight-year-old's whine in his voice, pitched deep now and soft like a proper Southern gentleman's. He was crooning that his mama had been the brightest ray of sunshine on the planet, and without her the world would be a blacker place.

I sat in the last pew of the packed sanctuary, twisting against the wood, brushing the powder-white sleeve beside me. I shouldn't have come. I felt too conspicuous; I didn't belong here. *A sense of closure*—what did that even mean? I'd lost the opportunity to reconcile with my mother. The long-imagined reunion was now reduced to holding a church bulletin with her photo on the front. I studied her, this unfamiliar lady, wispy-haired, blank-faced, prune-necked, her shoulders drooped inside a hefty pink blouse, a faux pearl button tight at her throat. Gradually I recognized the smile, the narrow crescent of teeth denting in her baggy cheeks. It was her worried smile.

"I'm sorry, Mama," I whispered and thought I might choke. I was sorry for too much: for robbing her of Barb and Ricky, for wanting to be nothing like her, for decades of absence. She'd sent me letters and cards for several years after my exile from Kingsfield, but I'd barely responded, so angry and depressed. I'd sent her a photo of me receiving my PhD, then I never wrote again. Would she be pleased I was here? I wasn't sure. Would she want me to reconnect with Billy? She probably would, and I looked at him again, this old drooping man weeping at the lectern.

I inhaled. The sanctuary, shadowy and small, was foreign and familiar at the same time. Here was the pulpit where Reverend Swanson had stood to preach about brotherhood. Here was the flaxen wood cross above the altar, and blond Jesus in all the stained-glass windows. I scanned the crowd, realizing some of these people may have been my former classmates. There were men with broad swaths of gray across their foreheads, women with hair dyed champagne blond, ash blond, golden blond, platinum. Their faces were leathered and mottled from exposure to more sun than their British-white skin could withstand, never meant for this latitude. Of course, not one of them was Black.

It would be so easy, I thought, to leave, to slip from the pew, creep through the door, and vanish. No one would suspect I was me. I'd told no one I was coming. I'd flown into Norfolk, rented a car, driven to Kingsfield, and shuffled anonymously into the sanctuary with the mob of mourners. I bent forward, intending to rise and slide away.

But then the pastor's voice boomed out, "Thank you, Billy." I stopped. With patting palms, the pastor steered Billy toward the front pew, seating him in a row of people who must have been Billy's family. I examined the backs of their heads: the copious straw-colored hair of his probable wife, the well-trimmed necks of sons, the butter-yellow heads of daughters, and, in the rows behind them, the twitching shoulders of grandchildren. This was a throng of relatives I'd never met, whose names I'd never even heard, emphasizing the fact I didn't belong here. In one of the stained-glass windows, blond Jesus was pointing, coincidentally, to the nearest exit.

But then a parade of mourners took turns at the lectern to praise our mama: Trudy was a giver, an exemplary wife and mother, a true Christian, a good neighbor, an excellent cook, a wiz with her sewing machine. Trudy was selfless till the end, requesting donations, in lieu of flowers, to research for liver cancer, which had, years ago, claimed her beloved husband—that pillar of the community and devoted family man, Dick McCoy.

*Dick McCoy.* The sound of it clattered like breaking glass in
my head. This was how he'd be remembered—just as he'd have
wanted, his history tidied up, smoothed down, whitewashed
like the brick facades on Main Street. I began to sweat. I knew
he was gone, but somehow I felt him surrounding me. I began to feel trapped in the pew, in this church, in this crowd of
Southerners, in 1963. I tried to catch my breath. Was I having a
panic attack? I needed to escape, but the organ started to play
and everyone rose—very slowly—and began to drone out a
hymn: *Blessed assurance, Jesus is mine...O what a foretaste of glory
divine...Born of his spirit, washed in his blood...* On and on it went,
on and on and on, like a turtle limping across a desert. When
the music ended at last, even the sitting down was slow. Then
the pastor read a Bible verse: *When you go through deep waters, I will
be with you. When you go through rivers of difficulty, you will not drown.
When you walk through the fire of oppression, you will not be burned
up...* I thought, unkindly, did these well-dressed white people
feel oppressed?

Abruptly, the service ended. All remained seated, and a silence descended, heavy and airless like a metal box clamped
down over me. I made a plan: I would say a brief hello to Billy,
nudging open the possibility of future communication, then I'd
melt away into the crowd and flee to my hotel, where I could
hide until my flight home to Chicago the next day. I spotted Billy at the front of the sanctuary, in a klatch of shoulder-patting
people. The mourners on either side of me began to rise—so,
so, *so slow.* Then they stood in the pew chatting, not moving. I
put an odd-feeling smile on my face, an attempt to look unlike
myself. I waited, and it occurred to me I could just phone Billy
later, from my hotel room. I didn't have to speak to him now.
There were probably still phone books in Kingsfield, with land-
lines listed. Yes, I decided: I'd leave now and call later. I was
about to stand and squirm through the crowd when an austere
voice came down from above, "I know who you are."

I looked up. It was the woman who'd sat next to Billy. She
was mountainous, with a long, bent face and parched hair hang-

ing in ropes past her shoulders. Her eyes were small and locked onto my face like the jaws of a pit bull. But then her bulky hand came trembling toward me, rested itself on my shoulder, and gave me a sympathetic squeeze. "I'm Linda, your brother's wife," and her lower jaw receded into a warm smile.

"I'm Willa McCoy," I said in my startling Northern accent.

Her smile tightened into a smirk. "I know who you are," she said. "Everybody knows who you are." I glanced around: this seemed unlikely. She asked, "How long you in town for?"

"Just for tonight, I leave tomorrow."

"Oh, that's a shame."

"Yes, I'm so busy at work right now." I said, though it wasn't true. It was summer. I wasn't even teaching summer school. I rose, as though to rush off. But she was standing at the end of the pew blocking my escape, and other people began to cluster around to grasp her hand.

One gray-haired couple lingered, and Linda said, "Willa, I bet you remember Mary and Ralph. They were in Barb's year at school." The woman was diminutive, the man so tall his torso slanted. I had no idea who they were. To Mary and Ralph, she said, "Y'all remember Willa, Trudy's other daughter?"

"Sure," Mary said in a teeny voice. "How're you, Willa?"

"We're so sorry for your loss," Ralph leaned in with droopy, sincere eyes.

"Thank you."

"Where are you now?" Mary squeaked, and I was tempted to say, *Standing in front of you.*

"Chicago," I replied.

"She's a *city girl*," Linda added, but not unkindly.

Ralph said, "We get WGN News from Chicago on the satellite. Lot goin' on there!" But he smiled, not judging. Mary began calling people over. "Y'all remember Willa, Trudy's other daughter?" Sad faces nodded at me; soothing voices greeted me. Everyone held my hand, petted my wrist. Here was the trademark Tidewater graciousness: everyone so mild, considerate, always offering to bring you a Coke.

Ralph said, "She's in Chicago now."

"You didn't come all that way by yourself?" A lady gasped, glancing around for a male stranger who'd be my husband.

"I did," I said. People oohed and ahhed.

Someone asked, "D'you have children, Willa?"

"I have two sons." This was another lie. But I knew these people didn't want to hear I was childless; it would make them unhappy and confused. I added, for credibility, "They live out West."

Someone else asked, "What d'you do in Chicago, Willa?" They were genuinely interested, asking questions to open little doors of connection, and I felt guilty for thinking critically of them. I felt guilty for lying, too, and was unclear as to why I told the next one. Instead of sharing my life's greatest achievement—being a college professor—I said, simply, "I'm a teacher."

"Oh, that's nice. What grade do you teach?"

"Kindergarten."

"How sweet!" Mary said joyfully, and I realized I was lying to avoid disrupting their expectations, to ensure they'd accept me, to feel I belonged. After all these decades, I still wanted to belong.

"How long you in town for?" someone else asked, and I had to tell the truth, because I'd already told Linda: "Just for tonight."

Linda rested her hand on my shoulder. "Well, thankfully you'll have time to come to the house this afternoon."

"Pardon?"

"We're havin' a barbecue. Mostly just family. You can have a nice long visit with everyone."

"I don't know your address," I said, as though this would prevent me from coming.

She laughed. "It's *your* address. We live in your old house. I'll tell Billy you're coming." She lumbered away toward Billy, and I couldn't move. Go back to my old house?

"You okay?" Mary asked, and Ralph said, "We got a vending

machine now down in the Fellowship Hall. Can I get you a Coke?"

"No, thank you." I watched Linda approach Billy, lean in, and whisper. His eyes snapped up, landed on me, then darted away. She kept speaking; he gazed down. She was insisting on something, or scolding him, or both. She was telling him to come speak to me, I realized—and he was refusing.

Well, fine. I didn't want to speak to him either. "Excuse me," I said and pushed past Ralph and Mary toward the exit. I'd come all this way, and he didn't want to speak to me. Well, fine. I yanked open the hefty door, and a furnace blast paused everyone's conversation. He still blamed me for what happened, for destroying the family, like my father had blamed me, and probably my mother did too. All those decades—she could've reached out to me. So there'd be no reconciliation for the last two McCoy kids, no closure here. I pushed through the viscera of heat toward my rental car, jumped in, and headed toward the hotel. I was fine: I'd lived this long without a brother. I'd be fine.

I turned onto Main Street. Downtown was eerily unchanged: it was the same five blocks of whitewashed brick facades, paper-mill stacks rising ghostly beyond them. A generation had grown old and unrecognizable, yet the town center had halted in time. I drove on and discovered Kingsfield had in fact expanded; along the railroad tracks stood big box stores and chain restaurants where the most impoverished Black people once lived. The town had burgeoned, predictably, from its unchanged heart.

At the hotel I checked in, found my room, plummeted onto the bed, and closed my eyes. Wouldn't it be nice, I thought, to fall asleep? But on the insides of my lids was Billy's down-turned face, his little-old-man frame, his hanging-open suit jacket. Like a statue he'd stood gazing at his shiny funeral loafers.

I texted Julie, *Help! It's awful. Billy wouldn't speak to me.*

Immediately she texted back: *Where are you now?*

*Hotel. Hiding. Billy's wife wants me to go to their house—MY OLD HOUSE!—for a BBQ.*

She texted: *Go.*
*What?*
*Go.*
*I am not OBLIGED to go.*
*True. Go.*
*I don't want to go.*
*Understood. This may be your last chance with Billy.*
Sometimes Julie sounded just like Ruth.

I went. By mid-afternoon, the heat had piled up on itself, like a mountain of rocks in the air. My armpits turned to ponds of sweat as I walked across the lot to my rental Honda. I sat in the car with the front doors open, all vents blasting the AC, then made myself close the doors and drive back toward downtown. Even with the windows up, the rotting-cabbage stench of the paper mill flooded the car. I turned, turned again. I didn't need the GPS.

I shouldn't be going, I kept thinking, but as I drew nearer the house, past weeping willows and crepe myrtles, I kept remembering Billy: little-boy Billy, my little brother romping toward me in his cowboy shirt, the top of his head shiny through his crew cut. His legs jittering, his face beaming when the *Mr. Ed* theme song began. Little-boy Billy standing outside our front door, watching my mother and me back away in the car, leaving for Albany. Before long, I was accelerating toward the house.

I idled in front of it for a moment to take it in: white clapboard, steep gray roof, shutters painted the color of dried blood. As a child I thought our house was not as nice as others, because the porch didn't wrap around. It didn't even extend the full length of the façade, and its roof rested on four plain square pillars, devoid of colonial flourishes. The house did not look smaller; it looked accusing.

The driveway was full of cars. I crackled across the narrow pass over the ditch and stopped behind a white van, which had a Confederate flag painted across its rear. I told myself, "May be my last chance," and got out of the car. I crossed the lawn, walked up the front steps, rang the front doorbell, and was seized by regret. *What the hell was I doing there?* I was too Northern, too urban. This was a terrible idea. I turned—I could still run away. But the door popped open and Linda said, "I'm so glad you came! Come in!" and reached through the door to tug me in. "You won't recognize the place."

I didn't. The living room had usurped the dining room, walls knocked through to create that trendy, open-concept look. The dining room and kitchen were now separated by an island with a granite countertop. The coat closet where I'd once hidden was a half-bath. The interior hummed with central air. Linda burbled, "Of course, we couldn't afford any of this till all our boys were grown."

"How many kids do you have?"

"Eight. All boys."

"*Eight boys?*"

She laughed. "Billy wanted a girl, so we kept goin'. Boy number eight I said, Okay honey, that's it. We got granddaughters now. Come on out and say hello." She led me through the alien space to the back door. "I told everyone you were a college professor in Chicago, hope that's okay. It was right there on your Facebook page."

"Oh, sure."

Linda opened the door with fanfare, revealing the backyard transformed into an elaborate garden. A multi-level pathway of small cedar decks led to one enormous one, which was packed with people under a green awning. This main deck was an entire outdoor room, complete with puffy weather-proof couches. What had my mother thought of this extravagance? Or had she, at the end of her life, made peace with expense? "Whaddya think?" Linda said coyly.

"It's gorgeous," I said truthfully. The cedar path was laced with marigolds, begonias, geraniums—hearty bursts of yellow, softly drooping petals of red, trumpets of purple and blue. At the edge of the yard was a row of maples that had grown wide enough to block the sun.

"Our son Danny designed the entire garden," she boasted, then led me to the main deck. "Everyone, here's your aunt Willa, from Chicago!"

They stared at me. They all had the pale elongated faces and globular noses endemic to the region, except for one woman, who looked vaguely Chinese. Linda said, pointing: "That's Rich, our oldest; his wife, Amy; Steve, married to Dawn; Danny, married to Lia; Brian; and Keith…" She went on. "Then the grandchildren—" Good god, would I be expected to remember their names too? The grandchildren ranged from babies to moody tattooed teenagers crammed together on one of the couches. Girlfriends were there, too, one of them dressed in the requisite hottie garb: crotch-length skirt, half a shirt, steep-heeled sandals. I cringed when I saw young women dressed this way, the expression of their sexual confidence conveniently coinciding with what men wanted to see.

I scanned the yard. Where was my brother?

"I got someone here *dyin'* to see you." Linda grinned, her face slick with liquid foundation and sweat, and my heart leaped. He'd changed his mind: he did want to talk to me. Suddenly, I couldn't wait.

I followed her inside and she called up the stairs, "Willa's here!" Footsteps thudded from above, but at the top of the steps, instead of my brother, appeared an old lady. She came down timidly, clutching the rail, stooped. Hanging on her frame was a pleated peach dress surely too formal for a barbecue. She was squealing, "Willa McCoy! Willa McCoy!" I gazed at her fervent sunken face. Her hair was like steel wool wrapped tight around her skull. Linda laughed and bounced up and clapped.

"Well!" I called out, searching for something familiar in the face.

Linda threw a large arm around my shoulder and gave it a squeeze, singing out, "It's Becky Cobb!"

"Becky—*Campbell?*"

She was at the bottom of the stairs now, smiling into my face with unnaturally white teeth. I recognized her olive eyes, the irises flecked with yellow-gold, outlined in bold moss-green. She grasped my hand. In an accent so thick I could barely comprehend her, she said, "Been Becky Cobb since 1970. Married Johnny Cobb!" Johnny Cobb—the dreamiest boy in junior high. Linda rested her hands on each of our shoulders. "You two come over and have a visit."

As we walked, Becky pulled out her phone and tapped its screen. We sat at the dining room table, Linda stationed delightedly behind the island. She shook a few red plastic cups off a stack and poured us diet Cokes.

"Here he is!" Becky tilted toward me to show a photo of an old man.

"Is that Johnny Cobb?" I gaped—all his beautiful hair gone.

"Yes," she replied wistfully, quietly, still in love. "He passed four years ago."

"I'm sorry."

"Here's the brood!" She scrolled through pictures of her children, grandchildren, and pets: Kates and Michaels, Bellas and Jasons, Snowballs and Gingers. Now I would never remember the names of Billy's kids. I nodded at each image. They were striking children, magnificent dogs, regal cats—but a hollowness opened up inside me. Once Becky had imagined herself on the African veldt, taking photos for *National Geographic*. Now she was showing snapshots of house pets on her phone. Still, her life had clearly been happy. Why did I have to judge?

"I can't believe you married Johnny Cobb."

"Yes, indeed! Quite the romance, dancin' at the senior prom," she said, her voice like slow syrup. "Year later we married. Florence and Sue were bridesmaids."

"Oh my god, Florence and Sue! Whatever happened to them?"

"Well, we were just inseparable after you left, best of friends. Sue married Stevie Hedgepeth and moved to Suffolk. Florence married Gene Beale and moved to Newport News."

"Well," I said, and a silence sprouted. "What about Joe Pedicini?"

"Oh, Joe. He went up North to college. Went on to law school, or somethin' I think. Last I heard he was livin' in Boston."

"Good for him!" I replied, too enthusiastically. She shifted, a look of suspicion flashing in her eyes. I said, "Do you know what happened to Patsy Beale?"

Becky glanced at Linda. "She went off to California, right? Some kind a nurse?"

"Nurse practitioner," Linda remembered and began hauling giant cellophaned bowls and plates from the fridge, setting them on the table, narrating as she went: "Gelatinous salad, ham biscuits, deviled eggs with capers and chives." Then she pulled out a bowl of green goop and gazed into it mournfully. "I made this one specially. One of Mama's favorites." Her voice jerked tearfully: "One bunch broccoli, mixed with one cup Miracle Whip, one quarter cup bacon bits." Then, in a brisk tone, she asked Becky, "You stayin' to supper?" They shared a slurpy exchange I did not understand. I glanced toward the staircase.

Then the back door flapped open and across the living room came two of the sons. Linda said, "Brian, Keith," for my benefit. The one who may have been Brian said, "Burgers ready, Mom." They continued ambling toward us. As they got closer, giddy grins overtook their faces. The one who was probably Keith pulled a red cap from behind his back and stroked it onto his head: *Make America Great Again.*

Linda barked, "I said no politics today."

"I didn't say anythin'."

Brian whined, "Kelly and them wanna eat inside. Too damn hot out there."

"That's fine," Linda said, so they moseyed out again.

Then Becky's phone chirped. "Oh, there's Katie!" She stood. "Gotta run!" We walked together to the front door, paused to smile at each other, and she said, "I always knew you'd do somethin' with your life. You on Facebook?"

"Yes! I'll send you a friend request." We shared a loose hug. She said, earnestly, "You take care," and left.

When I turned, Linda was wiping down the table, the sponge spiraling aggressively around the surface. I asked, "Where's Billy?"

"Upstairs. He'll be down. He's havin' a hard time with Mama's passin'."

The back door flung open again and a parade of people came in with platters of burgers. A few couples and most of the kids remained outdoors, but this group was more than enough to swamp the table. Linda said, "Leave a chair for Aunt Willa, please."

"Who's Aunt Willa?" said Keith, or was it Brian? The other one was still wearing the hat. With no reply, Linda pried a Chinet plate from the stack, snatched a burger, flipped off the top bun, and wheezed a circle of French's mustard onto the underside of it. She announced, "I'm takin' up a plate to Dad," and a quiet deference drifted over the group. Her hands sped through the assembly: a slice of American cheese, pickle, tomato. "I'll be right back," she said, stringent and matriarchal. "Y'all behave yourselves."

I stood to the side as everyone grabbed plates and food and drinks. I felt like a space alien. But one of the wives sweetly handed me a plate, and we exchanged smiles. By the time I dished myself some potato salad, everyone was seated; the only empty chair was, awkwardly, at the foot of the table, where Ricky used to sit. I sat.

"Don't you want a burger?" said one of the wives.

"Maybe she's a *vegetarian*," Brian snorted.

"No," I said, and all the faces turned toward me, curious, bemused, puzzled, hostile. "Just not very hungry."

Another wife asked me, "What do you do in Chicago, Willa?"

Sitting across from her, Brian said, in the irritated tone of a husband, "I told you she's a college professor."

"Okay," said the wife. "I was just askin' a question to be polite."

"Well, don't ask a question you already know the answer to. Why would you ask a question you already know the answer to?

Why wouldn't you ask a question you don't know the answer to? Makes no sense to ask a question you already know the answer to."

The wife's gaze shifted from his face to his clavicle. After a suitable silence, a different wife asked me, carefully, "What do you teach?"

"History," I said.

"Ahhh," one of them said sarcastically.

Keith bellowed, "Steve here's a college teacher, too, up at SRU. Teaches biology."

"Really?" I sounded too surprised. The man who must have been Steve, seated at the head of the table, shot me a dark, squinty look. There was something familiar about him—his narrow head, his small circular ears.

Brian continued, "Steve writes books, too," and grinning with some inside joke, prodded him. "Tell her about your new book, Steve."

In a mumble he said, "I don't think Aunt Willa's gonna wanna hear about it, it bein' not too politically correct."

My face twisted. I hated when people said that. "Do y'all know the origin of that phrase?" I asked.

Faces turned toward me again, some genuinely curious. I leaned forward. "A professor at the University of Chicago coined the term in the 1980s. The man hated women being on the faculty, so he used it against them. It's clever how the phrase works. It sounds like an objection to people shutting down discussion, but that's exactly what it does—shuts down discussion."

"That so?" Steve replied, smirking, eyes narrowed in an assumption of superiority. My breath caught. Of course he seemed familiar: he resembled my father.

"You wanna tell me about your book?" I asked, driven by an old impulse to engage the patriarch.

"Why, *sure*, Aunt Willa."

Keith shrieked out a hyena laugh, and one of the wives said, exasperated, "*Y'all*."

Steve said, "The title is, *The Evolution of Intelligence.*"

"Oh?" I said, with a creeping sense of dread.

"Tell her from the start!" Keith said. Silently one of the wives rose from the table, crossed the room, and went out the back door.

"Well, it goes back a little *before* the 1980s, Aunt Willa. By a couple million years." A few of the men chuckled. Steve had obviously rehearsed what came next: "When early humans migrated north out of Africa, they had to adapt to their colder climate. Am I right? They lost their skin pigmentation because they needed more UVB light for their bodies to manufacture vitamin D. Am I right? So why would anyone think that was the *only* adaptation? Only one adaptation? There'd have to be several adaptations. Doesn't that make sense to you?" I caught myself nodding along and stopped. He went on. "So, to survive those cold winters, the white European people evolved a great-er level of intelligence. They needed the ability to plan ahead and delay gratification. That's why Blacks commit more crimes than whites. Blacks don't have that ability to plan ahead, or *delay* gratification. They never developed their intelligence, like the people who migrated north."

After a prickly stretch of silence, during which one woman blew her nose, I said slowly, deliberatively, "So, what you're saying is, people from the North are smarter than people from the South."

A teenager at the table burst out a laugh. But Steve smiled, his head wagging with pity. "I feel sorry for you, Aunt Willa."

"Why's that, *Steve?*"

"You got a serious case of liberal self-loathing. You feel guilty about bein' smarter and wealthier than Blacks, am I right? What you gotta understand, it's not *our fault*. We're just better'n they are. Blacks are poor 'cause they're not as smart as us. *We* are not to blame. You liberals gotta quit blamin' white people and wake up to the reality, Aunt Willa, 'cause these are danger-ous times we're livin' in." When I didn't respond, he elaborated: "White genocide's already underway."

I couldn't recall the last time I'd encountered this kind of hatred face to face. I'd been living in my liberal bubble. My thoughts scattered like confetti on a wind, and a memory from years ago popped into my head. It was something I'd heard in a podcast, in an interview with a man involved in the Rwandan genocide of the 1990s. The event was horrific, one ethnic group slaughtering people of another ethnic group—their neighbors—with machetes. In the interview, the killer spoke sorrowfully, shamefully: "It was like devils got into me, like devils. I cannot explain it any other way. I felt I could not control myself—it was like devils." It had made me think of the Bible verse about the devils that flew into the swine, which made them run down a steep place into the water and drown. Hatred of the other, I thought, is like a preternatural evil—like devils invading your soul—that hurl you down to your own demise. I didn't believe in actual devils, but I believed the outcome was the same.

I pitched forward. "Black people are poorer because of redlining and other laws that prevented them from accumulating wealth the—"

Steve's head started wagging again. "You liberals—"

"What's the point of using that phrase, *you liberals*?" I snapped, and my skin caught fire. I never should have come back, *never*—I'd been right to stay away forever. These people were awful, all of them—rednecks and hillbillies—they were all alike, refusing to question their own beliefs or acknowledge a different perspective, clinging to some phony pride, their little egos too fragile to withstand the possibility they might ever be wrong, their male identities all shriveled up like shrunken heads because they still equated "female" with inferiority and rejected anything associated with women—qualities like empathy, adaptability, compassion, resilience, genuine strength. I wanted to throw a chair at Steve. I yelled at him, "I was once a racist like you, and I realized it was wrong!"

Of course, it wasn't facts and arguments that had made me see this; it was lived experience. It was walking alongside the other; it was proximity.

Steve was silent, and I thought maybe I'd made an impression. Then he said, in a tone laden with contempt, "*You liberals* always resort to name-callin'. A person's got a different viewpoint, and you start the name-callin'." Then he stated: "I am not a racist."

I gazed at him, and everyone else gazed at him, and the house bathed in a humming silence until the back door banged open. More sons came in, marching in together and forming a line where the arched doorway used to be. One of them said to Steve, "What're you doin'?"

Steve replied, "Havin' a conversation, Danny. Nothin' wrong with that."

Danny gripped his hands into fists and slammed them onto his waist. Three other brothers did the same. Then Danny yelled, "It's bad 'nough you spreadin' your hateful ideas all over the county, you have to bring it up at *Grandma's funeral?*"

"Grandma's funeral's over," Keith-in-the-hat said.

Brian continued, "We got a *right* to our opinion, Danny," and I was about to wail back at him when we heard footsteps coming down the stairs—thumping, racing, angry mom footsteps. Everyone contracted, including me, in an attempt to be less visible. Linda's face appeared, crimson, her voice a foghorn: "What is goin' on down here? As if I didn't know! Keith, take off that damn hat!" He whipped it off and bunched it up in his lap. She raged on: "Y'all finally get to meet your aunt Willa and *this* is what you talk about?"

In a wilting whine, Brian said, "We're sorry, Mom."

"Lord help me!" she gasped, and in a suffocated voice bellowed, "We're *family*," and stormed outside.

At the table, we remained in a drum of silence, until one of the wives inquired, timidly, "Aunt Willa, do you have children?"

I looked at her, her face smooth and freckled, young and soft, so eager to please. "Yes," I said. "I have two sons. They live out West."

"Oh, that's nice. What're their names?"

I paused. What would their names be? "Luke and John."

"Oh, I like those names."

People finished eating and rose from the table a few at a time, milled around, meandered back outside. I stayed inside. I stood at the back window for a while and watched Billy's off-spring mingle and merge into one big group, then splinter off into factions, and I thought how human history followed this pattern: unify, split, unify, split. As the yard began to fade into early twilight, I tried to recall it as it had been—that adequate plot of raggedy grass, my father standing with his legs planted in a firm upside-down V, smacking a softball from one hand to the other, and Billy beyond him, wriggling, jubilant, his tiny hands clasping his bat. I turned and went up the stairs.

At the top I paused to look up and down the hall: the up-stairs was unaltered. At one end were the two bedrooms for the kids—mine and Barb's, Ricky's and Billy's; at the other end, my parents' room and the bathroom. I tiptoed toward my par-ents' room and peered in. Billy wasn't there. I crept back down the hall and peeked into the room that was once mine. It had been painted blue, but the furniture was the same, twin maple headboards and the chest of drawers, standing in their original spots. Barb's voice rang in my head: *Willa.* I stepped back and turned toward the boys' room. The door was open a crack. I poked my face in.

Billy—old-man Billy—sat limp in a desk chair. I pushed the door open and looked at him, and he looked at me, his face blotched and pulled with grief, his eyes raw and bald. The win-dow blinds were closed but still the room was light and he was discernible, even in the shadow where he was trying to hide. I examined every contour of his forehead, cheeks, and chin, every pockmark. Somewhere in this form was the Billy I knew. He spoke, his voice rickety: "Where you been, Willa?"

Trying to soften my Northern accent, I said, "Downstairs."

"No," he said.

I was silent, confused.

He wheezed, "Where you *been*, the last fifty years?"

The room swarmed with bits of dust. I could tell it had been painted recently, a pale pink, and the bed in the room was a double. "Was this Mama's room?"

"Yeah," he said wearily. "Toward the end. We brought her back from assisted livin' to spend her last coupla years here, like she wanted. She died here, like she wanted."

I couldn't speak. The bed was made up tidily now with a floral mauve spread and pillowcases to match. I said, "This used to be your room."

"Yeah, tables turn. Child of the parent, parent of the child."

I said nothing. He'd taken care of our mother all these decades by himself. As the youngest daughter, I would have been expected to do that. Billy's voice returned, sturdier: "Why'd you abandon us, Willa?"

"What?" I half shrieked. "I didn't abandon you. They sent me away! They didn't want me and they sent me away!"

"*He* sent you away. Wasn't Mama sent you away. Wasn't me! One day I was a happy little boy with a big brother and two big sisters, next day I was all alone."

I listened to the silence of the house. There was a pressure to it, all that silence. "I'm sorry."

"He was *mean* after you left."

"He was always mean."

"He was *worse* after you left. Treated Mama like crap. Me too."

My eyes began to sting. "I'm sorry."

"Mama and I stuck together. Thank God for Mama. She was all I had."

Sadness hung over us for a long while. I said, "Then you met Linda."

"Yeah, yeah. Thank God for Linda."

"I bet Mama loved those grandbabies."

A grin pressed across his face. "Yeah, yeah." His eyes clouded and his shoulders shook once with a melancholy laugh. "Tell you though, she and I both wished a few of 'em had been girls. Don't know how anyone can have so many kids and none of 'em girls. If one of 'em had been a girl, Mama had the prettiest name picked out: Willow. Like a willow tree. Isn't that pretty?

Willow Barbara, that's what Mama and I said we'd name a girl if Linda ever had a girl; Linda was fine with that."

My throat turned to cotton. He twisted in the chair and peered at me, saying nothing for a bit. Then, "Did you ever have children?"

For a moment I pictured my fictitious sons, Luke and John, out West, rock-climbing together, tall and handsome, forever twenty-something, one blond, one dark. I replied, "No."

"No," he echoed. "Mama and I didn't think so. We figured you would've let us know."

"I have students. It's a little like having children."

He squinted at me again, but not in a hostile way—more in a way that suggested he should be wearing glasses. He asked, "You been happy?"

"Yeah, yeah." This was true. I'd had plenty of time to ponder this topic. I was proud of who I was, appreciative of my place in history: I'd had the opportunity to be who I was supposed to be, mostly.

Billy's eyes remained on mine. I could tell he wanted to say something more but didn't know what, so he said, "Linda says you're leavin' tomorrow, back to Chicago."

"Yeah."

"Will you come back again? For a visit? Before another fifty years go by?"

A smile crawled across my face. "Sure."

He smiled too—a fleeting grin—before his face returned to its sagging grief. He leaned forward, for a moment looking like he might throw up, and burst out, "Mama's gone!" and sobbed, sobbed until I had to rush over and fold my arms around him. His soft-haired head rested in the nape of my neck; his tears drenched my skin.

"Don't leave me alone so long, Willa."

"I won't," I whispered.

"Come back soon. Come back for Thanksgivin'. Will ya do that? Whole family'll be here. You can get to know everyone better."

I paused, then eked out a less enthusiastic, "Okay."

Then it occurred to me: Thanksgiving was months away. I'd have time to collect my thoughts, line up my references, craft a good, solid argument against Steve's hateful rhetoric. Human beings were 99.9 percent genetically identical. I didn't imagine I could change the horrible Steve, but he wouldn't be the only person at the table—there'd be wives and daughters and sons—all of them equally important, none of them extraneous. I knew how to plant seeds.

Billy coughed and said, "Okay then. It's settled. Thanksgivin'."

I smiled at him, and he gazed past my shoulder, as though at something behind me. His eyes had a glassy emptiness that reminded me of my mother's: a look of desolation, of too much loss, of a resignation born of powerlessness and defeat, a stinging acceptance of life's limitations. I studied the side of his hollow cheek and sensed his decades of disappointment. Of course, Billy didn't want a political debate at Thanksgiving; he wanted a sister.

I bent down to hug him goodbye and wondered if I could ever again feel I belonged here—if I could belong in two places and encompass the past as well as the present. Could I bring all the dark history together with the light of my ordinary daily routines? Maybe I could still grow to encompass both North and South. But how could I ever embrace the person I was then?

Once, Ruth had told me, *Forgive yourself.* I heard her voice now, clear as a ringing bell. *Forgive yourself,* she'd said. *But don't forget. Learn.*

# ACKNOWLEDGMENTS

For all the support and enthusiasm I've received for this novel, I'm deeply grateful. I thank Abby Geni, the best writing teacher I've ever had, for her brilliant guidance in revising the work. I also thank Rebecca Makkai and everyone at StoryStudio-Chicago who provided me with a much-needed writing community. I am especially grateful to Louise Marburg, my first reader and invaluable friend, who kept me writing the first draft at breakneck speed and read every version since.

I thank my dear friends, Terry Stirling and Arlene Borthwick, who provided me with period details that made the novel more authentic to its place in history. Thanks also go to Dion Ewald for his help with research, to Mark Spann for his unfailing encouragement and wisdom, and to Laurel DiGangi for her ninth-inning brilliance.

I thank my publishers, Jaynie Royal and Pam Van Dyk at Regal House Publishing, for their acceptance, expertise, guidance, and formidable Author's Guide, which answers every possible question an author might (and might not) have.

Much gratitude goes to my gifted sister, Connie Busch, who joined me on trips back to southeast Virginia for research and helped me recreate the world we inhabited long ago. My father, St. Elmo Nauman, Jr., also contributed details that proved integral to the story. Thank you to my wonderful daughter, Maggie O'Brien, an astute reader whose insights and suggestions strengthened the book. Finally, a very special thank you goes to my mother, June Anderson, who is no longer here to celebrate with us. Thank you, Momma, for always believing in me as a writer, for providing countless details and ideas for this novel, and for holding my hand tight the day the Klan marched.

# Author's Note

The decision to avoid the "N" word in this novel was highly intentional. Adult Willa, as the narrator, would not have used it. Moreover, I, as the author, didn't want to use it. Other racial slurs and the events of the novel seemed disturbing enough. Some readers may interpret this choice as timidity. I disagree. Of course, authenticity and language are important, but so is not gratuitously harming other people. The theoretical linguistic and literary articles I read on this issue did not, in my mind, outweigh Jamaican author Delta McKenzie's blunt comment on the "N" word in fiction: "I don't need to read it and you don't need to use it."